THE ICE TWINS

S. K. Tremayne is a bestselling novelist and award-winning travel writer, and a regular contributor to newspapers and magazines around the world. Born in Devon, the author now lives in London.

S. K. Tremayne has two daughters.

THE ICE TWINS

S. K. TREMAYNE

HarperCollins*Publishers*

HarperCollins*Publishers*
1 London Bridge Street
London SE1 9GF

www.harpercollins.co.uk

Published by HarperCollins*Publishers* 2015
1

A catalogue record for this book
is available from the British Library

ISBN: 978-0-00-756304-3

Set in Sabon LT Std by Palimpsest Book Production Ltd,
Falkirk, Stirlingshire

Photographs © S. K. Tremayne

Printed and bound in Great Britain by
Clays Ltd, St Ives plc

MIX
Paper from
responsible sources
FSC
www.fsc.org **FSC C007454**

FSC™ is a non-profit international organisation established to promote
the responsible management of the world's forests. Products carrying the
FSC label are independently certified to assure consumers that they come
from forests that are managed to meet the social, economic and
ecological needs of present and future generations,
and other controlled sources.

Find out more about HarperCollins and the environment at
www.harpercollins.co.uk/green

Author's Note

I would like to thank Joel Franklyn and Dede MacGillivray, Gus MacLean, Ben Timberlake, and, in particular, Angel Sedgwick, for their help with my research for this book.

Anyone who knows the Inner Hebrides will quickly notice the very strong resemblance between 'Eilean Torran' and the real Eilean Sionnach, off Isleornsay, in Skye. This is no coincidence: the book was inspired, in part, by a lifetime of visiting that beautiful tidal island, and staying in the whitewashed cottage under the lighthouse.

However, all the events and characters described herein are entirely fictional.

Editorially, I want to thank Jane Johnson, Helen Atsma, Kate Stephenson and Eugenie Furniss: without their encouragement, and wise advice, this book would not exist.

Finally, I owe a debt of gratitude to Hywel Davies and Elizabeth Doherty, for sowing the original seed, which grew into an idea: twins.

For my daughters

1

Our chairs are placed precisely two yards apart. And they are both facing the big desk, as if we are a couple having marital therapy; a feeling I know too well. Dominating the room is a pair of lofty, uncurtained, eighteenth-century sash windows: twin portraits of a dark and dimming London sky.

'Can we get some light?' asks my husband, and the young solicitor, Andrew Walker, looks up from his papers, with maybe a tinge of irritation.

'Of course,' he says. 'My apologies.' He leans to a switch behind him, and two tall standing lamps flood the room with a generous yellow light, and those impressive windows go black.

Now I can see my reflection in the glazing: poised, passive, my knees together. Who is this woman?

She is not what I used to be. Her eyes are as blue as ever, yet sadder. Her face is slightly round, and pale, and thinner than it was. She is still blonde and tolerably pretty – but also faded, and dwindled; a thirty-three-year-old woman, with all the girlishness long gone.

And her clothes?

Jeans that were fashionable a year ago. Boots that were fashionable a year ago. Lilac cashmere jumper, quite nice, but worn: with that bobbling you get, from one too many washes. I wince at my mirrored self. I should have come smarter. But why should I have come smarter? We're just meeting a lawyer. And changing our lives completely.

Traffic murmurs outside, like the deep but disturbed breathing of a dreaming partner. I wonder if I'm going to miss London traffic, the constant reassuring white noise: like those apps for your phone that help you sleep – by mimicking the ceaseless rushing sounds of blood in the womb, the mother's heartbeat throbbing in the distance.

My twins would have heard that noise, when they were rubbing noses inside me. I remember seeing them on the second sonogram. They looked like two heraldic symbols on a coat of arms, identical and opposed. The unicorn and the unicorn.

Testator. Executor. Legitim. Probate . . .

Andrew Walker is addressing us as if we are a lecture room, and he is a professor who is mildly disappointed with his students.

Bequeathed. Deceased. Inheritor. Surviving Children.

My husband Angus sighs, with suppressed impatience; I know that sigh. He is bored, probably irritated. And I understand this; but I also have sympathy for the solicitor. This can't be easy for Walker. Facing an angry, belligerent father, and a still-grieving mother, while sorting a problematic bequest: we must be tricky. So his careful, slow, precise enunciation is maybe his way of distancing, of handling difficult material. Maybe it is the legal equivalent of medical terminology. *Duodenal*

4

hematomas and serosal avulsions, leading to fatal infan-
tile peritonitis.

A sharp voice cuts across.

'We've been through all of this.'

Has Angus had a drink? His tone skirts the vicinity of anger. Angus has been angry since it happened. And he has been drinking a lot, too. But he sounds quite lucid today, and is, presumably, sober.

'We'd like to get this done before climate change really kicks in. You know?'

'Mr Moorcroft, as I have already said, Peter Kenwood is on holiday. We can wait for him to come back if you prefer—'

Angus shakes his head. 'No. We want to get it done now.'

'Then I have to go through the documents again, and the pertinent issues – for my own satisfaction. Moreover, Peter feels . . . well . . .'

I watch. The solicitor hesitates, and his next words are tighter, and even more carefully phrased:

'As you are aware, Mr Moorcroft, Peter considers himself a long-standing family friend. Not just a legal advisor. He knows the circumstances. He knew the late Mrs Carnan, your grandmother, very well. He therefore asked me to make sure, once again, that you both know exactly what you are getting into.'

'We know what we are doing.'

'The island is, as you are aware, barely habitable.' Andrew Walker shrugs, uncomfortably – as if this dilapidation is somehow his company's fault, but he is keen to avoid a potential lawsuit. 'The lighthouse-keeper's cottage has, I am afraid, been left to the elements, no one has been there in years. But it is listed, so you can't completely demolish and start again.'

'Yup. Know all this. Went there a lot as a kid. Played in the rock pools.'

'But are you truly apprised of the challenges, Mr Moorcroft? This is really quite an undertaking. There are issues concerning accessibility, with the tidal mudflats, and of course there are various and salient problems with plumbing, and heating, and electrics in general – moreover there is no money in the will, nothing to—'

'We're apprised to the eyeballs.'

A pause. Walker glances at me, then at Angus again. 'I understand you are selling your house in London?'

Angus stares back. Chin tilted. Defiant.

'Sorry? What's that got to do with anything?'

The solicitor shakes his head. 'Peter is concerned. Because . . . ah . . . Given your recent tragic bereavement . . . he wants to be absolutely sure.'

Angus glances my way. I shrug, uncertainly. Angus leans forward.

'OK. Whatever. Yes. We're selling the house in Camden.'

'And this sale means you will realize enough capital to enable renovations to Ell—' Andrew Walker frowns. At the words he is reading. 'I can't quite pronounce it. Ell . . .?'

'Eilean Torran. Scots Gaelic. It means Thunder Island. Torran Island.'

'Yes. Of course. Torran Island. So you hope to realize sufficient funds from the sale of your present house, to renovate the lighthouse-keeper's cottage on Torran?'

I feel as if I should say something. Surely I must say something. Angus is doing all the work. Yet my muteness is comforting, a cocoon, I am wrapped in my silence. As ever. This is my thing. I've always been quiet,

6

if not reserved; and it has exasperated Angus for years. *What are you thinking? Tell me. Why do I have to do all the talking?* And when he says that, I usually shrug and turn away; because sometimes saying nothing says it all.

And here I am, silent again. Listening to my husband.

'We've already got two mortgages on the Camden house. I lost my job, we're struggling. But yeah, I hope we'll make a few quid.'

'You have a buyer?'

'Busting to write a cheque.' Angus is obviously repressing anger, but he goes on. 'Look. My grandmother left the island to me and my brother in her will. Right?'

'Of course.'

'And my brother, very generously, says he doesn't want it. Right? My mother is in a home. Yep? The island therefore belongs to me, my wife, and my daughter. Yes?'

Daughter. Singular.

'Indeed—'

'So that's that. Surely? We want to move. We really want to move. Yes, it's in a state. Yes, it's falling down. But we'll cope. We have, after all' – Angus sits back – 'been through worse.'

I look, quite intently, at my husband.

If I was meeting him now, for the first time, he would still be very attractive. A tall, smart guy in his thirties, with three days of agreeable stubble. Dark-eyed, masculine, capable.

Angus had a tinge of stubble when we first met, and I liked that; I liked the way it emphasized his jawline. He was one of the few men I had met who could happily own the word handsome, sitting in that large, noisy, Covent Garden tapas bar.

7

He was laughing, at a big table, with a bunch of friends: all in their mid-twenties. Me and my friends were on the next table over. Slightly younger, but just as cheerful. Everyone was drinking plenty of Rioja.

And so it happened. One of the guys tossed a joke our way; someone came back with a teasing insult. And then the tables mingled: we shifted and squashed, and budged up, laughing and joking, and swapping names: this is Zoe, this is Sacha, this is Alex, Imogen, Meredith . . .

And this is Angus Moorcroft, and this is Sarah Milverton. He's from Scotland and he's twenty-six. She's half English, half American, and she's twenty-three. Now spend the rest of your lives together.

The rush-hour traffic grows louder outside; I am stirred from my reverie. Andrew Walker is getting Angus to sign some more documents. And oh, I know this procedure: we've signed so very many documents this last year. The paperwork that attends upon disaster.

Angus is hunched over the desk, scribbling his name. His hand looks too big for the pen. Turning away, I stare at a picture of Old London Bridge on the yellow-painted wall. I want to reminisce a little more, and distract myself. I want to think about Angus and me: that first night.

I remember it all, so vividly. From the music – Mexican salsa – to the mediocre tapas: luridly red *patatas bravas*, vinegary white asparagus. I remember the way other people drifted off – gotta get the last Tube, got to get some sleep – as if they all sensed that he and I were matched, that this was something more important than your average Friday-night flirtation.

How easily it turns. What would my life be now, if we'd taken a different table, gone to a different bar? But we chose that bar, that night, and that table, and by midnight I was sitting alone, right next to this tall guy: Angus Moorcroft. He told me he was an architect. He told me he was Scottish, and single. And then he told a clever joke – which I didn't realize was a joke until a minute later. And as I laughed, I realized he was looking at me: deeply, questioningly.

So I looked right back at him. His eyes were a dark, solemn brown; his hair was wavy, and thick, and very black; and his teeth were white and sharp against his red lips and dark stubble, and I knew the answer. *Yes*.

Two hours later we stole our first drunken kiss, under the approving moon, in a corner of Covent Garden piazza. I remember the glisten of the rainy cobblestones as we embraced: the chilly sweetness of the evening air. We slept together, the very same night.

Nearly a year after that, we married. After barely two years of marriage, we had the girls: identical twin sisters. And now there is one twin left.

The pain rises inside me: and I have to put a fist to my mouth to suppress the shudder. When will it go away? Maybe never? It is like a war-wound, like shrapnel inside the flesh, making its way to the surface, over years.

So maybe I have to speak. To quell the pain: to quiet my thoughts. I've been sitting here for half an hour, docile and muted, like some Puritan housewife. I rely on Angus to do the talking, too often; to provide what is missing in me. But enough of my silence, for now.

'If we do the island up, it could be worth a million.'

Both men turn to me. Abruptly. She speaks!

'That view,' I say, 'is worth a million by itself, over-looking the Sound of Sleat. Towards Knoydart.'

I am very careful to pronounce it properly: Sleat to

rhyme with slate. I have done my research; endless research, Googling images and histories.

Andrew smiles, politely.

'And, ah, have you been there, Mrs Moorcroft?'

I blush; yet I don't care.

'No. But I've seen the pictures, read the books – that's one of *the* most famous views in Scotland, and we will have our own island.'

'Indeed. Yes. However—'

'There was a house in Ornsay village, on the mainland, half a mile from Torran . . .' I glance at the note stored in my phone, though I remember the facts well enough. 'It sold for seven hundred and fifty thousand on January fifteenth this year. A four-bedroom house, with a nice garden and a bit of decking. All very pleasant, but not exactly a mansion. But it had a spectacular view of the Sound – and that is what people pay for. *Seven hundred and fifty k.*'

Angus looks at me, and nods encouragement. Then he joins in.

'Aye. And if we do it up, we could have five bedrooms, an acre – the cottage is big enough. Could be worth a million. Easily.'

'Well, yes, Mr Moorcroft, it's worth barely fifty thousand now, but yes, there is potential.'

The solicitor is smiling, in a faked way. I am struck with curiosity: why is he so blatantly reluctant for us to move to Torran? What does he know? What is Peter Kenwood's real involvement? Perhaps they were going to make an offer themselves? That makes sense: Kenwood has known of Torran for years, he knew Angus's grandmother, he would be fully *apprised* of the unrealized value.

Was this what they were planning? If so, it would be

seductively simple. Just wait for Angus's grandmother to die. Then pounce on the grandkids, especially on a grieving and bewildered couple: shell-shocked by a child's death, reeling from ensuing financial strife. Offer them a hundred thousand, twice as much as needed, be generous and sympathetic, smile warmly yet sadly. *It must be difficult, but we can help, take this burden away. Sign on the line . . .*

After that: a stroll. Ship a busload of Polish builders to Skye, invest two hundred thousand, wait for a year until the work is done.

This beautiful property, located on its own island, on the famous Sound of Sleat, is for sale at £1.25 million, or nearest offer . . .

Was that their plan? Andrew Walker is gazing at me and I feel a twinge of guilt. I am probably being horribly unfair to Kenwood and Partners. But whatever their motivation, there is no way I am giving up this island: it is my exit route, it is an escape from the grief, and the memories – and the debts and the doubts.

I have dreamed about it too much. Stared at the glowing pictures on my laptop screen, at three a.m., in the kitchen. When Kirstie is asleep in her room and Angus is in bed doped with Scotch. Gazing at the crystal beauty. Eilean Torran. On the Sound of Sleat. Lost in the loveliness of the Inner Hebrides, this beautiful property, on its very own island.

'OK then. I just need a couple more signatures,' says Andrew Walker.

'And we're done?'

A significant pause.

'Yes.'

Fifteen minutes later Angus and I walk out of the yellow-painted office, down the red-painted hall, and exit into the damp of an October evening. In Bedford Square, Bloomsbury.

Angus has the deeds in his rucksack. They are finished; it is completed. I am looking at an altered world; my mood lifts commensurately.

Big red buses roll down Gower Street, two storeys of blank faces staring out.

Angus puts a hand on my arm. 'Well done.'

'For what?'

'That intervention. Nice timing. I was worried I was going to deck him.'

'So was I.' We look at each other. Knowing, and sad. 'But we did it. Right?'

Angus smiles. 'We did, darling: we totally did it.' He turns the collar of his coat against the rain. 'But Sarah . . . I've got to ask, just one more time – you are absolutely sure?'

I grimace; he hurries on: 'I know, I know. Yes. But you still think this is the right thing? You really want' – he gestures at the queued yellow lights of London taxis, glowing in the drizzle – 'you really, truly want to leave all this? Give it up? Skye is so quiet.'

'When a man is tired of London,' I say, 'he is tired of rain.'

Angus laughs. And leans closer. His brown eyes are searching mine, maybe his lips are seeking my mouth. I gently caress one side of his jaw, and kiss him on his stubbled cheek, and I breathe him in – he doesn't smell of whisky. He smells of Angus. Soap and masculinity. Clean and capable, the man I loved. Love. Will always love.

Maybe we will have sex tonight, for the first time in too many weeks. Maybe we are getting through this. Can you ever get through *this*?

We walk hand in hand down the street. Angus squeezes my hand tight. He's done a lot of hand-holding this last year: holding my hand when I lay in bed crying, endlessly and wordlessly, night after night; holding my hand from the beginning to the end of Lydia's appalling funeral, from *I am the resurrection and the life* all the way through to *Be with us all evermore*.

Amen.

'Tube or bus?'

'Tube,' I say. 'Quicker. I want to tell Kirstie the good news.'

'I hope she sees it like that.'

I look at him. No.

I can't begin to entertain any uncertainty. If I stop and wonder, then the misgivings will surge and we will be stuck for ever.

My words come in a rush, 'Surely she will, Angus, she must do? We'll have our own lighthouse, all that fresh air, red deer, dolphins . . .'

'Aye, but remember, you've mainly seen pictures of it in summer. In the sun. Not always like that. Winters are dark.'

'So in winter we will – what's the word? – we'll hunker down and defend ourselves. It'll be an adventure.'

We are nearly at the Tube. A black flash flood of commuters is disappearing down the steps: a torrent being swallowed by London Underground. I turn, momentarily, and look at the mistiness of New Oxford Street. The autumn fogs of Bloomsbury are a kind of ghost – or a visible memory – of Bloomsbury's medieval marshes. I read that somewhere.

I read a lot.

'Come on.'

This time I grasp Angus's hand, and linked by our fingers we descend into the Tube, and we endure three stops in the rush-hour crowds, jammed together; then we squeeze into the rattling lifts at Mornington Crescent – and when we hit the surface, we are practically running.

'Hey,' Angus says, laughing. 'Is this an Olympic event?'

'I want to tell our daughter!'

And I do, I do. I want to give my surviving daughter some good news, for once, some nice news: something happy and hopeful. Her twin Lydia died fourteen months ago today – I hate the way I can still measure the date so exactly, so easily – and she has had more than a year of anguish that I cannot comprehend: losing her identical twin, her second soul. She has been locked in an abyssal isolation of her own: for fourteen months. But now I can release her.

Fresh air, mountains, sea lochs. And a view across the water to Knoydart.

I am hurrying to the door of the big white house we should never have bought; the house in which we can no longer afford to live.

Imogen is at the door. The house smells of kids' food, new laundry and fresh coffee; it is bright. I am going to miss it. Maybe.

'Immy, thanks for looking after her.'

'Oh, please. Come on. Just tell me? Has it all gone through?'

'Yes, we've got it, we're moving!'

Imogen claps her hands in delight: my clever, dark-haired, elegant friend who's stuck with me all the way from college; she leans and hugs me, but I push her away, smiling.

'I have to tell her, she knows nothing.'

14

Imogen grins. 'She's in her room with the Wimpy Kid.'

'Sorry?'

'Reading that book!'

Pacing down the hall I climb the stairs and pause at the door that says *Kirstie Lives Here* and *Knock First* spelled out in clumsily scissored letters made from glittery paper. I knock, as instructed.

Then I hear a faint *mmm-mmm*. My daughter's version of Come in.

I push the door, and there is my seven-year-old girl, cross-legged on the floor in her school uniform – black trousers, white polo shirt – her little freckled nose close to a book: a picture of innocence but also of loneliness. The love and the sadness throbs inside me. I want to make her life better, so much, make her whole again, as best I can.

'Kirstie . . .'

She does not respond. Still reading. She sometimes does this. Playing a game, mmmNOT going to talk. It has become more frequent, this last year.

'Kirstie. Moomin. Kirstie-koo.'

Now she looks up, with those blue eyes she got from me, but bluer. Hebridean blue. Her blonde hair is almost white.

'Mummy.'

'I've got some news, Kirstie. Good news. Wonderful news.'

Sitting myself on the floor, beside her, surrounded by little toys – by her penguins, and Leopardy the cuddly leopard, and the Doll With One Arm – I tell Kirstie everything. In a rush. How we are moving somewhere special, somewhere new, somewhere we can start again, somewhere beautiful and fresh and sparkling: our own island.

15

Through it all Kirstie looks at me. Her eyes barely blinking. Taking it all in. Saying nothing, passive, as if entranced, returning my own silences to me. She nods, and half smiles. Puzzled, maybe. The room is quiet. I have run out of words.

'So,' I say. 'What do you think? Moving to our own island? Won't that be exciting?'

Kirstie nods, gently. She looks down at her book, and closes it, and then she looks up at me again, and says:

'Mummy, why do you keep calling me Kirstie?'

I say nothing. The silence is ringing. I speak:

'Sorry, sweetheart. What?'

'Why do you keep calling me Kirstie, Mummy? Kirstie is dead. It was *Kirstie* that died. I'm Lydia.'

2

I stare at Kirstie. Trying to smile. Trying not to show my deep anxiety.

There is surely some latent grief resurfacing here, in Kirstie's developing mind; some confusion unique to twins who lose a co-twin, and I am used to this – to my daughters – to my daughter – being different.

From the first time my own mother drove from Devon, in the depths of winter, to our little flat in Holloway – from the moment my mum looked at the twins paired in their cot, the two identical tiny babies sucking each other's thumbs – from the moment my mother burst into a dazzled, amazed, giddy smile, her eyes wide with sincere wonder – I knew then that having twins was something even more impressive than the standard miracle of becoming a parent. With twins – especially identicals – you give birth to genetic celebrities. People who are impressive simply for existing.

Impressive, and very different.

My dad even gave them a nickname: the Ice Twins. Because they were born on the coldest, frostiest day of the year, with ice-blue eyes and snowy-blonde hair. The

17

nickname felt a little melancholy: so I never properly adopted it. Yet I couldn't deny that, in some ways, the name fitted. It caught their uncanniness.

And that's how special twins can be: they actually had a special name, shared between them.

In which case, this piercingly calm statement from Kirstie – Mummy, I'm Lydia, it was *Kirstie* that died – could be just another example of twin-ness, just another symptom of their uniqueness. But even so, I am fighting panic, and the urge to cry. Because she's reminding me of Lydia. And because I am worried for Kirstie.

What terrible delusion is haunting her thoughts, to make her say these terrible words? Mummy, I'm Lydia, it was Kirstie that died. *Why do you keep calling me Kirstie?*

'Sweetheart,' I say to Kirstie, with a fake and deliberate calmness, 'it's time for bed soon.'

She gives me that placid blue gaze, identical to her sister's. She is missing a milk tooth from the top. Another one is wobbling, on the bottom. This is quite a new thing; until Lydia's death both twins had perfect smiles: they were similarly late in losing their teeth.

Holding the book a little higher, Kirstie says,

'But actually the chapter is only three more pages. Did you know that?'

'Is it really?'

'Yes, look it actually ends here, Mummy.'

'OK then, we can read three more pages to the end of the chapter. Why don't you read them to me?'

Kirstie nods, and turns to her book; she begins to read aloud.

'I had to wrap myself up in toi-let paper so I didn't get hypo . . . hy . . . po . . .'

Leaning closer, I point out the word and begin to help. 'Hypoth—'

'No, Mummy.' She laughs, softly. 'No. I know it. I can say it!'

'OK.'

Kirstie closes her eyes, which is what she does when she really thinks hard, then she opens her eyes again, and reads: 'So I didn't get hy-po-thermia.'

She's got it. Quite a difficult word. But I am not surprised. There has been a rapid improvement in her reading, just recently. Which means . . .?

I drive the thought away.

Apart from Kirstie's reading, the room is quiet. I presume Angus is downstairs with Imogen, in the distant kitchen; perhaps they are opening a bottle of wine, to celebrate the news. And why not? There have been too many bad days, with bad news, for fourteen months.

'That's how I spent a pretty big chunk of my sum-mer holidays . . .'

While Kirstie reads, I hug her little shoulders, and kiss her soft blonde hair. As I do, I feel something small and jagged beneath me, digging into my thigh. Trying not to disturb Kirstie's reading, trying not to think about what she said, I reach under.

It is a small toy: a miniature plastic dragon we bought at London Zoo. But we bought it for Lydia. She espe-cially liked dragons and alligators, all the spooky reptiles and monsters; Kirstie was – is – keener on lions and leopards, fluffier, bouncy, cuter, mammalian creatures. It was one of the things that differentiated them.

'When I got to school today . . . every-one was acting all strange.'

I examine the plastic dragon, turning it in my hand. Why is it here, lying on the floor? Angus and I carefully boxed all of Lydia's toys in the months after it happened. We couldn't bear to throw them away; that was too final, too primitive. So we put everything – toys and clothes, everything related exclusively to Lydia – in the loft: psychologically buried in the space above us.

'The prob-lem with the Cheese Touch is that you've got it . . . un-til you can pass it on to some-one else . . .'

Lydia adored this plastic dragon. I remember the afternoon we bought it; I remember Lydia skipping down Regent's Park Road, waving the dragon in the air, dreaming of a pet dragon of her own, making us all smile. The memory suffuses me with sadness, so I discreetly slip the little dragon in the pocket of my jeans and calm myself, listening to Kirstie for a few more minutes, until the chapter is finished. She reluctantly closes the book and looks up at me: innocent, expectant.

'OK darling. Definitely time for bed.'

'But, Mummy.'

'But, Mummy nothing. Come on, Kirstie.'

A pause. It's the first time I've used her name since she said what she said. Kirstie looks at me, puzzled, and frowning. Is she going to use those terrible words again?

Mummy, I'm Lydia, it was Kirstie that died. Why do you keep calling me Kirstie?

My daughter shakes her head, as if I am making a very basic mistake. Then she says, 'OK, we're going to bed.'

We? *We?* What does she mean by 'we'? The silent, creeping anxiety sidles up behind me, but I refuse to be worried. I am worried. But I am worried about nothing.

We?

'OK. Goodnight, darling.'

This will all be gone tomorrow. Definitely. Kirstie just needs to go to sleep and to wake up in the morning, and then this unpleasant confusion will have disappeared, with her dreams.

'It's OK, Mummy. We can put our own 'jamas on, actually.'

I smile, and keep my words neutral. If I acknowledge this confusion it might make things worse. 'All right then, but we need to be quick. It's really late now, and you've got a school day tomorrow.'

Kirstie nods, sombrely. Looking at me.

School.

School.

Another source of grief.

I know – all-too-painfully, and all-too-guiltily – that she doesn't like her school much. Not any more. She used to love it when she had her sister in the same class. The Ice Twins were the Mischief Sisters, then. Every schoolday morning I would strap them in the back of my car, in their monochrome uniforms, and as I drove up Kentish Town Road to the gates of St Luke's I would watch them in the mirror: whispering and signalling to each other, pointing at people through the window, and collapsing in fits of laughter at in-jokes, at twin-jokes, at jokes that I never quite understood.

Every time we did this – each and every morning – I felt pride and love and yet, also, sometimes I felt perplexity, because the twins were so entire unto themselves. Speaking their twin language.

It was hard not to feel a little excluded, a lesser person in either of their lives than the identical and opposite person with whom they spent every minute of every day. Yet I adored them. I revered them.

And now it's all gone: now Kirstie goes to school alone, and she does it in silence. In the back of my car. Saying nothing. Staring in a trance-like way at a sadder world. She still has friends at the school, but they have not replaced Lydia. Nothing will ever come close to replacing Lydia. So maybe this is another good reason for leaving London: a new school, new friends, a playground not haunted by the ghost of her twin, giggling and miming.

'You brushed your teeth?'

'Immyjen did them, after tea.'

'OK then, hop into bed. Do you want me to tuck you in?'

'No. Mmm. Yes . . .'

She has stopped saying 'we'. The silly but disturbing confusion has passed? She climbs into bed and lays her face on the pillow and as she does she looks very small. Like a toddler again.

Kirstie's eyes are fluttering, and she is clutching Leopardy to her chest – and I am leaning to check the nightlight.

Just as I have done, almost every evening, for six years.

From the beginning, the twins were horribly scared of total darkness: it terrified them into special screams. After a year or so, we realized why: it was because, in pitch darkness, they couldn't see each other. For that reason Angus and I have always been religiously careful to keep some light available to the girls: we've always had lamps and nightlights to hand. Even when the twins got their own rooms, they still wanted light, at night, as if they could see each other through walls: as long as they had enough light.

Of course I wonder if, in time, this phobia will dwindle – now that one twin has gone for good, and cannot ever be seen. But for the moment it persists. Like an illness that should have gone away.

The nightlight is fine.

I set it down on the side table, and am turning to leave when Kirstie snaps her eyes open, and stares at me. Accusingly. Angrily? No. Not angry. But unsettled.

'What?' I say. 'What is it? Sweetheart, you have to go to sleep.'

'But, Mummy.'

'What is it?'

'Beany!'

The dog. Sawney Bean. Our big family spaniel. Kirstie loves the dog.

'Will Beany be coming to Scotland with us?'

'But, darling, don't be silly. Of course!' I say. 'We wouldn't leave him behind! Of course he's coming!'

Kirstie nods, placated. And then her eyes close and she grips Leopardy tight; and I can't resist kissing her again. I do this all the time now: more than I ever did before. Angus used to be the tactile parent, the hugger and kisser, whereas I was the organizer, the practical mother: loving them by feeding them, and clothing them. But now I kiss my surviving daughter as if it is some fervent, superstitious charm: a way of averting further harm.

The freckles on Kirstie's pale skin are like a dusting of cinnamon on milk. As I kiss her, I breathe her in: she smells of toothpaste, and maybe the sweetcorn she had for supper. She smells of Kirstie. But that means she smells of Lydia. They always smelled the same. No matter what they did, they always smelled the same.

A third kiss ensures she is safe. I whisper a quiet goodnight. Carefully I make my exit from her bedroom, with its twinkling nightlight; but as I quietly close the door, yet another thought is troubling me: the dog.

Beany.

23

What is it? Something about the dog concerns me; it agitates. But I'm not sure what. Or why.

Alone on the landing, I think it over. Concentrating.

We bought Beany three years ago: an excitable springer spaniel. That's when we could afford a pedigree puppy.

It was Angus's idea: a dog to go with our first proper garden; a dog that matched our proximity to Regent's Park. We called him Sawney Bean, after the Scottish cannibal, because he ate everything, especially chairs. Angus loved Beany, the twins loved Beany – and I loved the way they all interacted. I also adored, in a rather shallow way, the way they looked, two identically pretty little blonde girls, romping around Queen Mary's Rose Garden – with a happy, cantering, mahogany-brown spaniel.

Tourists would actually point and take photos. I was virtually a stage mother. *Oh, she has those lovely twins. With the beautiful dog. You know.*

Leaning against a wall, I close my eyes, to think more clearly. I can hear distant noises from the kitchen downstairs: cutlery rattling on a table, or maybe a bottle-opener being returned to a drawer.

What is it about Beany that feels wrong? There is definitely some troubled thought that descends from the concept *dog* – yet I cannot trace it, cannot follow it through the brambles of memory and grief.

Downstairs, the front door slams shut. The noise breaks the spell.

'Sarah Moorcroft,' I say, opening my eyes, 'Get a grip.'

I need to go down and talk to Immy and have a glass of wine and then go to bed, and tomorrow Kirstie – *Kirstie* – will go to school with her red book bag, wearing her black woollen jumper. The one with *Kirstie Moorcroft* written on the label inside.

In the kitchen, I find Imogen sitting at the counter. She smiles, tipsily, the faint tannin staining of red wine on her neat white teeth.

'Afraid Gus has nipped out.'

'Yes?'

'Yeah. He had a minor panic attack about the booze supply. You've only got' – she turns and looks at the wine rack by the fridge – 'six bottles left. So he's gone to Sainsbury's to stock up. Took Beany with him.'

I laugh, politely, and pull up a stool.

'Yes. Sounds like Angus.'

I pour myself half a glass of red from the open bottle on the counter, glancing at the label. Cheap Chilean Merlot. It used to be fancy Barossa Shiraz. I don't care.

Imogen watches me, and she says: 'He's still drinking a bit, ah, you know – excessively?'

'That's a nice way of putting it, Immy: "a bit excessively". He lost his job because he got so drunk he punched his boss. And knocked him out.'

Imogen nods. 'Sorry. Yes. Can't help talking in euphemisms. Comes with the day job.' She tilts her head and smiles. 'But the boss was a jerk, right?'

'Yes. His boss was totally obnoxious, but it's still not great, is it? Breaking the nose of London's richest architect.'

'Uh-huh. Sure . . .' Imogen smiles slyly. 'Though, y'know, it's not all bad. I mean, at least he can throw a punch – like a man. Remember that Irish guy I dated, last year – he used to wear yoga pants.'

She smirks my way; I force half a smile.

Imogen is a journalist like me, though a vastly more successful one. She is a deputy editor on a women's

25

gossip magazine that, miraculously, has a growing circulation; I scrape an unreliable living as a freelancer. This might have made me jealous of her, but our friendship is, or was, evened out by the fact I got married and had kids. She is single and childless. We used to compare notes – *what my life could have been.*

Now I lean back, holding my wine glass airily: trying to be relaxed. 'Actually he's not drinking as much as he used to.'

'Good.

'But it's still too late. For his career at Kimberley.'

Imogen nods sympathetically – and drinks. I sip at my wine, and sigh in a what-can-you-do way, and gaze around our big bright Camden kitchen, at all the granite worktops and shining steel, the black espresso machine with its set of golden capsules: all of it screaming: this is the kitchen of a well-to-do middle-class couple!

And all of it a lie.

We *were* a well-to-do middle-class couple, for a while, after Angus got promoted three times in three years. For a long time everything was pristinely optimistic: Angus was heading for a partnership and a handsome salary, and I was more than happy for him to be the main earner, the provider, because this allowed me to combine my part-time journalism with proper mothering. It allowed me to do the school run, to make cooked but healthy breakfasts, to stand in the kitchen turning basil into organic pesto when the twins were playing on one of our iPads. For half a decade we were, most of the time, the perfect Camden family.

Then Lydia died, falling from the balcony at my parents' house in Devon, and it was as if someone had dropped Angus from a height. A hundred thousand pieces of Angus were scattered around the place. His grief was psychotic.

A raging fire of anguish that could not be quenched, even with a bottle of whisky a night, much as he tried. Every night.

The firm gave him latitude, and weeks off, but it wasn't enough. He was uncontrollable; he went back to work too soon and got into arguments, then fights. He resigned an hour before he was sacked; ten hours after he punched the boss. And he hasn't worked since, apart from a few freelance design jobs pushed his way by sympathetic friends.

'Sod it, Imogen,' I say. 'At least we're moving. At last.'

'Yes!' she says brightly. 'Into a cave, right, in Shetland?'

She's teasing. I don't mind. We used to tease each other all the time, before the accident.

Now our relationship is more stilted; but we make an effort. Other friendships ended entirely, after Lydia's death: too many people didn't know what to say, so they said nothing. By contrast, Imogen keeps trying: nurturing the low flame of our friendship.

I look at her, and say,

'Torran Island, you remember? I've shown you photos, every time you've come here, for the last month.'

'Ah yes. Torran! The famous homeland. But tell me again, I like it.'

'It's going to be great, Immy – if we don't freeze. Apparently there are rabbits, and otters, and seals—'

'Fantastic. I love seals.'

'You do?'

'Oh yes. Especially the pups. Can you sort me out a coat?'

I laugh – sincerely, but guiltily. Imogen and I share a sense of humour; but hers is wickeder. She goes on. 'So this place. Torran. Remind me. You still haven't been there?'

'Nope.'

'Sarah. How can you move to a place you've never even seen?'

Silence.

I finish my glass of Merlot and pour some more. 'I told you. I don't *want* to see it.'

Another pause.

'Uh-huh?'

'Immy, I don't want to see it for real, because – what if I don't like it?' I stare into her wide green eyes. 'Mmm? What then? Then I'm stuck here, Imogen. Stuck here with everything, all the memories, the money problems, everything. We're out of cash anyway, so we'll have to move to some stupid tiny flat, back where we started, and – and then what? I'll have to go out to work and Angus will go stir crazy and it's just – just – you know – I have to get out, we have to get out, and this is it: the way of escape. And it does look so beautiful in the photos. It does, it does: so bloody beautiful. It's like a dream, but who cares? I want a dream. Right this minute, that's exactly what I want. Because reality has been *pretty fucking crap for a while now.*'

The kitchen is quiet. Imogen raises her glass and she gently chinks mine and says: 'Darling. It will be lovely. I'm just going to miss you.'

We lock eyes, briefly, and moments later Angus is in the kitchen; his overcoat speckled with cold autumn rain. He is carrying wine in doubled orange plastic bags – and leading the dampened dog. Carefully he sets the bags on the floor, then unleashes Beany.

'Here you go, boy.'

The spaniel shivers and wags his tail and heads straight for his wicker basket. Meanwhile I extract the wine bottles, and set them up on the counter; like a small but important parade.

'Well, that should last an hour,' Imogen says, staring at all the wine.

Angus grabs a bottle and unscrews it.

'Ach. Sainsbury's is a battleground. I'm not gonna miss the Camden junkies, buying their lemon juice.'

Imogen tuts. 'Wait till you're three hundred miles from the nearest truffle oil.'

Angus laughs – and it is a good laugh, a natural laugh. Like a laugh from before it all happened. And finally I relax; though I also remember that I want to ask him about the little toy: the plastic dragon. How did that end up in Kirstie's bedroom? It was Lydia's. It was boxed and hidden away, I am sure of it.

But why ruin this rare and agreeable evening with an interrogation? The question can wait for another day. Or for ever.

Our glasses replenished, we sit and chat and have an impromptu kitchen-picnic: rough slices of ciabatta dipped in olive oil, thick chunks of cheap saucisson. And for an hour or more we talk, companionably, contentedly – like the three old friends we are. Angus explains how his brother – living in California – has generously forgone his share of the inheritance.

'David's earning a shedload, in Silicon Valley. Doesn't need the cash or the hassle. And he knows that we DO need it.' Angus swallows his saucisson.

Imogen interrupts: 'But what I don't understand, Gus, is how come your granny owned this island in the first place? I mean' – she chews an olive – 'don't be offended, but I thought your dad was a serf, and you and your mum lived in an outside toilet. Yet suddenly here's grandmother with her own island.'

Angus chuckles. 'Nan was on my mother's side, from Skye. They were just humble farmers, one up from

29

crofters. But they had a smallholding, which happened to include an island.'

'OK . . .'

'It's pretty common. There're thousands of little islands in the Hebrides, and fifty years ago a one-acre island of seaweed off Ornsay was worth about three quid. So it just never got sold. Then my mum moved down to Glasgow, and Nan followed, and Torran became, like, a holiday place. For me and my brother.'

I finish my husband's story for him, as he fetches more olive oil: 'Angus's mum met Angus's dad in Glasgow. She was a primary school teacher, he worked in the docks—'

'He, uh . . . drowned, right?'

'Yes. An accident at the docks. Quite tragic, really.'

Angus interrupts, walking back: 'The old man was a soak. And a wife-beater. Not sure tragic is the word.'

We all stare at the three remaining bottles of wine on the counter. Imogen speaks: 'But still – where does the lighthouse and the cottage fit in? How did they get there? If your folks were poor?'

Angus replies, 'Northern Lighthouse Board run all the lighthouses in Scotland. Last century, whenever they needed to build a new one, they would offer a bit of cash in ground rent to the property owner. That's what happened on Torran. But then the lighthouse got automated. In the sixties. So the cottage was vacated. And it reverted to my family.'

'Stroke of luck?' says Imogen.

'Looking back, aye,' says Angus. 'We got a big, solidly built cottage. For nothing.'

A voice from upstairs intrudes.

'Mummy . . .?'

It's Kirstie. Awakened. And calling from the landing.

This happens quite a lot. Yet her voice, especially when heard unexpectedly, always gives me a brief, repressed, upwelling of grief. Because it sounds like Lydia.

I want these drowning feelings to stop.

'*Mummyyy?*'

Angus and I share a resigned glance: both of us mentally calculating the last time this happened. Like two very new parents squabbling over whose turn it is to baby-feed, at three a.m.

'I'll go,' I say. 'It's my turn.'

And it is: the last time Kirstie woke up, after one of her nightmares, was just a few days ago, and Angus had loyally traipsed upstairs to do the comforting.

Setting down my wine glass, I head for the first floor. Beany is following me, eagerly, as if we are going rabbiting; his tail whips against the table legs.

Kirstie is barefoot, at the top of the stairs. She is the image of troubled innocence with her big blue eyes, and with Leopardy pressed to her buttoned pyjama-top.

'It did it again, Mummy, the dream.'

'Come on, Moomin. It's just a bad dream.'

I pick her up – she is almost too heavy, these days – and carry her back into the bedroom. Kirstie is, it seems, not too badly flustered; though I wish this repetitive nightmare would stop. As I tuck her in her bed, again, she is already half-closing her eyes, even as she talks.

'It was all white, Mummy, all around me, I was stuck in a room, all white, all faces staring at me.'

'Shhhhh.'

'It was white and I was scared and I couldn't move then and then . . . then . . .'

'Shushhh.'

I stroke her faintly fevered, blemishless forehead. Her

31

eyelids flicker towards sleep. But a whimpering, from behind me, stirs her.

The dog has followed me into the bedroom.

Kirstie searches my face for a favour.

'Can Beany stay with me, Mummy? Can he sleep in my room tonight?'

I don't normally allow this. But tonight I just want to go back downstairs, and drink another glass, with Immy and Angus.

'All right, Sawney Bean can stay, just this once.'

'Beany!' Kirstie leans up from her pillow, and reaches a little hand and jiggles the dog's ears.

I stare at my daughter, meaningfully.

'Thuh?'

'Thank you, Mummy.'

'Good. Now you must go back to sleep. School tomorrow.'

She hasn't called herself 'we', she hasn't called herself 'Lydia'. This is a serious relief. When she settles her head on the cool pillow I walk to the door.

But as I back away, my eyes fix on the dog.

He is lying by Kirstie's bed, and his head is meekly tilted, ready for sleep.

And now the sense of dread returns. Because I've worked it out: what was troubling me. The dog. The dog is behaving differently.

From the day we bought Beany home to our ecstatic little girls, his relationship with the twins was marked – yet it was, also, differentiated. My twins might have been identical, but Sawney did not love them identically.

With Kirstie, the first twin, the buoyant twin, the surviving twin, the leader of mischief, the girl sleeping in this bed, right now, in this room, Beany is extrovert:

32

jumping up at her when she gets home from school, chasing her playfully down the hall – making her scream in delighted terror.

With Lydia, the quieter twin, the more soulful twin, the twin that used to sit and read with me for hours, the twin that fell to her death last year, our spaniel was always gentle, as if sensing her more vulnerable personality. He would nuzzle her, and press his paws on her lap: amiable and warm.

And Sawney Bean also liked to sleep in Lydia's room if he could, even though we usually chased him out; and when he did come in to her room, he would lie by her bed at night, and tilt his head, meekly.

As he is doing now, with Kirstie.

I stare at my hands; they have a fine tremor. The anxiety is like pins and needles.

Because Beany is not extrovert with Kirstie any more. He behaves with Kirstie exactly as he used to with Lydia.

Gentle. Nuzzling. Soft.

The self-questioning surges. When did the dog's behaviour change? Right after Lydia's death? Later?

I strive, but I cannot remember. The last year has been a blur of grief: so much has altered I have paid no attention to the dog. So what has happened? Is it possible the dog is, somehow, grieving? Can an animal mourn? Or is it something else, something worse?

I have to investigate this: I can't let it lie. Quickly I exit Kirstie's room, leaving her to her reassuring nightlight; then I pace five yards to the next door. Lydia's old room.

We have transformed Lydia's room into an office space: trying, unsuccessfully, to erase the memories with work. The walls are lined with books, mostly mine. And plenty of them – at least half a shelf – are about twins.

When I was pregnant I read every book I could find on this subject. It's the way I process things: I read about them. So I read books on the problems of twin prematurity, books on the problems on twin individuation, books that told me how a twin is more closely related, genetically, to her co-twin, to her twin sibling, than she is to her parents, or even her own children.

And I also read something about twins and dogs. I am sure.

Urgently I search the shelves. This one? No. This one? Yes.

Pulling down the book – *Multiple Births: A Practical Guide* – I flick hurriedly to the index.

Dogs, page 187.

And here it is. This is the paragraph I remembered.

Identical twins can sometimes be difficult to physically differentiate, well into their teenage years – even, on occasion, for their parents. Curiously, however, dogs do not have the same difficulty. Such is the canine sense of smell, a dog – a family pet, for instance – can, after a few weeks, permanently differentiate between one twin and another, by scent alone.

The book rests in my hands; but my eyes are staring into the total blackness of the uncurtained window. Piecing together the evidence.

Kirstie's personality *has* become quieter, shyer, more reserved, this last year. More like Lydia's. Until now I had ascribed this to grief. After all, everyone has changed this last year.

But what if we have made a terrible mistake? The most terrible mistake imaginable? How would we unravel it? What could we do? What would it do to all of us? I know one thing: I cannot tell my fractured husband any of this. I cannot tell anyone. There is no point in dropping this bomb. Not until I am sure. But how do I prove this, one way or another?

Dry-mouthed and anxious, I walk out onto the landing. I stare at the door. And those words written in spangled, cut-out paper letters.

Kirstie Lives Here.

3

I once read a survey that explained how moving house is as traumatic as a divorce, or as the death of a parent. I feel the opposite: for the two weeks after our meeting with Walker – for the two weeks after Kirstie said what she said – I am fiercely *pleased* that we are moving house, because it means I am overworked and, at least sometimes, distracted.

I like the thirst-inducing weariness in my arms as I lift cases from lofty cupboards, I like the tang of old dust in my mouth as I empty and scour the endless bookshelves.

But the doubts will not be entirely silenced. At least once a day I compare the history of the twins' upbringing with the details of Lydia's death. Is it possible, could it be possible, that we misidentified the daughter we lost?

I don't know. And so I am stalling. For the last two weeks whenever I've dropped Kirstie off at school, I've called her 'darling' and 'Moomin' and anything-but-her-real-name, because I am scared she will turn and give me her tranced, passive, blue-eyed stare and say *I'm Lydia. Not Kirstie. Kirstie is dead. One of us is dead.*

We're dead. I'm alive. I'm Lydia. How could you get that wrong, Mummy? How did you do that? How?

And after that I get to work, to stop myself thinking.

Today I am tackling the toughest job. As Angus has left, on an early flight to Scotland, preparing the way, and as Kirstie is in school – *Kirstie Jane Kerrera Moorcroft* – I am going to sort the loft. Where we keep what is left of Lydia. *Lydia May Tanera Moorcroft.*

Standing under the hinged wooden trapdoor, I position the unfeasibly light aluminium stepladder, and pause. Helpless. Thinking again.

Start from the beginning, Sarah Moorcroft. Work it out.

Kirstie and Lydia.

We gave the twins different-but-related names because we wanted to emphasize their individuality, yet acknowledge their unique twin status: just as all the books and websites advised. Kirstie was named thus by her dad, as it was his beloved grandmother's name. Scottish, sweet, and lyrical.

By way of equity, I was allowed to choose Lydia's name. I made it classical, indeed ancient Greek. Lydia. I chose this partly because I love history, and partly because I am very fond of the name Lydia, and partly because it was not like Kirstie at all.

I chose the second names, May and Jane, for my grandmothers. Angus chose the third names, for two little Scottish islands: Kerrera and Tanera.

A week after the twins were born – long before we made the ambitious move to Camden – we ferried our precious, newborn, identical babies in the back of the car, through the freezing sleet, home to our humble apartment. And we were so pleased with the result of our name-making efforts, we laughed and kissed, exultantly, as we parked – and said the names over and over.

Kirstie Jane Kerrera Moorcroft.

Lydia May Tanera Moorcroft.

As far as we were concerned, we had names that were subtly intertwined, and apposite for twins; we had names that were poetic and pretty and nicely paired, without going anywhere near Tweedledum and Tweedledee.

So what happened then?

It is time to sort the loft.

Climbing the stepladder, I shove hard against the trapdoor – and with a painful creak it flies open, quite suddenly, slamming against the rafters with a smash. The sound is so loud, so obtrusive, it makes me hesitate, tingling with nerves: as if there is something up here, asleep – which I might have just woken.

Pulling the torch from the back pocket of my jeans, I switch it on. And direct it upwards.

The square of blackness stares down at me. A swallowing void. Again, I hesitate. I am trying to deny that frisson of fear. But it is there. I am alone in the house – apart from Beany, who is sleeping in his basket in the kitchen. I can hear the November rain pattering on the slates of the roof above me, up there in the blackness. Like many fingernails tapping in irritation.

Tap tap tap.

Anxieties stir in my mind. I climb another rung on the stepladder, thinking about Kirstie and Lydia.

Tap Tap Tap. Kirstie And Lydia.

When we brought the twins home from hospital, we realized that, yes, we might have sorted the names satisfactorily, but we still had another dilemma: differing between them in person was much harder.

Because our twins matched. Superbly. They were amongst the most identical of identicals, they were the kind of brilliant 'idents' that made nurses from other wards cross long corridors, just to ogle our amazing twins.

Some monozygotic twins are not that identical at all. They have different skin tones, different blemishes, very different voices. Others are mirror-image twins, they are identical but their identicality is that of a reflection in the mirror, left and right are switched: one twin will have hair that swirls clockwise, the other will have hair that swirls anti-clockwise.

But Kirstie and Lydia Moorcroft were true idents: they had identically snowy-blonde hair, exactly matching icy-blue eyes, precisely the same button-noses, the same sly and playful smiles, the same perfect pink mouths when they yawned, the same creases and giggles and freckles and moles. They were mirror images, without the reversal.

Tap, tap, tap . . .

Slowly and carefully, maybe a little timidly, I ascend the last rungs of the ladder and peer into the gloom of the attic, following the beam of my torch. Still thinking. Still remembering. My torch-beam picks out the brown metal frame of a Maclaren twin buggy. It cost us a fortune at the time, but we didn't care. We wanted the twins to sit side by side, staring ahead, even as we wheeled them around. Because they were a team from birth. Babbling their twinspeak, entirely engrossed in each other: just as they had been from conception.

Through my pregnancy, as we went from one sono-gram to the next, I actually watched the twins move closer, inside me – going from body contacts in week 12, to 'complex embraces' in week 14. By week 16, as

40

my paediatrician pointed out, my twins were occasionally kissing.

The noise of the rain is more persistent now, like an irritated hiss. *Hurry up. We're waiting. Hurry up.*

I do not need encouragement to hurry. I want to get this job done. Briskly I scan the darkness – and my torch-beam alights on an old, deflated Thomas the Tank Engine daybed. Thomas the Tank Engine leers at me, dementedly cheerful. Red and yellow and clownish. That can definitely stay. Along with the other daybed, which must be up here. The blue one we bought for Kirstie.

Daughter one. Daughter two. *Yellow and blue.*

At first, we differentiated our babies by painting one of their respective fingernails, or toenails, yellow or blue. Yellow was for Lydia, because it rhymed with her nickname: Lydee-lo. *Yell-ow*. Blue was for Kirstie. Kirstie-*koo*.

This nail-varnishing was a compromise. A nurse at the hospital advised us to have one of the twins tattooed in a discreet place: on a shoulder-blade, perhaps, or at the top of an ankle – just a little indelible mark, so there could be no mistake. But we resisted this notion, as it seemed far too drastic, even barbaric: tattooing one of our perfect, innocent, flawless new children? No.

Yet we couldn't do nothing. So we relied on nail varnish, diligently and carefully applied once a week, for a year. After that – until we were able to distinguish them by their distinctive personalities, and by their own responses to their own names – we relied on the differing clothes we gave the girls; some of the same clothes that are now bagged in this dusty loft.

As with the nail varnish, we had yellow clothes for

Lydie-lo. Blue clothes for Kirstie-koo. We didn't dress them entirely in block colours; a yellow girl and a blue girl, but we made sure that Kirstie always had a blue jumper, or blue socks, or blue bobble hat, while the other was blue-less; meanwhile Lydia had a yellow T-shirt, or maybe a dark yellow ribbon in her pale yellow hair.

Hurry now. Hurry up.

I want to hurry, but it also seems wrong. How can I be businesslike up here? In this place? The cardboard boxes marked L for Lydia are everywhere. Accusing, silent, loaded. The boxes that contain her life.

I want to shout her name: Lydia. Lydia. Come back. Lydia May Tanera Moorcroft. I want to shout her name like I did when she died, when I stared down from the balcony, and saw her little body, splayed and yet crumpled, still breathing, but dying.

And now I am gagging on the attic dust. Or maybe it is the memories.

Little Lydia running into my arms as we tried to fly kites on Hampstead Heath and she got scared by the rippling noise; little Lydia sitting on my lap earnestly writing her name for the first time, in waxy scented crayon; little Lydia dwarfed in Daddy's big chair, shyly hiding behind a propped atlas as large as herself. Lydia, the silent one, the bookish one, the soulful one, the slightly lost and incomplete one – Lydia the twin like me. Lydia who once said, when she was sitting with her sister on a bench in a park: *Mummy, come and sit between me so you can read to us.*

Come and sit between *me*? Even then, there was some confusion, a blurring of identity. Something slightly unnerving. And now beloved Lydia is gone. Isn't she? Or maybe she is alive down there, even as her stuff is

42

crated and boxed up here? If that is the case, how would we possibly untangle this, without destroying the family?

The complexities are intolerable. I am talking to myself.

Work, Sarah, work. Sort the loft. Do the job. Ignore the grief, get rid of the stuff you don't need, then move to Scotland, to Skye, the open skies: where Kirstie – Kirstie, Kirstie, Kirstie – can run wild and free. Where we can all soar away, escaping the past, like the eiders flying over the Cuillins.

One of the boxes is ripped open.

I stare, bewildered, and shocked. Lydia's biggest box of toys has been sliced open. Brutally. Who would do that? It has to be Angus. But why? And with such careless savagery? Why wouldn't he tell me? We discussed everything to do with Lydia's things. But now he has been retrieving Lydia's toys, without telling me?

The rain is hissing, once again. And very close, a few feet above my head.

Leaning into the opened box, I pull back a flap to have a look, and as I do, I hear a different noise – a distinctive, metallic rattle. Someone is climbing the stepladder?

Yes.

The noise is unmistakable. Someone is in the house. How did they get in without my hearing? Who is this climbing into the loft? Why didn't Beany start barking, in the kitchen?

I stand back. Absurdly frightened.

'Hello? Hello? Who is it? Hello??'

'All right, Gorgeous?'

'Angus!'

He smiles in the half-light which shines from the landing beneath. He looks definitely odd: like a cheap

43

horror movie villain, someone illuminated from below by a ghoulish torch.

'Jesus, Angus, you scared me!'

'Sorry, babe.'

'I thought you were on the way to Scotland?'

Angus hauls himself up, and stands opposite. He is so tall – six foot three – he has to stoop slightly, or crack his dark handsome head on the rafters.

'Forgot my passport. You have to take them these days – even for domestic flights.' Angus is glancing beyond me, at the ripped-open carton of toys. Motes of dust hang in the air, between our two faces, caught by my torchlight. I want to shine the torch right in his eyes. Is he frowning? Smiling? Looming angrily? I cannot see. He is too tall, there is not enough light. But the mood is awkward. And strained.

He speaks. 'What are you doing, Sarah?'

I turn my torch-beam, so it shines directly on the cardboard box. Crudely knifed open.

'What it looks like?'

'OK.'

His silhouette, with the downstairs light behind him, has an uncomfortable shape, as if he is tensed, or angry. Menacing. Why? I talk in a hurry.

'I'm sorting all this stuff. Gus, you know we have to do something, don't we? About – About—' I swallow away the grief, and gaze into the shadows of his face. 'We have to sort Lydia's toys and clothes. I know you don't want to, but we have to decide. Do they come with us, or do we do something else?'

'Get rid?'

'Yes . . . Maybe.'

'OK. OK. Ah. I don't know.'

Silence. And the ceaseless rain.

We are stuck here. Stuck in this place, this groove, this attic. I want us to move on, but I need to know the truth about the box.

'Angus?'

'Look, I've got to go.' He is backing away, and heading for the ladder. 'Let's talk about it later, I can Skype you from Ornsay.'

'Angus!'

'Booked on the next flight, but I'll miss that one too, if I'm not careful. Probably have to overnight in Inverness now.' His voice is disappearing as he clambers down the ladder. He is leaving – and his exit has a furtive, guilty quality.

'Wait!'

I almost trip over, in my haste to follow him. Slipping down the ladder. He is heading for the stairs.

'Angus, *wait*.'

He turns, checking his wristwatch as he does.

'Yeah?'

'Did you—' I don't want to ask this; I have to ask this. 'Gus. Did you open the box of Lydia's toys?'

He pauses. Fatally.

'Sure,' he replies.

'Why, Angus? Why on earth did you do that?'

'Because Kirstie was bored with *her* toys.'

His face has an expression that is designed to appear relaxed. And I get the horrible sensation that he is lying. *My husband is lying to me.*

I'm lost; yet I have to say something.

'So, Angus, you went into the loft and got one out? One of Lydia's toys? Just like that?'

He stares at me, unblinking. From three yards down the landing, with its bare pictureless walls and the big dustless squares, where we have already shifted furniture.

My second-favourite bookcase, Angus's precious chest of drawers, a legacy from his grandmother.

'Yes. So? Hm?? What's the problem, Sarah? Did I cross into enemy territory?' His reassuring face is gone. He is definitely frowning. It is that dark, foreboding frown, which presages anger. I think of the way he hit his boss. I think of his father who beat his mother: more than once. No. This is my husband. He would never lay a finger on me. But he is very obviously angry as he goes on: 'Kirstie was bored and unhappy. Saying she missed Lydia. You were out, Sarah. Coffee with Imogen. Right? So I thought, why not get her some of Lydia's toys. Mm? That will console her. And deal with her boredom. So that's what I did. OK? Is that OK?'

His sarcasm is heavy. And bitter.

'But—'

'What would you have done? Said no? Told her to shut up and play with her own toys? Told her to forget that her sister existed?'

He turns and crosses the landing – and begins to descend the stairs. And now I'm the one that feels guilty. His explanation makes sense. Yes, that's what I would do, in the same situation. I think.

'Angus—'

'Yes?' He pauses, five steps away.

'I'm sorry. Sorry for interrogating you. It was a bit of a shock, that's all.'

'Tsch.' He looks upwards, and his smile returns. Or at least a trace of it. 'Don't worry about it, darling. I'll see you in Ornsay, OK? You take the low road and I'll take the high road.'

'And you'll be in Scotland before me?'

'Aye!'

He is laughing now, in a mirthless way, and then

he is saying goodbye, and then he is turning to leave: to get his passport and his bags, to go and fly up to Scotland.

I hear him in the kitchen. His white smile lingers in my mind.

The door slams, downstairs. Angus is gone. And quite suddenly: I miss him, physically.

I want him. Still. More. Maybe more than ever, as it has been too long.

I want to tempt him back inside, and unbutton his shirt, and I want us to have sex as if we haven't had sex in many months. Even more, I want him to want to do that to *me*. I want him to march back into the house and I want him to strip away my clothes: just like we did, in the beginning, in our first years, when he would come home from work and – without a word passing between – we would start undressing in the hall and we would make love in the first place we found: on the kitchen table, on the bathroom floor, in the rainy garden, in a delirium of beautiful appetite.

Then we'd lie back and laugh at the sheen of happy sweat that we shared, at the blatant trail of clothes we'd left behind, like breadcrumbs in a fairy tale, leading from the front door to our lovemaking, and so we'd follow our clothes back, picking up knickers, then jeans, then my shirt, his shirt, then a jacket, my jumper. And then we'd eat cold pizza. Smiling. Guiltless. Jubilant.

We were happy, then. Happier than any other couple I've known. Sometimes I actively envy us, as *we were*. Like I am the jealous neighbour of my previous self. Those bloody Moorcrofts, with their perfect life, completed by the adorable twins, then the beautiful dog.

And yet, and yet – even as the jealousy surges, I know

47

that this completion was something of an illusion. Because our life wasn't always perfect. Not *always*. In those long dark months, immediately following the birth, we almost broke up.

Who was to blame? Maybe me; maybe Angus; maybe sex itself. Of course I was expecting our love-life to suffer, when the twins arrived – but I didn't expect it to die entirely. Yet it did. After the birth Angus became a kind of sexual exile. He did not want to touch me, and when he did, it was as if my body was a new, difficult, less pleasant proposition, something to be handled with scientific care. Once, I caught sight of him in a mirror, looking at me: he was assessing my changed and maternal nakedness. My stretch marks, and my leaking nipples. A grimace flashed across his face.

For too long – almost a year – we went entirely without lovemaking.

When the twins began sleeping through the night, and when I felt nearer to myself again, I tried to instigate it; yet he refused with weak excuses: too tired, too drunk, too much work. He was never home.

And so I found sex elsewhere, for a few brief evenings, stolen from my loneliness. Angus was immersed in a new project at Kimberley and Co, blatantly ignoring me, always working late. I was desperately isolated, still lost down the black hole of early motherhood, bored of microwaving milk bottles. Bored of dealing with two screaming tots, on my own. An old boyfriend called up, to congratulate the new mother. Eagerly I seized on this minor excitement, this thrill of the old. Oh, why not come round for a drink, come and see the twins? Come and see me?

Angus never found out, not of his own volition: I ended the perfunctory affair, and simply told my husband, because the guilt was too much, and, probably, because I wanted to punish my husband. *See how lonely I have been.* And the irony is that my hurtful confession saved us, it refuelled our sex life.

Because, after that confession, his perception of me reverted: now I wasn't just a boring, bone-weary, conversation-less new mother any more, I was once again a prize, a sexual possession, a body carnally desired by a rival. Angus took me back; he seized me and recaptured me. He forgave me by fucking me. Then we had our marital therapy; and we got our show back on the road. Because we still loved each other.

But I will always wonder what permanent damage I did. Perhaps we simply hid the damage away, all those years. As a couple, we are good at hiding.

And now here I am: back in the attic, staring at all the hidden boxes that contain the chattels of our dead daughter. But at least I have decided something: storage. That's what we will do with all this stuff.

It is a cowardly way out, neither one thing nor the other, but I cannot bear to haul Lydia's toys to far northern Scotland – why would I do that? To indulge the passing strangeness of Kirstie? Yet consigning them to oblivion is cruel and impossible.

One day I will do this, but not yet.

So storage it is.

Enlivened by this decision I get to work. For three hours I box and tape and unpack and box things up again, then I grab a quick meal of soup and yesterday's bread, and I pick up my mobile. I am pleased by my own efficiency. I have one more duty to do, just one more doubt to erase. Then all this silliness is finished.

'Miss Emerson?'

'Hello?'

'Um, hi, it's Sarah. Sarah Moorcroft?'

'Sorry. Sarah. Yes, of course. And call me Nuala, please!'

'OK . . .' I hesitate. Miss Emerson is Kirstie's teacher: a bright, keen, diligent twenty-something. A source of solace in the last horrible year. But she has always been 'Miss Emerson' to the kids – and now to Kirstie – so it always seems dislocating to use her first name. I find it persistently awkward. But I need to try. 'Nuala.'

'Yes.'

Her voice is brisk; it is 5 p.m. Kirstie is in after-school club, but her teacher will still have work to do.

'Uhm. Can you spare a minute? It's just that I have a couple of questions, about Kirstie.'

'I can spare five, it's no problem. What is it?'

'You know we are moving very soon.'

'To Skye? Yes. And you have another school placement?'

'Yes, the new school is called Kylerdale, I've checked *all* the Ofsted reports, it's bilingual, in English and Gaelic. Of course it won't be anything like St Luke's, but . . .'

'Sarah. You had a question?'

Her tone is not impatient. But it expresses busyness. She could be doing something else.

'Uh, yes. Sorry, yes, I did.'

I stare out of the living-room window, which is half open.

The rain has stopped. The tangy, breezy darkness of an autumn evening encroaches. The trees across the street are being robbed of their leaves, one by one. Clutching the phone a little harder, I go on,

'Nuala, what I wanted to ask was . . .' I tense myself, as if I am about to dive into very cold water. 'Have you noticed anything odd about Kirstie recently?'

A moment passes.

'Odd?'

'You know, er, odd. Er . . .'

This is pitiful. But what else can I say? Oh, hey, Miss Emerson, has Kirstie started claiming she is her dead sister?

'No, I've seen nothing odd.' Miss Emerson's reply is gentle. *Dealing with bereaved parents.* 'Of course Kirstie still misses her sister, anyone can see that, but in the very challenging circumstances I'd say your daughter is coping quite well. As well as can be expected.'

'Thank you,' I say. 'I have just one last question.'

'OK.'

I steel myself, once again. I have to ask about Kirstie's reading. Her rapid improvement. That too has been bugging me.

'So, Nuala, what about Kirstie's skill levels, her development. Have you noticed anything different, any recent changes? Changes in her abilities? In class?'

This time there is silence. A long silence.

Nuala murmurs. 'Well . . .'

'Yes?'

'It's not dramatic. But there is, I think – I think there's one thing I could mention.'

The trees bend and suffer in the wind.

'What is it?'

'Recently I've noticed that Kirstie has got a lot better at reading. In a short space of time. It's a fairly surprising leap. And yet she used to be very good at maths, and now she is . . . not quite so good at that.' I can envisage

Nuala shrugging, awkwardly, at her end of the line. She goes on, 'And I suppose you could say that is unexpected?'

I say, perhaps, what we are both thinking: 'Her sister used to be good at reading and not so good at maths.'

Nuala says, quietly, 'Yes, yes, that is possibly true.'

'OK. OK. Anything else? Anything else like this?'

Another painful pause, then Nuala says: 'Yes, perhaps. Just the last few weeks, I've noticed Kirstie has become much more friendly with Rory and Adelie.'

The falling leaves flutter. I repeat the names. 'Rory. And. Adelie.'

'That's right, and they were,' Nuala hesitates, then continues, 'well, they were Lydia's friends, really, as you no doubt know. And Kirstie has rather dropped her own friends.'

'Zola? Theo?'

'Zola and Theo. And it was pretty abrupt. But really, these things happen all the time, she's only seven, your daughter, fairly young for her year.'

'OK.'

My throat is numbed. 'OK.' I repeat. 'OK. I see.'

'So please don't worry. I wouldn't have mentioned this if you hadn't asked about Kirstie's development.'

'No.'

'For what it's worth, Sarah, my professional guess is that Kirstie is, in some way, compensating for the absence of her sister, almost trying to be her sister, so as to replace her, to moderate the grief. Thus, for instance, she has worked to become a better reader, to fill that gap. I'm not a child psychologist – but, as I understand it, this might not be unusual.'

'No. No. Yes.'

'And all children grieve in their own way. This is probably just part of the healing process. So, when are you leaving? It's very soon, yes?'

'Yes,' I say. 'This weekend.'

The phone feels heavy in my hand.

I gaze at the elegant houses across the street; the parked cars glinting under the streetlights. The twilight is now complete. The sky is clear. I can see all the many plane lights circling London, like little red sparks: rising from a vast and invisible fire.

4

Angus Moorcroft parked outside the Selkie Hotel, climbed from his cheap, tinny rental car – hired last night at Inverness Airport – and gazed across the mudflats, and the placid waters, to Torran. The sky was clean of cloud, giving a rare glimpse of northern sun: on a cold November day. Despite the clarity of the air, the cottage was only just visible, peering above the seaweedy rocks, with the white lighthouse behind.

With a hand shielding the sun, Angus squinted at his family's new home. But a second car disturbed his thoughts – squealing to a stop, and parking. An old blue Renault.

His friend Josh Freedland got out, wearing a chunky Arran jumper, and jeans faintly floured with the dust of granite, or slate, or marble. Angus waved, and briefly looked down at his own jeans. He was going to miss good suits and silk ties.

Josh approached.

'The white settler has arrived!'

The two men hugged, slapping backs. Angus apologized for his own lateness, for missing the original flight – Josh told him not to worry.

This response had a certain irony, in Angus's mind. There was a time when it was Josh who was always late. When Josh was the most unreliable man in Great Britain. Everything was changing.

As one, they both turned, and gazed at the view across the Sound.

Angus murmured. 'You know, I'd forgotten just how beautiful it is.'

'So, when *was* the last time you were here?'

'With you. And the gang. That last summer holiday.'

'Really?' Josh smiled, in frank surprise. 'Junkie overboard! Junkie overboard!'

It was a catchphrase from that memorable holiday: when they'd come up here as college kids, to Angus's granny's island. They'd spent an epic weekend drinking too much, laughing too much, being obnoxious and loud, annoying the locals – and having enormous fun. They'd nearly sunk the rowing boat as they sculled back from the Selkie in the sweet, violet, Scottish summer gloaming: the twilight that never went totally black. Seals had emerged: perpendicular, and observing them. 'Junkie overboard' was born from one spectacularly intoxicated episode, when Josh, completely mashed on Ecstasy, had tried to embrace one of these seals, then fallen in the cold black water – at maybe 11 p.m.

It was a potentially lethal accident, but they were twenty-one years old and obviously immortal. So Josh just swam to the island, fully clothed – and then they'd got drunk, all over again, in that cranky, beautiful lighthouse-keeper's cottage.

'How long ago was that? Fifteen years? Jesus!' Josh was chatting away, hands in pockets. The cool sunny wind tousled his ginger Jewish hair. 'But we had fun, didn't we? All that cider we drank in Coruisk. You seen any of the gang?'

'Not so much.'

Angus could have added *for obvious reasons*. But he didn't have to. Josh knew all the facts.

This last year, following Lydia's death, Angus had turned to Josh, above all others: for long consoling phone calls, and the odd one-sided session in the pub, when Josh came down to London. And Josh had done his duty, listening to Angus talking about Lydia. Talking until the words turned to spit, until the words were a bodily fluid being purged, drooling from his mouth; talking until whisky and sleep blotted everything.

Josh was the only man who had seen Angus really cry about his dead daughter: one, dark, terrifying evening, when the nightflower of anguish had opened, and bloomed. A taboo had been broken that night, maybe in a good way. A man crying in front of a man, snot running, tears streaming.

And now?

Josh was checking something on his phone. Angus surveyed distant Torran Island once more. It was a long way across the mudflats: much further than he remembered. He'd have to walk down to the foreshore, then hike all the way around the big tidal island of Salmadair, then cross the causeway to the smaller, secondary tidal island of Torran. It would take thirty or forty minutes at the very least.

And this walking distance mattered, because the old island rowboat had long ago rotted to nothing. Which meant they had no boat. And until they acquired a new boat, he, Sarah and Kirstie would have to trek these dank, slippy, treacherous mudflats to access the island, and they could only do that at low tide.

'Know anyone with a cheap dinghy? To sell?'

Josh looked up from his phone.

'Mate, you haven't sorted a *boat*?'

'No.'

'Gus, come on. Really? How can you live on Torran without a boat?'

'We can't. But we'll just have to, until I buy one. And money is an issue.'

'I can give you a lift in mine, right now?'

'No, I want to walk across the mudflats. Test it.'

Angus's friend was tilting his head, offering a sceptical smile.

'You do remember those mudflats are dangerous, right?'

'Er. Yeah.'

'Seriously, Gus, at night – after civil twilight – you don't want to cross those mudflats. Even with a torch, you could break an ankle on rocks, get stuck in the mud, and then you're fucked.'

'Josh—'

'In Skye, no one can hear you scream: half the houses along the shore are empty. Holiday homes. In winter the tide will come in, cold and lethal: you'd drown.'

'Josh! I know all this. It's my island! Practically lived here as a boy.'

'But you nearly always came in summer, no? In winter, days are five hours long, or less. Mate. Think about it. Even *with* a boat, Torran can be very tricky in winter. You can still be stranded for days.'

'All right. Aye. I know winters are tough. I know it won't be easy. But I don't care.'

Josh laughed. 'Sure. I get it. I think.'

Angus pressed on: 'So, you mentioned, on the phone, the tides. This afternoon?'

Josh glanced at the receding sea, then back at Angus. 'I emailed you a link earlier: official Mallaig tide tables, with all the details.'

'Haven't had a chance to check: on the go since breakfast.'

Josh nodded. He was training his gaze, thoughtfully, on the mudflats and the seaweed, drying in the feeble sun. 'OK. Well, low-tide today is four p.m. You've got an hour either side of that, max. So we have half an hour to kill; till about three.'

Another silence descended between them, momentarily. Angus knew what came next. Gently, his friend enquired: '. . . how's Kirstie?'

Of course. This is what you have to ask. How's Kirstie? How *is* Kirstie?

What should he say?

He wanted to tell the truth. Maybe six months ago Kirstie had begun behaving very peculiarly. Something truly strange and disturbing had happened to his surviving daughter: to her persona. Things got so bad Angus nearly went to a doctor: and then, at the last moment, Angus had found a remedy. Of sorts.

But Angus was unable to tell anyone, not even Josh. Especially not Josh, because Josh would tell Molly, his wife, and Molly and Sarah were fairly intimate. And Sarah could not be allowed to know about this; she must not be told, ever. He simply didn't trust her with this. He hadn't trusted her, for so many months, in so many ways.

So it had to be lies. Even with Josh.

'Kirstie's good. Given the situation.'

'OK. And Sarah? Is she doing, y'know, all right now? Doing better?'

Another inevitable question.

'Yes. She's fine. We're all fine. Really looking forward to moving.' Angus spoke as calmly as he could. 'Kirstie wants to see a mermaid. Or a seal. A seal would probably do.'

'Hah.'

'Anyway. We've got time to kill? Shall we have a coffee?'

'Uh-huh. You'll notice a few changes in here,' Josh said, as he pushed the creaking door of the pub.

He wasn't wrong. As they stepped inside the Selkie, Angus gazed around: surprised.

The old, stained, cosy, herring-fisherman's pub was transformed. The piped pop music was replaced with piped modern folk – bodhrans and fiddles. The muddy carpeted floor had evolved into expensive grey slates.

At the other end of the bar a chalked sign advertised 'squab lobster'; and in between the boxes of leaflets from local theatres, and stacks of pamphlets on sea-eagle spotting, a chubby teenage girl stood behind the beer-pumps, toying sullenly with her nose-ring – and obviously resenting the fact she had to take Josh's order for coffees.

The metamorphosis was impressive, but not exceptional. This was yet another boutique hotel and gastropub, aiming itself at rich tourists seeking the Highlands and Islands experience. It was no longer the scruffy, vinegar-scented local boozer of two decades back.

Though, as it was mid-November, and a weekday afternoon, locals were the only clients to service, right now.

'Yes, both with milk, thanks, Jenny.'

Angus glanced across to the corner. Five men, of varying ages and virtually identical crew-neck jumpers,

60

sat at a large round wooden table. The pub was otherwise deserted. The men were silent as they squinted back at Angus over their pints.

Then they turned to each other, like conspirators, and started talking again. In a very foreign language.

Angus tried not to gawp. Instead he asked Josh, 'Gaelic?'

'Yep. You hear it a lot in Sleat these days, there's a new Gaelic college down the road. And the schools teach it, of course.' Josh grinned, discreetly. 'But I *bet* they were speaking English before we walked in. They do it as a joke, to wind up the incomers.'

Josh lifted a hand and waved at one of the men, a stubbled, stout, handsome guy, in his mid-forties.

'Gordon. All right?'

Gordon turned, and offered his own, very taciturn smile.

'Afternoon, Joshua. Afternoon. Ciamar a tha thu fhein?'

'Absolutely. My aunt was struck by lightning.' Josh tutted, good-naturedly. 'Gordon, you *know* I'll never learn it.'

'Aye, but maybe one day ye can give it a try now, Josh.'

'OK, I will, I promise. Let's catch up soon!'

The coffees had arrived: proffered by the bored bargirl. Angus stared at the twee little cups in Josh's rough, red, stonemason's hands.

Angus yearned for a Scotch. You were meant to drink Scotch, in Scotland, it was expected. Yet he felt awkward downing booze, in the afternoon, with sober Josh.

It was a slightly paradoxical feeling: because Josh Freedland hadn't always been sober. There was a time when Josh had been the very opposite of sober. Whereas the rest of the gang from Uni – including Angus – had mildly dabbled in drugs, then got bored and returned to booze, Josh had spiralled from popping pills at parties, into serious heroin addiction: and into darkness and dereliction. For years it seemed that Josh was slated for total failure, or worse – and no could save him, much as they tried, especially Angus.

But then, abruptly, at the age of 30, Josh had saved *himself*. With Narcotics Anonymous.

And Josh had gone for sobriety the same way he'd gone for drugs: with total commitment. He did his sixty meetings in sixty days. He completed the twelve-step programme, and entrusted himself to a higher power. Then he'd met a nice, affluent young woman in an NA meeting, in Notting Hill – Molly Margettson. She was a cocaine addict, but she was cleaning her scene, like Josh.

They'd promptly fallen in love, and soon after that Josh and Molly had married, in a small poignant ceremony, and then they'd exited London, stage north. They'd used the money from selling her flat in Holland Park to buy a very nice house, here in Sleat, right on the water's edge, half a mile from the Selkie, in the middle of the place they had all loved: near to Angus's grandmother's island.

The beautiful Sound of Sleat, the most beautiful place on earth.

Now Josh was a stonemason and Molly, remarkably, was a housewife and businesswoman: she made a decent living selling fruits and jams, honeys and chutneys. She also did the occasional painting.

Angus stared across the pub. Pensive. After years of

feeling sorry for Josh, the truth was, he now envied him. Even as he was happy for Josh and Molly, he was jealous of the purity of their lives. Nothing but air, stone, sky, glass, salt, rock and sea. And Hebridean heather honey. Angus too wanted this purity, he wanted to rinse away the complexities of the city and dive into cleanness and simplicity. Fresh air, real bread, raw wind on your face.

The two friends walked to a lonely table: far away from Gordon and his Gaelic-speaking mates. Josh sat and sipped coffee, and spoke with his own conspirator's smile.

'That was Gordon Fraser. He does everything, fixes shit from Kylerhea to Ardvasar. Toasters, boats, and lonely wives. If you need a boat, he could probably help.'

'Yes, I remember him. I think.' Angus shrugged. Did he really remember? How much could he recall, from so long ago? In truth, he was still shocked by his own miscalculation of Torran Island's nearness to the mainland. What else had he remembered wrongly? What else had he forgotten?

More importantly, if his long-term memory was unreliable, how reliable was his judgement? Did he trust himself to live, peacefully, with Sarah on this island? It could be very difficult: especially if she was opening the boxes, shining lights into the darkness. And what if she was lying to him? Again?

He wanted to think about something else.

'So, Josh, how much has it changed? Declined? Torran?'

'The cottage?' Josh shrugged. 'Well you really *should* prepare yourself, mate. As I said on the phone, I've been doing my best to keep an eye on it. So has Gordon – he loved your gran – and the local fishermen stop by. But it's in a state, no denying it.'

'But – the lighthouse keepers?'

Josh shook his head. 'Nah. They only come once a fortnight, and they're in and out, polish a lens, fix a battery, job done, head back to the Selkie for a jar.'

'OK.'

'We've all done our best, but, y'know, life, it's busy, man. Molly doesn't like using the boat on her own. And your gran stopped coming here four years ago, so it hasn't really been inhabited since then, at all.'

'That's a long time.'

'Too right, mate. Four long Hebridean winters? Damp and rot and wind, it's all taken a toll.' He sighed, then brightened. 'Though you did have some squatters for a while, last summer.'

'We did?'

'Yeah. Actually they were OK. Two guys, two girls – couple of lookers. Just kids, students. They actually came in the Selkie one night, bold as bollocks. Gordon and the guys told them all the stories – Torran was haunted – and they freaked. Left next morning. Didn't do that much damage. Burned most of your gran's remaining firewood though. Fucking Londoners.'

Angus acknowledged the irony. He remembered when he and the gang, from London, had been the same: sitting in this pub, listening to the folktales of Skye, told by locals, in return for a dram, those tales designed to while away the long winter nights. His granny had also told these stories of Skye. The Widow of Portree. The Fear that Walked in the Dark. And och, the Gruagach – her hair as white as snow, mourning her own reflection . . .

'Why haven't you been up since?'

64

'Sorry?'

Josh persisted: 'It's fifteen bloody years since you've been here. Why?'

Angus frowned, and sighed. It was a good question: one he had asked himself. He struggled towards an answer.

'Don't know. Not really. Maybe Torran became a kind of symbol. Place I would one day return to. Lost paradise. Also it's about five million miles away. Kept meaning to come up, especially since you guys moved here, but of course . . .' And there it was again, that fateful pause. 'By then we had the girls, the twins. And. That changed everything. Cold Scottish island, with yowling babies? Toddlers? All a bit daunting. You'll understand, Josh, when you have kids with Molly.'

'*If* we have kids.' Josh shook his head. Stared down at the stains of milky coffee in his cup. 'If.'

A slightly painful silence ensued. One man mourning his lost child, another man mourning the children he hadn't yet had.

Angus finished the last of his lukewarm coffee. He turned in the uncomfortable wooden pew and glanced out of the window, with its thick, flawed, wind-resistant bullseye-glass.

The glass of the window warped the beauty of Torran Island, making it look ugly. Here was a leering landscape, smeared and improper. He thought of Sarah's face, in the semi-dark of the loft, warped by the uncertain light. As she peered into the boxes.

That had to stop.

Josh spoke up: 'The tide must be out now, so you've got two hours, max. You *sure* you don't want me to come with, or give you a lift in the RIB?'

'Nope. I want to squelch across.'

The two exited the pub into the cold. The wind had keened and sharpened as the tide had fallen. Angus waved goodbye to Josh – *I'll come round the house tomorrow* – as Josh's car skidded away, chucking mud.

Opening the boot, Angus hauled out his rucksack. He'd packed the rucksack, very carefully, this morning, at his cheap Inverness hotel, so he had everything he needed for one night on the island. Tomorrow he could buy stuff. Tonight he just had to get there.

Across the mudflats.

Angus felt a pang of self-consciousness: as if someone was watching him, mockingly, as he adjusted the straps of his rucksack, distributing the weight. Reflexively he glanced around – looking for faces in windows, kids pointing and laughing. The leafless trees and silent houses gazed back. He was the only human visible. And he needed to be on his way.

The path led directly from the Selkie car park, down to some mossed and very weathered stone steps. Angus followed the route. At the bottom of the steps the path curved past a row of wooden boats – their keels lifted high onto the shingle, safe from approaching winter storms. Then the path disappeared completely, into a low maze of seaweedy rocks, and grey acres of reeking mud. It was going to take him half an hour, at least.

And his phone was ringing.

Marvelling at the fact he could get a signal – hoping faintly, futilely, that there might also be a signal on Torran – Angus dropped his rucksack on to the pebbles, and plucked his mobile from his jeans pocket.

The screen said *Sarah*.

He took the call. The fourth, from his wife, of the day.

'Hello?'

'Are you there yet?'

'I'm trying. I was about to cross. I'm at Ornsay. Just seen Josh.'

'OK, so, what's it like?'

'I don't know, babe.' He tutted. 'Told you: I'm not there yet. Why don't you let me get there, first, and I'll call you back as soon as I can.'

'OK, yes, sorry. Hah.' Her laughter was false. He could tell this even on a cell phone, from six hundred miles away.

'Sarah. Are you all right?'

A hesitation. A distinct, definite pause.

'Yes, Gus. I'm a bit nervous. You know? That's all . . .'

She paused. He frowned. Where was this going? He needed to distract his wife, get her focused on the future. He spoke very carefully.

'The island looks lovely, Sarah. Beautiful as I remember it. More beautiful. We haven't made a mistake. We were right to move here.'

'OK. Good. Sorry. I'm just jangling. All this packing!'

Sarah's anxiety was still there, lurking. He could tell. Which meant he had to ask; even though he didn't want to know any answers. But he had to ask: 'How's Kirstie?'

'She's OK, she's . . .'

'What?'

'Oh. It's nothing.'

'Sorry?'

'It's nothing. Nothing.'

'No, it's not, Sarah, it's clearly not. What is it?' He gripped his frustration. This was another of his silent wife's conversational stratagems: drop a tiny unsettling hint, then say 'it's nothing'. Forcing him to gouge the information out of her; so he felt guilty and bad – even when he didn't *want* the information. Like now.

67

The tactic drove him crazy, these days. Made him feel actually, physically angry.

'Sarah. What's up? Tell me?'

'Well, she . . .' Another long, infuriating pause stopped the dialogue. Angus resisted the temptation to shout *What the fuck is it?*

At last Sarah coughed it up: 'Last night. She had another nightmare.'

This was, if anything, a relief to Angus. Only a nightmare? That's all this was about?

'OK. Another bad dream.'

'Yes.'

'The same one?'

'Yes.' A further wifely silence. 'The one with the room; she is stuck in that white room, with the faces staring at her, staring down. It's nearly always the same nightmare. She gets that one, always – why is that?'

'I don't know, Sarah, but I know it will stop. And soon. Remember what they said at the Anna Freud Centre? That's one reason we're moving. New place, new dreams. New beginning. No memories.'

'All right, yes, of course. Let's talk tomorrow?'

'Yes. Love you.'

'Love you.'

Angus frowned, at his own words, and ended the call. Slipping his phone in his pocket, he hoisted his heavy rucksack – feeling like a mountaineer attempting a summit. He could hear the clink of a heavy wine bottle inside, knocking against something hard. Maybe his Swiss Army knife.

Picking his way through, he edged along rocks and sand, trying to find the safest route. The air was redolent with the heady smell of rotting seaweed. Seagulls wheeled above, calling and heckling. Haranguing him for something he hadn't done.

The tide was way out, exposing old grey metal chains, slacked in the mud, linked to plastic buoys. Whitewashed cottages regarded him, indifferently, from the curving wooded shoreline of mainland Skye, to his right. On the left, Salmadair was a dome of rock and grass, encircled by sombre firs; he could just see the top of that big unoccupied house, on Salmadair, owned by the billionaire, the Swedish guy.

Josh had told Angus all about Karlssen: how he only came here for a few weeks in the summer, for the shooting and the sailing, and the famous views over the Sound: to the waters of Loch Hourn and Loch Nevis, and between them the vast massif of Knoydart, with its snow-iced hills.

As Angus trudged along, hunched under the weight of his rucksack, he occasionally lifted his head to look at these same brooding hills. The great summits of Knoydart, the last true wilderness in western Europe. Angus realized, as he surveyed the view, that he could still distinctly remember the names of Knoydart's enigmatic peaks. His granny had taught him so many times: Sgurr an Fhuarain, Sgurr Mor, Fraoch Bheinn.

It was a poem. Angus was not a fan of poetry, yet this place was a poem.

Sgurr an Fhuarain, Sgurr Mor, Fraoch Bheinn.

He walked on.

The silence was piercing. A kingdom of quietness. No boats out fishing, no people walking, no engine noise.

Angus walked, and sweated, and nearly slipped. He wondered at the windless tranquillity of the afternoon, a day so still and clear he could see the last ferry, in the blue distance, crossing from Armadale to Mallaig.

Many houses, hidden in the firs and rowans, were totally shuttered for the winter. That accounted for much of the quiet: for this sense of desolation. In a way, this sheltered, stunning, southern peninsula of Skye was increasingly like one of the richest quarters of London: emptied by its own desirability, used by the wealthy for a few days a year. An investment opportunity. A place to store money. Other, less alluring parts of the Hebrides paradoxically had more life, because the houses were cheaper.

This place was cursed by its own loveliness.

But it *was* still lovely. And it was also getting dark.

The walk took him fifty difficult minutes, because the dark grey mud sucked at his boots, slowing him down, and because at one point he went wrong: climbing up onto Salmadair proper, heading unconsciously for the billionaire's house with the huge, glass-walled living room, which suddenly reared in front of him, in the gathering gloom, protected by its rusty twines of barbed wire.

He'd taken the wrong path left. Instead of skirting Salmadair's shingled beach.

Angus remembered Josh's warnings about the mudflats at night. You could die out there. People die.

But how many really died? One a year? One a decade? It was still much safer than crossing a London road. This place was crime-free; the air was clean and good. It was much safer for kids. Safer for Kirstie.

Pressing between gorse bushes, slowly negotiating the beaten path, Angus scrambled over some very slippery rocks – gnarled with old barnacles, which scraped his fingers. His hands were bleeding a little. He was scratched and weary. The north wind was perfumed with seagull shit and bladderwrack, maybe the scent of

70

newly chopped pine-wood, carried all the way from Scoraig and Assynt.

He was nearly there. In the dregs of the afternoon light he could see the exposed tidal causeway of rocks and grey shingle, littered with smashed crabshells. A slender green pipe snaked across the Torran causeway, burying itself in and out of the sands. He recognized the waterpipe, just as he recognized this part of the route. He remembered walking it as a boy, and as a very young man. And here he was again.

The lighthouse, the cottage, lay beyond, in the last of the cold, slanted sunlight. In just two minutes he would press the doorway, into his new home. Where his family would live: as best they could.

Reflexively, he looked at his phone. No signal. Of course. What did he expect? The island was entire and of itself: alone and isolated, and as remote as you could get in Britain.

As he ascended the final rise, to the lighthouse-keeper's cottage, Angus turned and looked back at the mudflats.

Yes. Remote as possible. That was good. He was glad that he had coaxed his wife into making the decision to move here: he was glad he had persuaded her into believing, moreover, that it was her choice. He'd wanted them far away from everything for months, and now they had achieved it. On Torran they would be safe at last. No one would ask questions. No interfering neighbours. No friends and relatives. No police.

5

Kirstie.

Glancing up, I see Kirstie's face, impassive, unsmiling, in the rear-view mirror.

'Nearly there, darling!'

This is what I have been saying since driving out of Glasgow; and, in truth, when I reached Glasgow I thought we *were* 'nearly there', it looked so close on Google Maps, we were halfway through Scotland, weren't we? Look, it can't take much longer. Just two more inches.

But instead, like a terrible endless story, told by a chuntering bore, the road has gone on, and on. And now we're lost amid the ghastliness of Rannoch Moor.

I have to remind myself why we're here.

Two days ago Angus offered money we didn't have, to fly us to Inverness, where he would pick us up, and leave all the moving to the men we'd hired.

But doing it this way seemed, somehow, a cheat – something in me wanted to drive the whole distance, with Kirstie and Beany; and someone had to bring the car, whether now or later. So I'd insisted Kirstie and I would make the entire journey, from the bottom corner to the very top of Britain, to meet Angus in the Selkie car park, in Ornsay, with the celebrated view of Torran.

Now I have regrets.

It is all so vast, and so bleak. Rannoch Moor is a bowl of green and dismal greyness, glacial in origin, presumably. Dirty, peat-brown streams divide the acid turfs; in places it looks as if the peat turf has been ripped apart then sewn back together.

I glance at Kirstie, in the mirror, then I glance at myself.

I truly don't want to, but I have to do this: I have to go over it all, yet again. I *must* work out what is happening with Kirstie, and whether it stems from the accident itself. From that terrible fracture in our lives.

And so.

It was a summer evening in Instow.

My father and mother retired to the little town of Instow, on the north Devon coast, almost ten years ago. They'd ended up with just enough money, salvaged from my dad's gently failed career, to buy a biggish house, overlooking the wide slothful river, at the point where it became an estuary.

The house was tall, with three storeys, and balconies, to make the most of the view. There was a proper garden, with a further, rabbity slope of meadow at the back. From the top floor there were glimpses of the sea between the green headlands. You could watch red-sailed boats heading for the Bristol Channel, as you sat on the loo.

From the start I liked my parents' choice, of Instow. It was a nice house, in a nice little town. The local pubs were full of sailors, and yachtsmen, yet they were without pretensions. The climate was kindly, for England: solaced

74

by southwestern breezes. You could go crabbing on the quayside, with bacon and string.

Inevitably and immediately, Instow became our default holiday home. A pretty, cheap, convenient bolt-hole for Angus and me, and then a place where we could take the girls, knowing they'd be looked after by their doting grandparents.

And my folks really doted. This was partly because the twins were so pretty and adorable – when they weren't squabbling – and partly because my wastrel younger brother was wandering the world, never likely to settle down: so the twins were IT. The only grandkids they were likely to enjoy.

My father was, as a result, always eager for us to come down and take another holiday; and my American mother, Amy – shyer, quieter, more reserved – more like me – was almost as fervent.

So when I got the call, from Dad, and he airily asked: What are you doing this summer? I readily agreed – to another vacation in Instow. It would be our seventh or eighth. We'd had too many to count. But all that free childcare was just so tempting. All those long, delicious sleeps, of adults on holiday, while the twins went off with Granny and Granddad.

And this was the very first night, of the very last holiday.

I'd driven down with the kids in the morning. Angus was delayed in London, but due later. Mum and Dad were out for a drink. I was sitting in the kitchen.

The large airy kitchen was where everything happened in my mum and dad's house, because it had one of the best views – and a lovely big table. All was quiet. I was reading a book and sipping tea; the evening was long, and beautiful: rosy-blue skies arched over the headlands

75

and the bay. The twins, already sunburned from an afternoon on the beach, were, I thought, playing in the garden. Everything was SAFE.

And then I heard the scream of one of my daughters.

That scream which will never go away. Never leave me.

Ever.

Here on Rannoch Moor I grip the wheel – accelerating. As if I can overtake the horror of the past and leave it dwindling in the mirror.

What happened next? Is there some clue, overlooked, that would unlock this awful puzzle?

For half a moment, sitting in that kitchen, I couldn't work it out. The girls were meant to be on the lawn, enjoying that languid summer warmth; but this awful scream came from *upstairs*. So I rushed up the steps in blinding panic, and raced along the landing, and looked for them – not there, not there, *not there* – and I knew, somehow I knew, and I ran into the spare bedroom – yet another bedroom with a balcony. Twenty feet up.

The fucking balconies. If there was one thing I hated about Instow, it was the balconies; every window had them. Angus hated them too.

We always told the twins not to go near them; the iron railings were too low, whether you were adult or child. Yet they were so tempting. Because they all had those blissful views of the river. Mum liked to sit on her balcony, reading Swedish thrillers, drinking supermarket Chardonnay.

So, as I ran up the stairs, it was the balconies that ripped me open with terrible anticipation, and when I stepped into the bedroom I saw the silhouetted figure of one of my daughters, dressed in white, standing on the balcony, shouting.

The irony is that she looked so pretty that moment. Her hair was caught by the setting sun: she was coronaed, gloried, flamingly haloed – she looked like a child of Jesus in a Victorian picture book, even as she was shouting, in icy and curdling terror.

'Mummy Mummy Mummy Lydie-lo, it's Lydie-lo, she's falling off, Mummy, help her, MUMMY!'

For a second I was paralysed. Staring at her.

Then, choking on my panic, I looked over the railing.

And, yes, there was my daughter – broken, down there on the decking, blood spooling from her mouth, like a filled-in speech bubble, red and glossy. She looked like an icon of a fallen human, like a swastika shape with her arms and legs splayed. A symbol.

I knew Lydia was doomed as soon as I saw her body shaped that way, but I rushed downstairs, and cradled her still-warm shoulders, and felt for her slivery pulse. And at that precise moment my mum and dad came back from the pub, walking up the path: walking straight into this appalling tableau. They stopped, and gazed, quite stricken – and then my mum screamed and my dad frantically called for an ambulance, and we argued about moving Lydia or not moving Lydia, and my mum screamed again.

And then we all went tearfully to the hospital and spoke to absurdly young doctors, to young men and women in white coats with that flicker of tired shame in their eyes. Murmuring their prayers.

Acute subdural hematoma, severe and stellate lacerations, evidence of retinal haemorrhage . . .

At one point, awfully, Lydia came to consciousness. Angus had arrived to be engulfed by the same horror, so we were all in the room – me and Angus, my father, all the doctors and nurses – and my daughter faintly stirred and her eyes slurred open, and she had tubes in her mouth, and she looked at us, regretfully, melancholically, as if she was saying goodbye, then she went under again. And she never came back.

I hate these memories. I remember how one doctor blatantly stifled a yawn as she was talking to us, after Lydia was pronounced dead. Presumably she'd done a long shift. Another doctor said we were 'unlucky'.

And monstrous as it was, he was, technically, right, as I discovered many weeks later – when I regained the mental capability to type words into a search engine. Most young children survive a fall of less than thirty feet, even forty feet. Lydia was unlucky. We were unlucky. Her fall was awkward. And this discovery made it all worse; it made my guilt even more unbearable. Lydia died because we were unlucky, and because I wasn't looking after her properly.

I want to close my eyes, now, to block the world. But I can't, because I'm driving. And so I drive on. Questioning the world. Questioning my memory. Questioning reality.

Who was the girl that fell? Is it possible I got it wrong?

The original and significant reason I thought that it was Lydia down there, dead, was because the twin who survived, *told me that.*

Mummy Mummy come quickly, Lydie-lo has fallen.

And naturally, when she said that, I took her at her word. Because there was no other immediate way of telling them apart. Because the girls were dressed so sweetly yet identically that day. In white dresses. With no blue or yellow.

This wasn't my doing. It was the twins themselves. For a few months prior to that holiday they'd asked – they had demanded – that we dress them the same, cut their hair the same, make them look the same. *Mummy, sit here between me and read to us.* It was as if they wanted to be re-absorbed into each other. As if they'd had enough of being individuals for a while. Indeed, sometimes the twins would wake up, in those final months, and tell us they'd had exactly the same dream. I didn't know whether to believe them. I still don't know now. Is that possible? For twins to have the same dream?

Is it?

Touching the pedal, I race around a corner; urging myself on, as if the answer can be found on the coast. But the answer, if anywhere, is in my mind.

Angus and I had acceded to the twins' impulsive wish – to be dressed exactly alike – because we thought it was just a phase, like tantrums or teething; and, besides, it was easy enough, by that time, to tell them apart by personality. By the different ways they bickered with each other.

But when I ran up the stairs and I saw one of my daughters, in her white dress, barefoot and totally distraught, there was no personality. Not at that moment. There was just one of the twins, shouting. And she was shouting *Lydie-lo has fallen.* And that's what gave me her identity. *Kirstie.*

Could we have got it wrong?

I do not know. I am lost in the hall of mirrored souls. And again that terrible sentence pierces me.

Mummy Mummy come quickly, Lydie-lo has fallen.

That's when my life cracked open. That's when I lost my daughter. That's when everything went black.

As it does now. I am shuddering with grief. The memory is so powerful it is disabling. Tears are not far away; my hands are trembling on the steering wheel.

Enough. I need to stop, I need to get out, I need to breathe air. Where am I? Where are we? Outskirts of Fort William?

Oh God. Oh God. *Just STOP.*

With a yank of the wheel I veer the car, fast and hard and straight into the forecourt of a BP garage, squirting grit with the wheels, almost smashing into a fuel pump.

The car gently steams. The silence is shocked.

'Mummy?'

I look up at the rear-view mirror. Kirstie is staring at me in the mirror as I smudge the tears from my eyes with the heel of my hand. I stare at her reflection, as she must have stared so many times into mirrors, seeing her own reflection. Yet seeing her dead sister as well.

And now Kirstie *smiles* at me.

Why? Why is she smiling? She is mute and barely blinking: and yet smiling? As if she is trying to freak me out.

A sudden fear ripples through me. Absurd and ridiculous, yet undeniable.

I have to get out of the car. Now.

'Mummy's just going to get a coffee, OK? I just – just need a coffee. Do you want anything?'

Kirstie says nothing. Clutching Leopardy with her two fisted hands. Her smile is cold, and blank, and yet somehow, knowing. It is the kind of smile Lydia would sometimes do, Lydia the quiet one, the soulful one, the more eccentric of the twins. My favourite.

Fleeing my own child, and my own doubts, I rush into the little BP shop.

'No petrol, thanks. Just the coffee.'

It's too hot to drink. I stumble out into the raw, sea-scented air, trying to stay in control. Calm down, Sarah, calm down.

80

A hot cup of Americano in hand, I climb back in the car. I take deep, therapeutic breaths. Slowing my heartbeat. And then I gaze in the mirror. Kirstie remains quiet. She has also stopped smiling, and turned away. As she scratches Beany behind the ear, she is staring out of the window at the suburban houses that straggle the road, to and from the garage. They look foolish, and English, and incongruous, with their polite windows and twee little porches, set against the grandeur and immensity of the Highlands.

On, on, on.

I turn the key, and pull away. We take the long road towards Fort Augustus; to Loch Lochy, Loch Garry, Loch Cluanie. It is so long, we have come so far. I think about life before the accident, the happiness, so easily shattered. Our life was made of brittle ice.

'Are we nearly there *now*?'

My daughter shakes me from my thoughts. I look in the mirror, again.

Kirstie is gazing at the summits of the mountains, which are veiled in grey mist, and returning rain. I smile in a reassuring way and say Yes and I drive my daughter, and Beany, and our hopes, along the dwarfed and single-track road that negotiates the endless wilderness.

But we are, indeed, nearly there. And now the distance I am putting between me and my old self, my old life, my dead daughter, her ashes scattered on Instow beach, feels right and good and necessary. If anything, I want to go further. This two-day journey from Camden to Scotland, overnighting in the Scottish Borders, has been so epic, it righteously underscores the life-change we are undertaking. This distance is so long there is no going back.

It feels like a nineteenth-century migration; as if we are pioneers heading for Oregon. So I grip the wheel and drive us out of the past; trying not to think who it is in the back of my car, which dancing and heraldic unicorn, which ghost of herself. It is Kirstie. It must be Kirstie. It is Kirstie.

'This is it, Kirstie, look.'

We are approaching Skye. The family's rusted Ford Focus is rattling through the touristic but rain-lashed port that is Kyle of Lochalsh – then we are steered along, by the high street, towards a great looping bridge. Abruptly the rain stops.

The grey, chopped-white waters of Loch Alsh flow beneath the soaring bridge – a gut-churning plunge. Then we swoop down onto a roundabout.

We have reached Skye. And the next little crowd of suburban houses soon yields to the emptiness.

It is a traumatized yet beautiful landscape. Islands and mountains are reflected in dark indigo waters to my left. Bow-backed moorland stoops down to the echoing shoreline. A boat drifts, alone. A plantation of firs is divided by a road that seems to go nowhere – disappearing into those dark, sombre regiments, then blackness.

It is harsh and daunting – and very handsome. Bright lozenges of late autumn sun blaze on the further hills, like organized fires, moving silently and very fast. And when we slow right down, on cattle-grids, I can see details: the way the dew in the grass is struck, by the sun, making tiny, shivering jewels.

We are just a few miles from Ornsay. The road is widening, and I begin to recognize the green hills and steely lochs from the pictures I have seen – from all those images on Google.

'I can see Dada!'

Kirstie points, eagerly. Beany growls.

I slow the car to a crawl, and follow my little girl's gesture, and yes, she is right. There are two men standing on a stone pier, in front of a big, white, gabled Victorian building, which is, in turn, staring out to the broad sea-channel. The men are recognizably Angus – and Josh Freedland. Josh's red hair is particularly distinctive.

This is it. Must be. That's the Selkie; and that's the pub car park on the seafront. And Ornsay village is, surely, the scattered outcrop of orderly gardens, converted crofts, and glassy-walled new-builds that surrounds the tiny harbour.

And that in turn means, most importantly of all – I lift my eyes like a worshipper in a church – that the little island with the little lighthouse, out there, in the Sound – that islet humbled by the beautiful vastness of oceans and mountains: that is our destination.

This is my new home; and its name is like a tolling bell.

Torran.

Five minutes of narrow lanes brings me to the car park and the Selkie, and the tinkling sound of nervous boats, moored and anchored in the wind: lanyards, spinnakers, bowsprits; I don't know what any of these words mean, but I will learn. I will have to acquire a new, maritime, seaworthy language, befitting someone who lives on an island. For all my anxieties, I quite like that idea. I want everything to be new.

'Hello, darling,' Angus is greeting Kirstie as she climbs, timidly, tentatively, blinking in the wind, from the back of the car; Leopardy is clutched, as ever, to her chest. The dog stirs, and barks, and follows my daughter, loping out onto the tarmac. 'Hello, Beano!' says Angus, and his smile widens. His beloved hound.

Amidst the sadness, I am pleased. Despite it all, I have successfully delivered the dog and the daughter.

'Say hello to Uncle Josh, sweetheart,' says Angus, as my seven-year-old gazes around, mouth half-open. Angus thanks me with another smile as our daughter says a polite and bashful 'hi' to Josh.

'Not too bad a journey?' Josh asks, eyeing me.

'Only two days,' I say. 'I could have done with a bit more driving.'

'Hah.'

'Perhaps next time, Angus, we can move to Vladivostok?'

Angus chuckles politely. He already looks more Scottish, here in Scotland. His cheeks are ruddier, his stubble is darker, he is definitely a bit dirtier: more rugged, salt-bitten and masculine. Instead of his architect's purple silk ties he has scratches on his hands and paint flecks in his hair. He's been here three days 'preparing the place' so as to make it habitable for me and Kirstie.

'Josh is going to give us a lift, in his boat.'

'You guys,' Josh says, kissing me warmly, on both sides of my face, 'you guys REALLY HAVE to get a boat. Torran is a nightmare without a boat, the tides will drive you doolally.'

I force a smile. 'Thanks, Josh, that's just what we need to hear, on our very first day.'

He grins in that boyish way. And I remember that I like Josh. He is my favourite of Angus's friends: it helps that he is a non-drinker – completely sober. Because he slows down Angus's boozing.

Like a team of explorers abseiling, we climb down

the steps of the pier, to Josh's boat. Beany goes second, chivvied by Angus, then leaping with unexpected grace into the vessel. Kirstie follows: she is excited, in that eerie calm way that Lydia used to get excited; her head is perfectly still, staring out, as if she is catatonic, but you can see the shine in her eyes. Enraptured.

'All aboard, shiver my timbers, Torran ahoy!' says Josh, for Kirstie's benefit – and Kirstie giggles. Josh poles the boat into the deeps and Angus gathers in the rope, very quickly, and we begin our miniature yet crucial voyage, rippling around the bigger tidal island, Salmadair, that divides Torran from Ornsay.

'That's where the packaging billionaire lives.'

Half my attention is given to Salmadair – but the other half is fixed on Kirstie's happy little face: her soft blue eyes gazing in wonder at the water and the islands and the enormous Hebridean skies.

I remember her shout of despair.

Mummy Mummy come quickly, Lydie-lo has fallen.

Again, it strikes me, with painful force, how those words are, really, the only evidence we have for believing it was Lydia that died, not Kirstie. But why did I believe those words?

Because there was no obvious reason for her to lie. At that moment of all moments. But maybe she was confused in some bizarre way. And I can see why she might have been confused, given that the twins were always swapping names, swapping their whole identities, during that fateful summer. When they were dressed alike, when they had the same haircut. It was a game they liked to play, that summer, on me and Angus. Which one am I, Mummy? Which one am I?

So maybe they were playing that game that evening? And then disaster happened. And the fatal blurring of

85

their identities froze over, and became fixed, like a flaw in ice.

Or maybe Kirstie is still playing this game. But playing it in the most terrifying way. Perhaps that is why she is smiling. Perhaps she is playing the game to hurt me, and to punish me.

But punish me for what?

'OK,' says Angus, 'this is Torran Island.'

6

The next five days are all about work, I do not have time to stop and breathe and brood or think too much. Because the cottage is a brutal nightmare. God knows what it was like before Angus 'prepared it' for our arrival.

The basic structure of our new home is pretty sound: two gabled white cottages, designed by Robert Louis Stevenson's father in the 1880s, and knocked into one family house in the 1950s. But the first hour's exploration of Torran cottage proves, beyond doubt, that no one has significantly touched the buildings *since* the 1950s.

The kitchen is indescribable: the fridge is rotten, there is black stuff inside. The whole thing will have to go. The cooker is usable, but demonically filthy: on the afternoon of Day One I spend hours cleaning it, till my knees burn from the kneeling, but when the evening light falls – so early, so early – I'm only halfway finished. And I have not even touched the deep ceramic kitchen sink, which smells like it's been used for butchering seabirds.

The rest of the kitchen is little better. The taps above the sink spout tainted liquid: Angus forgot to tell me that our only running water would be provided by a thin plastic pipe from the mainland – and this pipe is exposed at low tide on the causeway. It hisses with leaks, and lets seawater in; at low tide I can actually *see* the leaks as I stare out the kitchen window – joyous little fountains of spray, squirting from the pipe, and saying hello to the sky.

Because of this saline taint, we have to boil everything. But still everything tastes of fish. Fixing the water supply is consequently essential – we can't keep humping bottled water from the Co-op supermarket at Broadford; we can't spare the cash or the effort. Yet filtering or purifying water with tablets is too tricky and time-consuming, as a long-term solution. But how do we tempt the water company to come out and help us, just three people who chose, of their own volition, to go and live on a ridiculously remote island?

Perhaps when the water company eventually come to our aid, they will also, out of pity, help us to get rid of the rats.

Because there are rats everywhere. I can hear them when I sleep – they wake me with their scrabbling in the walls, playing and tumbling, dancing and squealing. The rats mean we have to keep all our food in wire baskets, in the kitchen, suspended from a metal clothes line.

I would like to put our food in the kitchen cupboards: but they are all damp and rotten; when I first opened the door of the very largest cupboard I found nothing but mould, dirt, and emptiness – and the small, white, intricate skeleton of a shrew, placed in the centre of the shelf.

It was like a beautiful museum piece, collected by an antiquarian: something strange and exquisite, something macabre but marvellous. I got Angus to throw it into the sea.

Now it is Day Five, and I am sitting here, smutted and tired, and alone, in the gathering darkness of a solitary lamp; I am letting the big fragrant woodfire crackle into nothing: because I like staring at the dying flames. Angus is snoring in our bedroom, on the large, old, wooden-sided bed he calls the Admiral's Bed. I've no idea why it has that name. My daughter is likewise asleep in her room, beside her precious nightlight, at the other end of the house.

The fire spits a huge spark onto the Turkish rug. I do not move because I know the Turkish rug is too damp to take flame. I am looking at a To Do list jotted on the notepad on my lap. It is sappingly long – and yet I am still writing in the semi-dark.

We must get a boat. Angus is negotiating every day with potential sellers – but boats are unnervingly expensive. Yet we can't risk buying something cheaper that might sink.

We also need the phone fixed: the ancient, black, 1960s Bakelite phone, that sits on the side-table in the chilly dining room, is freckled with hard drops of old paint, and is mysteriously singed on the bottom. Someone must once have put it on a hot stove, I think. Perhaps they were blind drunk from whisky, as they tried to keep out the cold, and not think about the rats.

Whatever the explanation, the phone-line pops and crackles so loudly, any voice on the other end is barely distinguishable; and I fear this is because the line is corrupted – rotted by seawater; which means that just buying a new receiver will not give us reception. There is of course no internet access, and no cell phone coverage. The isolation is intense.

But what can I do?

Finish the list.

I listen to the creak of the old house, bending in the low Sleat wind. I listen to the gristly noise of the wood-fire, its salt-watered logs reluctantly burning. All my clothes smell of woodsmoke.

What else? We have yet to unpack all our crockery and glassware: they're all in the boxes laboriously ferried across, by Josh and Angus and the removal men. We're still drinking red wine out of jam jars.

Underlining the word *boxes*, I stare around.

Some of the walls have strange, unsettling paintings of dancers, and mermaids, and Scottish warriors: prob-ably the work of returning squatters, over the years. They will have to go, they are a little eerie. The lumber-room at the back of the kitchen is even worse – a centuries-old mess; I'll leave that to Gus. Beyond that, the big shed outside is dilapidated, and filthy with gull feathers. And the walled garden is weedy, rocky, and will take years to redeem.

And then there's the toilet, by the bathroom, which actually has a cardboard sign on the cistern, written in Angus's grandmother's elderly hand: *Please leave the stone on the seat, it is to keep out the mink.*

I write: *Fix Toilet* on my To Do list. Then I write *Kill Mink*.

And then I stop, and half smile.

Despite it all, I can still find satisfaction here, a glimpse of future contentment, even. This is a proper project, and it is enormous, and daunting, yet I like the way this huge undertaking encompasses me, and commands me. I know for sure what I will be doing for thirty months: turning this beautiful horrible house into a lovely home. Bringing the dead back to life.

There it is. I have no choice. I just have to get on with it. And I am eager to obey.

There are also some serious pluses. The two larger bedrooms and this living room are habitable spaces; they have plastered walls, and functional radiators. The potential of the other bedrooms, and the dining room, and scullery, is obvious. This place is big.

I also like the lighthouse, especially at night. It flashes every nine seconds, I reckon. Not so brightly that it keeps me awake; in fact it helps me sleep, like a metronome, like a very, very slow maternal heartbeat.

And, lastly but most importantly, I adore the views. Even though I expected this scenery, it still amazes me. Every day.

Sometimes I find myself standing, paintbrush in hand, bucket of white spirit by my feet, open-mouthed – and then I come to, and realize that I've spent twenty minutes in silence, watching the rays of sunlight spear the tawny mountains, goring the darkened rocks with gold; watching the white clouds drift languidly, over the snow-chafed hills of Knoydart: Sgurr nan Eugallt, Sgurr a'Choire-Bheithe, Fraoch Bheinn.

Pen in hand, pad on lap, I write down these words. *Sgurr nan Eugallt, Sgurr a'Choire-Bheithe, Fraoch Bheinn.*

Angus is teaching me these words. These beautiful, liquid, salt-soaked Gaelic names, that stream into the culture, like the burns from the Cuillins tumbling into Coruisk. We drink whisky at night, together, and he shows me the Gaelic names on the map: and I repeat these mysterious vowels and consonants. Laughing, lightly but contentedly. Snuggled under the rug. Tender and together. With my husband.

Now Angus is asleep in our bed, and I am keen to join him. But for the last time today, I write down the names of the hills: as if they are an incantation that will protect this little family. The Moorcrofts. Alone on their very own island, with its little silver beaches, and its inquisitive seals.

The pen is almost dropping from my hand. I can feel myself nodding towards sleep; I have the deep satisfying tiredness, born of hard physical labour.

But I am woken.

'Mummy, Mummy . . .??'

A voice calls me. Muffled by doors and distance.

'Mummy!? Mama?!'

It must be another nightmare? Dropping my pad, I pick up a torch, turn it on – and walk the dark cold hallway to her room. Her door is shut. Is she talking in her sleep?

'Mummy . . .'

Her voice sounds odd. For a moment I am ridiculously paralysed at the door. I don't want to go in.

I am scared.

This is absurd, but my heart flutters with sudden panic. I can't go into my own daughter's room? Something unexpected holds me back, as if there is an evil beyond, a silly, childish, horror-film fear of ghosts is fluxing through me. Monsters under the bed, monsters behind the door. My daughter might be in there, smiling at me, in that way. The way she did in the car. Trying to confuse me, to punish me. You let my sister die. You weren't there.

But this is nonsense. This is just memories of my father shouting at me. He always shouted so much, as his career faded. Shouted at my cowering mother. I would hear the shouting behind doors like monsters, or thunder, and closed doors agitate me.

So. No. I am a better mother than this.

Suppressing my nerves, I twist the knob. And step over the threshold, and peer into the gloom within.

At once my anxiety flees: and I am suffused with concern – Kirstie is sitting up in her bed, and she is certainly not smiling: tears are streaming down her face. What is wrong? Her nightlight is still on, though its illumination is feeble. What has happened?

'Baby baby – what's wrong what's wrong, what is it?'

I swoop to her side and embrace her, and she cries, quietly, for several minutes, as I rock her from side to side, tight in my arms. She is wordless and harrowed.

It must surely be another nightmare. Slowly she sobs, and sobs. And the sea accompanies her grief, I can hear the waves outside, yearning and restless. Inhaling and exhaling. I wonder who left the window open? Maybe Angus. He has a thing about fresh air.

Gradually my little girl whimpers into silence. And I hold her face between two hands, feeling the warm damp tears on my fingers:

'Come on, darling. What is it? Was it another bad dream?'

My little girl shakes her head. She emits a stifled sob. Then she shakes her head again, and lifts a finger and points.

A big printed photograph lies on her bed. I pick it up – and feel the instant pain it evokes. The quality of the photo is poor – printed out from a computer – but the image is nonetheless stark. It is a cheery photo of Lydia and Kirstie on holiday in Devon, maybe a year before the accident; they are on the beach at Instow, smiling in their twin pink Duplo Valley hoodies from Legoland, holding buckets and spades, slightly squinting in the sun: but smiling happily at me, and my cameraphone.

The grief tumbles, like a ceaseless waterfall, stained brown by peat.

'Kirstie, where did you get this?'

She says nothing. I am bewildered. Angus and I long ago decided to keep most photos – all photos, if possible – hidden from our daughter, to ward off the memories. Perhaps she found it in one of the unsorted packing cases?

I gaze at the picture again, trying to ignore my own storms of sadness. But it is so hard. The twins look desolatingly happy. Sistered in the sun, and each other's closest relative. In a way, I suddenly, realize, my surviving daughter is now orphaned.

Kirstie leans away from me, in her soft pink pyjamas, and she plucks the photo from my hand and then she turns it, and she shows it to me in the quarter-light and says:

'Which one is me, Mummy?'

'Darling?'

'Which one is *me*? Mummy? Which one?'

Oh, help. Oh, God. This is unbearable: because I have no answer. The truth is, I do not know. I literally cannot distinguish between them; in this photo, there are no visual clues. Should I lie? What if I get it wrong?

Kirstie waits. I say nothing: I mumble nonsense words, comforting noises, trying to work out what lie to tell. But the lack of a proper answer is making things worse.

For a tight little second she stares at me, and then

Kirstie starts howling: she falls back onto the bed, flailing her arms, tantruming like a two-year-old. Her scream is terrible and rending, her wails are desperate; but I can distinctly hear the words:

'Mummy? Mummy? Mummy? Who am I?'

7

It takes an hour to calm my daughter all over again, to pacify her enough so that she finally goes to sleep – clutching Leopardy so tight, it's as if she is actively trying to strangle him. But then *I* am unable to sleep. For six dusty hours, next to snoring Angus, I lie there, eyes bright and fierce and upset, and I turn over her words in my mind.

Who am I?

What must that be like, to not know who you are, to not know which one of 'me' is dead?

At seven a.m. I rise, urgent and desperate, from the tousled bed and I call Josh on the crackly phone and he yawningly agrees to give me a dawnlit boat-ride to our car, parked by the Selkie, as the tides are against us. Of course, Angus is all questions as he ambles sleepily into the dining room; as I put the phone down. Why are you phoning Josh? Where are you going so early? What is going on? Yawn.

Words stop in my mouth even as I try to reply. I don't want to tell him the truth, not yet; not unless I have to, it's too bizarre and frightening – I'd much rather lie. Maybe I should have done more lying, in the past. Maybe I should have lied about that affair, all those years ago; perhaps the damage was done, by me, to our marriage, and we never quite recovered. But I do not have time for guilt: and so I explain that I have to leave early, to drive to Glasgow, to research an article, because I have a commission from Imogen, and I need the work because we need the money. I tell him Kirstie had another nightmare, so she needs a lot of comfort while I'm gone.

A nightmare. Just a nightmare.

The lie is feeble; yet he seems to accept it.

Then Josh arrives in the boat, scratching the sleep from his eyes, and we steer around Salmadair to Ornsay and I run up the steps of the pier and I jump in the car and I drive madly down to Glasgow – from Kyle to Fort William to the centre of the city, calling in a favour from Imogen as I go. She knows one of Scotland's best child psychiatrists. Malcolm Kellaway. And I know this because I read some of Imogen's articles months back, where she'd praised him in a piece about modern motherhood. Now I demand her help.

'Can you get me an appointment? Right now?'

'What?'

'Immy. Please.' I am gazing at the haunted bleakness of Rannoch Moor, simultaneously steering, and phoning. I don't think there are any police around, to arrest me for careless driving. Little lochs shine dirty silver, in the occasional breaks of sun.

'Please, Immy. I need this.'

'Well. Yes . . . yes, I could try. He could call you back. But, um, Sarah – are you sure you're OK?'

'Yes?'

'Sarah – it's just – you know—'

'Imogen!'

Like a friend – like the friend who has been with me all the way – she gets the message, and she stops asking questions, and she rings off, to do my bidding. And sure enough: his office calls me as I drive: he has agreed to see me with four hours' notice.

Thank you, Imogen.

And now here I am in Kellaway's office in George Street. The psychiatrist, Dr Malcolm Kellaway, is sitting on a leather swivel chair behind his slim metal desk. His hands are pressed exactly flat together, as if in the most pious prayer; his twinned fingertips are poised to his chin.

He asks, for the second time. 'Do you honestly believe that you might have made a mistake? That evening, in Devon?'

'I don't know. No. Yes. I don't *know.*'

Silence resumes.

The Glasgow sky is already blackening outside, and it is barely two-thirty p.m.

'OK, let's go over the facts again.'

And so he goes over the facts, again. The facts of the matter; the case in hand; the death of my daughter; the possible breakdown of my surviving child.

I listen to his recitation, but really I am staring at those dark swirling clouds outside, beyond the square windows with the sooty granite sills. *Glasgow.* This is such a Satanic city in the winter – Victorian and dour, exultantly forbidding. Why did I come here?

Kellaway has more questions of his own.

'How much of this have you discussed with your husband, Mrs Moorcroft?

'Not so much.'

'Why not?'

'Just that – I don't want to make it any worse than it is, I mean, before I know, for *sure*.'

Again the doubts assail me: what am I doing here? What is the point? Malcolm Kellaway is easily middle-aged, yet wears jeans which make him seem unconvincing. He has annoyingly effete gestures, a silly roll-neck jumper, and rimless spectacles with two perfectly round lenses that say *oo*. What does this man know about my daughter that I don't? What can he tell me that I can't tell myself?

Now he gazes at me, from behind those glasses, and he says,

'Mrs Moorcroft. Perhaps it's time to move on from what we know, to what we don't know, or can't know.'

'All right.'

'First things first.' He sits forward. 'Following your phone call this morning, I have done some research of my own, and I have consulted with colleagues at the Royal Infirmary. And I'm afraid there is, as I suspected, no reliable way of differentiating between monozygotic twins, especially in your pretty unique circumstances.'

I gaze back at him. 'DNA?'

'No. Afraid not. Even if we had' – he winces as he speaks the next words – 'a large enough sample from your deceased daughter, standard DNA tests could almost certainly not discern any difference. Identical twins are just that: identical – genetically identical as well as facially and physically identical. This is actually a problem for police forces; there have been cases where two twins have escaped conviction for crimes because the police are unable to identify which particular twin did the deed, even when they have DNA samples from the crime scene.'

'What about fingerprints, aren't they different?'

100

'Yes, there is sometimes a slight difference there, in fingerprints and footprints, even in identicals, but of course your daughter, ah . . . there was a cremation, wasn't there?'

'Yes.'

'And neither girl was fingerprinted before.'

'No.'

'You see the difficulty.'

He sighs, with unexpected vigour. Then he stands, and walks to the window and gazes at the streetlights outside, which are switching on. At three p.m.

'It is rather an intractable problem, Mrs Moorcroft. If both daughters were alive, there are other ways we *could* differentiate them, from now on – maybe using patterns of branching blood vessels in the face, facial thermography, but when one is dead, and you want to do it retrospectively . . . Then naturally it is pretty much impossible. Anatomical science is not going to help us.'

He turns, and regards me in my disconcertingly deep leather chair. I feel like an infant, my feet barely touching the ground.

'But maybe this is all unnecessary.'

'Sorry?'

'Let's be positive, Mrs Moorcroft. Let's look at it a different way, and see what psychology can tell us. We know that loss of a co-twin is especially distressing for the surviving sibling.'

Kirstie. My poor Kirstie.

'Identical twins who lose their co-twin have significantly higher scores on four of the eight GEI bereavement scales – they suffer more from despair, guilt, rumination and depersonalization.' He sighs, briefly, but goes on: 'In the light of this intense grief, especially the

101

depersonalization, the major possibility is that your daughter Kirstie is simply hallucinating, or delusional. Doctors at Edinburgh University did a study on this subject, on co-twins who lose the other twin. They found that outright psychiatric disorder is elevated in twins whose co-twins have died, compared with twins both living.'

'Kirstie is going mad?'

He is framed by the dark window behind.

'Not mad, more disturbed; perhaps quite severely disturbed. Consider what Kirstie is going through alone: she herself is a living reminder of the deceased sister. Every time she looks in a mirror, she sees her dead sibling. She is also experiencing, vicariously, your confusion. And your husband's confusion. Consider, likewise, how she must dread the approach of solitary birthdays, of facing a life of comparative isolation, after being a twin since birth – she is surely experiencing a loneliness none of us can really comprehend.'

I am trying not to cry. Kellaway continues,

'The bewilderment must be profound. Also, a surviving twin may well feel guilt and contrition after the co-twin's death: guilt that she was chosen to live. The guilt is further compounded by seeing the grief of her parents, especially if the parents are warring. So many divorces follow this kind of thing, they are sadly universal.' He looks directly at me. Clearly expecting a response.

'We don't argue.' Is all I can say. Quite weakly. 'I mean – maybe we did, at one point: our marriage went through, you know, a rough patch, but that's behind us. We don't argue in front of my girl. I don't think we do. No.'

Kellaway walks to the second window, and stares out at the streetlights while talking: 'The guilt and the grieving, and the sudden engulfing loneliness, can combine to unbalance the mind of the surviving twin in rather extraordinary ways. If you look at the literature of bereaved twins, as I have done, there are many examples of this. When one twin dies, the other will take over their characteristics, becoming more *like* the twin that died. An American study found one twin whose brother died at the age of twelve; the surviving twin became so like his dead brother his parents were convinced the living twin had, as they put it, the 'spirit of his dead brother within him'. In another example, a twin in her teens who lost her sister, took on that sister's name, voluntarily, so she could' – Kellaway half-turns, and looks at me – 'stop being herself. That is the phrase she used, she wanted to *stop being herself*. She wanted to *be* her dead twin.'

A pause.

I have to reply, 'So your conclusion is that Kirstie *is* Kirstie, but that,' I am trying to speak as calmly as I can, 'but she is pretending to be Lydia, or thinks she is Lydia, to get over the guilt, and her grief?'

'It's a very strong probability, in my mind. And it's as far as I can go without a proper consultation.'

'But what about the dog? What about Beany?'

Kellaway walks back to his swivel chair, and sits himself down.

'The dog is perplexing. Yes. To a certain extent. And you are of course right: dogs can differentiate by scent between identical twins, even if the best DNA tests cannot. Yet it is also known that bereft and surviving twins often make very close bonds with pets. The pet replaces the dead sibling. My guess, consequently, is that Kirstie and Beany the dog have formed this closer bond, and Beany is behaving in a different way in response to this fonder attachment.'

The Glasgow rain is now falling on the window, quite heavily. And I am at a loss. I had come so close to believing that my darling Lydia was back, and yet it seems Kirstie lives. I imagined it all. The whole thing. And so did Kirstie? My heartbreak has intensified: pointlessly.

'What do I do now, Doctor Kellaway? How do I deal with my daughter's confusion? Her grief?'

'Act as normal as possible. Continue as you are now.'

'Should I tell my husband any of this?'

'Up to you. It might be better to let it lie – but this, of course, is for you to decide.'

'And then? What's going to happen then?'

'It's difficult to say for sure. But my best guess is that this state of disturbance will pass, once Kirstie sees that you still regard her as Kirstie, still love her as Kirstie, don't blame her for being Kirstie; she will become Kirstie, once more.'

He makes this speech like a peroration. With an air of finality. My consultation is clearly over. Kellaway escorts me to the door, and hands me my raincoat, like a doorman at a classy hotel; then he says, much more conversationally:

'Kirstie is enrolled at a new school?'

'Yes. She starts next week. We wanted time to adjust. You know . . .'

'That's good. That's good. School is an important part of normalization: after a few weeks there, she will, I hope, and believe, begin to make new friends, and this present confusion will pass.' He offers me a wan but apparently sincere smile. 'I know it must be cruel for you. Almost intolerable.' He pauses for a moment, and his eyes meet mine. 'How are you doing? You haven't talked about yourself? You have been through an incredibly traumatic year.'

'Me?'

'Yes. You.'

The question stumps me. I gaze at Kellaway's face, his mild and professional smile.

'I'm doing all right, I think. The move is a distraction, but I like it. I reckon it can work. I just want all this to be over.'

He nods, once more. Pensive behind his spectacles.

'Please do stay in touch. Good afternoon, Mrs Moorcroft.'

And that is that. The door to his office shuts behind me, and I take the new steel-and-blond wood staircase to the main door, stepping out into the damp streets of Glasgow.

Streetlights make misty haloes in the freezing rain, the cold pavements are almost empty. There's just one woman in black fighting an umbrella in the wind. And it's me.

My Holiday Inn Express is just around the corner. I stay in the hotel all evening, get a takeaway curry delivered, eat it on my over-firm hotel bed with a plastic spoon, straight out of the plastic trays, gazing apathetically at the TV. Trying not to think about Kirstie. I watch nature programmes and cookery programmes until my mind is numb with the pointlessness. I feel nothing. No grief no angst, just quietness. Maybe the storm is past. Maybe this is it. Maybe life can go on.

My early breakfast is as plastic as dinner; I am glad to get in the car and head north for The Wilds. And as the grey council estates surrender to the greener fields, then wider forests, then proper mountains, graced with lean streaks of early snow, my mood elevates.

Surely Kellaway is right: he is a nationally renowned child psychiatrist. Who am I to argue? Kirstie Moorcroft is Kirstie Moorcroft, thinking otherwise is ridiculous. My poor child is confused, and guilt-ridden. I want to hug Kirstie for an hour when I get home. Then begin our lives again. In the sweet cold air of the Hebrides.

Loch Linnhe stretches blue and dark grey along my left, and beyond it I can see the thread of walls and hedgerows that is the Road to the Isles, which winds through woods and wilderness to the fishing port and ferry terminal of Mallaig.

I check the time on my dashboard as I drive. I've been told that if you get the right ferry, from Mallaig to Armadale, the Road to the Isles shaves two hours off the journey to Ornsay, as you don't have to loop north to Kyle.

Pulling into a lay-by, I call the cheery lady at Calmac, the ferry company. The news is good. Next sailing one p.m. I can do it easily. So I phone the cottage on Torran to tell Angus and through the crackles I can hear him saying, 'Good, good' and 'I'll pick you up in the boat.'

'The boat? We finally have a boat?'

Crackle. 'Yes. Dinghy. I . . .' *Crackle.*

'That's great—'

Hiss. Crackle. KKkkkkrackle.

'I'll pick you up at Ornsay pier when . . .' His voice fades out in a minor storm of static. This landline is going to collapse completely, soon.

'Two thirty. Two thirty!! Angus. Meet me at Ornsay at two thirty.'

I can barely hear him reply. I think he said OK.

But we have a boat.

We have a boat!

When I reach the harbour at Mallaig, with its coast-guard officers, and its chatting fishermen, and the cheery

106

crabbers and prawn boats lined along the harbour, the air of busyness gives me a rush of extroversion. Briskly I drive my car on to the ferry and sit there, half smiling, half dreaming, handing my change through the window to a handsome Polish guy in a vast anorak, who is splurging tickets from a clever machine.

And then I offload, and excitedly skid the car along the main Sleat road to Ornsay – we've got a boat! A real boat of our own! Accelerating and animated I crest the last serious hill south of Ornsay.

It's a bleak hump of moor, yet, often, strangely busy – because this is where the locals park their cars, at all hours, to catch a proper mobile signal: to access the Net on smartphones. It is also the last visual obstacle before Ornsay. And so, as I speed down the other side, I see it. My new home.

And my heart properly lifts.

Torran. Beautiful Eilean Torran.

For the first time since we moved here, I feel a serious attachment. Despite the rawness and the squalor, I am falling for the very real beauty of our new home: falling for the glory of the waters surging south past Salmadair; swooning over the lonely grandeur of Knoydart, between the sea lochs. The beauty is hurtful: like the pain of something beginning to heal.

I never want to go back to London. I want to stay here.

Eilean Torran. Our island.

Lost in my rhapsodies, I drive down through the village and park outside the Selkie, by the pier; and there indeed is Angus, with Kirstie in her pink coat protectively sheltered under his arm, and she is smiling shyly, and he isn't smiling at all. He is looking at me, oddly, and I know something is wrong.

'So,' I say, disguising my fears, what can be wrong now? 'How much did you pay?'

'Five hundred quid from Gaelforce – chandlers in Inverness. Josh helped me bring her back. Two point five metres, inflatable. Bit of a bargain.' He gives me a hard, handsome, unconvincing grin – and leads me to the pier, pointing down to a lurid, orange, inflatable dinghy, floating in the calm Ornsay waters. 'Josh is worried that this won't be man enough after a big night at the bar. But that's bollocks.'

'OK.'

Kirstie is clutching Leopardy with one hand, and her father's large fist with the other. Waiting to get in the boat with Mummy and Daddy and go home. Her dad goes on: 'Seen plenty of yachties get back to their vessels in this sort of thing. These are light enough to drag up the beach, solo. And as we've got no safe running mooring, seems crucial. Right?'

'Erm.' I've no idea what to say; I know nothing about boats. I'm still pleased about the boat; but there *is* some mood here. Something amiss.

'Let me get in first,' says Angus. 'And I'll help you guys aboard.' He jumps down the stone steps, then climbs into the dinghy, which wobbles under his weight. He turns and opens his arms to our daughter, and says:

'OK, Kirstie, do you want to come down first, before Mummy.'

I gaze at him. My eyes wide. Wondering. Thinking. Kirstie looks at me and says:

''Magine you had a dog and a cat and another cat called Hello Bye Bye and Come Here and you were in the park with them, shouting.'

'Yes?'

She is softly giggling to herself, her white teeth shining,

small teeth growing, one tooth wobbling. She is laughing properly now.

'If you were shouting in the park with them, Mummy, with the cat and the dog and you were shouting Hello and Bye Bye and Come here, they'd be running around everywhere, they wouldn't know what to do!'

I force a smile. This is the kind of joke – the kind of spontaneous nonsense concept – Kirstie would enjoy with Lydia; they would concoct these strange whimsical fantasies and they would get wilder and wilder and then they would both laugh, together, as one. But now there is no one here to play this game with her.

I try to laugh. It is blatantly phoney. Kirstie stares at me and now she looks sad, with the cold blue waves behind her.

'Had a dream,' she says. 'Bad dream again. Granddad was there in the white room.'

'What? Darling?'

'Sarah!'

Angus's voice is sharper than the cold Ornsay wind.

'Sarah!'

'What?'

'Can't you help her?' His eyes are fixed on mine, and he goes on. 'Help Kirstie into the boat.'

Taking her hand I lift her down into the boat, then follow. Kirstie is distracted, now, staring grief-struck at the waves. I lean close to my husband. And hiss at him:

'What happened?'

He shrugs. And his voice drops to a whisper. 'Another dream. Last night.'

'The same nightmare?'

'Yes. The faces. Nothing important. It will stop.' He turns, forcibly brightening, and smiling. 'OK, guys, welcome to HMS *Moorcroft*. Let's go!'

I gaze from Angus's measured and bogus smile to my daughter's bonny blonde head, turned away from me, and I consider this recurring dream. She's had it for months, on and off. And now her grandfather was there? Why is Angus dismissing this out of hand? It has to be symbolic. It has to mean something. Yet I can't work it out.

Angus is starting the outboard motor. The wind is kicking and brisk. Kirstie is leaning over the side of the boat, looking down at the waves. I worry that her anorak hood is down, she must be getting cold. But the boat successfully guides us to Torran; Kirstie jumps out, and runs up the path to the house: apparently in a brighter mood, glad to be home. Beany waits for her at the kitchen door: where he often can be found.

As if he doesn't want to go indoors.

We linger, as Angus tries to teach me how to tie the boat to the iron railings of the lighthouse.

'No, like this,' he says. 'Do it like this.'

I try to master the knot; and I fail, again, in the dimming light. He smiles and chides me,

'Milverton. You're such a landlubber.'

'And what are you, Gus, some old sea dog?'

He laughs. And the mood between us is better, again. Eventually I get the knot half-right – though I'm not sure I'll remember it.

We go inside and the mood is definitely good. There is a purposeful sense of family. A big pot of tea sits on the dining table; mugs are poured and cake is eaten and decisions are made; we are a couple working on a home. The sweet smell of new paint fills the cottage, as Angus goes into the lumber-room and chops wood, to build a fire, while I cook supper.

I note, as I slice the eyes out of potatoes, and stare

at the twinkled lights of Ornsay village, how the primitive conditions of our life are reverting us to traditional male and female roles. Angus would often cook in Camden, but he rarely does it here: this is because his strength and time is needed for arduous, masculine tasks. Chopping and lifting and bricklaying.

And yet, I don't mind that. Indeed, I quite like that. We are a man and a woman on an island, self-reliant and surviving, working as a team: and doing male and female things. It is old-fashioned, but it is not unsexy.

Over dinner we sip cheap Co-op wine and I hold Angus's hand and say, 'Well done on the boat.' He mumbles something about water hazards and basking sharks. I don't particularly know what he is saying, but I embrace the sound of it. We live somewhere with basking sharks.

As the big fire consumes the logs, and we open a second bottle of red, Kirstie happily retreats to her room with a magazine. Angus gets out a book of knots and tries to teach me some special boating knots – the bowline, the cleat hitch, the stopper – with a length of thin rope.

We are snuggled under the rug, again. I gaze at the slender grey rope, and do my best. But the knot falls apart in my hand, for the seventh time.

Angus sighs, patiently.

'Good job you're not into bondage,' he says. 'You'd be useless.'

I look up at him. 'But it wouldn't be me tying the knots, would it?'

He pauses, and he laughs. That old, deep, very sexy laugh. Then he leans and kisses me gently on the lips, and it is a husband's kiss, a lover's kiss. And I know the sexual chemistry is still there. Somehow, it has survived. Through everything. And I am actually happy, or something close to it.

For the rest of the evening, Angus and I do more work on the house: he is grouting the bathroom, and installing new pipes. I am contentedly painting away some of the squatters' murals: they are just too creepy.

Positioning a chair, I prepare to tackle the second mural. The harlequin. But then I stop, paint-roller in hand. And I look up. The harlequin looks down. With its white sad face.

From nowhere, the realization pierces me.

The white room, the sad faces, staring down. The constant repetitive nightmare. And now her grandfather?

I've worked it out. I've worked out Kirstie's dream. And everything has changed again; and I am frightened.

8

He gazed at his wife. At least they weren't drinking wine out of jam jars any more. At least they had gone beyond that, into a world of actual wine glasses.

This was something, but not enough. He was sweating around Skye, trying to find work, all kinds of work, any work, building pig sties and loft extensions, building garden sheds if he had to, all his wife had to do was unpack the rest of the crockery, which seemed to have taken her about a month. Or at least six days. Yes, they'd been working hard on the house. Together. And working quite well – getting along better, despite it all. And yes, she'd had her commission in Glasgow, but what was that all about, truly? He didn't quite believe it. Imogen seemed vague and evasive when he'd rung her, yesterday, from the Selkie, and asked her: what was his wife doing in Glasgow?

Straining not to drink his wine in one gulp, he listened to her talk about telepathy.

Telepathy?

Sarah gazed his way. Then she went on.

'Gus, think about it: I mean – the dream. Kirstie is

dreaming about Lydia. And she is dreaming about Lydia in hospital. Must be, right? So maybe she is imagining herself *as* Lydia, at that horrible moment: when she woke up for a second and saw us all – her family, the nurses, the doctors. Her grandfather was there, he was in that room. The white room in hospital.'

'But, Sarah, I—'

'But Kirstie has no idea that her sister Lydia woke up, that she was conscious for one final moment. No one has ever told her. So—' His wife's expression was now quite panicked 'Gus. How else would she have known about the hospital? How?'

'C'mon, Sarah. Calm down.'

'No, seriously, think about it. Please?'

Angus shrugged and said nothing, trying to express, with the disdain in his expression, how much contempt he had for this idea.

'Angus?'

Again he said nothing. Deliberately returning her silences, as a punishment. He felt a surge of anger, that she should try and ruin it all. Again. Just as they were beginning to settle in.

Setting down his glass, he gazed at the mad scribbles of rain on the dining-room window. How was he going to make this house waterproof? And windproof? As Josh had warned him: when the Skye winds and rains kicked in, Torran cottage was actually colder inside than out, thanks to some kind of refrigeration effect, from the intense dampness of so many years without proper heating.

'Angus, talk to me.'

'Why? When you're blathering nonsense?'

He was trying to restrain himself: Sarah hated being shouted at, she'd fracture into tears if he really raised

116

his voice. The legacy of her domineering father. But then she'd gone and married a brusque man, himself, not entirely unlike her father.

Her fault then? Or maybe it was no one's fault: just the repeating patterns of families. Angus was no different, he was not immune to the tedious reiterations of genes and environment: right this minute, he wanted a proper drink. He wanted a big glass of proper whisky like his failed and sweary old man, who beat the wits out of Angus's mother at least once a month. And then fell in the river and drowned. Good. There's all the drink you'll need, you old bastard.

'What is this crap? Sarah?'

'How else did our daughter learn about Lydia, in hospital?'

'You don't know that she is dreaming about this.'

'A white room, with sad faces, staring down, and her grandfather is there? It has to be, Gus, what else could it be? The imagery is so so stark, it's horrible. God.'

Was she on the verge of tears again? Something in Angus wanted her to cry: the way he had nearly cried, when Kirstie said what she said.

His wife had it easy.

Angus resisted the urge to terrify her with the truth. Instead he laid a big hand on his wife's small white hand, her tiny, pretty, ineffectual hands that couldn't tie a reef knot to fix the boat; yet these were the small white hands that he'd loved. Once. Could he ever love her properly again? Love her doubtlessly and purely, untroubled by resentment, or a desire for revenge?

'Sarah, maybe your dad told her? You know what he's like after a couple. Or your mum. My brother. Anyone could have said something about hospitals, and she overheard it, then imagined the rest. Think how

117

horrible it must be. The concept. To a child. Hospital. Rooms. Death. It'd lodge in the memory. That's why she's dreaming of it.'

'But I don't believe anyone did tell her, or said anything she might have overheard. Only my family knew that Lydia woke up. And I asked them.'

'You what?'

Silence.

'You asked your mum and dad??'

Another pause.

'Jesus Christ. Sarah? You've been ringing people up, telling them all this, all our private stuff? How is that going to help?'

His wife sipped from her wine, and shook her head, her lips thinned and whitened by suppressed tension.

Angus stared intently at the wine in his glass. Feeling a draining sense of futility: as if he were sitting in a bath and the water was glugging away down the plug-hole, making him colder, and heavier: transported to a nastier planet. They were shivering in this cottage; they were drowning in tasks and challenges, and maybe it was helpless.

No. He had to keep halfway positive. For Kirstie.

Tomorrow he'd try again. Maybe that architectural office in Portree, he'd take his portfolio in once more. They were close to offering him a part-time gig. They just needed one more nudge. Look, see, I used to design parts of skyscrapers, I think I can manage a sheepfold. Maybe he would beg. Help, I need a job, I need ten grand, because my daughter is living in a house that's literally like a refrigerator.

'Gus, there are lots of stories of twins having telepathy, some link – you know we used to talk about it and and . . . You know, they had the same *dreams*. Remember

118

when they would start laughing, instantly, the same moment, and we had no idea what it was?'

Angus sat back and rubbed his eyes with a dusty hand. He listened to the house. Kirstie was in her room playing with the old iPad. He could just about hear the distant clicks and whistles of the computer game, dueting with the crinkle of rain on the dining-room window. His daughter was lost in a computer world, and he couldn't blame her: it beat reality.

And the reality was: Angus did remember the times when Kirstie and Lydia would laugh simultaneously, for no reason. Of course he remembered: he would stare at them in astonishment when, from nowhere, the twins would both start giggling, in different chairs, at the same time, without apparently communicating. Sometimes this happened when they were in different rooms. He'd walk from one room to another and find them both in identical fits of giggles, with no identifiable cause.

He remembered so much. He remembered one time Lydia was reading Roald Dahl's *Big Friendly Giant* in her bedroom, and he found that Kirstie was on the same page, downstairs. He remembered watching them once as they walked home from school, Kirstie walking in front, at a funeral pace, doing a kind of slow goose-step, and then he saw Lydia walking behind her, thirty yards behind, walking exactly the same way, as if they were both in a kind of trance. Why did they do that? To freak people out? Or was it because there really was some kind of mental link? Yet he didn't and couldn't believe that. He'd read the science: there was no such thing as twin telepathy. Just the ordinary miracle of identical genes.

He gazed at the smears of the rain. The harshness of outdoors beckoned, and appealed.

Something in him wanted to be out there in the wind and the cold, scrambling the cruel ridges of the Black Cuillins, getting battered by the winds up by the Old Man of Storr. But he was in here, waiting for his wife to talk. She was finishing her wine, the last of the bottle. Would they open another? He always relied on her to police his drinking. And yes he wanted another bottle, already, at five p.m.

'Angus, please. Just think about it. Couldn't there have been some kind of telepathy? What about those twins in Finland, who died at the same time, in a road crash. What was it—'

'Ten miles apart. On the same night. Yep. And?'

'Isn't that amazing, doesn't that prove something?'

'No.'

'But—'

'Sarah, even if there was some mental link between them once, which I don't believe, but even if there was – Lydia has been dead over a YEAR. And the dreams only started a few months back.'

The rain seemed to pause. His wife gazed at him.

He went on, 'Even if you think twins can send each other dreams, from a distance, I really don't think twins can contact each other through the ether – when one of them is DEAD. Do you?'

A silence ensued. He barked with laughter.

'Unless you're saying that Lydia is coming back, as a wee ghostie? A little phantom, floating about, talkin' to her twin. Where is she now? In the wardrobe, holding her own head?'

It was a joke. He was making an attempt at humour.

But with a cringing dizziness, he realized that he'd touched on a truth. Sarah wasn't laughing; or frowning; she was just staring at him, as the Hebridean rain

120

returned, as the rain ate deeper and deeper into the cement and mortar of this stupid house.

'Oh, fuck this! You believe in ghosts now, Sarah? Get-a-fucking-grip. Lydia is dead, Kirstie is a confused and unhappy little girl. That's all. She just needs her parents to be sane.'

'No. It's not ghosts, it's something else.'

'What?'

'I . . .'

'What?'

'It's . . .' She tailed off into silence.

He felt like screaming. What. The. Hell. Is. It? His anger was overtaking him. Barely keeping control, he said, as evenly as possible, 'What is it, Sarah? What's the big mystery?'

'I – I don't know. The dreams, though, what about the dreams?'

'They're just fucking DREAMS!' He sank his head into his hands. Overdramatically. Yet sincerely.

For ten seconds neither of them spoke, then Sarah stood up, and took the empty wine bottle into the kitchen. Angus watched her as she went; the jeans were hanging off her hips. There was a time when they would have solved this tension by fucking. And he still wanted her; he still fancied her even when he resented her.

What would happen, if they went to bed? Their sex was always rough: Sarah liked it that way. It was one of the reasons he had fallen for her: her surprising, animalistic sexuality. Bite me, slap me, fuck me. Harder. But if he got rough with her now, and if his latent anger surfaced: where would it end?

Sarah came back from the kitchen. Not holding another wine bottle. His mood sank even further, if that was possible. Could he open one later without her

121

looking at him? He had to stop drinking so much. Kirstie needed her dad relatively sober and sensible. Someone had to be on the watch.

But it was so hard: maintaining the lies. And this place wasn't helping as he'd hoped. The cold, grey grisliness of November was ghastly enough, and this was just late autumn. What would real winter be like? Maybe the severity and brutality would help: they would have to pull together.

Or maybe it would end them.

She was hovering in the room, not sitting down.

'Sarah, is there something you're not telling me? You've been like this for a while – since Glasgow maybe. If not before. What's happened?'

His wife regarded him and said, as ever,

'It's nothing.'

'Sarah!'

'I'm sorry I mentioned it. I have to get Kirstie's clothes ready, I haven't even unpacked them, they only arrived this morning and' – he reached for her hand and held it, she went on – 'she starts at the new school in a few days.'

He kissed her hand, not knowing what else to do. But Sarah pulled away with a silent, apologetic smile, and she turned and exited the dining room, through the unpainted door, scuffing in her three layers of socks on the cold stone floor. Angus watched her go. Sighing urgently.

Ghosts?

It was ridiculous. If only the problem was just ghosts.

Ghosts would be easy. Because ghosts didn't exist.

Angus stood, and decided to busy himself with hard manual labour, to purge the sadness, and the anger. The endorphins might help his mood. They needed more wood chopped, and the light was fading.

Pacing through the kitchen he opened the battered door at the back, by the sinks and mops, that led to the lumber-room. Where the rats cavorted in ecstasy every night.

All kinds of crap was stored here, in this barnlike space: stacks of decrepit furniture, waiting to be sawed into kindling, the odd sack of coal, dating from maybe the Second World War. Pans and bottles were heaped in piles – like whole villages of refugees had stayed, then fled; there were heaps of plastic sacks and reels of blue nylon twine and pyramids of ancient porcelain flagons, most of them cracked. His grandmother had been a hoarder, a proper islander – a survivalist before her time, when it was necessary not fashionable, grabbing anything that drifted on to the beach. Hey, look, laddie, this could be useful. Keep that.

Selecting a few logs for chopping, Angus slipped on his plastic goggles, flexed his fingers into moist old gloves, and kick-started the electric saw.

For two hours he buzzed and sawed, in the dim thirty-watt light of the lumber-room bulb. The full moon rose over the rowans of Camuscross, as the clouds cleared. Beany nosed the door open and loped into the middle of the scattered, fragrant sawdust, and sat there, tail wagging slowly, and gazing at the puffs of yellow wood-dust spitting from the logs.

'All right, boy. All right?'

The dog looked sad. He'd looked sad ever since they'd got here. Angus had expected him to like Torran, indeed relish it – an entire and beautiful island, with rabbits and seals and birds to chase, and messy muddy rock pools? – better than the littered, brick-and-concrete labyrinth of Camden. No?

Yet the dog was often morose, as now: his muzzle posed between his paws.

Angus set down the saw; he had three plastic tubs full of chopped logs. He stripped off the sweaty plastic goggles and tickled Sawney Bean behind the ear, with his thickly gloved fingers.

'What is it, old pal? It's just an island?'

The dog whimpered.

'Kill some rats, Beano? There are lots of rats.'

Angus made a chomping motion with his mouth, then faked two paws with his fists. Trying to mimic a dog catching vermin.

'Nom nom nom. Rats, Beano? Rats? You're a bloody dog. Descended from centuries of ratters. No?'

Beany yawned, anxiously. And he laid his muzzle between his sphinxlike paws once again. Angus felt a flux of sympathy. He loved this dog. He'd spent endless happy hours walking woodlands around London, with Beany.

But this mood-switch was perplexing.

On reflection, Angus realized the dog had been acting very strangely ever since they'd arrived. Sometimes hiding in corners of the house, as if he was scared; at other times refusing to come in. And he acted differently around Sarah. He'd been acting differently around Kirstie and Sarah for a long time.

Could the dog have witnessed what really happened that night in Devon? Was Beany there, upstairs, when it happened? Could a dog remember or comprehend a human event like that?

Angus's breath was misting in the damp raw air. The lumber-room was bitterly cold, now that he'd stopped fighting the logs with the saw. So cold that the windows were actually icing up.

Just like that day the twins were born: the coldest day of the year.

He stared at the thin crackles of rime.

And now the grief hit Angus, like a blow to the back of his knees: as it often did. Like a hard rugby tackle. Making him crumple, and lean to the dusty stacks of planks for support.

Lydia, his little Lydia. Lying there in hospital with the tubes in her mouth, opening her regretful eyes, once, to say goodbye. As if to say sorry.

Lydia, his Lydia. Little Lydia. His darling daughter.

He'd loved her too, loved her just as much as Sarah. Yet somehow his grief was deemed as lesser? Somehow the mother's grief was seen as more important: *she* was the one allowed to crack up, *she* was the one given permission to cry, *she* was the one allowed to agonize for months about her favourite. OK, he'd lost his job, but he'd kept looking for more work through the agony and almost none of it was his fault. This was the enraging thing. She was far more to blame, infinitely more. He wanted to hurt his wife for what happened. Punish her. Hurt her badly.

Why not? His daughter was dead.

Angus plucked a hammer from a shelf. It was a claw hammer. Vicious and slightly rusted. Its fangs stained brown, as if there was already old blood on the steel. It was heavy, but it had a satisfying weight, just the right weight. It asked to be swung, hard, downwards, cracking something open. Finally. An explosion of redness. Like whacking a melon, soft pulp flying everywhere. Would the steel claws stick?

The rain had stopped and the sea was grey beyond the windows. Angus stared at the stained bare floorboards, despairing.

A low whimper brought him to proper consciousness. Beany was staring at him, head-tilted, and sad, and yet inquisitive. As if he could sense Angus's absurd and terrible thoughts.

Angus looked to the dog. Calmed himself. And spoke:

'Hey, Beany. Shall we go outside? Find a seal to chase?'

The dog barked softly and whisked his tail; Angus carefully replaced the steel claw hammer on the shelf.

9

It could be any school in Britain. Low-rise and airy, with a biggish playground with gaily painted swings and slides, and lots of parents looking sleepy, careworn and guiltily relieved as they drop off the little ones. It's just the setting that marks it out: sea to the left, and big sombre mountains behind, scarred with early December snow. And then, of course, there is the screwed-in sign on the gate.

Rachadh luchd-tadhail gu failteache

Underneath is a smaller, English translation.

All Visitors Must Report To Reception

Kirstie holds my hand, tightly, as we walk from our car between the sleeker city cars, and dirty Land Rovers, and approach the glass doors. Other mothers and fathers are greeting each other, personably, and affably, in that enviable, relaxed, chit-chatty, small-talking way that I have never quite mastered, and will find even harder here, amongst strangers.

Some of the parents are speaking Gaelic. Kirstie is as silent as her mum. Nervous and tense. She is in her new blue-and-white Kylerdale uniform under her quilted

129

pink anorak; when I pull the anorak off, at the school doorway, the uniform looks painfully big, verging on clownlike. And the shoes are clunky. And her hair is badly brushed: by me.

My guilt invades. Did I buy the wrong size of clothes? And why didn't I brush her hair properly? We were in such a rush. Angus wanted to cross to the mainland early: he's landed a part-time job at an architectural practice in Portree, far enough away that he will have to stay there overnight, whenever he gets work. This is good, financially, but it means transport is even more complicated.

So we all had to go, together, this morning, on our solitary boat. And I was forced to speed things up: brusquely spraying on the detangler, dragging the brush through my daughter's fine, white, fairysilk hair – as Kirstie stood between my knees – fidgeting with her toy, and singing a new made-up song to herself.

And now it is too late: Kirstie's hair looks messy.

My protective instinct reaches out. I desperately do not want her to be laughed at. She will already be dauntingly lonely, starting at a new school, well into the autumn term, without her sister. And the confusion about her identity is still there: lurking. Sometimes she calls herself 'we' not 'I'. Sometimes she calls herself 'other Kirstie'. She did it this morning.

Other Kirstie?

It is bewildering and painful, which is why I haven't addressed it. I merely hope that Kellaway is right, and school will somehow resolve it all: the excitement of new friends and new games.

So here we are.

We loiter at the school door as all the other children

go straight to their classes, chattering, laughing, hitting each other with their plastic rucksacks. Toy Story, Moshi Monsters. A woman with big glasses perched on a big nose, and a very sensible plaid skirt, gives me a smile of reassurance, and holds open the glazed door.

'Mrs Moorcroft?'

'Yes, er?'

'Checked you on Facebook. So sorry! Just curious to know who the new parents might be.' She tilts an indulgent expression at Kirstie. 'And this must be little Kirstie! Kirstie Moorcroft?' She ushers us in. 'You look just like your photos! I'm Sally Ferguson. Lovely to have a new girl at school. Please just call me Sally.' She looks back at me. 'The school secretary.'

She is waiting for me to respond. But I cannot. Because Kirstie is talking.

'I'm not Kirstie.'

The secretary smiles; she must think this is a joke. A game. A child hiding behind the sofa, holding up a puppet.

'Kirstie Moorcroft! We've seen your photos! You are going to love this school, we teach in a very special language—'

'I'm NOT Kirstie, I'm Lydia.'

'Uh—'

'Kirstie is dead. I am *Lydia*.'

'Kkkirr . . .?' The woman tails off. And looks at me. Understandably confused.

My daughter repeats herself. Loudly. 'Lydia. I am Lydia. We are Lydia. Lydia!'

The hallway of the school is silent apart from my daughter, shouting these lunatic words. Sally Ferguson's smile has faded, very quickly. She glances my way, with

131

a panicked frown. There are lots of happy Gaelic phrases printed on paper tacked to the wall. The school secretary tries one more time.

'Ah . . . um . . . Kirss—'

My daughter slaps at Sally Ferguson as if she is a wasp. 'Lydia! You have to call me Lydia! Lydia! Lydia! Lydia! Lydia Lydia Lydia Lydia LYDIA!'

The woman backs away, but my little girl is quite out of control now. She is giving us a full-on toddler's supermarket tantrum: except we are in a school, and she is seven, and she is claiming that she is her dead sister.

'Dead, Kirstie-koo is dead. I'M LYDIA! I am Lydia! She is here! Lydia!'

What do I do? I try to make normal conversation, absurdly, 'Um, it's just a thing, a thing – I'll be back to pick her up at—'

But my efforts can barely be heard as my daughter screams again, 'Lydia LYDIA LYDIA LYDIA LYDIA LYDIA – Kirrrstie is DEAD and I HATE her I'm *Lydia*!'

'Please,' I say. To Kirstie. Abandoning my pretence. 'Please, sweetheart, please?'

'KIRSTIE IS DEAD. Kirstie is dead, they killed her, they killed her. I am Ly-DDDDEEE-YYYAAAA!'

And then as quickly as it started, it blows itself out. Kirstie shakes her head, stomps over to the far wall, and sits down in a little chair, under a photo of school-kids working in the garden, with a cheery inscription in felt-tip pen.

Ag obair sa gharrad.

My daughter sniffs, then says, very quietly. 'Please call me Lydia. Why can't you call me Lydia, Mummy, that's who I am? Please?' Her teary blue eyes are lifted. 'I'm not going to school less you call me Lydia *please*. Mummy?'

I am paralysed. Her pleading sounds painfully sincere. I have no choice.

The silence prolongs into agony. Because now I have to explain everything to the school secretary at the worst possible moment, in the most awkward way; and to do that I need Kirstie out of here. I need her in that school.

'OK, OK. Mmm—' My childish stutter returns. 'Mrs Ferguson. This is *Lydia*. Lydia Moorcroft.' I am frightened, and mumbling. 'I'm actually enrolling Lydia May Tanera Moorcroft.'

A long silence. Sally Ferguson looks at me, with intense confusion. From behind those big thick glasses.

'Pardon me? Erm. *Lydia?* But . . .' She flushes bright red – then she reaches to a desk, behind an open, sliding window, and takes up a sheet of paper. Her next words are more of a whisper. 'But it says here, quite clearly, that you are enrolling *Kirstie* Moorcroft? That was the application. Kirstie. Definitely. Kirstie Moorcroft?'

I deeply breathe. I go to speak, but my daughter gets there first. As if she has overheard.

'I'm Lydia,' says Lydia. 'Kirstie is dead then she was alive but then she is dead again. I am Lydia.'

Sally Ferguson blushes, once more, and says nothing. I am feeling too dizzy to respond: teetering on the edge of dark absurdity. But with an effort, I speak: 'Can we let Lydia join her new class and I can explain.'

Another desperate silence. Then I hear children singing a song down a corridor, raucous and happy.

'Kookaburra nests in the old gum tree, Merry merry king of the bush is he! Laugh, kookaburra LAUGH—'

The incongruity makes me nauseous.

Sally Ferguson shakes her head; then she edges closer to me and says, quietly: 'Yes . . . That seems sensible.'

The school sec turns to a good-looking young man,

in skinny jeans, pressing through the glass doors from the cold outside. 'Dan, Daniel, please – do you mind – can you take, ahh, *Lydia* Moorcroft to her new class, Year Two, end of the corridor. Jane Rowlandson.'

'*LAUGH, Kookaburra, LAUGH—*'

Dan nods a languid amiable *Yes* and squats down, next to Lydia, like an overkeen waitress taking an order:

'Hey, Lydia. D'you want to come with me?'

'*Kookaburra sits in the old gum tree, Counting all the monkeys he can see-ee.*'

'I'm Lydia.' Kirstie is fiercely folding her arms. Scowling. Bottom lip jutting. As stubborn a face as she can manage. 'You must call me Lydia.'

'Sure. Of course. Lydia! You'll like it, they're doing music this morning.'

'*Stop, Kookaburra, Stop, Kookaburra, That's no monkey, that's me.*'

At last: it works. Slowly she unfolds her arms and she takes his hand – and she follows Dan towards another glass door. She looks so small, and the door looks so huge and daunting, and devouring.

For one moment she pauses and turns to give me a sad, frightened smile – and then Dan escorts her into the corridor: she is swallowed up by the school. I must leave her to her lonely fate; so I turn to Sally Ferguson.

'I have to explain.'

Sally nods, sombrely. 'Yes please. In my office. We can be alone there.'

Fifty minutes later I have given Sally Ferguson the basic yet appalling details of our story. The accident, the death, the confusion of identity, over fourteen months. She looks suitably and honestly horrified, and also sympathetic, but I can also detect a hint of sly delight in her eyes, as she listens to this narrative. I am very definitely livening up another dull schoolday. This is something she can tell her husband and her friends tonight: you won't believe who came in today, a mother who doesn't know the identity of her surviving twin, a mother who wonders if her supposedly dead and cremated daughter has actually been alive for fourteen months.

'That's a remarkable story,' says Sally Ferguson. 'I'm so so sorry.'

She takes her glasses off and puts them on again. 'It is amazing that there is, ah, no scientific way . . . of . . .'

'Knowing? Of proving?'

'Well, yes.'

'All we know is that – I mean, I think – If she wants to be Lydia for now maybe we *have* to go along with it. For now. Do you mind?'

'Well no, of course. If that's what you prefer. And that's fine in terms of enrolment. They are . . .' Sally searches for the words 'Well, they were the same age, so – yes – I'll just have to update the records, but don't worry about that.'

I get up to leave; quite desperate to escape.

'So sorry, Mrs Moorcroft. But I'm sure everything will be all right now, Kirstie – I mean – your daughter. Lydia. She will love it here. Really.'

I flee towards the car park and in the car I buzz the windows down and race back up the coast, the wind is biting cold, a knifing westerly off the Cuillins, from the Butt of Lewis, from Saint Bloody Kilda, but I don't care. I want the freezing cold. I squeal past Ornsay and head for Broadford, which feels like London after the remoteness of the Sleat peninsula. Here there are shops and post offices and people on pavements – and a big bright warm café, with very good wifi connection and a very good mobile signal. I want vodka, but coffee will have to do.

I sit on a comfy wooden chair by a big table, and with the fattest mug of cappuccino at my side, I take out my phone.

Mum. I need to call Mum. Urgently.

'Sarah, darling, I just knew it was you! Your father was in the garden, we're having an Indian summer down here.'

'Mum.'

'Is everything all right? Has Kirstie started at her new school?'

'Mum, there's something you need to hear.'

My mother knows me enough to realize what my tone of voice implies: her chatter ceases. She waits.

And I explain. I explain as I did to Sally Ferguson. As maybe I am going to have to explain with everyone else.

I do it quickly so I don't choke up. I tell her there is a possibility that we got it wrong: the identity of the twin that died. We don't know. We are trying to find out. It is all so absurd yet so cruelly real. As real as the mountains of Knoydart. My mother, who can anyway be easily as silent as me, stays respectfully silent throughout.

'My word,' she says at the end. 'My word. My. Well. Goodness. Poor Kirstie. I mean—'

'Mum, please don't cry.'

'I'm not.'

She is crying. I wait. She keeps crying.

'It's just that it brings back so many memories. That awful night. The ambulance.'

I wait for her tears to subside, fighting my own

emotions into submission. I have to be the strong one here. Why?

'So, Mum, we need to get to the bottom of this, if we can, because – because we need to decide if she is Kirstie or if she is Lydia. Then settle on it, I guess. I don't know. Oh, Jesus.'

'Yes,' my mum says. 'Yes.'

A few more stifled maternal sobs pass me by. I watch the traffic outside the café, heading for Kyle or Portree. The long winding mountain road that snakes past Scalpay and Raasay. Angus took that road this morning.

Our conversation drifts into practicalities, and trivialities. But I have a serious question for my mother.

'Mum, I want to ask you something.'

She sniffles. 'Yes, darling?'

'I need to know, to search out any inconsistencies, find out any clues.'

'What . . .'

'Is there anything about that night, that weekend, before the accident. Did you notice anything different about the girls, or different between them? Something you haven't told me, because it didn't seem relevant?'

'Different?'

'Yes.'

'What does that mean, Sarah?'

'I don't know. It's just – maybe I can differentiate them? Even now. Were they behaving differently, was there anything weird, any reason why there was this confusion in my daughter's head?'

My mother is entirely silent. A soft snow is now falling outside, the first of the winter. It is just a few brief flurries. It floats like the lightest confetti in the sharp sad air. Across the street, a small child, walking

137

with her mother, stops and points at the spangled nothingness, her face ignited with joy.

'Mum.'

More silence. This is an unusually prolonged pause,
even for my mother.

'Mum?'

'Well.' My mum puts her thoughtful, lying voice on.
'No. We don't need to dig it all up do we?'

'Yes, we do.'

'Well, I can't think of anything.'

*She is lying. My own mother is lying. I know her
too well.*

'Mum, there is something. What is it? What? You
have to tell me, no more evasions. Tell me.'

The snow is thinning to nothing: just a trace of
silvering in the air. The ghost of snow.

'I can't remember.'

'Yes, you can.'

'But, darling, I really can't.'

Why is she lying about this?

'Mum. Please.'

The next silence is different. I can hear her breathing.
I can almost hear her thinking. I can see her down
there in Devon, in the hallway, with the photos from
my dad's career on the wall, framed and faded, and
dusty. Photos of him receiving awards for long-fogotten
ads.

'Well, darling, there was something maybe, but it's
nothing. Nothing.'

'No. It's not nothing. It might not be.'

This is so obviously where I get it from: the propensity
to silence, the refusal to reveal.

I can see why Angus occasionally wants to
strangle me.

'It's nothing, Sarah.'

'Tell me, Mum. Tell me!'

I actually sound like Angus.

My mother takes a deep breath, 'All right, I . . . I just remember the day you arrived Kirstie was quite upset.'

'Kirstie?'

'Yes, but you didn't notice, you were so distracted, what with . . . everything. And Angus was late of course, late arriving, very late that night, and, I asked Kirstie what it was, what was upsetting her so, and, she said it was something, to do with Daddy. That he had upset her somehow, I think. Something like that, that's all I remember, it's surely nothing.'

'No, it might not be. Thanks, Mum. Thanks.'

The dialogue dwindles. We express our motherly and daughterly love. My mum asks if I am all right,

'I mean,' she adds, 'all right in yourself?'

'Yes. I am all right.'

'You're sure? You sound, darling, a little, you know, like you did. Sarah, you really do not want to go back there. Not like you were.'

'Mum, I am managing, I really am, apart from this Lydia thing. I actually like the house, despite the rats under the bed. And I love the island. You must see it.'

'Of course, of course we will.'

To get her off the subject, I ask about my brother Jamie: and it works. My mum laughs softly, and affectionately, and says he is sheep-farming in Australia. Or felling trees in Canada. She's not entirely sure. It is a family joke that Jamie is so wandering, and prodigal: a family joke we use, to get us through the bad times, and the awkward conversations. Like now.

Then Mum and me say goodbye. And I sit there in

the café, and order another coffee. Wondering about this conversation I've just had. Why was Angus late that night arriving at Instow? Before the accident the story was: he might be working late. Yet when we tried to call him at work, he wasn't there. It later emerged – he later explained, further – that he'd stopped by Imogen's house, from work, to pick up some of the twins' things: as they'd recently had a sleepover there.

Childless Imogen always liked having children around.

At the time I didn't question this story. Not remotely. I had too much grieving to do; it all made sense anyway. But now?

Imogen?

No. This is stupid. Why am I doubting my husband? Apart from the drinking, he's been there for us all along. Loving, devoted, resourceful, miserable, Angus. My husband. And I need to trust him, as I have no one else.

And anyway there's nothing more I can do about Kirstie's troubles this minute; I've got to do some of my own work.

I have to earn, by writing. Angus's new, part-time job in Portree will bring in a few quid, but a few quid is not enough. We need more income. Consequently whatever I can add will be crucial in keeping us on Torran.

And I want to stay on Torran, so very very much.

So I open my laptop, and spend two hours sending emails: the accumulated ideas, notions and necessary communications of forty-eight hours. I send a bunch of emails to editors in town: maybe I can write something about Torran and Sleat, about local folklore, the Gaelic revival, anything.

Sipping my cappuccino, looking at the cars driving in and out of Broadford Co-op, I consider, once more, my growing infatuation with our island. It's like a teenage crush on an uncaring, hard-to-please boy. The more difficult Torran is, the more I want to own it, to make it mine.

A few hard hours later and my work is done; I must go back to school to pick up Kirstie. I am going to be late, so I press the pedal, but then I skid over the snow-slicked cattle grid, and almost shunt into a stunted oak, mournfully guarding a farm track to my left.

Slow down, Sarah, slow down. I need to remember the road is dangerous pretty much all the way, from Broadford to Ardvasar. But then everything is slightly dangerous here.

A lonely snowflake hits my windscreen, and is exterminated by the wipers. I look at the low balding hills. Shaved by winds and deforestation. I think of the people wrenched from this landscape by poverty and the Highland Clearances. Skye used to be populated by twenty-five thousand people. A century later it is half that. I often consider the scenes of that emigration: the crying farmwives, the sheep-dogs quietly killed, the babies screaming as they quit their beautiful, hostile homeland, and sailed west. And now I think of my daughter.

Screaming.

I have decided what to do about my daughter. I don't want to do this. But I have to. The awfulness this morning clinched it.

I arrive at the school. With an effort, I flash an unconvincing smile at some of the other mothers, and then I turn and look to the cheery paper sign on the glass door saying *Failte* and I wonder where is she, where is my daughter?

All of the other children are pouring out: a cataract of giddy energy and Gaelic chatter and Lego Movie lunchboxes, a mob of small people running into parental arms and then, finally, the last, slow, reluctant child emerges from the door. A little girl with no friends. Talking to no one.

My daughter. Now an only child. With her sad little rucksack. In her sad uniform. She walks up to me and buries her face in my stomach.

'Hello you,' I say.

I put an arm around her, and guide her to the car.

'Hey. How was the first day at school?'

My cheeriness is absurd. But what else can I do? Be doomy and suicidal? Tell her everything is indeed awful?

Kirstie straps herself in the child seat, and gazes out the window at the grey tidal waters of the Sound, and the pink and orange lights of Mallaig: with its port and its railway station, and its symbols of escape and civilization and the mainland, now dimming in the distance. The winter darkness is already shrouding, at three-fifteen.

'Sweetie. How did it go at school?'

She is looking out of the window, still. I persist.

'Moomin?'

'Nothing.'

'Sorry?'

'No one.'

'Oh, OK.' What does this mean? *Nothing* and *no one*? I turn the radio on and sing along to a happy tune as I have a brief exultant urge to drive the car straight into Loch na Dal.

142

But I have a plan and we are going to stick to it. We just need to get to the boat, then get to the island.

Then I will do what I am so afraid of doing.

This wretched and terrible thing.

10

The boat is there, waiting, lashed to the pier that juts from the car park outside the Selkie. The lighthouse and lighthouse-keeper's cottage look innocent in the distance, white and lovely, yet humbled by the dark, framing mountains of Knoydart. I stop the Ford and park.

It takes me four or five tugs of the outboard to get the engine ticking over. It used to take me ten. I am getting used to this, and I am steering the boat better. I can even tie knots.

Kirstie sits, slightly red-eyed, yet calm, at the other end of the dinghy, looking first at me, then at the rocky beaches of Salmadair, as we putter across in the chilly breeze. Her blonde hair sweetly curls and kicks in the wind. She looks so pretty – her retroussé profile is framed by the waters. I love her so much, my little girl. I love her because she is Kirstie and I love her because she reminds me of Lydia.

And, of course, part of me wants my little Lydia back. Part of me sings at this idea. I have missed Lydia intensely: the way we would sit and read together for entire afternoons, the way we would sometimes just sit, quiet but happy; Kirstie was always bouncing around, much less patient. The idea that Lydia could have returned, from the dead, is a kind of miracle. Terrifying but a miracle. Maybe all miracles are frightening? But if I get Lydia back, if this really is Lydia here, now – then Kirstie dies.

What am I thinking? This is Kirstie, as I am about to prove. In the cruellest of ways. If I can find the ruthlessness to see it through.

Kirstie asks, in the biting sea wind, 'Why's it called Salmadair, Mummy?'

This is good. A normal conversation.

'I think it means island of psalms, darling, there used to be a nunnery here.'

'When, Mummy? What's nunnery?'

'A nunnery, with people who prayed, they used to pray here, many years ago, a thousand years ago?'

'Before we were a baby?'

I ignore the troubled syntax, and nod. 'Yep. Long time before then.'

'Now there's no nuns there?'

'No. Are you cold?'

The wind is really kicking at her hair; her pink rain-coat is unbuttoned.

'No it's all right. The wind is making my hair blow all over my face but I like hair in my face.'

'OK. We're nearly there.'

A seal rises to the right – bottling – looking at us with those orphaned eyes, sad, and wise; then with an oily, whiskered plop it disappears and Kirstie smiles her gap-toothed smile.

The Sleat waves are kind, and ferry us onto the beach beneath the lighthouse. I drag the dinghy – which is

146

just light enough – above the tideline, where crabs scuttle, and a dead salmon rots, pecked by herring gulls.

'Pooh,' says Kirstie, pointing at the smelly fish carcass. Then she runs up to the cottage and pushes the never-locked door and disappears inside. I can hear Beany barking softly in greeting. He used to bark loudly and happily. I knot the boat, and follow. The kitchen is cold. The rats are quiet. The harlequins dance on the stained white wall of the dining room. The stone is kept on the loo seat, so as to keep out the mink.

Angus is absent, doing his overnight thing in Portree. We are alone on the island and that's just fine.

Kirstie pats and strokes Beany then she goes to her room to read, and I prepare supper in the shadows of the kitchen, where the wire baskets swing overhead in the half-light, preserving our food from the rats. I can hear the respiration of the sea, it sounds like someone doing exercises. There is a calmness. Before the storm?

I gird myself for what I am about to do.

I should, perhaps, have done this three weeks ago: I am going to do a test on Kirstie, one she cannot fake or fail. The idea half-occurred to me this morning, as I contemplated Lydia, screaming at the school; it only really formed this afternoon.

My experiment will rely on my daughter's phobia: her hatred of darkness.

Whenever this phobia was triggered, both twins screamed: but they screamed in a unique way, they screamed differently. Kirstie would yell, and pant, and shout: making a tremulous version of horrified words. Lydia would go into a simple shriek: very high-pitched. Ice-shattering.

147

I've only heard this scream a few times. It is different to any other vocalization. Which is probably why I only clearly thought of this today. And one of those occasions was when we had a power cut, in Camden. Two years ago, plunging the twins into total darkness: the blackness they always feared.

When this happened, they both had that phobic, instant reaction. But Kirstie panted and yelled; Lydia emitted that piercing shriek.

And now I am going to trigger this phobia deliberately. By jailing her in sudden dark. Her reaction will be instinctive, and reflexive, she won't be able to fake or fabricate it; so it will tell me the truth. My plan is cruel, it makes me faint with guilt, but I see no alternative. Allowing this confusion to go on is crueller.

I have to do it now or I will lose myself in doubt, and self-hatred.

Kirstie gazes up at me as I enter her bedroom. She looks very sad. She has made this bare room a little more homely, with her books on a shelf and her pictures of pirates on the wall. But it is still a spare, lonely room, bereft of her twin. Her radio is playing Kids Pop. One Direction. There is a wicker basket full of toys. But she hasn't moved them much. Only Leopardy is huddled into her bed. Both twins loved Leopardy. Maybe Lydia loved Leopardy a little bit more?

Her sad eyes are unbearable.

'Darling,' I say, tentatively. 'Tell me what happened today at school.'

Silence.

I try again: 'Did you have a good day? Your first day? Tell me about your teachers.'

More silence, more One Direction. She closes her eyes and I wait and I wait and I can sense she is going to

148

tell me; then, yes, she slowly leans in to me, and she says, in a very tiny voice,

'No one wanted to play with me, Mummy.'

My heart breaks open.

'Oh. I see.'

'I kept asking people, but no one would play with me.'

The pain in me is burning, I want to cuddle my daughter, protect her.

'OK, sweetie, it's just your first day, darling, that happens.'

'So I played with Kirstie.'

I stroke her hair, gently, as my heart races.

'Kirstie?'

'She played with me, like we always play.'

'OK.'

What do I do? Get angry? Cry? Shout? Explain that Lydia is dead and she *is* Kirstie? Maybe I don't even know myself, which one is dead.

'But then, when I was playing with Kirstie-koo . . .'

'Yes?'

'Everyone laughed at me, Mummy. It was . . . It made me cry, they were all laughing.'

'Because you were really alone?'

'No! Kirstie *was* there! She was there! She's here! She's here!'

'Darling, she's not here, she's—'

'She's what?'

'Kirstie, your sister – she – she—'

'Just say it, Mummy, just say it, I know she's dead you told me she's dead.'

'Sweetheart—'

'You keep saying she's dead but she comes back to play with me, she was here, she was at school, she *plays* with me, she is my *sister*, it doesn't matter if she's dead, *she's still here*, still here, I'm here, we are here – why do you keep saying we're dead, when we're not we're not *we're not.*'

This howling speech ends in angry, noisy tears: Kirstie flings herself away from me and she crawls to the end of the bed and she buries her hot flushed face in the pillow and – I am helpless. I sit here, pathetic, the Terrible Mother. What have I done to my daughter? What am I still doing? What am I about to inflict?

Should I have ignored her confusion in the first place, in London? If I had never entertained any suspicion, if I had insisted she was Kirstie, she might have stayed Kirstie. But now I have to do *this.*

Bad mother. Evil mother.

I wait a few minutes for her anger to subside. The radio plays more tinny pop music: 'The Best Song Ever'. Then Britney Spears.

At last, I put a hand on Kirstie's ankle. 'Moomin.'

She turns. Red-eyed, but calmer. 'Yes.'

'Kirstie?'

She does not flinch at the name. I am sure now that she is Kirstie. My Lydia is dead.

'Kirstie, I'm just going into the kitchen for a second to get a hot drink. Do you want something? Something to drink?'

She eyes me. Blank-faced. 'Fruit Shoot.'

'OK. You read a book and I'll get us a drink.'

Kirstie seems to accept this. She reaches out for Wimpy Kid, and as she does I quietly close the curtains. So that not a chink of light can get through: it's not difficult, the moon is clouded, and there are no street-lights on Torran.

Then, as discreetly as I can, I bend to the floor, as if I am picking up toys. But I am secretly unplugging her nightlight.

Kirstie does not notice. She reads on, her lips slightly moving. Lydia used to do that.

Now I have one final task: turn off the main light and shut the door. Kirstie will be slammed into total darkness; engulfed in the worst of her fears. There are tears not far from my own eyes, as I walk to the door.

Can I do this? How can I not do this?

Quickly I slap the light off, then I step outside Kirstie's bedroom and shut the door. The hall beyond is also gloomy, barely lit by the light from the living room down the way. Kirstie's bedroom will be immersed in total dark.

I wait. There is a fierce burn of guilt in my chest. Oh, baby. Kirstie. I'm sorry. I'm so sorry.

How long will it take for her to scream?

Not long.

Not long at all.

Three seconds after I shut the door she screams: and it is a high, piercing, shrill distinctive scream, like something thin and metallic being sheared in two. It is unmistakable and horrible; it is piercing and unique.

Opening the door I snap on the light and rush to my bewildered and horrified daughter, wailing in her bed.

'Mummy Mummy Mummy—!'

I am cradling her in my arms; crushing her to myself.

'Sorry, darling. I'm so sorry, I'm so sorry, I forgot, I forgot about the light, I'm sorry, I'm sorry, I'm sorry. I'm so so so sorry.'

But in the middle of my stabbing guilt there is just one appalling thought.

It was Kirstie that died.

This is Lydia sitting here.

We got it wrong, fourteen months ago.

11

Angus calls me on the phone next morning. It is a Saturday. He wants me to come over and pick him up from the Selkie pier at five p.m.

'It will be dark.'

He can barely hear me over the popping static of our sea-chewed landline.

'What? Sarah? What?'

'Won't it be dark? Angus?'

'Full moon—' he says; I think.

The line frazzles into nothingness. I check my watch: eleven a.m. In six hours I will have to meet my husband in Ornsay, and then tell my husband that we made the most grievous error, that Kirstie is dead and Lydia is alive. How will he react? Will he even believe me?

I step out of the kitchen onto the cracked paving stones and look east, at the chalky pillar of the lighthouse, with the sea, and the snow-talced Knoydart mountains beyond. For some reason the sight – the mere existence – of the lighthouse always comforts and soothes me. A calming beacon, serene and aloof. Flickering every nine seconds at night, signalling the world: here we are. Angus, Sarah and *Lydia* Moorcroft. We three.

I can see Lydia, she is solitary, playing down there in her new blue wellingtons, wading in the rock pools, looking for little fish and pulsing urchins. It seems so easy to call her Lydia. She is Lydia. Lydia is back. Kirstie has gone. I am mourning for the second time, yet quietly and guiltily jubilant. Lydia has returned from the crematorium. My second daughter, the one who loves rock pools, the one who loves staring at the sea urchins, watching their delicate contracting softness, is alive, once again.

Lydia turns and looks at me, then she runs up the incline of salty grass to the kitchen, to show me some shells she has collected.

'Hey, very nice.'

'Can I show them to Dada?'

'Of course you can, Lydia. Of course.'

The shells are wet and sandy and graciously freckled with blue striations, fading to yellow and cream. I wash the grit from them, under the uncertain spatter of the tap, and hand them back.

'Keep them safe, Daddy is coming home later.'

When I have changed her boots for trainers, she disappears happily to her room. In the silence, I make soup to dispel my anxious thoughts: we eat a lot of soup, it's easy to reheat in this nightmare of a kitchen. I can freeze and microwave it back to life when the prospect of real cooking defeats.

The time passes without terrors. It's four-thirty p.m, and dusk is upon us when I peer my head around Lydia's door and ask her to come and get Dad at the Selkie.

She stands there, in her pink leggings, and her pink trainers with the glowing lights in the heel, in her draughty bedroom. Shaking her head.

154

'But Daddy wants to see you.'

'Nn. Don't want to.'

'Lydie-lo. Why not?'

'Just not. Just not. Not now.'

'Lydia, you'll be alone on the island.'

It seems so easy to call her Lydia. Maybe I knew, subconsciously, she was Lydia all along.

Lydia shakes her head. 'Don't mind!'

I have no desire to fight my daughter this afternoon, I've too much to worry about confronting Angus. And there is no reason why Lydia won't be safe on Torran, as long as she doesn't stray. It's an island. The tide is out. I'll be gone for thirty minutes. She is seven and she can sit safely in a house on her own. We don't have balconies.

'OK, then come here. Just promise to stay in your room, OK?'

'Yes.'

Giving her a hug, I button her blue cardy. Then I kiss her shampoo-scented hair and she retreats, obediently, to her room.

The dark has gathered itself, and surrounds the island. I grab a torch to follow the path, down to the shingled beach by the lighthouse, where I drag the boat off the grassy rocks. Unslipping the ropes, I haul the deadweight of the anchor aboard, as if it is a small body I am hoping to jettison, into the concealing waters of the Sound.

Angus it seems, was right; the night is clear and calm and the torch is unnecessary, the moon is ripe and bright, giving the waters a luminescence.

And there he is: my husband waits on the Selkie pier, with the lights of the pub behind. He is in dark jeans – but a V-neck jumper with a checked shirt: a compromise between island life and an architect's job. He seems energized, smiley, maybe happy from his first day of proper work in a while?

'Hey, gorgeous the boatwoman. Bang on time.'

Angus leaps down the steps and into the dinghy and kisses me, he smells of whisky but not too much. Perhaps a quick warming glass in the Selkie.

'How's Kirstie?'

'She's . . .'

'What?'

'Nothing.'

The outboard Yamaha motor slices the cold, black, moonlit waters, as I steer us around Salmadair. The big house of the billionaire is dark and empty. The black fir trees defend it, in their legions.

'Sarah?'

The boat is hauled up safe above the bladderwrack. The moonlight guides us to the cottage. Lydia hears us and she runs out from her room to hand her dad the shells she found; he cups them in his big hands and says,

'Hey. Sweetheart. These are beautiful. Really, lovely. Thank you.' Angus leans and gives her a kiss on her small pale forehead. Then she skips back to her room, past the painting of the Scottish clan-woman.

I sit Angus at the dining table and I make us both tea. He is very silent. As if he is expecting something big. Does he already suspect? Surely not.

As calm as I can, I pull up a chair, and sit down opposite. And I say: 'I've got something to tell you.'

'OK.'

My breathing is deep, but even. I continue, 'It wasn't Lydia who fell off the balcony, it was Kirstie. We got it wrong. We made an error. The girl in that room – our surviving daughter – she is Lydia.'

He says nothing. He sips his tea, his dark brown eyes fixed on mine. Not blinking. But fierce. Like a predator, watching.

I feel a sudden sense of peril. Of being menaced, as I did in the attic. My childhood stammer momentarily returns. 'I sh – I sh.'

'Sarah. Slow down.' He glares. Dark, and brooding. 'Tell me.'

'I turned off all the lights in her room. To make her scream.'

His frown deepens. 'What?'

'Remember how the twins screamed differently when they were really scared, when that phobia was triggered? Remember? The power cut? So I did it again. Plunged her into darkness. Yes I know, it was horrible but—' the guilt is getting to me. I hurry on '—but it's not something you could fake, is it? That scream was a reflex, it's fear, it is an instinctive difference, so – so that's it – she screamed like Lydia when she was in the dark. So she is Lydia. She must be.'

He sips hot tea again. I wish he'd respond normally. Or in any way. Maybe cry. Shout. Do something. React badly.

But all I get is this menacing stare. He swallows tea and says: 'That's it? A scream? A scream is your only evidence?'

'No – it's not just that, God, there's so much *more*.'

'OK. Tell me. Slow down. What else?'

Angus wraps his big hands around his mug. Tight. He takes another gulp, his eyes never leaving mine.

'Tell me, Sarah. Tell me everything.'

He is correct, he needs to know *everything*; and so, like someone purging a night of alcohol, I chuck it all up. Voiding myself of lies and evasions, redeeming myself with the truth. I tell him about the behaviour of the dog, the literacy issues, the switch of friends, the tantrum in the school, the weeks of strangeness, the way our daughter will only now let me call her Lydia. I tell him about the trip to Kellaway in Glasgow, and how it convinced me, for a moment, that I was wrong, but then the doubts crept back. More persuasive and convincing than ever before.

'She is *Lydia*,' I say, in conclusion. Staring at my husband who stares back.

I can see the teeth grinding in his jaw, under the stubble. I stumble on,

'We – I – made some mistake, somehow, Gus, it was just because of that one line, that sentence, after the accident, I presumed too much, maybe Lydia got confused – remember they were swapping identities at that time, playing games, fooling about, wearing the same clothes, asking for the same haircuts. Remember all that and then the accident, who knows, maybe there *was* some telepathy, when Kirstie was in hospital, we cannot know for sure, some mingling of their minds, like – like the way they mingled in the cot, sleeping in the same bed – sucking each other's thumbs.'

Angus still says nothing. During my soliloquy. But his grip on his mug is so hard I can see the straining whiteness of his knuckles. As if he is going to pick it up and smash it in my face. He is angry and he is going to be violent. I am scared yet not scared. Angus is going to hit me, to ram the Edinburgh Castle coffee mug in my face. I am telling him his favourite twin is dead and that mine has been resurrected.

But I don't care, I have to say it.

'The girl in that room is Lydia. Not Kirstie. We cremated Kirstie, Lydia is still alive.'

158

Here it comes. His reaction. Angus drains the last of his tea. He puts the mug down on the stained and dusty table. The moon is white and horrified outside, I can see her through the windows. Gawping.

At last he speaks.

'I know it's Lydia.'

I gaze his way. Stunned into muteness.

He shrugs at my bewilderment. Yet he is also tensed, and muscled. Then he says, 'I've known for a while.'

I am dumbed. He sighs, loudly.

'Guess we'd better get the death certificates changed.'

My silence is pathological.

Angus stands. And goes into the kitchen. Pans and plates rattle in the sink. Beany skitters into the dining room, then stops and looks at me; his unclipped claws have scratched the cold flagstones. We need a carpet in here, or some rugs. Everything is bare and cold and hard.

From somewhere I find the energy to respond. I go into the kitchen, where Angus is washing cups under the spattery water of the tap in the big ceramic sink. Our water coughs forth, belching and uncertain, like rain from a storm overflowing from a gutter. My husband's thick fingers rinse and clean the mugs. Obsessively.

'Josh and Molly have invited us for dinner next Thursday. They've got some London friends staying, there's a big wedding at Kinloch.'

'Angus.'

'Also, heard some good news at the Selkie. They may be putting up a mobile mast, back of Duisdale, might give us proper reception. We won't have to drive up that bloody hill.'

'Gus!'

His back is facing me as he methodically does the

159

dishes; he is gazing at the dark kitchen window – the kitchen that faces landwards, over the tidal flats, towards the line of low bald hills behind the Selkie, a horizon of deepest blue against the stars and darkness.

But I can also see his face, reflected in the window glass by the kitchen lights. He does not realize this. And I can see intense anger on that handsome face: a twisting, suppressed rage.

Why?

He clocks me looking at him, and the anger disappears. It is hidden away very quickly. Now he sets the mug to dry on a rack and he turns, plucking a tea towel, carefully drying his fingers of the suds.

He speaks at last.

'About six months ago . . .' He pauses, and drops the tea towel on top of the fridge. Looks up again. 'Lydia came to me and told me what she told you. That she was Lydia. That it was Kirstie that died. That we got it wrong. That you got it wrong. That we all got it wrong.'

The dog is in the kitchen, whimpering, for no apparent reason. Sensing the tension, perhaps? Angus glances at Beany, and nods.

'I also noticed the dog. Behaving differently. With Lydia.'

'Beany? You—'

'So. Adding it up, I thought – Well, I thought Lydia might be right. Or, rather, telling the truth. That's why I got Lydia's toy out.'

'She asked for the toy?'

'No.'

'Sorry. What? I don't see . . .'

'It was a test, Sarah. An experiment. Just like yours.'

I gaze. I can hear the rats in the lumber-room. Why

160

doesn't Beany kill them? The dog is pathetic. Morose, depressed, frightened.

'Sorry? What kind of *test*?'

'To see how she reacted. Testing Lydia. Or testing Kirstie. See if she reacted differently to her own toy, Lydia's toy.'

'And? Did she?'

'Yep. I got the little dragon out, secretly. Without her knowing. Got him from the attic. And I put him in her room, mixed with all the other toys. And then I watched her without her knowing. See how she responded.'

'You watched her secretly?'

'Yes. And as soon as she realized it was there, she went straight for the dragon. She clearly preferred Lydia's toy. Entirely unprompted. But emphatic.'

But of course: now I get it. The logic is clear – and gratifying. That's Angus. Logical and sensible, clear yet creative: an engineer, a problem solver. He thought of a subtle test, for our daughter, with a toy. Much less distressing than mine.

'So you knew all along, or you suspected, so – you agree? You really think she is Lydia?'

Angus leans back, his hands on the edge of the sink, as he faces me. Defiant, or maybe contemptuous? Or am I just imagining this? My confusion is a whirlpool; and I am drowning.

'But, Gus, why didn't you tell me *then*?'

'Didn't want to upset you. Wasn't sure.'

'That's it? That's your reason?'

'What else? What did you want me to do? You'd barely gotten over, you hadn't gotten over Kirstie's death. Then I slope up and say, Oh, by the by, you got it wrong at the accident? Wrong daughter. Come on, Sarah. Really? Was I really going to do that? To add to your pain?'

His frown softens to something else. Not quite a smile; but not a scowl either. Angus shakes his head and, as he does, I see a glisten in his eyes, the wetness of emotion. Not tears, but close. And I am pained for him, as I am pained for all of us. This must be so very hard for him. He's been dealing with this alone. And here I am, being the accuser. For months he has been coping with the desperate knowledge as best as he could. And he has lost Kirstie as he thought he lost Lydia.

I say, 'So she is Lydia?'

'Yes. If that's what she believes, and it seems that is the case, then that's who she is. We have no choice. It's Lydia, Sarah. Kirstie died. There. That's it. That's that.'

He swallows emotion. Then, across the kitchen, he opens his arms, beckoning. And I feel a surrendering inside me: I am tired of this renewed and anxious hostility between us. We need to be a family, to move on together. Lydia Moorcroft and her parents. I cross the kitchen and he hugs me and I rest my face on his shoulder.

'Come on,' he says. 'Let's make some dinner. Me, you and Lydia. And Beany the useless dog.'

I manage to laugh, and I almost mean it. And so we go into the living room. Angus builds a big fire and I cook up some pasta and then Angus calls, gently, down the hall into Lydia's bedroom,

'Lydia, Lydie-lo,' and she comes running out and this is a moment, this is such a moment – yet she just hugs him around his waist as high as she can reach her arms, and he tousles her blonde head, and kisses the top of her head, and he says Lydia Lydia and I can see that he means it.

Her calls her Lydia, I call her Lydia, she thinks she is Lydia. She is Lydia. That's it.

How easily an identity is changed.

Too easily?

We need to mark this. We can't just switch from one name to another, one identity to another, as if it's an everyday occurrence. We'll have to do something serious and symbolic. Perhaps a funeral; yes, almost certainly a funeral. My daughter Kirstie is dead and that needs to be remembered. Properly.

But that can wait. Right now I want this evening to be a resolution, to be final, to be some kind of catharsis for us. And it is: up until the time when I've cooked dinner and Angus finishes the washing up, again, and Lydia is playing with Beany on the rug in front of the roaring and comforting wood fire.

Then my mind casts back. Thinking of Angus's expression in the window. He was furious. There was a deep, fierce anger there. It was as if I'd uncovered a terrible secret, and he hated me for it; but what was that secret?

My husband paces into the living room. And squats by the hearth.

I watch him as he pokes the fire, shifting logs, shouldering and levering, so that a raw gash of burning vermilion is revealed in the charred and flaming wood-logs, and the golden sparks fly up. He looks masculine. A man and a fire. I like Angus's masculinity: tall and dark, a sexy cliché.

But something in his account is disquieting, still. He was prepared to let Lydia go on being Kirstie, possibly for ever, just to avoid upsetting me? Really? Does that make sense? I know I did the same to him, but that was only for a few weeks, and I always intended to tell him in time. So maybe it was more the case that he wanted Lydia to stay Kirstie, because he preferred

Kirstie? So he kept it quiet? But even that seems bizarre, and wrong.

Angus sits next to me on the sofa and puts an arm around my shoulder. This is it: or this is meant to be it. The moment. Us three, a family. Cosy in our cottage, which is now halfway habitable: the bathroom is grouted, half the walls are painted. The kitchen still offends but it is clean and usable. And here we are. The dog, the daughter, the cold bright night outside, the flashing of the lighthouse, calling out to all the other lighthouses, along this lonely coast: to Hyskeir and Waternish, to Chanonry and South Rona.

This is what I dreamed of all those nights when I gazed at the laptop screen, and the crystal images of Eilean Torran, with the cottage by the sea. And everyone and everything forgiven. Or forgotten.

Yet I am having to force myself not to shrink away from my husband's touch. I sense Angus knows something else. And he's still not telling me. And whatever it is, it is so bad he will lie, and has lied for months. Maybe fourteen months.

Or maybe I should get a grip and let it all be.

The fire crackles. Lydia plays. Our melancholic dog snores, and dreams, his muzzle twitching. Angus reads a big book about a Japanese architect of concrete churches. Tadao Ando. I sip some wine then yawn myself from half-sleep, I need to do a few chores before I can sleep properly: so many of Lydia's school things need sorting.

Making my way into the big bedroom I switch on the pretty feeble side light. There's a folded note on the bed. A note?

My heart sends out the alarm. The note has big childish letters on the front.

164

To Mummy.

My fingers are trembling – and I am not sure why – when I open the note and read. And now my heart trembles, too.

Mummy. She is in here with us. Kirstie.

12

Angus sat in the bedroom watching Sarah get ready for supper at the Freedlands'. There was a time when this would have been a sensuous interlude: his wife would half-turn, and ask him to zip the back of her dress; he would oblige, sowing delicate kisses on the whiteness of her neck; then he would watch her dab perfume *there* and *there*.

Now he had to resist the urge to walk out, or worse. How long could he do this? *And now he had to pretend that Kirstie was Lydia.*

His wife slipped on her shoes, nearly ready. Angus regarded the fine muscles of her shoulders, revealed by her backless dress, as she curved to smooth her tights. The softness of the skin above her spine; the subtle beauty, glinting. He still desired her. But it was all meaningless now.

Perhaps he could convince himself, over time, that Kirstie was Lydia? He thought he knew the whole of it, understood everything, but there *was* a strangeness here. Kirstie was acting differently. She *was* acting like Lydia, the dog *was* behaving oddly and differently. And he believed Sarah about the scream. Could Angus have got it wrong, too?

No, this was stupid. He was getting lost in these reflections. A labyrinth of darkened glass.

'Can you go and get Lydia?'

She was asking him, directly.

'Angus? Hello? Lydia. We need Lydia ready. Now. Can you go and get her please?'

Her instructions were clipped, and careful. Much like everything she said, now. It had the troubling subtext: *We know this is a nightmare but we have to try. Or pretend.*

'Yes, OK.'

He walked towards Kirstie's room. No, he walked towards Lydia's room. He had to pretend she was Lydia. He had to start believing she was Lydia, he had to think she was Lydia, for the moment, to keep the family stable. It was like learning a foreign language: he had to think in that language.

Angus knocked and opened the door.

His little girl was dressed, uncomfortably, in a summery frock, and spangly sandals. Just standing there. In the middle of the room. Unspeaking, and alone. Why was she doing that? Increasingly his daughter's behaviour unnerved him: again he felt a tingling panic. Time was running out. He had to rescue her from this madness. But he didn't know how.

She asked, 'Will there be other kids there, Dada?'

'Maybe,' he lied. 'Think Gemma Conway has kids.'

'Gemma who?'

'Conway. You'll like her, she's a bit weird and woolly, but she knows everything about everything—'

'No she doesn't, Dada, no one knows everything about everything, except maybe God and I don't know if HE is clever enough to know all that?'

Angus gazed at his daughter. This was new, this God stuff. Where did it come from? Kylerdale School was Church of Scotland, but it didn't seem especially tambourine-bashing; maybe she had new friends who were religious. The Hebrides were fiercely devout in places; they still locked playing fields on the Sabbath, out there on Lewis.

But then he remembered his daughter had no friends. She kept telling him this: *Daddy, no one will play with me.*

It cut him to pieces. Because it was no wonder no one would play with her: all the other children probably thought she was crazy. The kid with a dead sister, come back to life. The freak.

And it was all her mother's fault. Could he ever forgive her? All he ever did was forgive her, time after time. Yet he needed to love and absolve Sarah, once again, if this was going to work.

But too often he felt the violent opposite of love.

'OK, let's go.' He shouted down the hall, 'Sarah? Sarah!'

'Yes, ready.'

The three of them assembled in the kitchen; Angus picked up the torch and guided his little family down the pebbled path to the lighthouse beach, where they climbed on board, and he poled the boat away, into the Sound, and then steered them towards the Selkie.

It was a cold night, clear and sharp; the stars were reflected perfectly in the waveless waters of the sea channel; Knoydart frowned, a row of black burqa'd women on a very dark purple horizon; the sea lochs shone under the moon.

Angus moored their boat at the Selkie pier, where the rigging of the other boats chimed in welcome.

The brief car journey to the Freedlands' big bright house was silent: each member of the family staring out of a different window, at a different darkness.

Angus had wondered if he should cancel this social engagement, given the ongoing horrors of his daughter's bewilderment: given *everything*. But Sarah had insisted they had to aim for normality. Even though they were struggling, they had to pretend they were doing OK – as if that might, magically, make things OK.

So here they were, in a simulacrum of nice London clothes, stepping inside the big angular house, and there in the enormous kitchen, doyenne of her expensive copper pans, was Molly. Laughing by the Aga, Lady Bountiful standing over trays of canapés. Two other couples were sipping Aperol spritzers from elegant glasses by the kitchen table, and everywhere Angus inhaled the smell of decent cooking: something he missed on Torran, with their primitive kitchen.

'Just a bit of roast pork, I'm afraid,' Molly said, apologetically, as she took their coats. 'Not quite up to Michelin tonight.'

They stepped into the open-plan living room, with its expansive windows, and its pricey views of the Sound of Sleat; flutes of something bubbly were dispersed.

'Here,' said Josh, 'I've actually got some nice wine: Trentodoc by Ferrari, proper Italian champagne, none of that prosecco rubbish.'

'How would you know, Josh? You haven't had a drink in ten years.'

'I can tell by the bubbles. I am still allowed bubbles.'

Everyone joked in a faintly effortful way: Molly made elegant introductions between the couples. Gemma Conway, who Angus had met once before in London, with Josh, then her husband Charles (rich, London, art

170

dealer) then a younger American couple, Matt and Fulvia (rich, New York, banking); there were no other children. These couples were here for the big posh wedding at Kinloch: to which he and Sarah were not invited.

Angus didn't care about the wedding, he cared about his daughter. Alone, again? Why couldn't these ridiculous people have brought at least one kid between them, someone for her to play with? Angus struggled with his irritation, even as the other adults doted, dutifully, on Lydia – for about three minutes of clear boredom – then returned to their glasses of sparkling Italian wine and grown-up conversation.

After that his daughter stood there mute and alone with Leopardy the Leopard under one arm and Angus wanted, fiercely, to save her from all this, and take her away, take her to live on Torran. Just the two of them. On his family's island. Eilean Torran.

Where they belonged. Where his grandmother had been happy. Where he'd been happy with his brother as boys. Where he could be happy with his little girl.

Angus listened and watched as his daughter asked her mother if she could go upstairs, and play video games.

'Mummy, please, I can play with Dada's phone, it's got Angry Granny on it and everything.'

'But—'

'Mummy. Please. I'll be quiet?'

Sarah rolled her eyes, meaningfully, at Angus, but he had no desire to keep *Lydia* down here: where she would be bored, and possibly start acting up. And he could imagine the ways she might act up, if she wanted.

His daughter was haunted. And he knew why.

'Let her go upstairs if she wants,' he said in a curt whisper, to Sarah.

His wife nodded, and turned, to explain to Molly – as

she returned from the kitchen. Molly was flushed from cooking, and distracted. She laughed and said:

'Of course! Of course she can go upstairs. God, I wish there were more kids here for Kirs, I mean, um um um, Lydia to play with, um . . .'

Molly paused, clearly embarrassed. Josh frowned at his wife; he and Molly had been told about the Kirstie–Lydia thing only the other day. Molly's mistake was entirely understandable. But awkward. The other guests were, it seemed, unaware of any of this. A puzzled silence descended on everyone, then Josh said:

'No, really, it's not for want of trying. We may have to adopt bloody llamas at this rate.'

Molly chuckled uncomfortably and the moment passed. Pleasantries were swapped. The wedding was discussed, then the weather. Charles asked Sarah about property prices and the value of Torran and holidays in the Maldives, and as the chatter drifted in its middle-class way Angus surged with unspoken resentment.

These rich people with their villas and their auctions and their stock options: what did they know? These people had never had to worry about anything. Why was he listening to this bourgeois prattle? His granny was a farmwife, his mum a humble teacher, his dad a drunken docker, a wife-beater, an alcoholic. Angus *knew*. And they didn't.

Angus drank.

And drank. And brooded. He wondered if he was able to keep it together for just an evening any more; he wanted to walk out as they sat down to langoustine, served with some of Molly's best mayonnaise and fresh bread.

The food was predictably delicious; his mood was worsening. He wanted to say it out loud: my life is nothing, it is falling apart, my daughter is dead and my other daughter is mad. And sometimes I have terrible and serious fantasies about hurting my wife because she wants to have a funeral for a child who is still alive.

He wanted to announce this, calmly. He wanted to watch everyone else turn and stare in horror. Instead Angus said:

'We need interest rates to stay low, of course.'

'Oh, they will, another crash would kill the country off completely, there'd be lepers on Pall Mall.'

The wine came: plentifully. Angus noticed that his wife was drinking too much, as well, almost as much as he was drinking.

'Oh yes just another.'

Just another, just another, just one more.

The main course was suckling pig – local – with excellent crackling, damson plum sauce, and a tremendously fashionable vegetable he could not identify, and then the conversation moved on to death, and ghosts.

Why the hell were they talking about this? At this time?

Angus ploughed his way through his tenth glass of wine. He sat back and slurped and wondered if his teeth were stained red by the wine, as Gemma Conway pronounced:

'Chatwin is rather good on this, in his Australian book, he says our fear of ghosts is a fear of predators, of being prey.'

Molly put down her fork, and came back: 'I'm sure I read that you can mimic ghosts, or the effect of ghosts, by subjecting people to a subsonic growl – you cannot hear it, the same growl used by predators to terrify their prey.'

'Really?'

'Yes. They've tested it, on people, the subsonic noise cannot be registered by the ear but we hear it in our minds, that's the nameless dread people describe when they experience ghosts!'

Try being me, thought Angus, try being me and my daughter, about six months ago, in Camden, if you want Nameless Dread.

He looked round the table. His wife still looked anxious: slurping wine too fast. And she was silent, of course. From nowhere, from the past, from some dim, barely understood part of himself, Angus felt an unexpected pang of sympathy for her, a sudden sense of fraternity, and mutuality. Whatever else divided him and Sarah – and it was so much, it was surely *too* much – they were going through this nightmare together. He could almost forgive her for everything else: as she was his comrade-in-arms, in this.

And he had loved her once, quite intensely.

But how did that work? How could he still entertain these feelings about Sarah even as he daydreamed, wildly, about making her suffer for what she'd done? Perhaps when you had a child together there was always a residual connection of love, even if it was later drowned. The love was still down there: like a sunken ship.

And when you shared the *death* of a child you were bonded for eternity. And they had not only shared the death of a child, they had shared it twice, and now they had resurrected the other. He and Sarah, they were grave robbers. Necromancers. Raisers of the dead.

Angus was drunk and confused and he didn't care.

Molly was still talking: 'And that's why people get spooked in old houses, cellars, churches, these places have echoes and resonances, timbres of the air, thanks to the topography, and these air vibrations cause the same subsonic vibrations as predators growling.'

'Almost too neat an explanation. For ghosts.'

'Has everyone got enough wine?'

'This suckling pig really is excellent, you totally killed it, Molly.'

'They say when people are mauled by cats, they go into a kind of quiescence, a kind of Zenlike state.'

'How would they know, if these poor wretches have been consumed by tigers? Do they interview them in heaven?'

'Charles!' Gemma playfully slapped her husband.

The New York woman spoke up: 'If that theory is right, it kinda makes the entire Bible a kind of growl by God, threatening everyone with death!'

'The booming voice of Jehovah. The fire in the trees. Is this wine really Rioja, Josh? Gran Reserva surely, it's terrific.'

'I'll have more wine, yes,' said Angus, 'thanks.'

He reclaimed his glass, full and heavy, and he drank half of it, in one deep slug.

'Does that disprove the existence of God, the fact it can be explained as a fear of predation, of death?'

Charles intervened: 'Well, I've always been of the opinion that we are meant to be believers. After all, children believe by nature – they are instinctively faithful. When my kids were six they implicitly believed; now they are grown up, they are atheists. It's rather sad.'

'Kids also believe in Santa. And the Easter bunny.'

Charles ignored his wife: 'Therefore life is, perhaps, a kind of corrosion? The pure true believing soul of the child is rusted, over time, polluted by the years—'

'You haven't read enough Nietzsche, Charles, that's your problem.'

'I thought you said his problem was internet pornography?' said Josh, and everyone laughed and Josh teased his pompous older friend again, and Gemma made a deprecating joke about calories, but Angus stared at Charles, wondering if he was, actually, quite profound. Every so often this annoying London art dealer said something startling or curious that everyone half ignored, and yet sometimes, somehow, right now, these remarks made Angus want to vehemently agree, and he wondered if Charles, the art dealer, knew the effect he was having. And then Charles said this:

'It's not so much my own death that is intolerable, it's the death of those around me. Because I love them. And part of me dies with them. Therefore all love, if you like, is a form of suicide.'

Angus stared. And drank. And listened. And Josh had an argument about rugby with Gemma and Sarah, and Angus wanted to shake this man by the hand, to lean over and say Yes, that's so true, everyone else is wrong. Why are they ignoring you? Everything you say is absolutely *right* – the death of those we love is so much worse than our own death, and yes all love is a form of suicide, you destroy yourself, you surrender yourself, you kill something in yourself, willingly, if you really love.

'I'm going to get Lydia,' said Sarah. She was standing up, beside him.

Angus was jolted from his reverie. He wiped the wine from his lips, and turned, and looked up. 'Yes. Good idea.'

The plates were cleared away; Angus helped. By the time he returned to the dining table, carrying dishes for the dessert – brown bread ice cream with some salted caramel thing, his daughter *Lydia* was there with her mother, by the big black windows that looked onto the Sound.

'She can have some ice cream?' said Molly. And Sarah touched Lydia on the shoulder.

'Oh yes, darling, ice cream, your favourite?'

Angus watched. There was something amiss with his daughter.

Lydia was staring at the darkened windows. The view of the moon on the waters, the silhouettes of firs and alders. But the uncurtained windows also, of course, reflected the light within the room: the table and chairs, the art on the walls, the adults and their drinks. And the little girl standing in her dress with her mother by her side.

Angus realized what was happening. Too late.

Lydia screamed:

'Go away, go away, I hate you!!'

And she ran at the window and she charged into the glass with her little fists raised – and the glazing cracked and shattered with a terrifying crash; and then there was blood. So much blood. Too much blood.

13

I can see the terror on Angus's face, on Molly's face, their fears are nothing compared to mine. I feel I've been here before. In Devon.

Lydia screams again, she has pulled back from the shattered window; her scarlet, bloodied hands poised vertically in the air, like a surgeon waiting to be gloved.

Angus and I approach our daughter, tentatively, trembling, as if we are approaching a feral animal – because she backs away as we get close. But as she retreats, Lydia stares at me. Alarmed. As if she is scared of *herself*.

I can hear Josh behind me, calling an ambulance, Yes, Maxwell Lodge, Ornsay Village, half a mile past the Selkie, by the chapel, yes, please right away, PLEASE.

'Lydia—'

'Lydie . . .'

She says nothing. Rigid and red-handed, imploring, she continues to retreat. Her quietness is almost as terrifying as the bleeding.

'Christ—'

'Lydia—'

'Josh, call the fucking ambulance!'

'I have, I am, I—'

'Lydia, babe, Lydie . . .'

'Get water, Molly, bandages – Molly!'

'Lydia, it's OK, it's OK, stay still – let me—'

'Mmmmmummmmy. What happened to me?'

Even as she speaks, Lydia is still backing away, her hands raised in the air. The blood runs down her bare elbow, dripping now onto the polished wooden floor.

'Please, Lydia?'

Behind me, Molly runs in with a bowl of water and tissues, and flannels, and once again Angus and I attempt to approach Lydia, on our knees, arms beckoning: but she evades us, sloping away, bleeding. Has she severed an artery, or is it just deep scratches?

I am kneeling on something hard and sharp. Glass.

I stand – but Angus runs past me and he grabs Lydia, in the corner, and holds her close to his chest; she is too shocked to elude him. He yells at me: 'Wash her hands, get the blood off, we have to see how bad this is.'

'Josh—'

'The ambulance is coming: ten minutes.'

'Baby, baby, baby.'

Now Angus is rocking Lydia backwards and forwards in his arms: saying *shhh, shhh, shhh*, comforting her, as I lean close. I begin to sponge and daub the blood from her fingers, with the cold flannels, and Molly's bowl of water. The sponged blood coils in the bowled water like red smoke. With a swoon of relief I can see she is not so badly cut; my daughter has lacerated her palms and knuckles, and ripped the skin in multiple places, but it does not look arterial, the wounds are not that deep.

But there is lots of this blood; lots of blooded tissues are piling up; Molly whisks them away like an attending nurse.

'Jesus,' Angus is whispering as he holds her tight. 'Jesus.'

Molly replaces the tissues with baby wipes, ointment, bandages.

'Hey,' I say, 'Lydia. *Sweetness.*'

She looks so vulnerably young here, in her father's embrace, in her party dress, with those cheery butterflies outlined in pink spangles on the front. She looks so young, and so damaged. Her white socks and pale pink sandals are speckled with blood, she has a tiny smear of blood on one of her bare oval knees.

What can I do? I know she is unhappy, and I know she is too young to be this unhappy; and I haven't forgotten the note on my bed. *Kirstie is still here.* Why did she write that? What is preying on her mind? What anguish and doubt? So my grief battles my fears, which tussles with my guilt, as I wash her little fingers. As I squeeze the water and wash the worst of the bleeding.

Then I say, again: 'Darling. Lydia. What happened just now?'

Of course, I know what happened. Or I can guess very well what happened. She looked in the window and she saw herself, but she saw the image of her dead sister. The identity confusion is sending her into ever darker places.

Sitting on her father's lap, Lydia shakes her head and hugs her dad closer, he is stroking her hair, gently, caressingly; she looks away from me, but speaks:

'Nothing.'

181

I daub at the bloodstains, they are almost gone now; it's my own fingers which are trembling. I really thought she had opened her wrists, in some horrible, infant suicide bid. Or maybe in fear of the ghost inside herself, the ghost she has become.

'Lydia, why did you break the window?'

Angus glares at me. 'We don't need to ask that, not here, not yet, for God's sake.'

I ignore him. What does he know? He wasn't there, in Devon, that evening. He's never been through this before, he's not been to that place of particular terror, hearing a shout, discovering that your daughter is dead.

'Sweetheart, what was wrong, with the window? Was it like a mirror?'

Lydia takes a deep breath, and she hugs her daddy one more time, then she sits up and lets me wipe the last of the blood from her knuckles.

She might need stitches, she will definitely need plenty of plasters and bandages. Most of all, Lydia needs love, calm and peace, and an end to all this scariness – and I don't know how we are going to find that.

Molly is on her hands and knees, brushing the chunks and angles of window glass into a dustpan; I wince, guiltily.

'I'm so sorry, Molly.'

'Please . . .' She shakes her head, and gives me a smile of very serious pity, which makes me feel worse. 'Sarah.'

I turn back to my daughter. I want to know.

'Lydia?'

Abruptly she opens her eyes very wide and stares at the broken window, its black jagged void, surrounded with fangs of glazing; then she turns to me and speaks, her voice quivering:

'It was Kirstie, she was here, she was in the window, Mummy, I saw her, but it wasn't like last time, not like then, that time she was saying things, saying bad things, it was scary Mummy, but I – I – I—'

'OK,' says Angus. 'Weeble, slow down.'

I stare at him.

Weeble?

That's what he used to call Kirstie. *Weeble*. It's a word from some TV ad when his mum was a kid: she taught it to him. *Weebles wobble but they don't fall down*. That's why he gave the word to Kirstie. Because Kirstie was the brave one, his favourite, the tomboy climbing trees, the roisterer doing fun things with Daddy, she would climb trees so high and yet she never fell down. Weeble.

He's calling her Weeble. He's hugging Lydia, and calling her Weeble, the same way he would tightly hug Kirstie. Hugging and kissing her. Does that mean he still thinks she is Kirstie? He knows something I don't? Or is this just the terror of the moment?

'Weeble,' he says, 'You don't have to tell us.'

'No.' Lydia shakes her head and gazes at me. 'I want to tell. Mummy?' Now she reaches out her arms and she climbs into my arms and together we sit, mother and daughter, on the fashionable Turkish rugs with her on my lap and she breathes in and out for a few seconds, and then she says, 'Kirstie was in the window upstairs too and I couldn't stop her, every time I looked she was there, every time, and she's dead and she's in the mirror at home, and now she was in here and she starts saying things, Mummy, bad things, horrid things. This was different, Mummy, and it makes me frightened. I'm so

183

frightened of her, make her go away now, please, make her go away, she is on the island and she is in the school and now she's everywhere.'

'OK, OK . . .' I soothe my daughter, stroking her head. 'OK.'

Josh appears in the door again: abashed, and pallid: 'The ambulance is here.'

We probably don't need the ambulance any more; we assuredly don't need some siren-wailing, life-saving dash to Portree; nevertheless we carry Lydia to the drive and we all clamber into the ambulance, and Josh and Molly and the Americans and Charles and Gemma Conway make their mumbled and heartfelt goodbyes; and then we are the afflicted little family driving through the darkened roads of Skye, past the star-crowned mountains, sitting in the back of the ambulance with a silent paramedic, and Angus and me not speaking.

Lydia lies on the stretcher, her hands lightly bandaged. She is inert and sad now. Passive. Expressionless. The ambulance speeds. I don't know what to say. There is nothing to say. Portree greets us with roundabouts, traffic, two supermarkets and a police station and I get an urgent yearning to be back in London. For the first time.

In the Emergency Room at the small, new Portree hospital they patch up Lydia's fingers with several delicate stitches, and ointments, and soothing creams, and proper bandages, and lots of nursing compassion offered in fluting Hebridean accents, and throughout it all me and Angus stare at each other, and say nothing.

Then the ambulance drivers take us back to Ornsay as a favour, so we don't have to pay for a taxi. Because Angus and I are, of course, over the drink-drive limit.

We only had to drive half a mile from the Selkie to the supper party so we didn't bother staying sober. Now it seems awful. The shame of it mixes with the shame of everything else. We are a shameful couple. Dreadful people. The worst parents of all. We lost one daughter to a fall and somehow we are losing the other.

We deserve all this.

Angus starts the boat and we divide the dark waters back to Torran and I put Lydia to bed; then both of us go to the Admiral's Bed and Angus tries to cuddle me and I push him away. I want to be left alone with my thoughts. He called her Weeble. I'm not sure what it means.

That night I have a dream: I am in the kitchen getting my hair cut and when I look in the mirror, I can see that all my hair has been cut off, and then I look down and see I am naked and people can see me through the dark windows; and I don't know who these people are, and they stare, and then I feel a cold kiss on my lips and when I wake up I want to masturbate, my fingers between my thighs; it is four a.m.

But as I put my face to the pillow again I get an overpowering sense of remorse, and guilt, like there is dark silt in my mind, churned up by the dream. What did it mean? Is this the guilt from my affair? All those years ago? Or the guilt from not being there, not being a good mother: when my daughter fell?

Angus is snoring and dead to everything. The moon looms through the window, over the Sound of Sleat, over the dark green Scots pines of Camuscross, over the gathered white yachts with their rigging stripped for the winter.

That morning we don't do anything; Lydia is obviously not going to school, her hands are still bandaged and her eyes are still clouded with unhappiness, and Angus seems content to stay at home, attending our daughter. The three of us drink tea and juice and then Lydia comes with me to the window and we look at a lonely seal on a rock out there on Salmadair, barking, sad, it looks crippled: like a creature with no limbs.

Then I hang some washing on the line – the day is cold but bright and windy. I gaze at the waters: Loch Alsh and Loch Hourn and Loch na Dal, all those rivers and estuaries, lit by slender dazzles of winter sun, as the clouds part and reform. The lochs seem so cold yet unruffled today.

Out on the water is a big blue boat, the *Atlantis*. I know this boat, I've seen it before. It's one of the glass-bottomed tourist boats out of Kyle, showing the trippers what lies beneath the chilly waters: the swaying forests of kelp, dancing slowly, like enchanted courtiers; the deep dark weeds and sharks. Then the violet, pulsing jellyfish, trailing their melancholy tentacles.

They say some of these jellyfish are venomous with their stings. I've always thought that this doesn't seem right. Somehow unjust. Cold northern waters with tropical dangers.

Pegging out the last shirts, and Lydia's now bloodless frock and white socks, I glance once more at the boat, then go back in to the cottage.

Angus has Lydia on his lap and they are reading Charlie and Lola books, the way he used to read Charlie and Lola to the twins years ago. I look at them. She is surely too old for these books, she looks – suddenly – a bit too old to be on Daddy's lap: I forget that she is growing up, despite all the horrors. Angus always liked to put Kirstie on his lap.

But perhaps all this regression is comforting. I glance

186

down. The Charlie and Lola book on the floor is *I Will Not Ever Never Eat a Tomato*; the one they are reading is *Slightly Invisible*.

I remember *Slightly Invisible*. I think it is about Lola's invisible and imaginary friend, Soren Lorensen. He appears in the books like a ghost, only half-drawn: icy and grey.

Kirstie always liked reading about Soren Lorensen, the imaginary friend of Lola.

And now I think again, obsessively, about the note on the bed. I have not forgotten it, this last week, despite the intervening scares. My little girl wrote that note. It had to be her. No one else could have written it, not unless Angus is trying to torment me. And even if he were trying to do that – and there seems no possible motivation for him – he surely couldn't have faked that handwriting, not so precisely.

But Lydia's and Kirstie's handwriting was, of course, identical. Lydia could easily have done it. That's just how she writes. Which means she really did it: she wrote it.

And what do I do about this? Grab Lydia and shake her until she confesses? Why should she suffer, when it is mostly our fault? We called Lydia Kirstie for a year, by mistake, because we made a tragic and stupid error, so inside herself Lydia must still be deeply confused as to where Kirstie has gone.

The remorse accumulates; I need to get out – from under its weight.

'I'm going to take the dinghy,' I say to Angus.

He shrugs. 'OK.'

'I just need a walk. Just need to get out of here for a bit.'

His smile is tepid. 'Sure.'

187

The tension between us remains, it is weakened only by the horror of the last day; we are too exhausted to mistrust each other. But the growing mistrust will return.

'I'll pick up some shopping at Broadford.'

'OK.'

He isn't even looking at me now, just helping Lydia to turn the page with her bandaged hands.

The sight of this pains me, so I step outside, march to the boat, and motor myself to the Selkie pier. Then I walk to the Freedlands' house, quickly step in the car, and drive the three or four miles across the Sleat peninsula to Tokavaig. I want to see the famous view of the Cuillins across Eisort.

The wind is steely and chilling, trying to push the car door closed; I zip my North Face jacket to my chin and stuff my fists in my pockets, and walk the beaches, gazing. And thinking.

The light here fascinates me even more than the light around Torran. It's not quite as beautiful as Torran, but it shifts with even more tantalizing swiftness, veils of rain and cloud conceal the mountain peaks, shyly, then you see bright spears of sunlight, lancing, and slanted, and golden.

They look so judgemental, the Black Cuillins. Like a row of inquisitors in black hoods. Their shark-toothed peaks rip at the heavy passing clouds, gutting them of rain. Yet still the clouds build and fall, in their endless and anguished turmoil, apparently without pattern.

But there is a pattern here. And if I stare long enough at the Black Cuillins across the waters of Eisort, I will understand it.

Angus loved Kirstie. But something that he did

frightened her. He loved her. But she was frightened of him?

The pattern. *The pattern.* I can find the pattern if I think hard enough; then I will understand everything.

We still haven't found a church for Kirstie's funeral.

14

The days mingle into each other: like the clouds over Sgurr Alasdair. Angus goes to work two or three days a week; I try and find freelance business. I get emails from London therapists, following up my grief from Kirstie's death. It seems trivial, and outdated, and irrelevant. All of it. Compared to what is happening to our daughter, right now.

She has to go back to school or we will never succeed on Torran; but she is clearly reluctant. Her bandaged hands are an excuse for her to stay home, but when the bandages are ceremonially removed, one evening, I decide, with Angus's concurrence: she has to try again at Kylerdale.

Next morning we take the boat, as a family, across the water to the Selkie. Lydia looks miserable and apprehensive, lost in her oversized school uniform with the stupid shoes. Her shy face peering out from the pink hood of her anorak.

Angus kisses me on the cheek and gets in Josh's car – he's getting a lift to Portree. I envy him this: he has a job and he seems to be enjoying it. At least he gets off the island, out of Sleat, and meets people.

Pensive and brooding, I drive Lydia to Kylerdale Primary. The morning is mild, with a spit of rain, all the kids are leaping up the path, scampering out of cars, heading for their classes, throwing off their coats and joshing each other. All except my daughter, who approaches the school gates with tiny steps. Will I be forced to carry her?

'Come on, Lydia.'

'Don't want to.'

'It will be much better today. The first weeks are always the worst.'

'What if no one plays with me again?'

I ignore my sympathetic pain.

'They *will*, darling, just give them a chance. There are lots of new kids here, just like you.'

'Want Kirstie.'

'Well, Kirstie isn't here any more. You can play with the other girls and boys. Come on.'

'Daddy likes Kirstie, he wants her back too.'

What is this? I hurry on. 'Here we go. Let's take off your coat, you don't need it now.'

Escorting her inside the glazed door, I share a silent glance with Sally Ferguson. She gazes down at my daughter.

'Hello, Lydia. Are you feeling better now?'

No response. I put a hand on Lydia's shoulder. 'Lydia, say hello.'

Still no response.

'Lydia?'

My daughter manages a bashful, reluctant, 'Hello.'

I look at Sally and she looks at me and she says, rather too breezily:

'I am sure everything will be fine today. Miss Rowlandson is telling stories about pirates.'

'Pirates! Lydia, listen, you love pirates—'

I gently push my daughter in the back, propelling her towards the corridor, and slowly – very slowly – she walks, looking at the floor, a portrait of introversion. Then she disappears into the school corridor. Engulfed.

When she is gone Sally Ferguson reassures me.

'We've told all the kids that Lydia lost a sister, and can be a little confused; they won't be allowed to tease her.'

I am meant to be soothed; but I'm not convinced that this is better. Now my daughter is indelibly marked out as odd: as the girl who lost a twin. The haunted sister. Perhaps the other kids have heard about the incident at the Freedlands'. Oh yeah, that's the crazy girl who smashed the window because she saw a ghost. *Look at the scars on her hands.*

'Thanks,' I say. 'I'll be back at three-fifteen to pick her up.'

And I am. By ten minutes past three I am waiting anxiously at the school gates with other mums, and a couple of dads, who I do not know: I painfully wish I did know these people because then I could casually chat, and then Lydia would see me interacting and, by example, it might help her to interact with her peers. But I am too shy to strike up conversations with these strangers: these confident parents with their big 4x4s and their banter; it strikes me once more how much of this is my fault – I have handed on my crippling shyness to Lydia.

Kirstie would probably have been fine here. Certainly better at interacting. She would have bounced around, singing her songs, making other kids laugh. Not Lydia.

The children rush out of the door at the allotted time, little boys run into their mothers' arms, girls walk out hand in hand, slowly everyone appears, and is embraced, and slowly the parents and kids disperse; until I am the last parent left in the playground, in the cloaking winter darkness, and then my daughter emerges, unhappy in the doorway, and a young blonde teacher, I presume Miss Rowlandson, shepherds her towards me.

'Lydia!' I say. 'Did you have a good time? Was it nice today? How were the pirates?'

I want to ask her: Did anyone play with you? Did you pretend Kirstie was alive?

Lydia takes my arm and I look at the young teacher and she weakly smiles, and blatantly blushes – and returns to her classroom.

In the car, and in the boat, Lydia will not talk. She is mute. She says a quiet thank you to food, but she says nothing else and goes to her room and reads. Then she walks down to the beach in the moonlight and stares at the shining rock pools, which capture the reflection of the silvery moon. I watch her from the kitchen. My daughter. Lydia Moorcroft. A solitary little girl, on an island, in the dark. Quintessentially alone.

And so the days go on, similarly cloudy, mild and damp. We plan the funeral: Angus agrees to do most of the phoning and paperwork, as he gets off the island more than me. I can sense his reluctance. I take Lydia to school every day, and she is silent; I pick her up from school every day, and she is silent. She is always the last to leave the classroom.

On the fourth morning I get to school early: I am going to try something different. With a choke of guilt, I push Lydia into a crowd of girls, from her year and her class, gathered at the school gate – and then I pretend to take a call on my mobile.

Lydia has no choice: she has to interact, or she will be standing there, quite painfully isolated.

I watch, pretending to converse on the phone. Lydia looks as if she is trying to talk – to join this group of her peers. But they are ignoring her. She looks desperately back, at me, for support, or consolation, but I act distracted, as if I am engrossed in my phone call. Then I stand nearer, eavesdropping.

My hopes rise. It seems as if Lydia is going to do it: my daughter is going to talk to a schoolmate, to communicate; she is shyly approaching a brunette girl: a slender, apparently confident child, chattering with her friends.

I listen as Lydia says in a nervous voice: 'Grace, can I tell you about my leopard?'

The girl – Grace – turns to Lydia. She gives my daughter a tiny appraising glance, then she shrugs, and doesn't even reply. Instead she looks away and talks to her other friends; and then the entire group of girls goes happily wandering off, leaving Lydia there, staring at her shoes. Rebuffed. And shunned.

Unbearable. I am wiping away barely hidden tears as I take her into the school building, as I walk to my car and start the engine. I hope the tears will go away, but they don't, they last all the way to Broadford, where I do my wifi work and answer my emails. And by noon the urge is irresistible.

I have to see for myself.

Climbing in the car I drive too fast, down the Sleat road, to Kylerdale School, on its green promontory, by the wind-tousled waves. The cold metallic sun has emerged: making Knoydart shine gold and bronze. Above a steely sea.

It's the end of lunchtime. All the kids will be in the playground, having eaten. I want to watch Lydia again: to see if things have improved. I want to discover if she is interacting, or if she is being teased and mocked.

But I don't want to be seen, myself: so I creep up the side of the playground, on a little-used path, which wanders down to the shingly beach just beyond. I am sheltered, by winter's thorny shrubbery, from the screaming happy kids beyond the chainwire.

Girls are hopscotching. Boys are ragtagging. I scan all the little pink faces, the white socks and blue trousers, looking for the blonde hair of my daughter. I cannot see her. All the kids are, apparently, out here playing. But Lydia?

Might she be inside? Reading on her own? I hope not. She must be out here. Please let her be out here, playing with someone else.

There she is.

I close my eyes and calm myself. Then gaze, properly.

Lydia is standing in the far corner of the playground. Entirely alone. The nearest child, a small boy, is ten yards away: with his back to her. But even though she is conspicuously alone, Lydia is doing something. What?

I go closer, still concealed by trees and bushes.

I am just a few feet distant, now. I see that Lydia is facing away from the school, from her classmates, isolated from the world.

She is quite alone – yet she is talking. Animatedly. I can see her lips move, and her arms wave. She is talking to the air, to the trees and the chainwire, she is actually smiling and laughing.

Now I can hear her.

'Nnneeooo nononon yes free up thrre up fff . . . Wakey wakey no yes paka. Sufffy suffffy nnnn. Mmmmm. Nana nana nana.'

As she says this Lydia waves her arms, then she stops, and listens, as if someone is talking right back at her.

But no one is talking back at her. Then she nods and laughs and babbles some more.

It's the nonsensical twin language she shared with Kirstie. The twins kept it going right to the end. We never worked out what it meant.

Lydia is talking to her dead sister.

15

'An t-Eilean Sgithenac – the winged isle – Skye.' Josh spun the wheel as they rocked south. 'That's about the only Gaelic I learned.'

Angus said nothing. The morning was bright and fiercely cold. Perhaps the first morning of proper winter.

'Molly's learned quite a bit more, she's into all that Celtic stuff. But it's all so bloody gloomy. I mean – you know that little cove near Ardvasar, Port na Faganaich, it's really cute, right?' Josh chortled, and went on: 'Then you find out what that means, Port na Faganaich? It means the Port of the Forsaken Ones, really. *Port of the Forsaken Ones*. Charming.'

Josh accelerated up a hill, momentarily leaving the sea behind, though you never left the sea behind for long, not on Skye. His friend buzzed open a window, and inhaled the icy fresh air.

'Winter, at last, love it. Proper cold, so where was I – yeah – and there's some lake here, Lagan, something. Lagan—'

'Lagan inis na Cnaimh.'

'That's the one. I keep forgetting you're a local. Yes.

Lagan inis. And that means – Molly told me last night – *the hollow of the meadow of bones*. For fuck's sake. Why? What's that doing for real estate values? Do you want to buy a nice bungalow in the hollow of the meadow of bones? No? OK, then we're building a condo, yeah, by the Ridge of the Night-hags.'

Josh chuckled at his own jokes. Angus stayed quiet. He already knew the quaint and macabre local folklore. He could remember it word for word: all the stories his grandmother used to tell him. They were sacred in his memory. Happy holidays and scary fables. Bonfires on Torran with his brother. His dad not there. Everyone happy. Listening to the old tales. *The bonny road which winds around the fernie brae – ach, that's the road to death and heaven, the auld place of the fairies . . .*

Angus gazed from the window of Josh's car, Torran was hidden now, behind headlands. He thought of Lydia – *Lydia* – and Sarah, alone, together, in the cottage. Sarah and . . . Lydia. He had to accept she was Lydia. It was for the best. It was his doing. His daughter with her damaged soul, and her scarred hands and wrists. She was harmed: by life, by death, by Angus.

And by her mother.

Now the car rattled over a cattle grid; they were crossing the top of the Sleat peninsula, east to west. Taking the road to Tokavaig. This narrow road cut through an expanse of brown and rolling moorland, studded with little silvery lochans, shivered by kittiwakes. It was not beautiful. But soon they would see Loch Eisort.

'It's just down here. Through the wood. And it's all broadleaf: oaks, hazel, wych-elms.'

Angus grunted a reply. 'My granny loved it here. Said

it was a sacred grove, called Doir'an Druidean, the Grove of Quarrelling.'

'Yeah? That true? The Grove of Quarrelling! Again! This stuff is priceless. No really, mate, you've got to tell Molly all this.'

Why was Josh being so upbeat? Angus guessed that his friend was trying to keep things happy, following the morbid events at the supper party. Josh and Molly had barely mentioned the incident since.

Yet they had to talk about it. Soon.

The car ducked between some gnarled old trees, and a summit of basalt rocks, then they began the hard descent, to the western shores of Sleat, and the tiny hamlet of Ord.

The view was just as Angus remembered, and quite spectacular: behind them the wide, green, heathery slopes were wooded with oaks and alders, these milder inclines faced onto the blue-grey calm of Loch Eisort, which reflected, in turn, the sobering grandeur of the Black and Red Cuillins, across the waters.

Soay was visible to the south. And Sgurr Alasdair sang on the western skyline, with its sister peaks. Their lofty snowcaps gazed into the darling wastes of water.

It was so beautiful, Angus felt a brief urge to cry. For Lydia, for Kirstie, even for Sarah; for all of them.

The two men got out of the car and walked down to the chilly loch shore. A seabird called from a distant island. A heron winged its slow and lonely way, down towards Loch a' Ghlinne.

Josh said, straight out: 'Are you all right, mate?'

'Yes. Yes I'm fine.'

'Just that you're a bit quiet? Is it – are you – are you still – y'know – if you want to talk about things?'

Angus shrugged, helplessly. In truth, this minute, he

wanted to tell his friend everything. He needed to unburden to someone, to explain and share the nightmare unfolding on Torran. His wife, his daughters, and the past that could never be properly examined.

The heron was a speck in the blue, and then nothing. Angus resolved: he was going to tell Josh, in a minute.

Angus shook his head and picked up a flat round stone and skimmed it on the water. One, two, three, *plop*. Then he turned to Josh and said, 'So, why have you brought me here?'

Josh grinned. 'Because we need you to build.'

'Sorry?'

'Could you build something here?'

Angus gazed. 'Me? Build? Don't get it, Josh. This is all owned by the Macdonald estate. All of Tokavaig and Ord. No?'

Josh smiled. 'Molly and me bought a patch of land, just up there, a few years ago. See, past the barbed wire – the field, with the blackthorns in the hedge.'

Angus nodded. Josh explained. 'It's about half an acre, maybe a bit more.'

'Half an acre of nettles and hazels? Nice for redstarts, but it's just a field.'

'We got planning permission. Last week.'

Angus gaped. 'You did?'

'We did. Yes, we really did. In fact we got permission for a five-bedroom cottage – and we'd love *you* to design it, mate. The council want us to build a *nice* place. You know, something serious: award-winning. Making the most of the view.'

Angus looked at the field, sloping down to the shell sands of the loch shore. At once, his thoughts teemed. He could already see it: first you'd level half the field away. Then you'd use the simplest and purest materials:

stone, wood, steel, slate. Then fill the whole place with gorgeous light: floor-to-ceiling windows, a glazed enfilade, make the entire thing half glass, so the place just melted into the air and sea and sky. At night it would shine.

'Gus?'

'It could be incredible.'

'Hah.' Josh grinned. 'So you're up for it? Good man! We want to rent it out, maybe to artists in the winter, and holidaymakers in the summer.'

'You have the cash?'

'Everything, mate, everything. Molly's inherited a hefty sum from her granny. Good job I married well!' He chuckled. 'Let's go back to my place, I can show you the papers.'

Angus walked to the car, slightly dazed. He wondered if this was Josh and Molly's way of helping him and Sarah through their anguish. If so, he was fine with that. Completely fine. He was pathetically grateful. A chance to build something good, a real design!

Josh drove them to the Freedlands' big airy house, with the enormous steel kitchen, and the pots of blueberries cooking on the stove, and Molly making him taste her latest jam. And the big window in the living room.

Angus tried not to think about that night. He tried not to look at that vast window, now repaired, as Josh commandeered the dining-room table, and showed him the paperwork. The Planning Permission. The capital investment required. The dream that could come true. The Freedland House in Tokavaig, winner of the Architecture Scotland Award, by Angus Moorcroft.

In Angus's mind, it was already a house, not a cottage: because it was going to be *big*. Maybe he could mix some larch cladding with Caithness stone; of course he would incorporate solar panels; maybe he could make the entire north face a door of sliding glass: so the house would literally open onto the Loch . . .

For a while, Angus was happily distracted, drunk on Rooibos tea and daydreams. Perhaps this was the turning point? Perhaps things could change now? As the afternoon faded to wintry dark, Angus decided. The moment had arrived. He was going to tell Josh.

At least half of the truth.

The papers were filed away. Angus put on his coat, and looked at Josh. Meaningfully. 'I'm going to have a quick one at the Selkie. Fancy keeping me company? We can talk some more.'

The sweet smell of stewing blueberries filled the house. Josh gave Angus that look which said *I understand*. They both said goodbye to Molly and walked downhill, through the sharp winter twilight, to the pub. Angus inhaled the cold Ornsay air as they walked; the frostiness malted with coastal scents – of lobster pots, and chopped wood, and sweetly rotting kelp.

'Let's sit outside,' said Angus. 'More private.'

Josh squinted at him, and agreed; Angus went inside the bar, bought two drinks, made his way outside again. Then he set the glasses on the wooden table, and gazed out towards Torran lighthouse, its beam now visible, in the tranquil chilliness of dusk.

Angus sipped his whisky. Trying to locate the courage. Josh broke the brief silence: 'So, mate, how is Lydia, now? She doing better?'

Angus shrugged, and sipped more fiery whisky. Savouring its smoky alcohol. Then he answered. 'Kinda. Sometimes. But . . . she's still acting up, too.'

'How?'

'Talking to her dead sister, acting like Kirstie was – or rather *is* – there with her.'

Josh stared. 'She does that a lot?'

'Yes. A lot. She does it at school. At home. In the car. Sometimes it's just normal talk, but often it's in their twin language – so it's eerie. Sometimes she moves and mimes, as if her twin is there, physically interacting. That is pretty strange to watch.'

'OK. OK. Jesus.'

'That's what freaked her out at your house, I reckon. She thought she saw the ghost of her sister in the window. Reflected.'

Josh nodded. 'Well, yeah, it would freak you, wouldn't it? Christ. I'm sorry.' Josh hesitated, sipped a little more juice, then leaned forward, a fraction.

'So. Does she really believe all this, Gus? Does your daughter, I mean, you know – does she—'

'Is she mad or is there really a ghost? Or is she just pretending?'

'Um.'

'Clearly there isn't a ghost.' Angus stared at Josh, without blinking. 'But nor is she mad.'

Josh frowned. 'So she's pretending? Is that it? Why on earth? Look, you don't have to tell me, of course, but . . .'

Angus said nothing, feeling the bitterness inside him. And the urge to confess. He was tired of lying. Tired of deceiving people close to him. But did he have the courage to be honest? He couldn't and wouldn't tell everything – ever. But he would unburden himself of something.

After one more drink.

Angus lifted his empty glass.

Josh nodded: 'Another?'

'Ardbeg. Double. But let me pay. You don't have to cough for my functional alcoholism, Josh.' He reached in the front pocket of his jeans for a note.

Josh managed a smile. 'Just this once I will subsidize your addiction.'

Collecting Angus's glass, Josh disappeared inside the bar. The faint noise of folk music filtered out, as the door swung open and closed. Through the glass door, the saloon of the Selkie looked happy and bustling. All the locals were in there: drinking their whiskies and McEwan's, enjoying a weekend of relaxation, talking about the football and the horses, and the weird new family on Torran.

Angus slumped forward, his arms crossed on the table, his forehead resting on his arms. Staring into deep, deep darkness. He was defeated by events.

The bar door opened.

'Hey,' Josh said, ferrying the drinks to the table. 'Gus. Come on. It's not that bad.'

Angus looked up.

'Yes it is.'

Josh sighed, and sat down opposite, in the shrouding dark. With the drinks set on the table, he was unwrapping a packet of cigarettes.

Angus raised an eyebrow: *Josh Freedland, smoking?*

Josh shrugged. 'Secret vice. Don't tell Molly! Yes I have the odd cigarette at weekends. You want one?'

'No thanks.'

More silence. Just the laboured breathing of the sea, and the wind in the birches.

Angus stared to his left: at Torran and the humble lighthouse, and the squat whiteness of the cottage. He could barely make out the lights of their little kitchen, through the gloom and mist. What might be happening in Torran cottage, right now?

Angus closed his eyes. He was going to do this. He opened his eyes.

'Josh, you asked about Lydia.'

'Yes.'

'You want to know the truth?'

'Yes. But only if you want to tell me.'

'I do. I think. Yes I do. You used to tell me that it was good to share, confess, that it helps, right? That's what got you off drugs? What they taught you at NA meetings?'

'Yeah.'

'OK, but what I'm about to tell you is a total secret, you must never tell anyone, ever. And I mean that. No one EVER.'

Josh nodded. Sombre in the gloaming. 'Understood.'

'All right. Good.' Angus took a deep breath, and rubbed his hand over his mouth, feeling his own stubble. The cold air seemed heavy. A dew falling on the Sound. Angus spoke, his words misting in the brisk night air: 'First you need some backstory.'

'OK.'

'You have to remember that Sarah always preferred Lydia. Lydia was quite emphatically her favourite.'

'All parents have favourites,' Josh said. 'Or so I'm told.'

'Yes, but this was exceptional. She really favoured Lydia, the quiet one, the soulful one, the one like her, the one who liked reading. She favoured her so much it became distressing to Kirstie. I tried to balance it out by being much nicer with Kirstie, but it didn't work. Father's love isn't as important or impressive. Can't match a mother's, not when they're young, anyway.'

A pause. Angus couldn't properly see his friend's expression in the evening light. And that was fine. It

207

made his confession more anonymous: like an actual religious confession, in a church, to a priest, the faces concealed. Angus continued,

'A couple of days before the accident, Kirstie actually told me she hated her mummy, 'cause of all this, and I got very sharp with her. In fact I almost slapped her. I've never slapped my kids before. Ever. But I was drunk, and I lost my temper.' He shook his head, and went on, 'And Kirstie was seriously upset. As you'd expect. First her mum favours her twin sister, then Daddy shouts?'

Again, Josh was silent. But the tip of his cigarette glowed, as Angus went on,

'And then the accident happened. You know. The balcony. After that, Sarah fell apart, and we all fell apart, and it got worse, and worse . . . And then, six months ago . . .' he paused, taking a deep sip of whisky, for courage. 'Six months ago my surviving daughter came to me and said to me: "Daddy, I did it. I did it. I killed my sister. I pushed her. 'Cause Mummy always liked her more, and now she's gone."'

Josh said, very quietly: 'My God.'

'Quite.'

'Jesus . . .' Josh extinguished the cigarette under his boot heel. The silence was painful. Then at last, he spoke again: 'But – Gus – could she – *did* she kill her? Can you believe her? Did you believe her?'

Angus sighed,

'Yes. Maybe. But she was just six when it happened, seven when she said this. Did she even know what she was saying? Do they ever really know what they are saying at this age? Trouble was: her new explanation made sense, Josh. She had a motive, her mum's absurd preference for Lydia. And it fitted with the evidence. I mean: why were Lydia's injuries so bad? From a

208

twenty-foot fall? Kids normally survive falls like that, of that distance. So – why?'

'Because . . .?'

'Because she fell from the top floor, not the middle floor. Kirstie actually told me: they were . . . up on the top floor, then the twins ran onto the balcony, and that's when Kirstie pushed Lydia . . .'

'Still don't quite picture it.'

Angus paused. Took a breath. And went on,

'It's like this, she pushed her off the top balcony, then she – I guess she raced down to the first floor to look over that balcony at what she'd done – as you would – and that's when Sarah came in and found her yelling – *Lydia has fallen Lydia has fallen*. So that's the explanation, that is what probably happened. Kirstie killed her sister. And it has happened in the past. I've done research. There is literature. Intense sibling rivalry in identical twins. Which can become murderous.'

'OK. But . . .' Josh was shaking his head. Angus could just about discern this, in the light from the pub. 'What's this got to do with the identity change?'

'When Kirstie came to me and told me this, I panicked. Totally lost it. Kirstie was determined to tell her mum and her friends and her teachers – everyone. And her mum was massively unstable at the time, there was no way she could hear this. And Kirstie also wanted to tell the police, because she had intense guilt. She was falling apart, my own surviving daughter. So, yep, I panicked.'

'Why?'

'Because! What happens if a six-year-old is accused of murder? What do the police do? Anything? Everything? Investigate? They would certainly investigate. There was circumstantial evidence backing her up. So I had to shut her up, calm her down, get her to disbelieve herself.'

'And . . .?'

'I did whatever I could. I stopped her talking. I told her not to tell me any more. I said I didn't want to know. I said no one needed to know. Then I told her Lydia wasn't really dead.'

'*What?*'

'I explained that no one dies really, they go to heaven but part of them always stays with us, too. I told her about Lydia waking up in hospital, told her that was Lydie coming back. I gave her Lydia's favourite toy – look she's still here! I convinced her that twins are special and they don't really die because they are the same person and if one of them survives then they are both here. I blurred the identity inside her, I told her you are Kirstie, but you will always have Lydia with you, because you are her twin sister, and now you can go on living for the two of you. And I told her all of this was a big, big secret between her and Daddy and she mustn't say anything about this, ever again.' Angus sat back. 'And I told her all of this because I was scared of Kirstie telling the truth, and of my family breaking up entirely, because—'

Angus gazed directly at the darkness of his friend's face, and went on. 'Imagine, Josh. Imagine if my daughter went to her mum and her grandparents and her teachers and her friends and said, "I am a murderer, help me, I killed my own sister." That would have been us finished. For ever. We couldn't have survived that as well as the accident. No way. No fucking way.'

The door to the pub opened, abruptly, as a drinker departed into the night.

At last, Josh spoke: 'So *you* sowed the confusion in her head, telling her she was Lydia as well as Kirstie. And now she thinks she is Lydia, because of what you said.'

'Yes. I calmed her down at the time, which is all I wanted, it did the job, but then the confusion in her head re-emerged. In the most appalling way. As her thinking she is Lydia.'

'But she really is Kirstie?'

'Yes.'

'What about the screaming thing?'

'Just a scream. Doesn't prove anything.'

'The dog? You told me about the dog.'

'Pets reattach themselves to surviving twins in different ways, they try to protect them. Also I wonder if the dog saw something. Sensed something. He was with the twins when it happened. And he's never been the same, I know that sounds insane, but it all sounds insane.'

'So Lydia really is still Kirstie.'

'Yes.'

'And you know this?' Josh shook his head, again, in the dimness. 'You know it's a lie. You know she is really Kirstie. Yet you go along with this charade, this pretence? You even let your wife plan a funeral for Kirstie?' His voice was sharpening, in the cold clear air. 'Really, Gus? It's just so fucked *up*. How could you *do* this?'

'Because I have no choice! I can't tell the truth to anyone – you're the only one that knows. If I told Sarah, she'd probably crack up – would that help? She might hate her surviving daughter. And also, why not let Lydia live, if this keeps the peace? Let her mum have her favourite back. For now.' Angus sighed, fiercely, and went on, 'And you know what? Sometimes these days I actually think of her as Lydia, as if she really is Lydia, I forget. And she does act like Lydia; it happens in twins who survive a co-twin's death. The point is: what does it matter, as long as the truth doesn't come out, that maybe, probably, one of my daughters killed the other?'

'But Kirstie *is* still here. Still here now. Still inside Lydia.'

'Yes.'

'Stuck inside Lydia. Fighting to be heard.'

'Yes.'

'Jesus,' said Josh. 'What a total fucking mess.'

Angus nodded, feeling a certain exhaustion. But also a certain relief. He had shared, and yes, it felt better. But the other problems remained; the deeper truths were concealed: his own guilt; Sarah's involvement; Sarah's responsibility. Stuff they couldn't tell anyone.

The lighthouse flickered across the Sound. Angus thought of his diminished and broken family, out there, in Torran cottage. His yearning for revenge had not gone away. His child had died. And the injustice burned.

16

It's Friday with a rumour of snow in the air when I go to Kylerdale School to pick up Lydia. I am desperate to help my daughter now. She needs friends, or she will be lost. She needs some reason to hope, to see a future here; she needs people to talk to who aren't ghosts.

I look beyond the blocky buildings to the waters of Sleat: the grey waves are scoured by the wind, everything is harsh, raw and sombre, making the gaily painted swings and wooden riding animals in the playground look totally incongruous: surreal invaders from a fatuously happy world.

A young, pale woman is standing on her own at the gates, staring at the glass door of the school, and the cheerful signs saying *Shleite* and *Sgoil*. I recognize this woman; Lydia has pointed her out to me as being 'Emily's mum': Julia Durrant.

Emily Durrant is another blow-in, another English girl at Kylerdale, and she seems to be the only other child with whom Lydia might just have connected. She is, at least, the only child Lydia has mentioned more than once by name, whenever I have carefully, anxiously and pretend-casually quizzed my daughter; 'Hey, how did it go today at school?'

I have no real idea if Emily likes Lydia; probably she doesn't. I am fairly certain none of the children at Kylerdale truly like or even know my daughter: they find her uncanny, and unsettling.

But I have no alternatives now, and so I grip my shyness and hide it somewhere inside me, and I approach Julia Durrant with her nice purple coat and her Ugg boots. Her slender face creases with a frown, even before I speak.

'Hello, I'm Sarah Moorcroft.'

'Yes, hello.'

'Lydia Moorcroft's mother.'

'Of course. Sorry. Yes.'

'I was just wondering, would your daughter like to come on a play date tomorrow? We live on Torran Island, the one with the lighthouse, it would only be for about four hours starting maybe eleven a.m. – we'll come and pick her up?'

'Well . . .'

She looks startled. Who can blame her? But I have to persist. I can't let Lydia's increasingly crazy loneliness go on. I must be rude, and aggressive: a horrible, pushy parent.

'You see, Lydia is a bit lonely to be honest so we'd *really* like it if Emily would come and play with her for a day, is eleven a.m. OK? You've not got anything planned? We'll do everything, that would be great.'

'Well . . . we had . . . I mean . . .'

She clearly wants to say no but she is wavering, because I am hardly giving her any choice. I feel sorry for this poor woman. Confronted by me. But I need to seal the deal. So I use *it*.

'Of course Lydia's still deeply confused after her sister's accident. You probably know what happened, her sister died, her twin, so she's – just – just finding it difficult to fit in, and it would be so lovely for her to play with Emily?'

What can Julia Durrant say now? *Oh, I don't care that your daughter has lost a sister? I don't care that you are a grieving mother of a difficult and lonely child?*

I can see the resistance crumbling in her expression: she is embarrassed for me, she is probably pitying me – and so what? Just as long as she agrees.

'OK,' she says, forcing an unreal smile. 'You know where we live, right, by the Post Office on the hill?'

'Yes. That's great.' I return an equally phoney smile. 'Lydia will be so happy. Angus, my husband, will come and pick her up at eleven and we'll drop her off at three, before it gets dark. That's great – thanks!'

With that we both turn and look to the glass door as the children are released from school: as always Lydia is the last, reluctant child to emerge from the door, when all her shouting, smiling classmates have dispersed.

I scrutinize her as she walks towards me. At least the scarring on her hands isn't too bad.

And now I grimace, inwardly, at my own thoughts. That is the extent of my optimism, this is me looking on the bright side: *the scarring isn't too bad.*

'Hello, you.'

I put an arm around her, and guide her to the car.

'Hey. How did it go at school?'

'Nothing.'

'Sorry?'

'Can we go home, Mummy?'

'OK. Sure.'

I turn the key and we drive away.

217

'I've got some nice news for you, Moomin.'

I look in the rear-view mirror. Lydia looks back at me. Hopeful yet sceptical. My pity grows, and I hesitate. Then I say,

'Emily is coming to play, with you, tomorrow.'

Lydia is silent as she absorbs this news. She gazes at me, mirror-wise. She blinks, once, and twice. And now I can see the softness of sad hope in her wide blue eyes. The silence goes on, as she dwells on this thought.

I know that weekends on Torran Island are achingly lonely for Lydia, worse even than the loneliness of school; however desolated she might be in her isolation on the playground, she is still surrounded by kids and she listens to lessons and at least the teachers engage with her.

On Torran it is just me. And Angus. And the sky and the clouds and the weeping grey seals and the whooper swans driven south by Arctic cold. I still love Torran – or, at least, I want us to love Torran, despite its harshness and pains – so I want Lydia to love it, too. And for that she needs company. On the island.

So I hope and believe she will be pleased by this news: the weekend play date.

At last she says: 'Really?'

'Yes.'

'Someone's coming to *play* with me? Play with *me*?'

'Yes, really. With you. Her mummy asked me just now if Emily could come. Won't that be fun?'

My daughter gazes, and then she bursts into a big, bright, hopeful smile. The biggest smile I've seen on her face for many weeks. Maybe many months. Then she tries to hide the smile: she is embarrassed by how pleased she is. And I am delighted by her smile. And I am terrified.

What if this goes wrong? She now has huge expectations. But I have to do it.

I try to rein in her excitement, but it is not easy. Throughout supper she keeps asking me what time is Emily coming, and if she can come earlier – and this makes Angus irritable. But Angus is irritable, or distant, all the time now. His moods are beginning to resemble the view of Torran in a rainstorm: I can still see him, when he's with us, he's right there. But the details are blurred.

Since the supper party he and I have moved further apart. I don't know what he's truly thinking any more. And he clearly doesn't know what I am truly thinking any more. When we work on the house, we do it with signals and monosyllables. As if we are not fluent in the same language.

Maybe it's because we have endured too much pain – but we have endured it differently, individually – and now we are separated. Maybe it's because he rather frightens me now, with his barely concealed anger – at the world, at the cottage, at life, and maybe at me. The strange thing is that I still desire him. Even as everything else in our relationship seems fractured and misshapen. Maybe there is some hope there.

But I don't have the energy to fix our relationship now. My thoughts are focused on my daughter.

Eventually at nine I put Lydia to bed and I'm so exhausted by her questions and chatter I go to bed myself, soon after.

At seven-thirty a.m. Lydia is shaking me awake, standing in the cold bedroom in her pyjamas, her face flushed and excited.

'Mummy, Mummy. Where's Emily?'

I groan from sleep. Angus remains unconscious, on the other side of the bed.

'Sorry?'

'Emily! Where is she? My new friend. Mummy, you said she is coming!'

I swing my legs from the bed, and yawn till my jaw cracks.

'Mummy?'

'She's coming, darling. But not yet.'

'When is she coming, Mummy? When?'

'Oh, God, soon, Lydie, soon. Let's make you some breakfast.'

Slipping on my dressing gown, I walk into the kitchen – and the first thing I see makes me almost vomit. There is a dead vole drowned in a jar of oil; its little corpse leaking black blood, which curlicues in the green oil. My God. Torran.

Where do these vile rodents come from? The rats and voles, the shrews and mice; they are remorseless, and numberless. Shuddering my disgust, I open the door, and I hurl the oil and its little black corpse onto the frosty beach, to be taken by the tide, and I come back inside and I think about the day and the Big Play Date. And abruptly I realize that, even though I do not believe in God, I am actually praying.

Please, God, make this work. Please, God, I will believe in You if You make this work.

And now Emily is here.

It is half past eleven and I am standing at the kitchen door and I can see Angus in the boat rounding the rocks of Salmadair, with a little person to his right: Emily Durrant. Even from a distance I can see the wariness in the little girl, in her posture. Lydia didn't go on the boat because she wants to welcome Emily to her island, on her island.

Lydia and I walk down to the lighthouse beach to

220

greet Emily Durrant. My daughter is jumping up and down in her blue wellingtons. The day is clammy and misty, but at least it isn't raining: the girls will be able to explore the rock pools, touch the fossils in the stones, they will comb the beach for all its rich treasures: plastic bottles of Nestlé water, fish boxes from Peterhead and Lossiemouth, antlers discarded by stags after the rut, floating on the tide from Jura.

I call out, 'Hello, Emily!'

The small, freckled, red-haired girl gives me a shy, uncertain glance as Angus helps her from the boat. By my side, Lydia is staring at Emily as if Emily is a celebrity. Lydia is amazed, wondrous, dazzled, an actual new friend! Come to her island! Emily is in a new black anorak, and new black wellingtons.

'Lydia, say hello to Emily.'

'Hello-Emily-thank-you-for-coming-thank-you!' My daughter says, all at once, and then she rushes forward and she hugs Emily and this is obviously too much and too gauche, for Emily Durrant, because she actively pushes Lydia away, with a scowl. Quickly I intervene, and separate the girls, and take them both by the hand, and then I say, brightly, 'Right, let's go inside, shall we have some orange juice? Some biscuits? Then, Lydia, you can show Emily all your favourite rock pools!'

'Yes yes!' says Lydia, bouncing up and down. 'Emily, do you want to see all our rock pools?'

Emily shrugs, unsmiling, as we trudge to the kitchen door. Then she says, 'All right.'

I feel serious sympathy for little Emily: this girl isn't being cruel or cold, she simply doesn't know my daughter, she has been forced into this play date. But I can't let this stop me. I just hope Lydia's inner niceness, and bashful charm – the charm of my lovely sweet

221

daughter, so delicate and funny when you get to know her – will do the hard work, and form a bond.

Angus offers me a stare as he passes into the cottage; as if this play date is going to be *my* fault if it doesn't succeed. Ignoring this, I give the girls their biscuits and juice and then I button up their coats, so I can send them out onto the rocks and beaches to play; I'm trying to sound as affable and relaxed and we-do-this-all-the-time-ish as possible.

'Thank you, Mummy, thank you, Mummy!'

Lydia is trembling with happiness as I do up her coat: she is so thrilled by the thought of her new playmate. In contrast, Emily stands there mute and resentful, but trying to be as polite as a seven-year-old can, which is: not very polite. She mumbles a minor thanks for the food and drink, and she slowly follows my unusually noisy daughter out of the kitchen door.

'C'mon, Emily, we've got crab shells and everything and mussels and seals, can I show you? Can I?'

It is painful to hear Lydia's supplications, her neediness. So I close the kitchen door and meditate on my hopes, wishing them away. I must not expect too much.

Angus hovers into the kitchen; pecks me on the cheek; his stubble is prickly, not sexy. He says, 'I've got to see Josh at the site in Tokavaig, then go to Portree in the morning. Planning office. Might stay overnight.'

'OK.'

I suppress my envy. He gets to do stuff. I have to look after Lydia.

'But I'll be back to pick up Emily.'

'OK.'

'About three.'

Again I note how our conversation is reduced to this: Where you are going, Why am I going, Who gets the boat, Who will buy food tonight. Maybe it is because we are scared of talking about the bigger things: what is happening to Lydia. Maybe we just hope that if we don't talk about it, the problem will melt away, like early drifts of snow on the lower slopes of Ladhar Bheinn.

He opens the door to the freshening air and trudges down to the lighthouse beach. As the door opens I pretend to myself I am *not* looking for Lydia and Emily, but I am. I want to be a non-interfering mother who can let her happy daughter run free, safe on her island, with her friend, but I am also the anxious mother of a friendless daughter and I am shredded with worries.

I can hear the dwindling buzz of the outboard motor, as Angus disappears around Salmadair. For a moment I stand at the kitchen window and watch a curlew, sitting on a rock, near the washing line. It is pecking at a winkle, tossing seaweed over its shoulder; then it hops on one leg to a slippy boulder, flaps irritably at the dampness, and makes its lonely cry.

Lydia.

She is there on the beach by the tidal causeway. My daughter is staring into the still pools of water. She is alone. Where is Emily?

I have to intervene.

Zipping up my windcheater, I stroll, casually, down the grass path, to the sands and shingles.

'Lydia, where's your new friend?'

My voice is absurdly calm.

Lydia is now digging something out of the sand with a stick. Her boots are smeared with grey mud and green seaweed and her soft blonde hair looks wild, near-feral. Her hood is down. An island child.

'Lydia?'

223

She looks up, with an expression halfway between guilt and sadness.

'Emily didn't want to play what I wanted to play, Mummy. She wanted to go look at the lighthouse, that is boring isn't it? So I came here.'

I can sense the panic of isolation in this statement. It's been so long, Lydia has forgotten how to socialize, to share, how to be a friend.

'Lydia you can't *always* do what you want to do. Sometimes you have to do what your friends want to do. Where is she?'

Silence.

'Where is she?'

The first strain of anxiety tightens in my throat.

'Sweetie, where is Emily?'

'Told you! By the lighthouse.' She stamps her foot. Pretend-angry. But I can see the hope, and the hurt, in her eyes.

'OK then, let's go and find her, I'm sure we can find something you both want to do.'

I take my dismayed daughter by the hand and haul her up onto the path – and together we march, lockstep, to the lighthouse, and there is Emily Durrant looking utterly fed up, and bored, and cold, her hands in her anorak pockets, standing by the lighthouse railings.

'Mrs Moorcroft, can I go home now?' she says. Flatly. 'I want to see my friends in the village this afternoon.'

I glance, immediately, at my daughter.

Lydia looks openly anguished, and hurt, by this inadvertently cruel remark. Tears are not far from her blue eyes.

Yet Emily is, of course, simply being truthful: Lydia is not one of Emily's friends and probably never will be.

Somehow I suppress my maternal anger. The urge to

protect Lydia. Because I am determined to give this another shot. 'Hey, girls, why don't we play rock-skipping?'

Emily pouts. 'But I want to go *home*.'

'Not yet, Emily, not quite yet – very soon. But we can have some fun first, we can skim rocks behind the lighthouse!'

This is one of Lydia's favoured games: skimming rocks over the flat stretch of water around the corner, where the waves are harboured by the basalt and granite blocks, set beneath Stevenson's noble lighthouse. She likes to play this game with Daddy.

Emily sighs heavily, and Lydia says, 'Please come, Emily. We can play this, I can show you. Please let me show you?'

'Oh, all right then.'

Together we painstakingly make our way down to the basalt blocks, and the flat stretch of water. We have to clamber, and trip over kelp, and step onto crusts of decaying seaweed. Emily wrinkles her nose.

When we reach the tiny beach, Lydia picks up a round stone and she shows it to Emily.

'See, you have to get a round one and then throw it kind of like a sideways thing?'

Emily nods. Clearly uninterested. Lydia leans back and skims a stone and it does three little cheery bounces and then she says: 'Your go. Your go! Emily!'

Emily does not move. Lydia tries again. 'Let me find you a stone, Emily. Can I find you a stone to throw?'

I watch on, helpless. Diligently Lydia searches the shingled little beach for a nice flat round stone, and she hands it to Emily, who takes it, and looks at me, and at the sea – and then she listlessly throws the stone; it does a half-hearted plop straight into the water. Then Emily shoves her hands in her pockets.

Lydia gazes at Emily in despair. I don't know whether to intervene, or how to intervene. At last my daughter says: 'Imagine if everyone in the world wanted to queue up to see a caterpillar?'

Emily says nothing. My daughter goes on, 'Imagine that, imagine if they did, you'd have to have a big café, but there'd be no one to give them food coz they'd all be queuing!'

It's one of Lydia's flights of fancy, her nonsense concepts: the ones she used to exchange with Kirstie, when they'd whoop with laughter, spiralling into ever dizzier realms of absurdity.

Emily shakes her head and shrugs at Lydia's idea and then she looks at me and says: 'Can I go home *now*?'

It's not Emily Durrant's fault, but I seriously want to slap her.

I am about to give up, to call Angus and say come and collect, or maybe I will just drag Emily on foot over the causeway and mudflats at low tide; which happens in less than an hour: one p.m. But then Lydia says, 'Emily, do you want to play Angry Granny on the big phone?'

And this changes things. Emily Durrant actually looks curious. The *big phone* is the iPad. Which we bought when we had money.

'It's an iPad,' I say to Emily. 'Got lots of games!'

Emily Durrant frowns. But it is a different frown, a good frown, a frown of confusion – and interest.

'Daddy won't let us uh play any computer games or stuff like that,' she says. 'He says they are bad for us. But can I play them here?'

'YES!' I say. 'Of course you can, sweetheart.' I am beyond worrying as to whether this will annoy the Durrants. I just need to rescue the day. 'Come on, you girls, let's go inside and you can play on the iPad and I'll make some lunch! How about that?'

This works. Emily Durrant looks properly enthused – even keen. Consequently the three of us climb back up the rocks and we skip into the cottage and I settle them both in the living room, where the woodfire is roaring, and the iPad is glowing. Emily actually giggles as she boots up one of the games. Lydia shows her how to do the first level of her favourite game: how to stop Angry Granny from running into a sheet of glass.

The girls look at each other – and they smile – and they giggle together, like friends, like sisters, like Lydia and Kirstie used to do, and I make another little prayer of thanks and gently, tentatively, hopefully I step outside the living room and go into the kitchen. I want to make pasta and meat sauce. All kids like pasta and meat sauce.

I can still hear them laughing and chattering in the living room. The relief is intense. This is not what I'd intended, what I had idealized. It's not two girls scampering around our lovely island, hunting for ark shells and cowries, pointing at harbour seals swimming upstream from Kinloch: it's two kids hunched over an iPad, indoors. It could be in London. It could be anywhere. But it will very definitely do. Because it could be the beginning of something better.

The minutes pass in relief and reverie. I sieve the penne, carefully make the sauce, and stare at little Ornsay Bay, and the hills over Camuscross, through the kitchen windows. The beauty of Torran and Ornsay is subdued today, but still impressive. It is always impressive. The fine pale greys of sea and sky. The rich dark russet of the dead winter bracken. The trumpeting of the whooper swans.

The sound of a girl screaming.

What?

It's Emily. And she is shrieking.

Desperately.

I stand, still, quite stuck. Rigid with fearfulness. Paralysed by a desire not to know what is happening. *Not again. Not here. Please no.*

Reflex takes over and I run into the living room and it is empty but then I hear the scream again – and it is coming from our bedroom, Angus's and mine, with the Admiral's Bed, so I step into this room: and Emily is standing in a corner sobbing, frantically. And pointing at Lydia.

'Her! Her! Her!'

Lydia is sitting on the bed and she is also crying, but in a different way. Helpless. Silent. Those silent tears that freak me out.

'Girls. What is it?! What's happened?!'

Emily screams like an animal, she runs from the room, right past me, I try to grab her but she is too fast. What do I do? I cannot let her run onto the beach, onto the rocks, not in this hysterical state, she might fall – anything might happen. So I pursue Emily into the kitchen where I corner her and she stands by the fridge, shivering, trembling, sobbing, and then screaming again.

'Her! It was her! Her talking! Her! In the mirror! In the mirror!'

'Emily, please, calm down, it's just—' I don't know what to say.

Emily screams in my face, 'Take me home. Take me home! I want my mummy! Take me home!'

'Mummy . . .'

I turn.

Lydia is in the kitchen door, her face streaked with misery. Standing in her pink socks and her little jeans.

'I'm sorry, Mummy,' she says. 'I just . . . I just said that Kirstie wanted to play too. That's all.'

This provokes even louder shrieks from Emily: she looks terrified of my daughter, she is hunched, backing away.

'Take me home! Pleeeeese, please get it away, get it away from me, get it away! Get them away from me!'

17

Angus comes quickly. Thirty minutes after I phone him – he was in Ord, which has a randomly good mobile phone signal – he appears in the dinghy, around the rocks of Salmadair.

I have calmed down Emily Durrant, in the meantime. She is still trembling, but the tears have stopped. I've given her cocoa and biscuits and I have kept her away from Lydia.

I have to keep other children away from my daughter.

Lydia is hunched on the sofa in the living room, pretending to read a book; she looks terminally lonely – and guilty, too: as if she has failed at something very important.

And the worst of it is: she has.

I cannot see now how she will ever make friends with anyone at Kylerdale. Whatever she did to freak out Emily – Talk her twin language? Pretend to interact with Kirstie? Talk about a ghost sister? – Emily will tell everyone at the school and all the children will listen to her and Lydia will become, even more, the strange kid from Torran. The spooky, lonely girl. With the voices in her head.

And the Durrants will loathe me in so many ways: for making their daughter play computer games, for making their daughter miserable and terrified.

We are doomed. Maybe it was a tragic error, moving here.

'Where is she?' says Angus, as he pushes into the kitchen and looks at Emily, standing at the furthest corner of the kitchen. 'Where is Lydia?'

I whisper back. 'She's in the living room, she's OK, considering.'

'Hm.' He is glaring at me. The play date has failed, catastrophically, and this is my fault. I arranged this, and it has gone horribly wrong.

'Please, Angus, just take Emily home.'

'I will.'

He goes over to Emily and, quite bluntly, he seizes her by the hand and leads her out into the dying light of the afternoon. I give him Emily's bag with her toy inside. The two of them traipse down to the boat and the motor starts; I turn in despair, and go back into the house.

It's just me and Lydia. Alone. Here.

I peer my head around the door of the living room – she is still reading but not really reading.

'Sweetie.'

She doesn't even look at me. Her white face is streaked by tears. The house is so quiet. Just the hymning of the wind and waves and the crackle of the hungry woodfire. I wish for a TV. I wish we had a hundred televisions. I wish we were back in London. I can't believe I want this, but I think I do.

Yet we can't go back. We are trapped here. On an island.

We have very little money. *I* have no money. We are putting everything into Torran, we have just enough for a basic renovation; but if we sell it now, barely developed, just half a shell, we will make nothing. We might even make a loss, and go bankrupt.

The night passes in frightened quietness, Sunday is listless and subdued; our daughter loiters in her room. I sense that if I try to console her, I might make things worse. But what else should I do? Angus is no help: by Monday morning he is barely speaking to me: there is rage in his movements, he cannot hide it. He clenches his fist at the breakfast table. It seems as if he is inches from punching me.

And I am beginning to feel genuine fear of this anger: the repressed violence it implies. Angus, after all, hit his boss. And Angus's drunken dad beat Angus's mum half to death. Is Angus that different? He certainly drinks, and he is angry all the time. I don't think he would ever touch Lydia, but I no longer feel entirely safe with him next to me. So close.

He gets up, wordless, and ferries his breakfast dishes to the sink. And then I shrug, and I let him take Lydia to school. Because I cannot face the mums and dads at the gate; especially not Emily Durrant's mum. Lydia is also silent. Everyone has been silenced.

When I am properly alone, I take the phone off the hook. I want to be undisturbed, I want time to think.

Then I go back to our bedroom and lie there, for five or six bleak, silent hours, staring at the ceiling and its stains of dampness. I consider my mother's words. About Kirstie's strange behaviour just before the accident. The way Angus was delayed that night, with Imogen.

There *is* some pattern here. What is it? I feel as if I am staring at one of those 3D puzzle-pictures and I have to let my eyes relax, and the reality will come into view.

Resting my face piously on my hands, my eyes slowly unfocus, and I gaze vacantly across the room. Then I realize I am staring at Angus's cherished chest of drawers. One of those items of furniture that *had* to come here from London.

It's been his since before we were married. A present from his grandmother: an old Victorian Scottish 'kist'. The drawers are lockable. And he keeps them locked.

But I know where he stores the key. I've seen him casually reach for it, half a dozen times; after all, we've been married ten years. You see things in ten years. He probably doesn't know that I know, but I know.

Crossing the room I reach behind the kist: and here it is. Lodged in a slot, at the back of the chest.

I pause. What am I doing?

The key slots in the first lock, and turns with antique and well-oiled ease. I grasp the brass handles, and pull the top drawer out. The house is very cold. I can hear seagulls swooping on the Torran winds, calling in that annoying way – needy, yet critical.

The drawer is full of documents. Career stuff. Architecture journals, some of them signed by stars of the trade. Richard Rogers, Renzo Piano, other people I don't know. Then a folder of CVs. Photos of buildings. Plans and projects.

The next drawer unlocks, and slides out. This looks more promising; though I'm not sure what the promise might be. There are letters and books. I lift one letter up to see, properly, in the ageing afternoon light.

234

The letter is from his grandmother.

My darling Angus, I'm writing from Torran to tell you we have a pair of otters breeding! You must come and see them, they play all day by the lighthouse beach, it's lovely to—

I feel the sense of wrongness, as I read this. What am I doing? Sleuthing my husband? Yet I don't trust him, because he's told too many shifting lies: about the toy, about the identity change. I am also increasingly scared of him. So I want to know. I want to understand the pattern. Dropping this letter, I reach for another.

A noise stiffens the air. That was a definite creak in the floorboards. Is that *Angus* coming back? So early? It's nearly three p.m., and low tide. He could have crossed the mudflats on foot. But why?

The creak repeats. The terror is like a cold injection, intramuscular.

Why was Kirstie frightened of Angus the day she died? Had she seen his violence? Did he slap her?

The creaking stops. It must have been the back door of the kitchen, swinging on a hinge. I didn't shut it properly.

The relief surges and I plunge into the second drawer again. Letters spill onto the floor. One is from his granny, again, another one is from his mum, a third from his brother, written in a bad schoolboy hand. I also find two typed letters about his dad; plus his father's death certificate. And then – my fingers tingle with unexplained anxiety – I see it.

A copy of *Anna Karenina*.
Anna Karenina?

Angus is not a reader of novels. He devours news-papers and architectural journals, he can be easily diverted by a volume of military history, like most men.

But novels? Never.

Why would he have a copy of *Anna Karenina*? And why would it be hidden?

I pluck it up, and flick the first few pages. And my fingertips go cold as they rest on the third page.

There is a brief, handwritten inscription, under the title.

For us, then . . . Love, Immy, xxx

I know that handwriting from Christmas cards, and birthday cards, and witty sarcastic postcards from Umbria, and the Loire, every summer. I've known this handwriting for all my adult life.

It's from Imogen Evertsen.

My best friend Immy.

And she's signed it with love. And added three kisses? To a famous novel about adultery?

Imogen Evertsen?

My breath is a faint vapour in the freezing bedroom. I urgently want to search the rest of the drawer, but I can't. I am halted by a noise, once again. And that sound is unmistakable.

There is someone else in the cottage. A door has slammed shut. I can hear footsteps.

18

Is this Angus? What do I do? What if he catches me sneaking through his stuff? The threat of his violence is suddenly very real.

Gathering all the letters I hastily shove them in the drawer, desperate, frantic, yet trying to do this in silence. The final letter is crammed into place, and I turn.

Numbering my own heartbeats.

The footsteps have ceased; I can hear a rattle. Someone is definitely in the kitchen: and they surely came in through the back door, knowing it would be unlocked.

So this must be Angus?

I urgently need to close the two drawers, gently, gently. The first drawer shuts – but with a squeak. Far too loud. I hesitate, wholly tensed.

Footsteps rattle, again. Is that a voice? A small, high, girlish voice? Could Angus be with Lydia? Why would he have collected her from school early? If not Lydia, then who?

Silence resumes. If they were voices: they have stopped. But as I push the second drawer shut, I hear the tread of footsteps, again. They are slow. And pains-taking. I get the terrifying sense that someone is stealthily crossing the floor: that whoever else is in the house is trying to be as quiet as possible, as they approach me. Why?

Now a door creaks, almost imperceptibly: and that's the dining-room door, I recognize the sound. So the person, the intruder, whoever it might be – surely Angus? – is slowly approaching me, in this bedroom. I have to speed up: fervently I lock the middle drawer, then I go to lock the top drawer, but the key slips through my perspiring fingers and I fumble, desperate, flailing, on the floorboards – the room is now dark, as the winter light falls outside – so where, where is the key? I am kneeling in my jeans in the dust like a burglar, this is pathetic, and wrong. But I must find the key.

Here. Biting back my panic, I lock the top drawer, slip the key in its hiding place and then I stand up, turn around, and smooth down my shirt and try to look normal as the footsteps come right to the doorway, and the bedroom door swings slowly open.

Nothing.

I stare at the empty rectangle, that gives on to the hall. A bad painting of a Scottish dancer stares at me. In the silence.

'Hello?'

Silence.

'Hello??'

Silence like a howl, like a shriek. My heart is the noisiest thing in the house. Thumping. Who is in the building, and how are they playing this game? Why would they want to scare me? I definitely heard foot-steps, this was no illusion. Someone is in here.

'Hello? Who is it? Who is there? Who is it?'

Nothing.

'Stop this! Angus? Lydia? Stop it.'

The darkness intensifies; the wintry afternoon light fades so quickly on cloudy days. Why didn't I turn on the lights before I began? The house is shrouded. The sea breathes in and out, exhausted. Very slowly I walk to the door, and peer out. The hall waits for me. Empty. I can see the shapes of furniture in the living room. The light is so murky. And it is so unbelievably cold. Torran Cottage is always chilly but this is exceptional. I realize I am shivering.

I lean and switch on the bedroom light, but it is feeble, sixty watts. Not much better than a yellow moon.

'My Bonnie lies over the ocean,'

It's a girl's voice. Coming from Lydia's bedroom.

'My Bonnie lies over the sea –'

But it's Kirstie's voice. Because I know that tune: it's Kirstie's favourite tune. The Scottish ballad her father loved to sing to her. Kirstie's voice is muffled and distant, yet lilting and happy.

'Bring back, bring back, O bring back my Bonnie to me . . .'

I grip myself. It cannot be Kirstie, of course. She is dead.

So this must be Lydia, in her room, pretending to be Kirstie. But how did she get in her room? Why is she here? Did Angus bring her over early? Why is she singing like Kirstie?

'Lydia! Lydia!' I am running to the bedroom, the door is shut; I press the door, and turn the knob, and I painfully hesitate at the last moment – filled with the obscene fear that I am going to see Kirstie in here. In her blue bobble hat. Buoyant, joking, bouncy. Alive. Or maybe she will be broken on the bed, bleeding and dying, as she was in Devon, after the fall. *A blooded body, singing.*

My daydreams are nightmares.

Taking a hold of myself, I push open the door and I scan the room and there's Lydia, in her school uniform, under her thick pink anorak, staring soulfully out of the window, at the sea, and the coast down to Ardvasar, gathering its darkness, under the starless sky. Her room is weirdly cold.

'But, Lydia, darling – why?'

She turns and smiles sadly at me. Her school uniform is still too big, she looks lonely as I have ever seen her; my heart throbs with sympathy.

'Were you singing?'

'Kirstie was singing,' she says, simply. 'Like she used to. I was listening and playing. She's gone now.'

I ignore this announcement. Because I can't bear the implications. My daughter really is going mad. So I ask questions, instead.

'What are you doing here? Lydia?' I look at my watch, its only three p.m.: her school will only just be emptying. 'Lydia? Lyddie-lo? What happened? How did— I don't— Why?'

'It was me. I brought her over.'

Angus's dark baritone breaks the spell. He is standing in the doorway, tall and looming.

'I got a call from the school.' My husband eyes me, significantly. His brown V-neck jumper is dusty. 'Called me about Lydia. Wanted me to pick her up.' He looks around Lydia's spartan bedroom, the cuddly toy giraffe toppled on the bed, the Charlie and Lola book on the floor.

'Christ,' he says. 'Why is it so cold in here? We have to fix the heating.'

240

He is frowning at me, in a meaningful way. I give Lydia a little hug and she smiles blankly, again, and then we, the caring parents, step outside. Angus and I close the door and we are standing next to each other, in the hall, and I feel as if I want to back away from him, he is too near, too tall, too male.

Angus says, 'The school secretary called me, they couldn't reach you, they said Lydia was very unhappy. Totally freaking. Because Emily Durrant refused to sit in the same class as her, and then lots of other kids did the same. They asked me to pick her up early.'

'But, why—'

'They want us to keep her out of school for a week.' He sighs, in a firm way; and rubs his stubbled chin. He looks older. Tired. His brown eyes seek mine. 'I've tried to get her to talk about it. But you know what she's like, Lydia, she can be so bloody silent.' He pauses, just enough to insult.

I want to hit him. I haven't forgotten the book. *Imogen Evertsen?* But my overriding thought is Lydia.

'Why a week? What's going to happen then?'

He shrugs. 'Don't know. They just said they want things to calm down. Anyway, I picked her up and brought her home.'

'Did you sneak into the house – I just – you gave me the fright—'

'Didn't realize anyone was here, to be honest. Lights were all out.'

He is lying. Again. I know it. *He is lying.* His eyes fix on mine. Maybe he knows I was looking in the chest. And perhaps he knows that I found the book, *and he doesn't care.* But what about Lydia? What must she be feeling now?

'I have to talk to her.'

'No, I'm not sure that—'

Pushing his big, controlling hand away, I creak open Lydia's door. She is sitting on her bed, her eyes glassy, reading the Charlie and Lola book again. As she used to do, years back. It must be like comfort food. She wants something reassuring. I wish her room had more light; and more heat. This cold is abominable.

'Lydia, what happened at school?'

She stays quiet, reading.

'Darling, I need to know if anyone did anything bad to you.'

Only the sea is talking, whispering to the sands and the rocks.

'Lydia . . .' I sit down on the side of the bed, and stroke her arm. 'Lydia. Please talk to me.'

'Nothing.'

There it is. Again. The discernible voice of her mother.

'Lydie-lo, please—'

'Nothing.' Her face lifts and her eyes burn. 'Nothing! Nothing happened!'

I stroke her arm again, but she reacts with greater fury.

'Go away!'

Lydia is screaming at me. Her pale, pretty face is pink with anger, and scrunched with loathing. 'Go away, I hate you, I hate you—'

'Lyd—'

I reach out another hand but Lydia slaps it, hard, much harder than I knew she could: the pain is quite stinging.

'GO AWAYYYYYY!'

'OK.' I stand. 'OK.'

'GO AWAYYYY!'

'OK, I'm going.'

And I am, I am retreating. Pitiful and defeated, the worst of mothers. I go to the door, and open it, and shut it behind me, leaving my daughter alone in her room. I can hear her sobbing like the sea, keening like the seagulls on Camuscross; there is nothing I can do.

I look at the door, it says *Lydia Lives HERE* and *Keep Out* in golden spangled letters. I resist the urge for tears. What's my crying going to do? How can my emotions help? A deep, quiet voice intrudes.

'I heard.'

Angus is standing three yards down the hall, at the open door to the living room. I can hear a woodfire crackling, and see warming lights.

'Hey.'

His arms are open. He wants to hug me. I want to slap him. Very hard. And yet, a part of me wants his hugs.

Because I still want sex.

If anything, I want sex *more*. I do. I think this is probably jealousy sex. It's that book signed by Imogen. It's made me jealous, but more desirous. I want to possess him, mark him, prove that he's still mine. The way he once repossessed me.

I also just want sex. We never have enough.

He comes close.

'There's nothing we can do, you're doing your best.' He comes closer still. 'She's confused, of course. But she will get better. She will. But maybe she needs help. Maybe we all need help. Perhaps you ought to speak to that guy again, the one in Glasgow. What was it? Kellaway?'

His hand is reaching for mine, I can see that he wants it as well.

Softening my gaze, I open my lips, and I lift my face

to his; and he sinks his mouth onto mine. And we are kissing as we have not kissed in a month. Perhaps three months.

And now we are stripping. Feverishly. Teenagerishly. I rip his jumper up, and off; he is unbuttoning the studs of my jeans. We topple, giddily, into the living room, he is picking me up, carrying me, and I want to be carried. *Just do it, Angus Moorcroft. Fuck me.*

He fucks me. This is good. This is what I want. Him taking me, like it was, like we used to. I don't want foreplay, I don't want fooling around; I want him inside me, resolving any doubts, just for a few minutes.

His kisses are strong and deep. He bites my shoulder as he turns me over, and fucks me again; I grasp at the pillows. Listening to him kissing me, biting me.

'I love you, Sarah.'

'Fuck you—'

'Sarah.'

I gasp into the pillow. 'Harder.'

'Ah.'

He has a hand around my neck, pressing my head into the pillow, as if he is going to break it, with one snap, I look around, and I can see the angry glitter in his eyes; so I push up, and push back, push him out of me; I turn over. I am hot and shining with sweat, and bruised, and ready to come, I take his hand and put it round my slender neck again.

'Fuck me like you fucked Imogen.'

He says nothing. He does not even blink. His thumb is light yet firm on the narrowness of my throat. My windpipe. He could press. He is strong enough. Instead he looks hard and furious into my eyes, and he rises up and pushes me back and he enters me again, and I say:

'Did she come? Did she come when you fucked her? Was it like this?'

He fucks me, his strong hand on my white neck, and I imagine him fucking her, fucking my best friend, and I want to hate him, and I hate him. But even as I hate him the orgasm comes, my orgasm, dizzying and irresistible.

As my own orgasm pulses away, ripples into nothing, he comes too: slumping forward, then not breathing, then breathing hard. Then receding. He slumps to my side. Two hearts beating, and the sea outside the window.

'I never had an affair with Imogen,' he says.

19

'There's a book, in your chest of drawers. Signed by her.'

We are both lying back, naked, perspiring, under the duvet, facing the ceiling. With that huge patch of damp, which looks bigger in the feeble light from the bedside lamp.

The twilight has turned to darkness; the window is open to the starlit sea.

'You looked?' he says.

'It was signed. It said *Love, Immy. Kiss kiss kiss.*'

He says nothing.

I turn, briefly, and glance at him, his handsome profile, silent, and staring upwards, like one of those knights on tombs in churches, carved in stone. Then I lie back, too, and gaze up.

'She gave you a novel. About adultery? You never read novels. She signed it with love and kisses. Now tell me you're *not* fucking her.'

'I'm not,' he says. 'Not sleeping with her. Not having an affair with her.'

And yet there is a pause here. Fatal, and revealing. He sighs, and goes on: 'But we did sleep together once.'

247

The cold breeze kicks at the half-drawn curtains.

I control myself. And ask the obvious question: 'When was this, Angus? Was it that night?'

'The night of the accident?' I sense him turn, towards me, across the pillow. 'No, Sarah. Jesus. No!! Everything I said back then was true. I just stopped by, I was just coming back from work. You have to believe me.'

I hesitate. Maybe I do believe him, on this point. He sounds halfway convincing.

But . . .

'But you said you did. With her?'

He sighs, again. 'It was afterwards, Sarah, after Kirstie fell. You were so, you know, so wrapped in your grief – mad with grief.'

'And you weren't?'

'No. Not saying that, course not. God. I was just as bad, I know, in my own way, all the booze. But you were untouchable. Wouldn't let me near you.'

I don't remember this. Don't remember being *untouchable*. But I will let it go, for now.

'So you turned to Imogen? My best friend? For someone to cuddle?'

'I just needed a female friend. You were out of reach. And we were always close, Immy and me, always got on. I mean – she was there the night we met, remember?'

I refuse to look at him. I gaze at the ceiling. I can hear a solitary bird outside. Piping and skirling. I see now why Imogen Evertsen stuck with me, when so many other friends fell away. She felt guilty. But her guilt made our friendship awkward: and for ever different.

'I still need to know.' Half turning. 'Tell me, Angus. When you slept with her.'

He takes a long breath.

'It was . . . I was in pieces, maybe a month after the

accident. We'd had a few bottles. We were talking. And she started . . . she leaned over and she kissed me. She was the one who, y'know, did that. And yes, I responded, but . . . But then I didn't, Sarah. I stopped her after the first night. I said no.'

'And the book?'

'She sent it a week after. Don't know why.'

I muse. So Angus stopped her. So what? At what point did he call a halt? Did they do it all night? A weekend? Did they kiss and laugh in the morning? Do I care? I am less vengeful than expected; more indifferent. This is just so weak. I have gone from fearing to despising my husband. And yet even now, as I want him away from me, I wonder what I would do without him: as we are stuck on this island.

I still need him, practically, even as I revile him.

'Sarah, I wanted a friend. To talk about the accident. Listen. Believe me. But Imogen got confused. Afterwards, she was wracked with guilt. Really truly.'

'How jolly fucking nice of her. To feel guilty. For screwing my husband.'

'I didn't want an affair. What else can I say?'

'Why did you keep the book?'

'Can't remember. Just did. Sarah, this is the truth. I never wanted anything serious and when she got romantic I said it wasn't going to happen and since then, she and me, we've just been friends, and she still loves you, she really does, she feels terrible that it even got that far.'

'Must send her a thank you card. Maybe give her a book?'

He is gazing away from me, now, gazing at the sea through the window. I can sense this. Corner of my eyes. He speaks,

'You seem to forget. I once forgave you.'

My anger is instant.

'You mean my so-called "affair"? Really?'

'Sarah—'

'After the birth?? After you ignored me for a year, when you just pissed off and left me surrounded by nappies, by two screaming twins? Totally alone?'

'I still forgave you.'

'But that wasn't your *best friend* I fucked. Was it, Angus? Did I fuck your *best friend*? Did I? Did I fuck your best friend right after your child died?'

He is silent, and then he says,

'OK. You think this is different. I get it.'

'Well done you.'

'But please, maybe get some perspective.'

'*What?*'

'Nothing really happened, anyway, Sarah. Nothing emotional. So you can hate me, and you can hate Imogen – but hate us for what we actually did – not what you think we did.'

'I think I'll work out who to hate, all by myself.'

'Sarah!'

Ignoring him, I rise from the bed and slip on my thick woollen dressing gown. The floorboards are scratchy and cold on my bare feet. I walk to the window. The moon is high over the Small Isles. A cloudless night in early winter. It should be beautiful. And it is beautiful. This place is so relentlessly fucking beautiful, it never stops. Whatever else is happening, the beauty goes on, like a terrible nightmare.

Angus makes more excuses, but I am barely listening.

For the first time, I see Angus as something truly inferior to what he was. Less masculine, less of a man, less of a husband, just so much less. I would probably walk out the door, right now, with Lydia, if I could.

But I cannot. I have nowhere to go: my best friend Imogen is no longer my best friend; my parents' house has too many memories.

We are trapped on Torran, financially, for now. I am trapped with my adulterous husband. Maybe in time I will forgive him. Perhaps three decades will do it.

'Sarah,' he says, again, like he will never stop saying it. But I walk out of the bedroom and into the kitchen, because I am hungry.

I make myself toast. And sit at the dining table. Munching mechanically, fuelling myself. Staring at the telephone. Thinking about Lydia.

I know I've got to call Kellaway: on that subject Angus is quite correct. I need to speak to Kellaway. I need to speak to him as soon as possible. I need his expert opinion on the strangeness. What is happening to my daughter? Maybe he could help with my so-called marriage. Is my lying husband still concealing something else?

Angus and I have one more confrontation in the evening. I am sitting in the living room, looking out at the rain. I used to like this rain sweeping up the Sound from the Point of Sleat. It made everything, somehow, into a sad Gaelic song: liquid and soft, lyrical yet indecipherable; the landscape was like a beautiful, disappearing language.

Now the rain just irks me.

Angus comes into the living room, a glass of Scotch in his hand. He's been taking the dog for a walk. Beany slumps by the fire, chewing his favourite bone-toy, and Angus falls into the armchair.

'Beany caught a rat,' he says.

'Only three thousand to go then.'

He smiles, briefly, but I do not smile. His smile disappears.

The fire crackles. The wind laments the state of the roof.

'Listen,' he says – leaning forward, annoyingly.

'I don't want to listen.'

'Imogen. And me. It was just one night. Really. Just a drunken mistake.'

'But you had sex. With my best friend. A month after our daughter died.'

'But—'

'Angus, there are no buts. You betrayed me.'

A dark flash of anger crosses his face. '*I* betrayed *you*?'

'Yes. In the worst possible way. As I was grieving.'

'Look—'

'It was a betrayal. Wasn't it? Or would you call it something else? What would that be, Angus? How would you phrase it? "Building my support network"?'

He says nothing, though he looks as if he wants to say a lot. The teeth are grinding in his mouth, I can see the muscles moving.

'Gus, I want you to sleep in the spare bed.'

He slugs whisky, wholesale. And shrugs. 'Sure. Why the fuck not? We've got lots of spare beds.'

'Don't give me that self-pitying shit. Not now.'

He laughs. With deep bitterness, and gazes at me, directly. 'Did you read all of *Anna Karenina*? You read everything you found?'

'I saw the inscription, Angus. Why? Did she put love-hearts halfway through?'

He exhales – and shakes his head. He looks very sad. He leans and morosely tickles the ear of his much-loved dog. I resist the urge to feel sorry for him.

Angus sleeps, as ordered, in one of the spare beds. In the morning I lie under the duvet and listen to him bathing and dressing, then gathering paperwork, plans for his precious house in Ord; I wait for the low churning sound of the outboard motor, indicating his departure. Then I rise, make breakfast for Lydia, get dressed, and prepare myself.

Lydia is on the sofa reading Wimpy Kid. She is off school, of course. Until things calm down. The idea of things ever being calm seems pitiable in its absurdity.

Closing the door that divides the living room from the dining room, I pick up the big clunky old phone. I dial Kellaway's office – but he is not there. His secretary tells me he's working from home this week. She won't, of course, give me his home number. *Give us your number and he will call back in a few days.*

But I'm not waiting for a few days. I need to talk to him right now. So I dial Directory Enquiries.

Who knows. I might get lucky, I deserve some luck.

I have a vague sense where Kellaway lives, an upmarket part of Glasgow. Imogen mentioned it; she visited him there, when she interviewed him.

Imogen. My ex-friend. Bitch.

My call gets through: I ask for a Dr M. Kellaway, in Glasgow. How many can there be? Surely only one, or two. It just depends whether he is ex-directory.

And my luck, it seems, pays out.

'M. Kellaway, Doctor, 49 Glasnevin Street; 0141 4339 7398.'

I scribble the number; the phone line hisses.

It's a cold Tuesday afternoon in December. He could be Christmas shopping with his wife. He could be skiing in the Cairngorms. I have no idea.

'Hello. Malcolm Kellaway?'

253

More luck. He is at home.

Now I have to ride this luck: I just have to dive straight in.

'Hi, Dr Kellaway. I'm so sorry to bother you at home but it is rather urgent and – well – I'm desperate, really desperate and I need your help.'

A long, static-filled pause. Then: 'Is that Mrs Moorcroft? Sarah Moorcroft?'

'Yes!'

'I see.' His voice-tone is mildly tetchy. 'How can I help?'

I have already asked myself the same: how is he going to help? And my answer is: by listening. I need to share this frightening drama. I want him to listen to everything that has happened since I last saw him.

And so, like a woman on her deathbed urgently dictating her will, I stand by the dining-room window, watching the ravens flustering above the shell-sands of Salmadair – and I tell him the lot: the scream, the tantrum with Sally Ferguson, the bloody smashed window, the fact Angus knew. The hysterical reaction from Emily Durrant. The horrors of the school. Even 'My Bonnie Lies Over the Ocean'. I tell him everything.

I expect him to be astonished. Maybe he is astonished. But his voice remains cool, and professorial.

'I see. Yes.'

'So what's your advice, Dr Kellaway? Please tell me. We're desperate here, Lydia is breaking up, in front of me, my family is falling apart, everything is falling apart.'

'Ideally we need a consultation, a discussion of therapies, we must go over things properly, Mrs Moorcroft.'

'Yes, but what advice can you give me now, here, right here, right now, PLEASE.'

'Please be calm.'

I'm not calm. I can hear the waves, outside. What would it be like, if one day they just stopped?

Kellaway goes on, 'Whether your daughter is Lydia, or Kirstie, I, of course, cannot say, if you believe that she is Lydia, and she accepts that, and you've been through all these adjustments – then yes, it is probably best to persist with that assumption, now, whatever the truth.'

'But what do we do about the strangeness, the singing, the mirrors, the – the – the—'

'You really want my opinion now, this way? Over the phone?

'*Yes.*'

'Very well. Here is one possibility. Sometimes the loss of a twin in childhood can produce in the surviving twin a kind of, ah, hatred of the parents – this is because the child implicitly trusts her parents, believing in their capacity to take care of her. So you see? When a twin dies, this parental ability to keep the child safe appears to fail, catastrophically, and this can be perceived, by the surviving twin, as something the parent should have prevented. This is true of all siblings, but extremely true of monozygotic twins.'

'What does *that* mean?'

'Lydia may be retreating from you because she blames you and mistrusts you. She may even be punishing you.'

'You're saying – she could be making stuff up to scare us? To trouble us? Because she thinks we are to blame for her sister's death?'

'Yes and no. These are just possibilities. You asked me for my opinion, and these are just that: opinions. Ideas. And . . . well . . .'

'What?'

'We really need to talk face to face.'

'No. Please. Tell me now. What about all this stuff, stuff about reflections, and photos?'

'Mirrors are known to be extremely perplexing for twins, at any time, likewise photos, as we have already discussed. But there are other factors to consider.'

'Yes?'

'Let me look at my notes, on my computer. I made them after your last visit.'

I wait. I am staring out to the Sound. I can see a crab boat puttering up the way to Loch na Dal, towards that white-painted hunting lodge: Kinloch. Where the Macdonalds live: the Macdonalds of Macdonald, Lords of the Isles since AD 1200. There is so much history here; there is too much history here. I am starting to hate it. I wanted a clean slate. A new break. This isn't it.

Too much history.

'Yes,' says Kellaway. 'Here we are. A surviving twin may also feel guilty after the death – guilty that he or, of course, she, was chosen to live. This much is self-evident. But this guilt is made worse if the parents seemed to have preferred the other child to live. It is all too easy for parents to idealize the dead child, especially if, in reality, they *did* prefer the dead child. So I have to ask, did either you or Angus have a favourite? Was there some preference for one daughter over another, did, for instance, her father prefer Kirstie?'

'Yes,' I say. Numbed.

'Then . . .' Kellaway falls uncharacteristically quiet. 'In that case, we must also look at other concerns.' He sighs. The dodgy phone line flares with white noise. Then he goes on, 'Of course depression is heightened in fathers and mothers of twins compared to singletons, and this is terribly compounded if one twin dies.

256

Especially if the parents themselves feel guilty. And then there's, well . . .'

'What?'

'We know the rate of suicide is elevated in co-twins who lose a twin.'

'You're saying Lydia could kill herself?'

The boat has disappeared, the herring gulls cry and complain.

'Well, it is possible. And there are other possibilities. Robert Samuels, the child psychiatrist, his theories are also relevant. But—'

'Sorry? Who? What?'

'No.' His voice is firm now. 'Mrs Moorcroft, I absolutely have to stop here. Samuels is it. I've really gone as far as I can over the phone. I'm sorry. I cannot go any further, professionally, in this ad hoc way. You really do need to come in to see me. Quite urgently. These things are far too delicate and complex to talk about, so casually, on the phone. Please call me when I am back at work, next Monday, and arrange a consultation, as soon as possible. Mrs Moorcroft? Will you do that? I will clear my diary for you next week. It is imperative you come and see me very soon. And bring Lydia.'

'OK, OK, yes. Thank you.'

'Very good. Now please stay calm. Keep your daughter calm, keep everything civil in your domestic situation, wait until you see me. Next week.'

What is he saying? He thinks I am panicking? – that I am losing control?

I am not losing control: I am angry.

Muttering a Yes and a Thanks, I put the phone down and gaze out at the Sound. Thinking hard.

So what did all that other stuff mean? Favourite kids? Preferred children? Suicide??

I go back into the living room. Lydia is asleep on the sofa, the book has fallen from her hands. She looks exhausted, and unhappy, even in her sleep. Fetching a blanket from a cupboard, I lay it over her, and kiss her frowning, unconscious forehead.

Her blonde hair is tousled; I prefer her hair like this, slightly wild. It offsets the formal, symmetric prettiness of her face. She and Kirstie were always pretty. Angus and I would revel in it. Everyone adored the pretty Moorcroft twins. Back in the day.

The fire needs banking up: I take some logs from the basket and lodge them in the flames. As I watch the flames grow, and regain, licking and spitting, the thoughts churn in my mind. Angus and Kirstie, Angus and Kirstie.

We still have to endure Kirstie's funeral. On Friday. She was *his* favourite.

20

'We brought nothing into this world, and it is certain we can carry nothing out. The Lord gave, and the Lord hath taken away.'

I do not believe any of this. But then, I cannot believe reality: that I am in another church having a different funeral for the daughter who *really* died. I cannot believe my family has collapsed. That everything has turned to ashes.

The vicar intones. I gaze around. Helpless now.

The church is Kilmore, half a mile down the coast from Lydia's primary. It is Victorian: dour and plain in the Scottish way, with an austere nave, bare oak pews, and three tall arched windows letting in a strained, meagre sunlight.

There are about twenty people inside, locals and family gathered with the dead, sitting in the uncomfortable pews, under the metal memorials to the sons of Lord and Lady Macdonald of Sleat: killed in Ypres and Gallipoli, South Africa and at sea; four sons of the British Empire, slain but not forgotten.

All the dead children.

'Lord, let me know mine end, and the number of my days.'

Angus told me – before we essentially stopped talking – that he'd had trouble finding a priest to do this job. The local vicar, or reverend, or preceptor, or whatever they term him, was apparently unkeen. It was all too strange and unsettling; maybe improper. Two funerals for one dead child?

But a friendly priest from Broadford was persuaded by Josh and Molly, and this church was the obvious choice – sad, but nobly situated, looking out to the waves, staring across the graveyard towards distant Mallaig, and wistful Moidart.

I Googled it a little. It has a history of druidic worship, and clannish violence. A previous church stands in the damp green precinct outside, but it is eroded by the Hebridean wind and rain into a ruin.

Now we stand in the last, Victorian church, my mother next to Lydia, just down the pew, with Angus, tall in his dark London suit, between us. His tie is not quite black. It has tiny red polka dots. I hate them. I hate him. Or at least, I no longer love him. He is sleeping permanently in another bedroom.

Lydia is dressed entirely in black. Black dress, black socks, black shoes. Black sets off her blonde hair and pale skin. Black and ice. She seems calm for the moment. Unruffled. Yet the trouble is still there, a sparkle of sadness in her eyes, like the promise of snow on a clear winter's day.

My mother has her arm draped protectively across Lydia's shoulders. I look down the pew to my surviving daughter, to smile at her, encouragingly. But she does not notice me: she is gazing at the bible in front of her, flicking its pages with her small hands, which still show the tiny complex scars from when she smashed the Freedlands' window. She is engrossed.

Lydia is such a reader.

The priest continues, saying his special words:

'O spare me a little, that I may recover my strength, before I go hence, and be no more seen.'

This sentence makes me want to cry; my tears have been brimming since the service began and they are now close to breaking, to overtipping me. To trick myself into not crying, I pick up a copy of the same bible Lydia is holding, and read what she is reading.

Am Bioball Gaidhlig.

The bible is in Gaelic.

Is Lydia really reading this? How can she understand Gaelic? Her school is bilingual but she has, of course, only been there a couple of weeks, and she is off school at the moment. Yet as I stare down the pew there she is: reading, absorbed, eyes flickering left to right, apparently reading Gaelic.

Perhaps she is just pretending to read, perhaps like me she is trying to distract herself, so she doesn't have to think about this funeral. And why not? Arguably, she shouldn't even be here: I wondered about keeping her away from the ceremony, to save her the distress; but then that seemed even more wrong than her being present: for the funeral of her twin sister.

'Lord, thou hast been our refuge, from one generation to another.'

I close my eyes for a second.

'Thou turnest man to destruction; again thou sayest, Come again, ye children of men.'

How long can I stall the tears?

I see Angus glancing across at me. Disapprovingly. He never really wanted this funeral. Yet, despite his reluctance, I let him organize pretty much everything to do with the service: I let Angus organize the priest, and sort out the death certificates, and notify the authorities of The Confusion. But I chose the liturgy. It is the same liturgy we had at Lydia's funeral – Lydia who is now standing under my mother's arm, two yards away, in this cold grey Victorian Gothic church that stares down the Sound towards Ardnamurchan.

The strangeness is immersive. It is as if we have all fallen into the cold deep waters of Lochalsh, where the eerie seaweeds dance and sway: languid, and bewitched.

'Out of the deep have I called unto thee, O Lord. Lord, hear my voice.'

Hear my voice? Whose voice? Lydia's? Kirstie's? I look around the church at the congregation. There are voices here I barely know: locals I have hardly spoken to. Molly and Josh gathered them, I think, to make up the numbers. They are here out of distant sympathy. *Oh, that poor couple, with the twins, the terrible mistake, we have to go, we can have lunch at the Duisdale afterwards, they do the scallops.*

There is my dad at the end of the pew, in his dusty black suit, which he wears these days only for funerals. He looks old and jowly, his once dark lustrous hair is now completely white, and sparse. His watery blue eyes still have a glint, though, and when he sees me looking across, he gives me a weak yet hopeful smile, trying to reassure, to comfort. He also looks guilty.

That's because my dad feels guilty about everything. The way he shouted at us kids when we were young. The way he was unfaithful to my mum and the way she stood by him nonetheless – making him feel guiltier. All that guilty drinking which damaged his career, which made him more resentful, a vicious cycle of very male frustration.

Like Angus.

And then Dad stopped the shouting and drinking, and he retired with what little he'd kept. And he learned to make Portuguese *cataplana* in the big kitchen at Instow. Where his great joy was the Twins, and their many happy holidays in Devon.

'I am the resurrection and the life, saith the Lord: he that believeth in me, though he were dead, yet shall he live.'

Something buried deep within me echoes this passage, quite ardently, because in my case it is literally true: even as my other daughter dies, for the second time, my Lydia is resurrected. Born again. And standing six feet away, reading a Gaelic bible, with scarred fingers.

I grasp at the railing of the pew. Keeping it together. Just keeping it together.

'Please rise.'

We are standing to sing a psalm and I stutter out the words, and I look at Molly across the aisle of the church, and she blushes – and gives me another one of those small, humble, you-can-get-through-it expressions; the same expression that everyone is wearing when they look at me.

'Merciful Father, whose face the angels of thy little ones do always behold in heaven; Grant us steadfastly to believe that this thy child hath been taken into the safekeeping of thine eternal love.'

It's nearly over. I am making it through. My little Kirstie, my little daughter, is being released. Her death is acknowledged, her soul is unclutched and sent to join the clouds that rinse the Red Cuillins. And again I don't believe any of this. Kirstie is probably still here. In her own way. In her twin.

The priest is stiffening his words as we approach the climax.

'O God, whose most dear Son did take little children into his arms and bless them; Give us grace, we beseech thee, to entrust the soul of this child, Kirstie Moorcroft, to thy never failing care and love.'

I have a tissue in my left hand and I am crushing it, with my fist, to stop myself crying.

Nearly done, Sarah, nearly there. I remember this so well. There's just one more line. Everything is repeated. And everything ends.

'The grace of our Lord Jesus Christ, and the love of God, and the fellowship of the Holy Ghost, be with us all evermore. Amen.'

The funeral is over, the ordeal is complete.

Now I'm crying. As we file out into the refined and delicate drizzle of a December day in Skye, my tears fall unabated. The swathes of rain are sweeping down the Sound, from Shiel Bridge to Ardvasar. Veiling and unveiling. I see Josh talking to Angus, my dad is holding Lydia's hand. My mum is stumbling; I wish my damn brother was here to help, but he is trawling salmon in Alaska. We think.

So let the tears fall. Like the endless sleet over Sgurr nan Gillean.

'It's such a view—'

'Yes. And such a pity.'

'Well now, Mrs Moorcroft, please don't be strangers, come over any time.'

'I hope the wee one is happy at the school. Hear we've bad weather coming!'

I stammer my answers, bewildered. My black heels

scrunching in the damp gravel of the churchyard path. Who are these people? With their pleasant fibs and lying pleasantries? I am nonetheless grateful for their presence, to stave off the moment. As long as there are people around, the terrible climax – which I know is coming – is temporarily postponed; so I shake hands and accept consolations, then I climb in a car by the church gate and Josh drives me and Lydia to the Selkie, where he and Molly have helped us arrange a kind of wake. Angus is driving my parents. He probably wants to do this so he can bicker with my dad in the car.

I sit in the back of Josh's car with Lydia, my arm around her slender shoulders. My daughter in black.

As Josh takes a curve, Lydia tugs at my sleeve, and says, 'Mummy, am I invisible now?'

I am so used to the strangeness I am barely fussed. I just shrug. And say: 'Let's look for otters later.'

The car pulls off the main road and rolls down to Ornsay village, with Torran looking beautiful beyond. A break in the clouds is shining a light directly on our white cottage and our white lighthouse, with Knoydart and Sandaig forbidding, and grey, beyond: the scene is so dramatic it is as if Torran is floodlit.

An empty stage, impatiently awaiting the actors. For the final scene.

Where am I going? A wake?

Can you have a wake for a person who has been dead over a year? Perhaps it is just an excuse for everyone to drown themselves in Old Pretender Beer, and Poit Dhubh whisky.

My dad, of course, needs little excuse. Twenty minutes after we have gathered in the pub he is downing his third or fourth very large glass and I can see the tiny beads of sweat on his forehead as he squabbles with

265

Angus. They've never got on. Two would-be alpha males. A clash of antlers in the forests of Waternish.

The tension of this moment has only made their antagonism worse. I hover at the edge of their conversation, wondering if I should try to make peace, wondering if I can be bothered. Dad is holding up his glass of pure malt Scotch, to the wintry light from the window.

'Here is the outcome of the mystical alchemy of distillation, turning the rain-pure water into that golden liquid of life, of the immortal Gaels.'

Angus looks at him. 'Prefer gin.'

Dad says: 'How *are* the loft extensions, Angus?'

'Grand, David, grand.'

'Guess this kind of local architecture, this vernacular stuff, it must allow you a lot of time off so you can come down here for a snifter.'

'Yeah. It's ideal for an alcoholic like me.'

My dad glowers. Angus glowers right back.

'So, aye, David, have you stopped making the TV commercials – what was it, tampons?'

How can they still be bickering? Today? After a child's funeral? But then again, why should they stop? Why not just carry on? Nothing is ever going to stop, it is all going to get worse and worse, until. Perhaps they are right to just carry on as they have always carried on: their mild and mutual dislike is a kind of normality, something comforting and reliable.

But even if they're not going to cease, I've heard enough of this verbal skirmishing for three lifetimes. Turning to my left, I see my mother standing just yards away, glass of red wine in hand. I walk over, and tilt a frown at Dad and Angus. 'They're at it again.'

'Darling, they like it. You know that.' She puts a

266

wrinkled hand on my arm. Her dreaming blue eyes are as bright as ever though; bright as my daughter's. 'I'm so glad that's over. You did well, Sarah. I was proud of you. No mother should have to go through what you've been through.' A glug of wine. 'Two funerals? Two!'

'Mum.'

'And what about you? Are you feeling better now? Darling? You know – inside? Are you and Angus OK?'

I don't want to get into this. Not today. Not now.

'We're OK.'

'Are you sure? It's just that you seem, I don't know, there's some tension, isn't there?'

I gaze back. Unblinking.

'Mum. We're fine.' What should I tell her? Hey, Mum, turns out my husband slept with my best friend, maybe a month after my daughter died? At least no one, here, has mentioned the marked absence of Imogen from the funeral; perhaps they sense the fracture. I did get several imploring emails from Imogen – and ignored them all.

My mother gleans the meaning from my silence, and moves on. Nervously.

'So, has the move helped? It is such a lovely spot here, despite all the weather you have. I can entirely see why you love it so.'

I nod; and my mother babbles away: 'And Lydia. Lydia! Of course it is terrible to say, but there is a chance, darling, that now Lydia is alone she may lead a more normal life, you know, twins are so different, now she is more normal, in the most terrible way, of course.'

'I suppose.' Part of me wants to be offended by this, but I do not have the energy. Maybe my mum is right.

267

She sips too much wine and a little dribbles down her chin, and she goes on:

'And of course they fought didn't they? Lydia and Kirstie? I remember you telling me, Lydia was the weaker one, in the womb, don't twins fight for nutrition? They were great friends, inseparable, but they certainly fought for your attention, and Kirstie complained more, didn't she?'

What is all this about? It barely matters; I am hardly listening. I can see Lydia at the edge of things. Lydia, standing in the doorway of the Selkie looking out, through the glass door at the rain.

How is she coping? What is she thinking? She is as alone as a human can be. The love and pity rises in me as nausea, once more, and I quit talking with my mum, and push through the drinkers to Lydia.

'Lydia, are you OK?'

She turns and gives me a brief smile. 'I'm still here, Mummy, but I'm not. Not any more.'

I stifle my pained response, and smile back. 'Are you annoyed by the rain?'

She frowns. Not understanding. I take her softly scarred hand and kiss it, and brush her pink cheek.

'Sweetheart. You're looking at the rain.'

'Oh,' she says, blankly. 'No. Not the rain actually, Mummy.' She points at the door, her thin arm elegant and somehow adult, in that long-sleeved black dress, 'I was just talking to Kirstie in the car, Mummy: she was in the mirror Daddy uses.'

'But—'

'But now she's gone, and I remember the priest saying she has gone to heaven, and I wanted to ask him where it was.'

'Lydia—'

'And no one would tell me, so I searched for Kirstie, Mummy, because I don't think she's in heaven, she's in here. With us, isn't she? Remember how we played hide and seek, Mummy, in London. Remember?'

Oh yes. I remember. The memory makes me sadder than sad. But I have to stay sane for Lydia.

'Of course, darling.'

'So I thought she was playing hide and seek again. And I looked in all the places like we used to hide when playing hide and seek at home, Mummy. But Kirstie was squeezed behind the wardrobe thingy over there.'

'What?'

'Yes, Mummy, I felt her hand.'

I gaze at my daughter. 'You felt your sister's hand?'

'Yes, Mummy, and it was scary. I have never felt her before. I don't want to find her if she is going to touch me, it's too scary.'

This is too scary for *me,* let alone my daughter.

'Lydia . . .'

How can I calm her? I have no idea. Because Lydia seems to be regressing. She is talking more like a five-year-old in her perplexity.

I need a child psychologist. I'll have an appointment with Kellaway, next week. But can I last until then?

'Mummy, do you ever talk to Kirstie?'

'Sorry?'

'Can you ever hear her or see her? I know she wants to talk to you.'

How can I distract my daughter? Perhaps I should ask her questions. Perhaps I should ask her some *serious* questions? It would, after all, be difficult to make things more distressing.

'Come on,' I say. 'Let's go outside. There may be otters by the pier.'

269

There won't be otters by the pier, but I want to talk to her alone. Obediently, Lydia follows me out, into the chilly afternoon air. The drizzle has gone, leaving a ghost of dampness behind. Together we walk to the pier, and kneel down on the moist concrete, and gaze at the rocks and shingle, the complex seaweeds wafting in the tide.

I've tried to learn the names of these seaweeds: scentless mayweed, sea milkwort, sea holly – the tidal shoreline plants. Similarly, I've tried to learn the names of the little fish that live in Torran's rock pools: the shanny, the butter fish, the stickleback, with its vivid, orange-scarlet scales.

But still something escapes me. Something vital. Still I don't quite grasp the language.

'No otters,' says Lydia. 'None. Never see otters, Mummy, not yet.'

'No. They are very elusive.'

I turn to my daughter. 'Lydia, do you remember if Kirstie was angry with Daddy, um, on the weekend that she fell?'

My daughter looks at me. Blank. Passive. 'Oh yes. She was.'

The moment tenses.

'Why?'

'Because Daddy kept kissing her.'

A herring gull calls, solitary, and maddened.

'Kissing her?'

'Yes, kissing and hugging.' Lydia is looking at me, unblinking, looking me honestly in the eyes. 'He was kissing her, and hugging her, and she told me she was scared. He did it a lot, all the time, all the time.'

She pauses, gazing blankly at me. I try not to show my thoughts, my lurid memories, returning: the way Angus kissed his daughters, especially Kirstie. Over the years. He was the hugger, the kisser. The tactile one.

270

I picture Lydia on his lap, after the accident with the window. The sense of awkwardness; the sudden thought that she was too old to be sitting on Daddy's lap. But he liked it?

The herring gull wheels away. I feel as if I am crashing. In mid-air. Falling to earth.

'Think it scared her, Mummy. Daddy scared her.'

Is this it? Is this what I was looking for, and not seeing?

'Lydia, this is very important. You have to tell me the truth.' I swallow my fury, and my grief, and my anxiety, together. 'Are you saying that Daddy kissed and hugged Kirstie, in a certain way? A way that made her upset? And scared?'

Lydia pauses. Then nods. 'Yes, Mummy.'

'You're sure?'

'Oh yes. But she still loved Daddy. He's Daddy. I love Dada. Can we look for otters over by the other beach?'

I restrain the urge to scream. I have to stay on top of this. I have to go off and talk to Kellaway again. Have to. NOW. Who cares if this is Kirstie's funeral?

My dad has wandered out of the pub. Sad, and genial, and drunk, with a glass in hand.

I grab him. 'Play with Lydia,' I say fiercely. 'Please. Look after her.'

He nods, vaguely, and half-smiles in a boozy way, but he obeys and bends to chuck his granddaughter under the chin. And I take my phone, and I walk down to the other end of the pier, where no one can hear.

First, I try Kellaway's office number. No answer. Then I try his home number; no answer.

What next? For several moments I stand here, looking across the mudflats and the incoming tide: towards Torran. The light has shifted again: now the island is

271

darkened and it is Knoydart that dazzles, in green and dark purple. Birch forests and emptiness.

Kellaway. I remember something he said. And where he stopped. And seemed hesitant. It was Samuels. The child psychiatrist Robert Samuels.

I need the internet for this. But where?

I'll have to drive. Crossing the pub car park, I climb inside the family car. The keys are in the ignition; Angus often does this, just leaves the keys in place. No one locks doors or cars around here. They take positive pride in their crimelessness.

Extracting the keys, I weigh them in my hand. As if they are valuable foreign coins. *Samuels, Samuels, Samuels.* Then I put the keys back in the ignition, and turn – and I floor the pedal – and now I am driving away from my daughter's funeral. I'm just going a mile, up the hill. To that place you can get a proper 3G signal. And internet access.

At the crest of the hill, I park. Like a local. And take out my smartphone again.

Now I enter the words in Google.

Robert Samuels. Child Psychologist.

Immediately his Wiki page flashes up. He works at Johns Hopkins. He is quite famous.

I scan his biography. The wind whispers in the firs and pines, like a faint chorus of disapproval.

Samuels is a busy man. He has loads of citations. I read the list: *The Psychology of Childhood Bereavement, Gesture Creation in Deaf Children, Risk Taking in Pre-pubertal Boys, Evidence of Paternal Abuse in Twins.*

My eyes rest on the words.

Paternal Abuse in Twins.

I click on the link but it just gives me a one-line summary. *Elevated levels of paternal sexual abuse in identical twins: a meta-analysis and proposed explanations.*

This is it. I am close. Nearly there. But I need to read the entire paper.

Breathing deeply, and calmly, I click two or three times until I find a copy of the paper. The site demands cash. I take out my card from my purse and type in my card-numbers, paying my money for the PDF.

And then I read it in twenty minutes: sitting here in my car, as the sun sets over the bald hills above Tokavaig.

It's a dense, but short article. Samuels has, it seems, collated dozens of cases of sexual abuse by fathers of twins, especially twin daughters, 'commonly the favoured twin'.

I read on, the phone trembling in my hand.

Signs of abuse include intensified rivalry between twins, 'self-harming by the abused and/or her co-twin', inexplicable expressions of guilt and shame, 'an appearance of happiness which cannot be trusted', 'the non-abused twin can exhibit as much psychological harm and mental disturbance as the abused twin if they are exceptionally close and privy to each other's secrets, as many twins are'; and then a final stab: 'self-harm or even suicide is not unknown in the abused twin'.

It all feels so normal. Reading this. Sitting here. In a car. Parked on a bleak twilit hillside. Learning that my husband, it seems, sexually abused Kirstie. Or at least got *way* too close.

Why didn't I see it? The special hugs: between Daddy and Kirstie, between Daddy and his little 'Weeble' – that stupid name, his icky term of endearment. And what about those times he would go into his daughter's bedroom, at night – when Lydia was awake and reading with me – leaving him alone with Kirstie?

This is surely it. This is the pattern I have been searching for, the pattern hidden everywhere I looked. Angus was abusing Kirstie. That's why she was frightened of him. She was always his special, special favourite. He liked her to sit on his knee whenever he could. I saw it. Hidden in plain sight. Lydia has confirmed it, Samuels predicted it.

He was abusing her. It confused her and scared her and in the end she jumped. It was suicide. And so much of Lydia's subsequent bewilderment and distress must come from this.

Because Lydia knew. Maybe she witnessed some of the actual abuse? Maybe Kirstie told her, long before she jumped. That would have upset Lydia so much she might even have pretended to be Kirstie, to deal with the trauma. To somehow pretend her sister had not died because of what her father did: Lydia went into denial about everything. Maybe that's why they were swapping identities that summer, trying to avoid Daddy?

The possibilities are endless and bewildering, but they all attain the same conclusion: my husband bears the guilt for the death of his daughter, and now he is tearing the other into pieces.

What do I do?

I could go up to the road to McLeods, the shop that sells stuff for deer stalkers: buy myself a big shotgun. Go to the Selkie. Kill my husband. Bang. The anger inside me is virulent.

Because, oh God, I need revenge. I do. I do. But my needs, right now, are irrelevant. I am not a murderer; I am a mother. And what matters is my daughter Lydia. For now, despite my fury, I just need a practical way out of here: a way for me and Lydia to escape this horror. So I have to stay calm, and be clever.

I stare out of the car window: a father is walking down the road with his toddler daughter. Maybe it's a grandfather, he looks old. Rather stooped in a Barbour jacket and knotted red scarf. He is pointing at a huge herring gull swooping down, pecking, dangerous, a white flash in the air.

Evidence of paternal sexual abuse.

The anger rises inside me: like fire.

21

Slipping the rope, Angus jumped in the boat, with the weekend's shopping from the Co-op.

The outboard motor kicked into life and Angus throttled up to speed: ploughing the waters. It was getting very dark already, and the weather was brewing something nasty to the north. There was a lick of cold rain in the air; the firs on Salmadair were bending in the sharpening wind. There were rumours of a real storm next week, perhaps this was the first hint.

The last thing they needed was a proper winter storm on Thunder Island. Yes, the funeral yesterday had gone OK, considering. Everyone had come and gone, the rituals had been completed.

But the dark, underlying cracks in the family were unresolved, the terrible confusion in Lydia, his contempt for Sarah, her mistrust of him because of Imogen.

He steered the boat, and frowned at the louring sky.

His guilt was intense. He may not have had sex with Imogen that night, but their flirtation *had* begun the night of the accident. The first unexpected touch, the different way they looked at each other: a lingering gaze. He'd known what she wanted, from that night on, and yes he'd encouraged it by staying, that night, much longer than planned. *Oh I can drive to Instow later.*

But it only got slightly serious after the accident. After Sarah fell apart. And in the end they'd only had sex a couple of times. He had, at the last moment, drawn back from Imogen – out of loyalty, however misguided, to Sarah: to his family. So his guilt and responsibility, however painful, was nothing compared to hers: compared to Sarah's.

The anger was urgent inside him. He tried to calm it. Sniffing the air. Cold and rainy. What would happen now?

Next week Lydia was meant to go back to school. How would that work? The Kylerdale teachers, perhaps regretting their hasty exclusion, had taken to calling the Moorcrofts, and imploring them: *Give us another chance.* Despite their pleas, Angus wanted to try a different school, or maybe home schooling; but Sarah was determined to have one last go, lest Lydia feel defeated.

But if she went back to Kylerdale – if she went to any school right now – Angus could envisage all kinds of terrors; they were obscene in their madness.

Perhaps, then, a proper winter storm would be fitting: a suitable backdrop to the intensifying strangeness. Because their lives had become melodrama. Or maybe some form of masked theatre. And all three of them were in disguise.

The waves lashed at the little dinghy. He was glad to make it to the shingly beach, under Torran lighthouse. He'd just finished dragging the boat out of the clutches of the highest tide, and dropping the shopping bags on the shingle, when Sarah's voice rang across the darkness.

He could see her, running towards him, in the beam of his head torch. Even in the semi-dark it was clear she was alarmed.

'Gus!'

'What is it?'

'Beany!'

He noticed Sarah was in a shirt, and soaking wet. The rain was getting heavier.

'What the hell?'

'He's gone, Beany's gone.'

'How? Where?'

'I was in the dining room, painting one of the walls, and Lydia came in and said she couldn't find him, so we searched, everywhere, he's gone, he's really gone – but—'

'I don't understand – it's an island?'

'We can hear him, Angus.'

'What?'

The lighthouse beam flicked on, for a second, making a moment of dazzling moonlight; Angus saw the pain on Sarah's face. He realized what she meant.

'He ran onto the flats? Christ.'

'He's stuck somewhere out there – we heard him howling about ten minutes ago.' She gestured, wildly, at the greyness and the blackness that divided Torran from Ornsay. The great expanse of sand and rock, and those sucking, pungent, dangerous tidal mudflats.

'Gus, we have to do something, but – but what? Lydia is going crazy. We can't just let him drown in the mud, in the next tide.'

'OK. OK.' Angus put a calming hand on Sarah's shoulder. And as he did, she flinched. She definitely *flinched*. What did she think he was going to do? There was certainly a new expression in her eyes: she was trying to hide it. And the expression said *I hate you.* She was that angry about Imogen?

He thrust the thoughts away. Had no choice. He'd deal with this later.

'I'll get my waterproofs.'

It took Angus five minutes to force himself inside his waterproof trousers and oily rain-jacket. He tucked the plastic of his trouser legs inside big green wellingtons. Sarah and Lydia stared at him as he strode into the kitchen, a rope tied around his waist. He slipped his head torch on and adjusted the tightness. It was going to be fearsomely unpleasant out there. A thick Skye fog was rolling in, as well. Probably the worst possible conditions to go onto the mud.

'Gus, please, be careful?'

"Course.'

He nodded at his wife. For some reassurance. Yet her anxious smile was, again, quite unconvincing.

Lydia ran and hugged him, making a crinkling noise as she embraced the plastic of his waterproofs. Angus gazed down at his only daughter. Felt a surge of love and protectiveness. Sarah said:

'You know you don't have to.'

But she tailed off. All three of them turned as one, and looked through the rain-speckled kitchen window at the darkness of the mudflats as a faint but unmistakable howl drifted on the wind. A dog. Howling. Loud enough they could hear it through the window pane.

His dog.

'Yes, I do,' said Angus. 'I have to try.'

'Please save Beany, please, please! Daddy, please: he'll be drowned if we don't. Please!'

Lydia was hugging him again, tight around his waist. Her voice trembled with tearfulness.

'Don't worry, Lydia,' Angus said. 'I'll get Beany back.'

He gave Sarah one final, bewildered glance. What was she playing at? How did this happen? Again, he didn't have time to work it through. However it had happened, Beany was out there in the dark, and needed rescuing.

Angus stepped outside the kitchen into the rough slap of the rain. The wind was quite spiteful now. And yet the fog was also flooding down the Sound of Sleat, from Kylerhea.

Slipping on his plastic hood, Angus trudged against the flailing wetness, towards the causeway, following the beam of his head torch. This was proper, hard, Ornsay winter rain: the kind of rain that soaked you twice: once as it fell, then again as it bounced back, spitting, from the rocks and silt.

The mud. The damn mud.

'Beano!' he shouted, into the rain-bittered wind. 'Beano! Beany! Beany!'

Nothing. The wind rappling his hood was so brutal it obscured any other noise. Angus tore off the hood of his waterproofs, he would just have to get wet; at least this way he could hear better. But where was the dog? Beany's pitiful howling had seemed to come from the southern edge of Ornsay's curving bay: the opposite side of the sullen mudflats.

But was it really a dog howling? Who was out here? What was out here? It was all so lightless. A dark brown spaniel would be very hard to see at night, in the mud, in good clear weather. This weather was the opposite. The fog was thickening along the shore, hiding every-thing. Obscuring the lights of Ornsay village. The Selkie was completely invisible, cocooned in freezing mist.

'Beany? Where are you! Sawney Bean! Sawney!'

Again, he heard nothing. The rain was near-horizontal: giving the wind a rasping edge, cutting coldly into his face. Angus strode forward – but he slipped on a kelp-slimed rock that came out of nowhere; the slip was serious – he fell to his knees, cracking a shin very painfully against the boulder.

'Fuck.' He put a hand in the gloop and lifted himself. 'Beany! Beany! Where the fuck are you? Beannnnyyy!'

Standing up, slowly, Angus bent himself into the driving cold rain. *Lean into the wind.* He took a deep breath of rain and air. He knew very well that in these conditions he was possibly risking his own life. What did Josh say? *In Skye, in winter, no one can hear you scream.* He could break a leg in this horrible, treacherous mud, get himself sucked in, and get himself stuck.

Of course Sarah would telephone someone, but it might take them an hour to rustle up a posse, and the tides rose very fast around Torran. He wouldn't drown in an hour, but he could freeze to death in the frigid, imprisoning water.

'Beany!'

Angus scanned the nothingness. Frantically wiping rain off his face.

There?

'Beany?'

There!

He heard it.

A small, pitiful, unmistakable howl. Weakening, but definitely there. Judging by the noise, the dog was three hundred, four hundred yards away. Angus took out his hand torch and switched it on, his hands slippy and damp, and numbed with iciness, fiddling to press the plastic switch.

That's it. Angus lifted the hand torch. Combining its

light with that of the head torch gave him a powerful beam of illumination. Directing it towards that spot, Angus stared, and stared, into the ghostly drifts of fog.

Yes. It was Beany. He was just a dim shape, but he was alive. And the dog was in mud up to his neck.

The dog was going to drown, very soon. Angus had at most a few minutes to reach the animal, before the waters engulfed him.

'Jesus. Beany. Beany!'

A pitiful whimper. A dying animal. What would this do to Lydia, if her Beany drowned? It would crack Angus open, too.

Angus began to run, but it was impossible. Every step was either sucked into mud, or dangerously skiddy. He almost toppled forward on one wet, seaweed-skinned boulder, made extra slick by the relentless rain. One bad fall and he could split his skull on a rock. Knock himself out. That would probably be fatal.

Perhaps he had made a mistake. Risking his own life this much. He thought of Sarah's deceptive smile. She'd planned this? No. Ridiculous.

He had to slow down, but if he slowed, Beany died.

He could crawl faster?

Dropping to his knees, Angus crawled. Through the mud. The rain was achingly cold, dribbling down his neck and shoulders, soaking through into his bones. He was shivering, feeling maybe the first hints of hypothermia, but he was nearly there. Fifty yards. Forty. Thirty.

The dog was dying. Only Beany's head was visible. Beany's eyes shone with terror in the beam of the torch. But Angus was getting close. And there was a wooden platform here, perhaps some scuppered boat, half-buried in the slime for decades. It was hard to see in the dark, but the wood provided a bridge to the patch of cold mud where Beany was stranded.

'OK, boy, OK, OK, I'm here, I'm coming. Hold on.'

Angus crawled across the wood. He was five yards from the dog, he was working out a rescue plan: he'd have to reach into the mud and yank the hound, bodily, from the gunge.

But then Beany moved. The incoming waters must have loosened the mud. The dog was half-swimming, half-struggling: rescuing himself. And he was wriggling away from Angus, up onto the shingle.

Angus called, in desperation, 'Beany!'

He heard a crack of splitting wood. As Angus lifted a knee, to stand, the wood beneath him snapped, and opened up.

At once Angus was plunged into a sump of cold seawater. Deep and silty, and very cold. There was no mud under here. He was flailing in freezing seas, in heavy boots and waterproofs. Desperate, he lunged for another spar of timber but it sank into gritty water. He was already up to his neck. Kicking at the void.

Across the mudflats, Torran lighthouse flashed through dark. A pale glow of silver. Then black.

22

Where is Angus? Why is he taking so long? Is he drowning? I hope so. And yet I don't. I do not know any more.

I am standing at the kitchen window, gazing over the dreary flats towards Ornsay, but it is pointless. In this fog and darkness, I could be staring into space: a deep grey saddening void. Without stars.

'Mummy, where is Daddy?'

Lydia tugs at the sleeve of my cardigan. Innocent, gap-toothed, blue eyes unblinking; her tiny shoulders are trembling with worry. Much as I loathe Angus, she cannot lose her dad; not like this. Perhaps I should have restrained Angus? But he would always have tried to save his dog, no matter what the danger.

The wind lashes the kitchen window with a whip of rain.

This is taking too long. Once again I read the various shades of grey that constitute the fog, the densely veiled moon, the misty shoreline of Ornsay. Nothing. Every nine seconds the lighthouse bestows a paparazzi flash of silver, but it reveals just glistening emptiness.

'Mummy! Where is Dada?'

I hold Lydia's hand. It is shaking.

'Daddy will be fine. He's just getting Beany; it's dark, so it's difficult.'

I wish I believed this. I wish I understood all this. I wish I knew whether I wanted my husband to live or die.

I'm not even sure how the dog got onto the mudflats: one minute he was in the dining room romping, as much as he does these days, with Lydia; I was in Lydia's bedroom ironing – and then Lydia screamed and I ran into the dining room and the dog was gone and the back door in the kitchen creaked open in the Hebridean wind.

'I want Daddy.'

Perhaps Beany saw one of the kitchen rats, and gave chase? Or maybe Lydia chased the dog away? Frightened him into fleeing? Beany always seemed so scared of Torran, or of someone, or something, in the cottage on Torran.

'Mummy, it's Beany! I heard him!'

Is she right? Was that a howling? Releasing her hand, I step to the kitchen door and pull it open. At once the ugly weather tries to push me back in, the angry rain, the bullying wind. Helpless, urgent, I shout, towards the mudflats, towards the dim shapes of anchored boats and sandbanks, and the ranked spires of dull fir trees. To where everything is smothered in mist.

'Angus! Beany! Angus! Beany!'

I may as well be shouting down a coal mine. Or in a locked and dripping cellar. The words are robbed from my mouth and whirled away on the gale. Taken south to Ardnamurchan and the Summer Isles.

288

Oh, the Summer Isles. The despair surges. Tragedy has chased us from London.

'Dada is coming back, Mummy?' says Lydia from the kitchen door. 'He's coming back. Like Lydia.'

'Yes, yes, of course he is.'

She is dressed in thin purple leggings and a little denim skirt, her Hello Kitty top is too thin. The cold will get at her. 'Go back inside, Lyddie, please. Daddy will be fine, he's just gone to get Beany. He will be back very soon, please, just go and read something, it won't be long.'

Lydia turns and runs into the dining room, I pursue her as far as the decrepit, paint-flecked Bakelite telephone on the dining-room window sill. The old receiver is ludicrously heavy and the dial ponderously slow. I grind out Josh and Molly's number. But it doesn't answer; their phone just rings and rings, perversely innocuous.

I try Josh's mobile. Again, nothing. 'Hi, this is Josh Freedland. If you're calling about work, try Strontian Stone—'

I slam the phone down. Angry now, angry at everything. Who can help us?

Gordon the boatman! Yes. Gordon. His number is in my mobile. Running into the bedroom, I snatch my barely used mobile from the cluttered drawer in the side table and wait – painfully – for it to switch on, and as I do Lydia wanders into the bedroom. From somewhere. She looks different. Her hair is wilder. She gazes at me, in that placid, trancelike way, as I shake my phone in frustration: Come on, come on, *come the fuck on*. She has Leopardy tucked under one arm. She eyes me dubiously, and says:

'Mummy, maybe it doesn't matter about Beany. Kirstie

didn't come back, maybe it doesn't matter if Beany doesn't come back.'

'What, Lyddie, darling? I'm trying to get a number—'

'Daddy comes back, doesn't he? Please, Mummy. Lydia doesn't mind. Kirstie is gone now, so it doesn't matter what he did. Can we get him off of the mud?'

The what? What is she saying?

I gaze at her. Bewildered. And with tears ready to roll. My tears for Kirstie, and what he did to her.

No. I have to look at the phone. Its happy friendly screen glows in the darkness of the badly lit cottage. It tells me that I have no signal. Of course. I press two buttons and I reach CONTACTS. G or F, G or F.

Gordon Fraser. Here's his number.

Running with the phone in hand to the dining room, I grab the heavy old receiver and dial, with frenzied patience, 3, 9, 4, 6, and the phone rings at the other end – pick up, pick up, *pick up* – and eventually I hear a crackled voice, frail and yet gruff, transported through the storm.

'Gordon Fraser.'

'Gordon, it's Sarah. Sarah Moorcroft from Torran.'

A slow, frustrating pause.

'Aye. Sarah. Well now. How are you?'

'We've got a problem, a big—' The line is popping and seething. 'Please.'

'I'm not—' Hissssss '—atching you—'

'F—'

'Sarah . . .'

'We need help, please help—' the landline goes dead, even the fuzz of static disappears, and I almost throw it at the wall in frustration: of all times, it chooses now to give up? But then the static whistles in my ear, so loud it hurts, and the line suddenly clears, and I hear that voice again.

'Are ye in some trouble now, Mrs Moorcroft?'

'Yes!'

'What exactly?'

'My husband, Angus, is on the mudflats – we lost the dog, he went out to save him, at low tide, in the dark, and now I'm worried, he's been gone so long, ages, I don't know what to do – I'm worried for him and—'

'On the mudflats, ye say?'

'Yes.'

'On his own, off Torran?'

'Yes!'

I can hear the disapproval in the hissy silence that follows.

'OK now, calm yerself, Mrs Moorcroft. I'll get some of the boys from the Selkie.'

'Oh thanks, thank you!'

I put the phone down before the line gives out on me, as if this is some deadly computer game and the phone is your life-force seeping away until you hear *bzzz game over*; and then I turn and there she is again: Lydia. I almost fall back against the wall in alarm, and surprise.

She is simply standing there. Blank-faced. Tranced. Eyes open wide and saddening blue, right behind me.

How did she do that? These floorboards creak from the slightest pressure. I heard nothing.

Lydia is a mere three feet away. Rigid and silent, and staring, her face pallid with anxiety. I didn't hear her come in. I certainly didn't hear her standing right behind me.

How does she do this? How many Lydias lurk in

291

this house? This is crazy. I have the dizzyingly insane sensation that there are two identical Lydias in this house, playing games in the shadows and cold, between the cobwebs and the rats, just like Lydia and Kirstie used to play games in London, especially that last summer: *this is me, no, it's me*, their girlish laughter ringing down the hallway as I first chased one then the other, hiding and seeking, trying to perplex me.

But this is my mind misting up; I need clarity.

'Daddy is coming back, with Beany, isn't he?'

Frowning and sad, she gazes. The pain inside her must be unbearable, losing a twin, and now frightened of losing her dog, and her daddy. That will complete her destruction.

As much as I despise Angus, he has to survive.

'Mummy, he is coming back, isn't he? Please, Mummy?'

'Yes!'

I kneel down and crush her into my arms and hug her tight tight tight. 'Sweetheart, Daddy will be coming back soon, I promise.'

'Promise?'

'Really promise. A million times. Come on, let's go into the kitchen and make some tea and wait for Daddy and Beany.'

I don't mean this. I just want an excuse to stand in the kitchen and look through the window, to see if anything is happening. And so, as I funnel brackish water from the vile tap into the kettle, my eyes fix, furiously, on the blackness.

Just blackness. Maybe a smear of moonlight as the clouds and fog part for a moment. Closer to hand, the pathetic light from our kitchen shows a green patch of cold wet grass, a silly oblong of lurid colour. Sodden washing flaps wildly, on the line. The wind's howling is unabating. As if it could go on for weeks.

This is real winter coming in now: the new regime announcing itself.

'Look, Mummy!'

Prickles of light pierce the murk. Misty beams from car headlamps. Torches maybe? Lights on boats? It must be Gordon and his friends: yes, there are shadows of men on the pier, their torch-beams mingling and crossing, like lights in wartime, seeking bombers above London. The men are clearly going out onto the water. The boats are rounding Salmadair, several of them, I can see them quite well now.

One mighty beam shines from a boat, rocking on the waves and the rippled sands: a handheld searchlight. Scanning the mud, I try to follow it, but then the mist thickens and I am defeated.

The entire Sound is a valley of fog. How will they find Angus in all that? Do I care?

Yes, I do. Maybe in the wrong way. I want him back and alive, so I can confront him.

'Let's go into the living room,' I say to Lydia.

'Why?'

'There's nothing to see.'

'What are those lights, Mummy?'

'Just people helping Daddy, that's all, everyone is helping out.'

I grasp her hand and lead her firmly into the living room and together we bank up the fire; it had almost extinguished itself in the last hour, neglected and unwatched. Now Lydia hands me the smaller logs, dutifully and carefully, and I feed them into the flames, which grow and thrive.

'Mummy, what would you like it to rain if it didn't rain water?'

'Sorry?'

Lydia looks at me, squinting, thoughtfully. Her pale pretty face has a smut of soot on the chin. And I smile, and try not to think about Angus or Kirstie or the hugging and the kissing and I say, 'What?'

'If rain wasn't water, what would you like it to be? I'd like it to be flowers, raining flowers – that would be so pretty.'

'Yes.'

'Or people.' She quietly laughs. 'That would be funny, wouldn't it, Mummy, raining people, everywhere, oh look, LOOK, it looks rainbow!'

She is pointing at the flames in the hearth: one particular small flame is jetting from the logs, purple and blue. Together we watch the flames and the fire, then we go back to the sofa and we sit cuddled under the blanket which smells of Beany, and we talk about the dog in a nice way, because I want to keep Lydia's anxious mind diverted. Lydia listens to me and she nods and she laughs, and so I laugh as well, but even within the laughter I can feel my sadness and anger.

This is still taking too long. Where is Angus? They cannot find him. They've lost him. I imagine the boys from the Selkie scouring the sands, from the boat, and tiring, and rubbing cold hands together and blowing warmth between fingers, not quite looking each other in the eye, knowing they have failed, there's no sign of him, we'll have to wait . . .

If Angus dies, would we survive? Maybe we would. At least there would be an ending.

The fire rises and the fire subsides. I stare at my

daughter as she stares at the fire, the flames reflected in her shining blue eyes.

'Sarah.'

What?

'Jesus.'

'Daddy!'

It's Angus. He is in the frame of the living-room doorway, covered in mud, almost a mud-man, his eyes like slots of dark life in the muck; but he is alive.

Behind him is Gordon and some other men, they are all laughing. Their voices fill the house, they smell of diesel and seaweed and thick oily mud – and Angus is alive. Lydia scampers off the sofa and runs to him and he holds her at a distance, and kisses her on the forehead.

'I know you want to hug me,' he says, walking painfully to the sofa. 'But I wouldn't advise it. This mud stinks.'

Lydia jumps up and down.

'Dadadada!'

'Jesus we thought—' I almost say, but I don't say it. For Lydia's sake. For everyone's sake.

Gordon interrupts: 'We fished yer husband out about ten feet off Ornsay pier.'

Angus looks sheepish. He comes near me and pecks me gently on the cheek. I try not to flinch. He gives me a strange, suspicious glance and says: 'I had no idea where I was – in the fog.'

I gaze past him.

There is no dog. Where is the dog?

'Beany?'

Lydia is gazing at her father, rapt, but also worried. 'Yes, Daddy, where . . .?'

Angus smiles, but his smile is faked.

'He escaped! He got out of the mud, and ran off. We'll find him tomorrow, but he's fine.'

I'm guessing this is a lie. Perhaps Beany got away, but there's no guarantee he will survive, or be found again. I'm not pressing this now. I lay a caressing hand on my husband's cold, muddy face; I want to slap him. Very hard. I want to punch him cold, and claw at his eyes. Hurt him.

This caress is for Lydia's benefit, and Gordon, for everyone but me.

'You must be freezing, Angus. Jesus, look at you – you need a bath!'

'A hot bath,' says Angus, 'is just about the best idea on earth, Sarah. Can you give Gordon and Alistair a glass of the Macallan, the good stuff. I promised them a dram. By way of thanks, for . . .' He glances at Lydia, he hesitates, and says: 'You know, just for helping out. Sarah?'

'Of course,' I say, and I force out the smile of fake relief.

Angus squelches his way carefully into the bathroom. I hear hot water being slowly poured: I turn to my daughter.

'Lydia, can you fetch some glasses, sweetie?'

Whisky is brought, and poured. The men apologize for their dampness and I say, Think nothing, and we sit on the sofa and the chairs, and the fire is refuelled. We sit and we drink, and Lydia gazes at the men, as if they are brilliant new animals in the zoo. Gordon looks around him, at the half-painted walls, and says:

'You've made a real go of the place, it's coming along nicely now. Good to see Torran cottage getting some attention.'

What can I say? The sadness dilates, until it fills the room. I mumble a faint thank you and no more.

We drink in silence. I can hear Angus splashing in the bath. I look at the door of the bathroom. We are all safe. Yet we are in real danger.

Breaking the silence, Gordon starts talking about Torran and Sleat, and the Gaelic college, I join in thankfully. I am happy to talk about anything. I don't care. What am I going to do about Angus?

Alistair, the younger man, red-haired and clean-shaven, rawly handsome, takes his third very large glass of Macallan, and interrupts Gordon's chatter: 'A thin place. That's what they called this.'

Gordon shushes him. Lydia is now fast asleep on the sofa, curled up. A soft, mist-blue blanket over her shoulder.

I tip my own Scotch; the firelight flickers. I am so tired.

'What?'

Alistair is clearly a little drunk. He burps and says sorry and then says: 'The locals, they used to call Torran a thin place. That means a place where there are spirits –' he chuckles into his glass – 'real spirits, where the spirit world comes close.'

'Ach, load of nonsense,' says Gordon, eyeing me, and then Lydia. Carefully. He looks as if he wants to clout his young friend.

'No,' Alistair says, 'it's true, Gordon. Sometimes I think they've a point, y'know, Thunder Island and all that, it's like there is something, an atmosphere. Remember when the squatters left? They were terrified.'

He clearly doesn't know any of our family history. Or he wouldn't go near this subject.

'Aye, a thin place. Where you can see the other world.' Alistair grins. And slurps down his Scotch, and looks at me. 'That's what they said.'

Gordon Fraser tuts loudly, and says again: 'Just pish. Sarah, I wouldnae listen to it.'

I shrug. 'It's OK. It's interesting.'

I am being sincere. I'm not fazed by historic folklore or ancient superstition: my present anxieties are disturbing enough. Gordon sips with delicacy his Scotch, savours the flavour, and then he tilts his glass at my sleeping daughter.

'Looks like it's time for us to be going.'

They make their departure swiftly. I wave to their boat as it disappears around the darkness of Salmadair. The lighthouse flickers in valediction. I notice the dinghy lashed to the railings; the shopping bags have all disappeared, snatched by the tides.

I go back inside the kitchen. I pull out the knife drawer.

And stare at the armoury. The gleaming knives. I like to keep them sharp.

Quickly, I shut the knife drawer, with the knives untouched. I am having fantasies about murder?

I walk across the living room and down the hall and I open the bathroom door – he is in the bath, rinsing himself, soaping his muscled arms, his hairy chest black-and-white with suds.

I hate his physical presence.

'You've got to go get some more shopping,' I say. 'Tomorrow. You left it by the boat and the tide has taken it. Taken all the bags.'

'What?' he says. Understandably bemused. I can see the thought processes in his head. *I nearly died saving the dog and she's talking about shopping?*

But I can't fake it any more. I just want him out of the house while I work out what to do. How to confront him properly.

'Tomorrow. Shopping. Thanks.'

23

We search for Beany all morning. Lydia shouts, desperately, as we circle the island, 'Beany! *Beany!*'

The tide is in. I don't think the poor dog is going to emerge from the waters. But Lydia is fraught:

'BEANY!'

As we scan the waters, we are cat-called by black-headed gulls. The oystercatchers look at us, sceptically, hopping further down the beach as my daughter runs, shouting, and yelling.

And then crying.

'Come on,' I say, placing an arm over her trembling shoulders. 'I'm sure Beany is fine. He probably ran off into the woods. We'll put up posters.'

'He's not coming back.' She shakes my hand away. 'He's dead. He's not coming back. NOT.'

With that she runs into the house. I have no notion of how to console her. The world itself is inconsolable: from the tearful grey seals on Salmadair, to the weeping wet rowans of Camuscross.

And now the hours melt into each other, imperceptibly. As Lydia reads in her room, I actually do some wall-painting. I'm not sure why. Perhaps because I have vague ideas that we must somehow finish the renovation, and sell the house. Soon.

When I need a break, I go into the kitchen to wash the paint from my fingers – and then I see Angus boating over, chalking the slate-grey water of the Sound with white backwash.

He's a solitary figure in his boat, standing, hand on the tiller, staring straight at me. Coming for us. Bringing the shopping, as requested.

The hatred uncoils. Abruptly. I hope his fucking boat hits a hidden block of basalt down there, under the lighthouse. I hope it is holed, and ripped. For all my desires to be logical, to have it out, to confront him with the evidence, I could easily watch him drown in those cold tidal waters and I would not budge. Not an inch. Right now, I would just stand here: and watch myself be widowed.

But of course the boat doesn't sink; Angus is quite expert at this island life, now. And he's probably being extra careful after the scare on the mudflats yesterday. With skill he slows the boat, and deftly beaches its stupid orange rubber, stepping out onto the grey shingle. He drags the dinghy out of any tide, takes out two big Co-op shopping bags, and marches up the slope to the cottage.

His walk is determined, fast. Maybe even menacing? The anxiety flashes through me.

Does he know that I know? How could he have guessed? He's obviously sensed my new hostility: but how could he have pursued my thoughts that far?

He's getting closer. The sense of purpose in his stride is unignorable. I edge back to the kitchen drawer, and gaze closely at the shiny cutlery, again – and this time

I do it: I pull out a kitchen knife. The biggest and the sharpest. Then I hold it in one hand, behind my back. I recognize the insanity of this, even as it seems perfectly explicable. *This is the correct thing to do.*

'Hello,' he says. Gruffer than normal, shunting through the door, dropping the bags to the kitchen floor. He is unsmiling. I have the knife in my hand, sweatily grasped, and badly concealed. Could I use it? Am I capable of actually stabbing my own husband?

Perhaps.

Yes definitely, if he goes for Lydia. Who knows if the abuse has stopped. Perhaps he is calling her *Kirstie*. Pretending his favourite is still alive.

Does all the confusion come from him?

'Where's Lydia?' he says.

His stubble makes him look villainous now, not handsome. More like a criminal on TV news: Do you know this man?

No, I don't.

What did he do to Kirstie? How could he do that? For how long? Six months? A year?

'She's asleep,' I say, and this is a lie. Lydia's in her room, reading. But I'm not letting him near our surviving daughter. If he tries I really will use the knife. 'She's exhausted, Gus, I think we should let her sleep.'

'But she's all right? Despite. You know.'

'Yes,' I say. 'Considering all that, yes, yes, she is doing OK. Angus, please let her sleep. She has to go back to school, she needs her rest. Please.'

And it is so hard for me to say please. To this man, this thing. He is monstrous now; an entirely inhuman presence, and I want him gone.

'OK,' he says, looking me deep in the eyes. And the charge of hatred passes between us; he does not strive

303

to hide it. We are two people on our very own island, with the ravens of Salmadair roosting and chattering, and we hate each other and we both know it; but I still don't quite know why *he* hates *me*: perhaps because he realizes that I have guessed his secret?

Perhaps that is why he looked so angry when I told him Kirstie was Lydia: he knew I was getting closer.

He turns to go to the dining room and I say: 'Angus, I think . . .'

'Yes?'

'Well, I've been thinking, while you were shopping.'

Can I mention my suspicions? No. I can't just come out and say it, here, on a Sunday afternoon, in this cold kitchen, where we hoped to be happy, where there are Dairylea cheese triangles in the fridge for Lydia's packed lunch, where the shelves are stacked with Crunchy Nut Cornflakes. I will have to say these terrible words sometime, I will have to say You Touched Her – but not yet, not now, not with Lydia still traumatized by everything; I want her to go to school tomorrow, Monday, she has to dive back in, or we will never rescue ourselves.

'Yes?' Angus is waiting, impatient. 'What is it?'

His jeans are dirty with motor oil. He looks properly unkempt, even dishevelled. Quite unlike himself. Maybe he is turning into his real self.

'Angus, you know that things aren't so good between us. I think maybe – just, you know, for Lydia's sake, for all of us, maybe you could spend a couple of days on the mainland.' I am still holding the knife behind my back, with one hand. He is staring at me as if he knows what I am doing and he does not give a fuck.

'Fine,' he says. 'Fine with me. Just fine.' And his dark eyes flash with darker contempt. 'I'll grab some work stuff and get a room at the Selkie. Costs nothing this time of year.'

So that wasn't hard. I hear the creak of the dining-room door as Angus shoves paperwork in a bag, then I hear noises from our bedroom. The wardrobe, his kist, footsteps. Is he really just going to come and go, so easily? It seems that way.

Slipping the kitchen knife back into the cutlery drawer, I take deep breaths of relief.

I am listening to the gulls, and the wind at the door; the fluttering of dried sea-wrack down on the beach. Ten minutes later – no more – Angus appears in the kitchen and says, 'Please hug Lydia for me.' His anger is gone now. He looks softer, he looks sadder, and a stupid pang of sympathy reflexes in me, sympathy for the man I once loved, sympathy for the father losing his daughters, until I remember what he has done.

'Yes,' I say. 'I'll do that.'

'Thank you,' he says, very quietly. 'I'll take the boat, but you can walk over at low tide and pick it up later? You guys will need the boat for school.'

'Yes.'

'OK then, Sarah.'

'Bye, Angus,' I say.

He looks at me. Is that contempt, or guilt, or despair? Maybe it is just a shrug. 'Bye.'

And now he shakes his head again, very slowly, very soberly, as if this is the last time we will ever meet, and I watch him hoist his bag and kick open the kitchen door, and stride down to the dinghy, where he tugs the motor into life and oars the boat onto the waters. I watch him to make sure he really is going; but as he dwindles around the Salmadair headland, Lydia rushes into the kitchen, barefoot in her primrose yellow leggings, and tear-streaked, and saying:

'Is that Daddy? Where is Daddy? Is he coming to say hello?'

What can I say? Nothing. In the midst of my anger, I forget that Lydia still loves her father. Despite everything. So I take her in my embrace, hold her firm between my arms, and I lay one protective hand on her blonde hair and now we turn and we are both facing out, towards the door and the sea, mother and daughter, and I say:

'Daddy had to do some work again.'

Lydia revolves, and she looks right up at me, imploring, supplicant, her blue eyes large, and puzzled, and sad:

'But he didn't say hello?? He didn't even come in and *see* me?'

'Darling—'

'He didn't say goodbye?'

'Sweetheart—'

She is distraught now. 'Didn't say goodbye to me!' Abruptly she twists and wrenches free and then she goes running through the open kitchen door, down the path, straight through the wet bracken and heather, right down to the lighthouse beach, and she is screaming: 'Daddy? Daddy! Come back, come back!'

But his boat is too far away, and he has his back to us, and the waves and the wind are drowning her words, her small childish voice, and he obviously cannot hear her as she screams, and sobs.

'Daddy! Daddy, come back, come back, come back to me, Daddy!'

And the ravens caw, and the seagulls soar, and I have sadness choking me so I try to stay calm: I watch a hooded crow watching Lydia from the stunted rowans by the lighthouse; the crows that swoop and bite the tongues from newborn lambs, so that they cannot suckle, so that they die in just a day.

My little girl is still shrieking.

And, oh, this is too much. I am scared she will run into the water and I run after her, sprinting down the path to the beach, and I take her by the hand, and I crouch beside her: 'Darling, Daddy is busy, he will be back very soon.'

'He came and went, he didn't say hello or bye-bye, he doesn't like me any more!'

I cannot process another second of anguish. I am content to lie. 'Of *course* he loves you. He is just so busy and he will be back very soon. Now come on, we've got to get you set for school tomorrow, come on, we can bake some cakes. Gingerbread men!'

Bake things. That's my solution. Baking cakes and biscuits. Gingerbread men. Bicarbonate of soda and those little silver sugar balls, and sugar and butter and ginger.

So that's what we do: we bake.

But the gingerbread men come out all wrong. Like deformed things, like gingerbread animals, and I try to make some desperate fun from the misshapen men, but Lydia stares at them in dismay, on the hot wire tray, and she shakes her head and runs to her room.

Nothing works. Nothing will ever work any more.

I wonder about Lydia's deep love for her father. If she witnessed the abuse, would she still love him *that* much? Truly? Maybe she didn't see anything, and Kirstie just told her. Or maybe the abuse didn't happen like that, or maybe it didn't happen at all, and maybe I am presuming too much, too quickly? For a moment, the doubts open up – dizzying, like vertigo. Perhaps I am wrong? Perhaps I am reaching for a cliché: sex abuse, paedophilia, modern-day witchcraft – because I am blinded by anger, or grief?

No. *No.* I have Lydia's own words, and the evidence of my own memory, and the science from Samuels. More likely is this: I just don't want to accept that I lived with and loved, for ten years, a man who was capable of touching his own daughter. Because what does this say about me?

Stepping outside, I throw the gingerbread men on the compost heap and look across the reeking mud to Ornsay.

Nothing.

Later that day Lydia and I walk across the mudflats at low tide, scrunching dead crabs under our wellingtons, and we get the boat from the pier at the Selkie, and then we steer the boat home and read books. In the evening, with a bottle of wine beside me, I iron her school uniform as she sleeps; and I've got half the windows open despite the cold.

Because I want piercing cold air to keep me sharp and logical. Am I doing the right thing in taking her back to Kylerdale?

When we were still just about communicating, Angus almost persuaded me she shouldn't go back. But the school secretary is adamant that things will be better; and, until we get a new placement, home schooling, I am sure, will only make her lonelier. She'd never leave the island.

So Kylerdale must be given one last chance. But as I iron, I listen to the waves of Torran wash up and down the shingles, breathing in, breathing out, and I worry. The waves sound like the fevered breathing of a child in a sickroom.

Finally I slide into bed and sleep. And I do not dream.

The morning sky is grey as a goose. I chide Lydia

into her school uniform, though all she wants to do is stay at home, and ask me where Daddy is.

'He'll be here soon.'

'Really, Mummy?'

I pull her school jumper over her head and lie. 'Yes, darling.'

'Mummy, I don't want to go to school.'

'Come on.'

'Because Emily will be there, and she hates me. They all hate me. She thinks there is something wrong with me, doesn't she?'

'No, she doesn't. She just got a bit silly. Come on. Let's put your shoes on. You can do that yourself today. You've had a week off, now it's time to get back to school. It'll be OK.'

How many lies can you tell your daughter?

'They all hate me, Mummy. They think that Kirstie is with me and she is dead, so I'm a ghost.'

'Enough, darling, enough. Let's not think about any of this, let's get you to school, everyone will have forgotten.'

But when we boat across, and climb in the car, and drive the few windy miles down the coast to Kylerdale, it is apparent everyone has not forgotten; the intensely embarrassed stare I get from the school secretary, climbing out of her Mazda, tells me this. And when we go to the cheery school door with its pictures of kids on their summer outing, and its bilingual list of Our Playground Rules – *Riaghailtean Raon-Cluiche* – the worst possible news is immediately confirmed. We are creating an atmosphere. And it is worse than ever.

'I don't want to go in, Mummy,' says Lydia, in a tiny voice, turning her face towards my stomach.

'Nonsense. You'll be fine.'

Other children are shoving past us.

'Look, everyone is going to assembly, hurry up.'

'They don't want me here, Mummy.'

She is so obviously correct: how can I lie? The sense of hostility is palpable. Whereas before the kids here mainly ignored her, now the other children look fearful. One boy is pointing at her and whispering, two blonde girls from Lydia's class are backing away from Lydia, as I push her towards the corridor, and into a day where she must survive, without me.

Closing my eyes, I steady my emotions, and walk through the cold to the car, trying not to think of Lydia, in that school, alone. If she suffers one more day of torment I will take her out, and we will give up. But I want to try one more time.

I need to go to Broadford to work, to plan things: so I drive fast and hard, taking the icy curves like a local, not some pootling tourist. In that way, if in no other, I have acclimatized, and slotted right in.

'Cappuccino, please.'

It's my normal rigmarole: double-shot capp and very good wifi, in the café diagonally opposite the Co-op, in the table that looks out the window at Scizzorz the hairdresser and Hillyard the fisherman's shop that sells oilskins and spear-guns and buckets of bait, and lobster pots to local drug dealers, or so it is said. I've seen those boats on the Sound, collecting the lobster pots: allegedly cached with heroin and cocaine. I didn't believe the rumours at first; but then I saw the fishermen driving BMWs in Uig and Fort William, and I wondered.

Everything here is more malevolent, and sinister, than it first appears. Sometimes things aren't remotely as you imagined, sometimes what you thought was reality does not exist at all.

Mummy, am I invisible now?

Opening my laptop, sipping my coffee, I send a brace of urgent won't-wait emails, then I do some research on child protection and parental abuse. It is a depressing trudge: there are so many words I don't want to see. Like *police*. An hour later, I make first contact with my solicitor – preparing for separation and divorce, for dislocation from Daddy.

And then I feel a throbbing in my jeans pocket and take out my phone. I am swallowing the taste of anxiety.

Six missed calls?

And they are all from Kylerdale School. In the last twenty minutes. I had the phone set to mute; I hadn't noticed the vibrations as I was so absorbed.

Something sharp breaks inside me, and I get a keen sense of dread: I know that a terrible thing is happening to Lydia at Kylerdale. I have to save her. Slapping change on the table, I run out of the café and jump in the car and skid back down the Sleat peninsula.

I'm driving so fast sheep scatter in damp grey fields as I accelerate past, slurring grit, skidding right, pulling up at Kylerdale School. It is playtime. I can hear the chanting.

'Bogan, bogan, bogan, bogan.' There are dozens of kids in the yard and they are pointing and chanting. But they are shouting at a wall, with a window. What is happening?

I open the gate to the playground – which is forbidden at normal hours but this is so far from normal, so fucking far – and now I am pushing through all these kids – as they keep shrieking and chanting, and yelling at the window in the white-painted bricks: 'Bogan! Bogan! Bogan!'

There is a teacher out here, trying to calm the

311

children, but the kids are panicked, hysterical, out of control, not listening to the teachers. But why are they screaming? What are they screaming at? I run over to the window and peer through the glazing, and there, in some kind of study, or an office, is Lydia, cowering in the corner.

She is on her own in this room and she has her hands over her ears, trying to block out the noise of the mobbing children outside. And there are tears running down her face, she is doing that silent eerie sobbing, and I am slapping on the window, trying to signal to Lydia, *I'm here I'm here, Mummy is here*, but Lydia is not looking and still the kids are screaming 'Bogan! Bogan!' And then I sense a hand on my shoulder and I turn and it is Sally the school sec, who says, 'We've been trying to call you, for an hour, we've been trying, we—'

'What happened?'

'We don't know, something in the classroom, it terrified the other children. I'm so sorry, we had to isolate Lydia. We put her in the stationery office, to protect her, till you got here.'

'Isolate her? Protect her?!' I am outraged. 'Protect her from *what*? Is that what you call protecting her?? Locking her in a room on her own?'

'Mrs Moorcroft—'

'Shutting her in by herself? How fucking frightened do you think she is?'

'But, but but – you don't understand – the teacher was with her. She must have stepped out. Everyone is unnerved. We tried to reach your husband as well, but—'

I am so angry, I am close to slapping this bitch. But I ignore her and I run into the school, shouting at some young man, Where is my daughter? Where is the

312

stationery room? and he says nothing. His mouth opens and closes, and then he points and I follow his gesture. Pushing my way into an empty classroom, I trip over tiny plastic chairs and buckets of papier mâché, and then I'm out in another corridor and I see a door that says *Stationery* and *Paipearachd Oifig* and now I realize, with a flux of nausea, how much I loathe this Gaelic crap.

The door is not locked, it opens when I turn the handle and there inside is Lydia: crouched in a corner, her hands still over her ears, her blonde hair sticking to her face from the dampness of her tears, and then Lydia looks up, and sees me and she drops her hands and yells, with sobbing relief, and terror, with a voice that rips through me like a knife, slicing me with guilt:

'Mummmmmyyyy!'

'What happened, baby, what happened?'

'Mummy, they are all shouting, they chased me, they chased me in here, they put me in here, I was so scared so—'

'It's all right.' I am hugging her smallness to my chest, tight as I can; trying to squeeze the terror out of her, hug the memories away. Smoothing the hair away from her pink face I kiss, once and twice, and kiss her again, and I say, 'I'm taking you out of here, now, right this minute.'

She looks at me: hopeful, yet disbelieving, and entirely desolate.

'Come on.' I tug her gently by the hand.

And we open the door, and then we retrace my steps to the school gate. No one stops us, or even talks to us: everyone is silent, teachers are standing in doorways, watching, blushing, saying nothing. I open the last glass door to the fresh sea air, and now we have to run the gauntlet of the kids, locked behind the wire in the playground, by the path that leads to the car park.

But the children aren't screaming any more. They are silent. All of them. Observing our departure. Several rows of silent, wondering faces.

Opening the car door, I strap Lydia into the child seat and we drive, in silence, the curving road to Ornsay. Lydia only speaks when we reach the boat and we are motoring back to Torran.

'Will I have to go back to school tomorrow?'

'No!' I say. Shouting above the sound of the outboard motor, and the slap of the agitated waves. 'You're never going back. That's it. We will find you another school.'

Lydia nods, her face hooded by her anorak, then she turns and looks at the water and the approaching light-house. What is she thinking? What has she been through? Why were the kids shouting? We beach the boat and I drag it to safety and we go into the kitchen where I cook up tinned tomato soup and buttery bread cut into soldiers. Comforting food.

Lydia and I sit in silence at the dining-room table in the bare grey dining room with the Scottish dancer painted on the wall. Something about this image chills me more than ever. Because it is coming back. I painted over half these figures: the dancer, the mermaid, yet they are re-emerging through my paint-layers. I didn't use enough paint.

The dancer looks at me, pale and inscrutable.

Lydia barely eats any soup. She dunks her bread in: eats half a soldier. She leaves the other half on the table, leaking red soup like blood. And now she just stares at the soup and says, 'Can I go to my room?'

And I want to say yes. Let her sleep. Let her dream this day away. But I have to ask first: 'The kids, in the school, what were they shouting? Bogan? What does it mean?'

Lydia looks my way as if I am stupid. She has learned some Gaelic at school; I have learned nothing.

'It means *ghost*,' she says, quietly. 'Can I go my room?'

I am fighting my fears. I spoon some soup in my mouth and point at her soup. 'Please eat some more, two more spoonfuls, for Mummy.'

'OK,' she says. 'Yes, Mummy.'

Obediently she eats two spoonfuls of soup then she drops the spoon and she runs out of the room and I hear her in her bedroom. The iPad clicks and whirrs. Yes. Let her play with that. Let her do what she likes.

For the next hour or two I divert my thoughts by planning our escape: sitting at the table with papers and laptop. We can't afford to go back to London. I don't want to go back to London. Maybe I could take Lydia and me to stay with Mum and Dad, just for a few weeks? But Instow is also haunted by memories.

My mind strays back to this afternoon. The screaming of the children.

Bogan bogan bogan bogan. Ghost Ghost Ghost Ghost.

Why would they shout that?

I cannot think about it. I mustn't think about it.

So what do I do? Plan The Future.

I would quite like to stay in Skye, if not on Torran. I've grown closer to Molly, so perhaps I could rent a cottage near Ornsay, to be near her. Then again, perhaps this is madness. Perhaps it is ridiculous to consider lingering here.

The fact is, I have no idea what to do, how to get out of this. What's worse, I will have to talk to Angus. Do we sell Torran, rent it out, or what? Lydia and I could do with the money from Torran Restored. But are we entitled to that cash? Why should he get anything, after what he did?

He should be in prison.

Dropping my pen, I rub my tired eyes. I need to lie down. Shutting the notebook, I walk into the bedroom I once shared with Angus. There is a mirror here: the last big mirror in the house. We have hidden all the others because they upset Lydia.

I stare at my image in the mirror. The afternoon light is wintry and feeble. I look wintry and feeble. Thin, and maybe even gaunt. I need to take better care of myself.

I gaze at my reflection. Lydia is standing there, in my reflection, Leopardy in her hand. She must have wandered into my bedroom. She is smiling. She has cheered up. Her smile is pert, serene, chirpy.

I turn and look at my daughter, for real. Standing there in my room. Quiet and alone.

'Hello, you. Feeling better?'

But she has stopped smiling. This is quick. Her expression has changed very quickly.

Then I realize she is not carrying Leopardy.

24

I gaze at my daughter. She looks right back at me, silent and questioning and younger than ever: as if she is going back in time, to when both twins were alive, six years old, five, four, down down down. I remember them playing bumps on the beach in Devon, banging their hips together; the memories swirl. I feel frightened and giddy: staring down at the past.

They are both here. They cannot both be here.

'Lydia.'

'Yes, Mummy?'

'Are you playing a funny game?'

'I don't understand, Mummy.'

'With Leopardy, darling, with Leopardy, are you playing a silly game?'

I swivel and check the mirror once more: there we are, mother and daughter, Sarah Moorcroft and her surviving daughter, Lydia Moorcroft. A little girl in bright yellow leggings, and a denim skirt with a cheery red bird embroidered on the front.

She carries no Leopardy. Yet she was carrying Leopardy in the mirror: I'm sure I saw it. Didn't I? And she was wearing Kirstie's perkier, happier smile. It was Kirstie I saw reflected. They both loved Leopardy, they would fight over him. Maybe they are fighting now. As they fought in my womb. As they fought for my milk.

They are *both* here in the cold white room, with the cold grey sky outside, fighting to see which one of them lives and which one of them dies, all over again.

I lean to the bed. I am unsteady.

'What's wrong, Mummy?'

'Nothing, darling, nothing. Mummy is just a bit tired.'

'You look different.'

Why is this bedroom so cold? The house, the cottage, is always cold, it always feels like the icy relentless sea has eaten into the bones of the place; but this is a new and different cold: my breath is misting before my mouth.

'It's freezing in here,' says Kirstie.

'Yes,' I say, and I stand. 'Yes, let's go into the living room and get the fire going properly.'

I take her little hand and it too is cold, like the hand of a corpse; I remember holding Kirstie's still-warm hand, desperately searching for her pulse, when I ran down the stairs at Devon to see if she was dead.

Is Kirstie really in this room now? The doubts engulf me. I look around the room at the white walls, at the crucifix next to the Scottish chieftain, at the old sash windows showing wet green heather and dark blue sea; a wind is truly picking up. Torran's few stunted trees are bending.

'Come on, Moomin.'

My voice is scratchy. I am trying not to show Lydia how scared I am: scared of this house. Scared of the island. Scared of what is happening to us. And scared of my daughter.

Lydia looks unfussed, and when we retreat to the living room she sits on the sofa, quite calm now, despite the trauma at school.

But as I kneel and stuff logs into the never-satisfied woodfire, I am not calm. The urgent wind is rattling the crappy window frames of Torran cottage and all those strange moments begin to coalesce. I stare into the flames as I feed the fire. What did I just see then? What happened with Emily Durrant, she was screaming something about a mirror?

And the incident today at the school. Bogan, bogan, bogan. *Ghost, ghost, ghost.*

Could we truly be haunted? I don't believe in ghosts. But it was Kirstie in that mirror. Yet Kirstie was and is identical to Lydia. So it was Lydia too; they are the ghosts of each other, Lydia is already the living ghost of Kirstie. I am living with a ghost as it is; why can't I believe in ghosts?

Because they do not exist.

Yet it was Kirstie in that mirror. Come back to say hello. Come back to talk to Mummy.

You let me jump, Mummy. It was your fault.

And it was my fault. Why wasn't I there? Why wasn't I looking after my daughters? I was the parent in charge. Angus was in London. I should have been there. I should have been there long before: stopping him from doing what he did. I should have seen the signs. *Elevated Levels of Paternal Abuse.*

Why didn't you stop him, Mummy?

'It's not your fault,' says Lydia, out loud, and I am so startled I drop a chunk of damp log onto the scruffy rug.

I stare at my daughter.

'What?'

'The school thing,' Lydia says. 'That wasn't your fault. It was Kirstie's fault. She keeps coming back, doesn't she? She frightens me.'

'Don't be silly, Lydie.' I pick up the log and install it in the flames; the heat raves and crackles, and it does not touch the cold. If I walk four yards from the fire my breath will be misting again. This fucking house.

'Anyway, Lydia, we're going to be leaving soon, so there's no need to worry about any of that any more.'

'What?'

'We're moving, darling. Leaving. Moving on.'

'Leaving the island behind?'

'Yes.'

Her face twists into a frown: maybe a panicked sadness.

'But you wanted us to come here, Mummy, and you said it was going to be better than before.'

'I know. But—'

'What about Kirstie? Kirstie is here. And Beany is here, we can't leave them behind, can we? And what about Daddy—'

'But—'

'I don't want to go anywhere – 'less Daddy comes too!'

Her anxiety is rising again, far too quickly. Everything disturbs her now; she is unapproachably fragile. What do I say?

'Oh, we'll see Daddy, too, sweetie, I promise. We just need to find a new house, with a road, and a TV – won't that be good? The next place will have a TV and heating and everything.'

Lydia says nothing. She stares at the blazing woodfire. I can see the faint glow of the flames on her anxious little face, reflected, as the darkness gathers. A raven's wing sweeping across the world. The windows are agitated by the wind. This is beyond Torran's normal brutal breezes. I can hear moaning from the pines on Salmadair as the wind races towards us, from Eisort and Tokavaig, from Ord and Sgurr Alasdair.

'She's in here now, isn't she?' says Lydia, very quietly.

'What?'

'Kirstie. Here.'

'What?'

My blood is tingling cold in my hands.

Lydia gazes at me, her expression a strange mixture of passivity and fear. 'She is here now, Mummy. Here. In this room. Look!'

I stare around the room, feeling something close to terror. Expecting my dead daughter to emerge from the frigid gloom of the hallway. But there is nothing. Just shadows of the furniture, dancing on the walls, enraged by the roaring flames of the woodfire.

'Nonsense, Lydia, we just need to get away. I'm going to make us some—'

A terrible noise interrupts me: I am so frightened, I laugh, nervously, when I realize it is the telephone. Just the phone? I am so alarmed and nervous, the old-fashioned bell of the phone is freaking me out.

Brought to my senses, I give Lydia a hug and a kiss then I run into the dining room, eager to hear a human voice, an adult voice, someone from out there, the place of sanity, the normal mainland where people live, and work, and watch TV; I hope it's Molly, maybe Josh, my folks, I wouldn't even mind if it was Imogen.

It's Angus.

The only person I don't want to talk to in the world is the only one who calls me. His sombre voice fills me with a yearning and bitter sadness. I can barely stop

321

myself slamming the phone down. And he is talking about the weather.

The fucking weather?

'Seriously, Sarah, they say it's going to be, ach, terrible. Big big storm. Think you should come off the island. I can come over in Josh's boat.'

'What? And stay with you, Gus? That will be so *nice*.'

'Really. Look at the wind, Sarah – look, and it's only just picking up. Just beginning. Remember I told you, these storms can last for days.'

'Yes. I get it.'

'And Torran is famous for it. Torran. Eilean Torran. Thunder Island. Remember? Sarah? Remember?'

I stare out of the window at the wintry darkness, as he talks. The last daylight has fled away to the west, I can see the final dim whiteness above Tokavaig. But the sky is clearing and a full moon is out. And if anything, the sea appears calmer than before, the trees have stopped that awful moaning. The only odd thing is those high, fragmented clouds: they are racing across the blue-black sky, silently and very fast.

'Looks fine to me, the wind has dropped. Gus, please stop ringing us, stop bothering us, you know, I, I, you know why—' I have to say it, I have to, I am going to say it. 'You know what you did. I've had enough of the lies. You know what happened. I know what happened. Let's stop lying, here and now.'

The phone line is dead quiet. As if it has finally failed. Then Angus says: 'What the fuck are you talking about?'

'You. Angus. *You*. You and Kirstie.'

'What??'

'You know what you did. I've worked it out. Lydia told me. About you touching Kirstie. Kissing her. Scaring her. And Dr Kellaway confirmed it, basically.'

'What? Sarah? This is drivel. What the fuck are you talking about?'

'You abused her. You were abusing her. Abusing Kirstie. Sexually. Touching her, that's what you did, you bastard, that's what you were doing, for months, for years – how long? The way she'd sit on your lap, the way you fucking *hugged* her – you were touching her, weren't you? Don't fucking deny it, that's why she jumped, she was scared of you, she jumped, didn't she, jumped, fucking jumped. She killed herself, and it was 'cause of you, her own *father*. Did you rape her? How far did it go? And now Lydia is screwed up, too, she doesn't know what to do, you've broken us, you've broken this family, you did this, you, and and—'

I've run out of hatred. The words fail in my mouth. I am trembling as I hold the phone. Angus is saying nothing. I'm not sure how I expect him to react. With anger? With flaming denial?

His answering voice is quiet: there is anger there, but he is calm.

'This is untrue, Sarah, all of it. Entirely untrue.'

'Oh yes? So—'

'I never touched Kirstie. Not like THAT. How could you think this?'

'Lydia told me.'

'I was tactile with Kirstie. I gave her hugs. Kisses. That's all. I tried to cheer her up. Be affectionate. And why? 'Cause you weren't, that's why.'

'You scared her.'

'I snapped at her. Once. Sarah, this is crazy. You are fucking crazy.'

'Don't you dare make this about me, don't you—'

'Shut up,' he says. 'Shut. The. Fuck. Up.'

Like a commanded child, I am silenced. He can still

somehow do this. Because when he does it I am seven years old again: and my dad is shouting. But Angus is not shouting, he goes on, very slowly and precisely:

'If you want the real truth, ask your daughter what really happened. Ask her to tell you what she told me, six months ago.'

'What?'

'Ask her, if you must. And have a look in the kist. Did you ever reach the bottom drawer, hmm? No?' His voice spits with anger. 'Then batten down the hatches, Sarah. This storm is coming. If you want to sit it out on Torran then – then there's nothing I can do. Fuck you. But keep our daughter indoors. Keep her safe.'

He has confused me. But maybe he is trying to confuse me. The anger rises again, inside me:

'Don't come near us, Angus. Don't come near us, don't speak to us, just – don't.'

I drop the phone.

'Mummy?'

It's Lydia. She is in the dining room: I didn't hear her come in. Because I was yelling at Angus.

'Mummy? What's happening?'

The realization is sickening. How much of that conversation did she witness? I just got carried away. I did not think. Did she hear me accuse her father of raping Kirstie? What have I done? Am I making it all worse?

My only choice is to pretend I said none of this, and act normal. I can hardly lean down to her and ask her whether she heard me accuse Daddy of rape.

'Nothing's happening, sweetness. Mummy and Daddy were just talking.'

'No you weren't, you were shouting.'

What did she hear? I force a smile. She is not smiling.

'What's wrong, Mummy? Why are you shouting at Daddy? Is it because of Kirstie, because she keeps coming back, because he wants her back?'

I want to say Yes.

But I control myself and I place a protective arm over Lydia's shoulder, and I guide her away from all this: into the kitchen. The kitchen feels like the kitchen in a drama, in a TV play. A stage set. A simulacrum of normality. But the walls are fake and the brightness is unreal and there is a strange darkness beyond, and there are people watching. A silent crowd, watching us onstage in the lights.

'Shall we have some tea? What do you want for tea?'

Lydia gazes, at me, then at the fridge. 'Dunno.'

'Anything you like, Moomin. Anything in the fridge.'

'Um . . . Cheese toastie.'

'Good idea! I'll make some cheese on toast, it won't take long. Why don't you go and play in the living room, let me know if the fire is doing OK.'

Lydia looks at me with a hint of suspicion – or wari-ness – then, to my intense relief, she slopes out. Now I can pretend that she didn't hear any of that *chat* with Angus.

Carefully, I take the bread from the wire basket above my head, then the Cheddar from the fridge. I glance out of the window: the strange grey clouds are racing again: very fast, across the appalled white face of the moon. The trees have begun to moan, once more, as the wind kicks up. Was Angus right about the storm?

I need to feed my daughter.

When the toasted cheese is melting and popping I slide it out from under the grill, then I serve it on a plate, and cut it into special bite-size pieces, and I take it into the dining room, where Lydia sits, patiently.

At the dining-room table. She is wearing blue socks now. She must have put them on just this moment. Leopardy has reappeared and sits on the table next to her: his inert, cuddly-toy smile is aimed directly at me.

Lydia picks up her little orange plastic-handled kids' knife and fork and she eats the cheese on toast placidly enough. She has a book by her plate. Usually I don't like her reading as she eats, but I am not going to stop her today. She seems remarkably and strangely contented, considering the terrors she has endured.

I look out of the window. The moon has disappeared behind bigger clouds; the trees are moaning much louder. Rain is hitting the windows. Angry and contemptuous. Lydia is eating and reading and humming a little tune: 'My Bonnie Lies Over the Ocean'.

Kirstie's nursery rhyme. She is humming it here.

O bring back, bring back, bring back my Bonnie to me.

I try to stay calm. But I have the intense, abrupt and overwhelming sense that this is *Kirstie*, sitting right here in front of me. Sitting in the semi-dark of the dining room, with the island cowering before an approaching storm, with the lighthouse flicking, desperately, urgently, signalling every nine seconds across the dark waters of the Sound: *Help, Help, Help*.

'Lydia,' I say.

She does not turn.

'Lydia.'

She does not turn. She eats and hums. Leopardy smiles at me: sitting on the table. I have to fight my way back to logic: this is Lydia, sitting here. I am letting the stress delude me.

Leaning back, I take deep breaths. Calming myself. Regarding my daughter. Trying to be objective. Now I remember what Angus said: *Ask her about what really happened, ask her what she told me six months ago.* Something in these words is quite piercing: and his denial of child abuse was halfway convincing. I don't believe him, and yet: I do have troubling doubts. Have I leapt to some terrible false conclusion?

What to do?

The storm is really picking up. I can hear doors, somewhere, slamming repeatedly, and helplessly. External doors, perhaps the shed. They sound bad: as if they could break. I need to secure everything: *batten down the hatches.*

So I don't have much choice what to do next. The weather is in command. Leaning across the table, I touch Lydia on the hand, to get her attention: she is wrapped up in her book, and she has stopped humming that frightening song.

'Darling, will you wait here – there's going to be some really bad weather tonight, and I have to go and check the cottage. Outside.'

She looks up at me, and she shrugs. Passive, distracted.

'OK, Mummy.'

I stand and step into the bedroom and I refuse to look at the mirror. I put on a thick jumper, then my sturdiest North Face anorak. Back in the kitchen I slip on my wellingtons, then I mentally brace myself, and open the kitchen door.

The wind is ferocious. Dead leaves, slips of seaweed, knots of dead bracken are flying through the cold dark air. The lighthouse looks diminished by the booming noise of the wind. Its flickering light is no longer any comfort.

I have to secure all the external doors. But the wind is so strong it almost tips me to the side, into the slippery grass, as I shuffle around the cottage walls. I have never encountered gales like this: not in soft southern England. Occasionally the wind hurls rain right in my face: it stings like cold grit, as if someone is flinging sharpness in my face. I am being threatened.

The shed door is flapping on its rusty hinges: they sound as if they are about to break. My hands are numb with rain and cold as I close the door and slide the wooden bar across.

I once wondered why all the external doors had these wooden bars. Now I know. For the storms of Thunder Island: Eilean Torran.

My task takes me twenty minutes. The most difficult part is dragging the soggy dinghy as high as I can manage, in the dark, and the screaming gales, and the horrid wetness. As I drag the boat, I almost fall, cracking one knee on the shingles, then righting myself.

'Jesus,' I say. 'Come on, Sarah!' I am shouting these words out loud, to myself. But my words are stolen by the gale and hurled into the sea.

'Come on!'

How high does the boat have to go, to be safe? I drag the boat all the way up to the lighthouse steps; then I weight it down with the anchor, and lash it to the lighthouse railings. My fingers are clumsy in the freezing blackness.

But there. Done. I can tie knots, just as Angus taught me.

Now I am running back, heading for the kitchen door, crouching down: tugging one side of my hood against the bitter rain. With an exultation of relief I drag myself into the kitchen, close the door behind me. The kitchen door has an internal wooden bar: I slide this across, too. The horrible moaning and howling is muffled, but still audible.

'Mummy, I'm frightened.'

Lydia is standing in the kitchen.

'The wind is so noisy, Mummy.'

'Hey, it's only a storm,' I say, giving her a hug. 'We've just got to sit it out. We'll be fine. We've got food and firewood. It will be like an adventure.'

'Is Daddy coming here to help?'

'Not tonight, darling, but maybe tomorrow. We'll see.'

I'm telling lies. Doesn't matter. The mention of Angus brings me back to his words: his denial of the abuse. And then that other phrase: Ask Lydia what she told me six months ago. I have to go deeper into this: it is going to hurt Lydia, but if I don't go deeper, her mother will go crazy, which is worse.

'Let's go in the living room, sweetie, I want to ask you something.'

Lydia looks up at me. Panicked.

'Ask me what?'

I lead her into the living room and draw the curtains against the rain and the wind, and the thumps of the wind on the roof – it sounds like slates being torn away – and then in front of the fire, as we sit huddled and cuddled together on the sofa, under a blanket that still smells faintly of Beany, I ask her: 'You know you said Daddy touched and kissed Kirstie?'

Her eyes flicker. Embarrassed?

'Yes, Mummy.'

'What did you mean by that?'

'What?'

'When you said it, did you mean—' I search for the words. 'Did you mean he touched and kissed her, the way Mummy and Daddy touch and kiss? Do you mean like that?'

329

She gives me all her attention. And her face is shocked. 'No. No, Mummy. No! Not like that!'

'So . . .' The darkness opens wide inside me. I might have made an atrocious error. Again. 'What did you mean, Lydie?'

'He was just cuddling her, because you wouldn't, Mummy. And then he shouted. That scared her. I don't know why he shouted.'

'You're sure?'

'Yes, Mummy. Sure. I'm sure. He didn't kiss her like Mummy and Daddy. No. No! Not like that!'

The darkness turns to blackness.

I take long breaths, with my eyes closed. Then I try again. 'OK. One more question, darling. What did you tell Daddy six months ago?'

Lydia sits there. Awkward. Stiff. Not quite gazing at me. Her eyes angry and wet, and frightened.

I repeat the question. Nothing.

Just like her mother and her grandmother. Nothing.

But I am determined to do this. I've come so far, I must get to the end. Even if it is causing her obvious distress. My rationale is that if I do all this on the same day then maybe it will fade into her memory as just one terrible day, the Day of the Storm.

I ask again. Nothing.

I try once more.

'Did Daddy ever ask anything about Kirstie, or did you ever tell him something about Kirstie, when he asked?'

She shakes her head. She is backing away from me: extracting herself from my embrace, edging up the sofa. The wind shrieks in the trees outside. This is horrific. I ask again. I have to know.

'Did you tell Daddy something six months ago?'

330

No response.

'Lydia?'

Silence. Then she breaks open.

'This is what Daddy did, this is what Daddy did, you're doing what Daddy did: STOP IT!'

What?

I reach out a hand, to calm my agitated daughter. 'What did you say, darling? What do you mean – this is what Daddy did?'

'Like you, like THIS, what you are doing *now*.'

'Lydia, tell me—'

'I'm not Lydia, I'm Kirstie.'

I have to ignore this.

'Lydia, what did Daddy say, what did you say? Tell me.'

The wind throws everything at the walls and doors. It feels as if the house is going to break.

'He did THIS. He kept asking me QUESTIONS about it, about the accident, so I told him, Mummy, I told him—'

'What, darling?' My blood is thumping even louder in my ears than the booms of the wind outside. 'Just tell me what you said.'

Lydia looks at me, gravely. She seems suddenly older. A vision of the adult she will become. And now she says, 'I told Daddy I did it, and I did, I did, I did it – I did something bad.'

'What? What do you mean? What did you do?'

'I told Daddy I did something bad. And I DID. Daddy didn't do anything. But I never told him about you, nothing about you, I told him 'bout me not you so he wasn't angry with YOU—'

'Lydia?'

'What??'

'Lydia. Tell me. Now. Tell me everything.'

'Tell you everything? But you *know*! You already *know* everything!' The wind duets with my daughter, screaming and repeating, 'Mummy, you know what happened. You *know it!*'

'No, I don't.'

'Yes you do yes you do.'

'No, I don't.'

'Yes you do YES YOU DO!' My daughter is trembling, and shrieking, 'It wasn't just me, it was never just me.' A sudden silence. Lydia looks straight at me. And then she screams in my face. 'MUMMY SHE DIED BECAUSE OF YOU!'

25

Angus sat in the Selkie, nursing a triple of Ardbeg: drinking by himself. The pub was virtually deserted, the only noise came from a few locals, including Gordon, finishing up their pints before they all headed home to sit out the storm. Angus had booked a berth upstairs: the Selkie was pricey in summer but a bargain in the winter depths.

He would have stayed with Josh and Molly again – they were normally very generous – but it didn't feel right. He was too angered by Sarah's outrageous accusation. He would make his friends uncomfortable.

Child abuse.

It was insane. The idea – the mere idea of the idea – entirely enraged him. Maybe it was a good thing he was stranded on Sleat, away from his family, because if he saw Sarah, after all these whiskies, he would probably kill her. Actually kill her. He would. He could. Just break her neck.

Now he could see his father in himself: kicking the shit out of the little woman. The difference was that he, Angus, was justified.

Child abuse.

Did you rape Kirstie?

He swooned with rage, but steadied himself with another slug of whisky. And another. What else could he do? It was all her fault, anyway.

Standing up and walking to the window, Angus gazed drunkenly through the thick glass at the island, now blurred by rain and dark.

How was his daughter doing, stuck on that island in the storm? Did Sarah have the sense to hunker down properly? Would she secure all the doors and windows, slide the necessary bolts? Would she lash the boat to the lighthouse railings? She wasn't an idiot. Perhaps she would do all this.

But she was also unstable, and had been so since their daughter's death. She'd recovered her senses in recent months but now she was, apparently, right back in the vortex. The whirl of her private insanity.

Child abuse.

Angus wanted to spit the words onto the floor. Bitch. Fucking cunt. Child abuse?

What lies was she pumping into his daughter right now?

He needed to get over there, and take control, but the tide was in, and the weather was too foul for anything but the biggest boat to cross in safety; Josh's RIB was not built for gales like this. And this storm could take several days to clear.

That meant, if he had to get to Torran by boat, he would be obliged to call the authorities and seek official help. He would need the police, the coastguard, the law. But if he brought them into this mess, everything would unravel: he might – he probably would – get arrested for child abuse. And even if he managed to prove the absurdity of that allegation, the police might then ask questions about the accident, and they might discover that the sister pushed the sister, that there was a murder, however childish.

And then, everything he had striven to do – to keep the family together, despite it all – would come flying apart. Their lives would be shattered, for the second time. A whirling nightmare of police, doctors, child psychologists. Sarah would crack when her guilt was revealed, when her denial was ripped away.

And yet she might crack anyway: because of his stupid outburst.

He shouldn't have said what he'd said about the kist. He'd just been lashing out, in his fury. Not thinking. Yet now, if she remembered this remark, and actually looked in the bottom drawer, she would see the truth and there was no guessing how she might react. Out there. When she was meant to be caring for his little girl.

Perhaps he should have destroyed the contents of the drawer, months ago. Yet he'd always kept it, in reserve. Spare ammunition. Once his daughter was safely grown up, he'd thought he might show it to her: *See, here, bitch, this is what YOU did. This is what REALLY happened.*

Too late.

Angus sat down, defeated, drunk, angry, trembling, on the hard uncomfortable chair. He was paralysed. He couldn't do anything until the storm passed, could he? But he was desperate.

'All right there, Angus?'

It was Gordon, passing out of the pub.

'Yer girls out on Torran?'

Angus nodded. Gordon frowned.

'Raw night for them to be alone, out there. That cottage is hellish cold in these storms.'

'I know.'

Gordon shook his head. 'And that thunder. Could drive a man to drink!' He glanced at Angus's whisky glass, and frowned again. 'Well now. If you need any help, ye know where to call me, any time.'

'Thanks, Gordon.'

Gordon sighed, blatantly dismayed by Angus's attitude, then opened the door to the blasting wail of the storm, and disappeared.

Angus stared out of the window again. The wind was so strong it was ripping small branches off the trees down the way: the car park of the Selkie was a mess of leaves, and twigs, and shrivelled bracken.

What was Sarah doing on Torran? What was she doing with his daughter?

He had to get out there as soon as the tide allowed. It didn't matter how dangerous it was: not doing anything was worse. He had to get out there and make Sarah see sense. Or calm her down. Or maybe silence her.

That, then, was his plan. Cross before dawn, at the next low tide, six a.m. And before then he would drink away the pain, and stifle the anger. Until he needed that anger.

26

I ask for the third time, maybe the fourth time. This is
too much.

'What do you mean, it was *me?*'

I cannot disguise the trembling fear in my voice.
Lydia has now stopped screaming, stopped crying; but
she is looking away from me. Leopardy is lying next
to her. She picks him up and hugs him close, as if he
is a better friend to her than me. Better than her own
mother.

'Lydia, what did I do? What do you mean it was me?'

'Not saying.'

'Come on, please. I won't be angry.'

'Yes, you will. Like you were before, in the kitchen
at Nannan's.'

The wind rattles the windows, like a burglar. Testing
the house. Finding the weak points.

'Lydia. Lydia, *please.*'

'Nothing. No one. Nobody.'

'Lydie-lo, please tell me. Please!'

She turns, eyes narrowed. I can hear the kitchen door
rattling in the gale; the wooden bolt creaking.

'You took the pills, remember, Mummy?'

'Sorry?'

She shakes her head. She looks very sad, but she is not crying.

'What do you mean, I took the pills?'

'Everyone said you were sick, Mummy. I was frightened you were going to die like Kirstie.'

'What pills?'

'Special pills. Oh, Mummy, you know? Daddy kept them.'

'He . . .'

Pills? I am getting the sense of dim memories, returning. I *did* take pills, after the accident. It was that therapist, who emailed me, who recommended the medication. Yes, I can vaguely remember that.

But why? Was there a special reason?

'Take them again, Mummy. You were better when you took them.'

'I really don't know what you are talking about, Lydia. We just have to sit out the storm.'

Lydia looks at me, imploring. Very young again: wanting her mother back. 'Mummy, I'm frightened by the storm. Please just take them. I know where Daddy kept them in the bedroom drawer. I saw him put them there for you.'

The kist. Angus's chest of drawers. I never looked in all of it, not thoroughly. And he mentioned the bottom drawer in the phone call. I haven't confronted this yet. Is there something else in there?

'OK,' I say. 'It's getting late now. Do you want to go to sleep?'

'No.'

'You sure?'

'No.'

'You can sleep in Mummy's bed, if you want.'

'No!'

Lydia is clutching Leopardy tight, as if she fears the wind will rip him from her arms. And why not? Because the moaning of the wind in the trees is like a pack of wolves. We are being stalked by the weather: it is a huge beast on the prowl, battering the windows, seeking prey. This has been going on for six hours, and it could last for three days.

'Want to go to bed with Leopardy.'

Thank God. Thank God.

'OK. Then let's do that.'

This is better: I can get Lydia to bed, then I can look in the chest of drawers. Sort this poisonous mystery once and for all: and then maybe we can both sleep through the worst of the storm; maybe we will wake up and the sky will be blue and clear, and Knoydart will sparkle with snow across Loch Hourn. I will have to apologize to Angus. What I said was awful; but he still betrayed me with Imogen.

What is in that chest of drawers?

It is surprisingly easy to get Lydia ready for bed. We run to her room and she rips off her clothes, and she dives into her pyjamas and she slips quickly under two duvets, and I tuck her in tight and she closes her eyes, with Leopardy clutched in her fists. I kiss her. She smells sweet, in a sad way. Nostalgic.

The rain thrashes at her window; I close the curtains so Lydia cannot see reflections of her dead sister. I am about to turn off the light when she opens her eyes, and says, 'Mummy, am I becoming Kirstie?'

Sitting on the bed, I take her hand, and squeeze. 'No. You are Lydia.'

She stares up at me, blue eyes trusting, and hopeful,

and desperate. 'But, Mummy I don't know any more. I think I am Lydia, but sometimes Kirstie is inside me and she wants to come out and sometimes Kirstie is in the windows and sometimes she is just here, out here, with us.'

I stroke my daughter's soft blonde hair. I'm not going to cry. Let the wind do all the lamenting: it is loud enough for all of us. I can hear terrible crashing outside: perhaps one of the doors is being wrenched away. Maybe I did not lash the boat properly. I do not especially care. We couldn't use the boat in this weather anyway: we would drown.

'Lydia, let's go to sleep. Tomorrow the storm will be over, I promise, and then everything will be better. Tomorrow we can go somewhere else.'

Lydia looks at me, as if she does not believe me. But she nods, and says:

'OK then, Mummy.'

'Goodnight.'

I kiss her once more and inhale her scent so that I can remember it; then I shut the light, and close the door, and I sprint to my bedroom and grab the little key, and open the bottom drawer of Angus's kist. The wind thumps the walls and the slates. It sounds as if someone is dragging something along the roof.

Or maybe like a madman trying to get in.

There. Lots of pill bottles.

Tricyclic antidepressants.

They clink as I grab them from the drawer and turn them in my hand. They have my name on them: Sarah Moorcroft. The latest of the bottles is dated eight months ago. I recognize the bottles. I dimly remember taking the pills. I have images of myself holding one. Popping a pill. In the kitchen in Camden.

So it's true: I took antidepressants after Kirstie died? And I've forgotten. This is hardly a revelation. My daughter had died. I was in a terrible state.

But there is a letter here in the drawer under the bottles. I see from the letterhead it's from Dr Malone. My own, regular GP. My doctor is in his sixties, and he's probably the last doctor to write real letters in England. But this letter is written to Angus? Why is my doctor writing to my husband?

I pick up the letter and read. The wind slows to a sad crooning. As if it is exhausted, for the moment.

The letter is all about me. It says I am suffering from Complicated Grief Disorder. It says I have 'deep abiding guilt' about the death of my daughter.

The letter shakes, slightly, in my hand. I read on.

Clearly she feels, or felt, responsible for some aspects of the accident, as a result of her adulterous liaison that night. The guilt is therefore too much to bear, causing this situation-specific memory loss, which may well be permanent. This is rare but not unknown, a distinct form of Transient Global Amnesia. She will recall certain minor fragments, lucidly, and build a false picture therefrom, but the crucial, more personally painful elements will be missing.

Bereaved parents, especially, are known to suffer this kind of amnesia if they are implicated in the death of a child. And when grief takes a morbid turn, as it has done with your wife, there is no remedy but time. However the pills she has been prescribed will alleviate the worst of her symptoms: the mutism, the insomnia, &c. As I say, if and when she makes a recovery, her memory of the most important events surrounding the accident will, very likely, be completely absent.

My advice is to treat this as a blessing: you can then move on, start with a clean slate, which is necessary, if you want to rebuild your family, as you have indicated. And you should make no reference to her psychological disturbance, as this may cause regression and deepen her depression. It is very important to restrict all knowledge of this to your immediate family circle, as you are doing now. Suicidality is a concern, if she ever learns the truth, from any source.

The letter goes on. It wishes Angus and me the best of luck. And then it signs off.

Adulterous liaison?

The first outlines of an old memory emerge in my mind. Like breath misting on cold glass. I remember that strange dream I had: naked, hairless, in the kitchen. Then sex.

And then, when I woke, that sensation of intense and painful guilt.

A lash of rain makes me turn to the window. The darkness is still out there. Trying to get in.

The noise is repeated, as if someone is finger-tapping, very urgently. Then I hear a ghastly shearing sound. Metallic and loud. The shed door being pulled from its hinges? Everything is being stripped down to the bones.

Thunder booms, on Thunder Island. I gaze down at all the dinky pill bottles on the floor. There are a few dusty tablets left. I could take one. But I want to stay sane and lucid and I want to recall the truth, however painful.

346

And I don't think I will need help in going to sleep. I am exhausted: I want to curl up right now. With a prayer. Please please please let the storm blow itself out, overnight.

Adulterous liaison?

Slipping off my clothes until I am down to my underwear, I load the bed with blankets, turn off the light, get into bed, and close my eyes. For half an hour my mind churns the day, as the wind whips at the windows. And then sleep claims me, sucking me under.

I am woken by Lydia.

She is a dim shape in the room. Standing by my bed.

'Scared, Mummy. The wind keeps trying to come into the bedroom.'

I am groggy, only barely awake. It is so very dark, I have no idea what time. Maybe two a.m., three a.m.?

The wind is busy outside: tearing things up, the rain is still gritty on the windows. This fucking storm. I am so tired.

I reach for the dim form of my daughter. Her warm little hand. I can't see her face so I am not sure if she is crying. Her voice is wobbly. I yawn widely and say: 'Come on then, get into bed with Mummy.'

Lydia leaps quickly under the sheets and snuggles up to me and I squeeze her hard, and inhale the sweet smell of her hair, and we cuddle up, spooning. Her warmth is a serious comfort; I fall asleep again, with a feeling close to tranquillity.

And when I wake up it is still dark outside and the wind is still howling, quite undefeated. Unabated. Contemptuous of my prayers. I feel like screaming *Shut up!* Shouting like my dad, like Angus.

And then I realize there is no Lydia in my bed.

347

But there is the shape of Lydia in the sheets, and the dent made by her head on the pillow.

Where has she gone?

Jumping up, I sleeve myself in my dressing gown and grab a torch, I run barefoot through the cottage – through the cold dark living room, and down the hall, to the door of Lydia's room. I push open the door and shine the torch on her bed and there she is: asleep in her bed, her little nightlight twinkling.

Just as I left her, hours ago. Clutching Leopardy.

She looks as if she hasn't moved all night. She surely hasn't moved all night. If Lydia had come to my room, she would have been obliged to walk through almost total darkness. And she'd never do that.

The fear cuts me deep inside: dicing me into little pieces of panic. If Lydia hasn't left her bed since I tucked her up, who was it that slipped into my bed last night? Who was that girl? Was I holding Kirstie? Was I clutching a ghost? A real, living, warm-blooded ghost?

This is too much. I am the crazy woman who took the pills. I cannot bear this any more. I look at the small, boxy clock on Lydia's bedside table. It is not even six a.m. It won't be light for another two hours.

This has to end. I am hovering on the very edge. I walk back, in the torchlight, into the living room and pass into the dining room, where everything is so cold. Even colder than normal. Why?

Because there is water on the floor; it stings my bare feet it is so cold. The water must have come from somewhere. I can feel it dripping on my shoulder. Timidly I shine the torch upwards.

A huge hole has been ripped in the ceiling: the slates have been stripped away, and a rafter has broken, falling through the plaster, ripping a hole that exposes us to the dark, stormy sky. The wind gusts over the hole; the rain gutters down, and into the cottage.

This is calamitous. We need help.

Stepping over to the window sill, I pick up the phone. It is dead. Of course. Everything is dead. The line has finally given out. One possible hope, I suppose, is the boat, but I can see through the dining-room window that this option is also ruled out. The lighthouse is still flashing, and when it flashes it shows the truth.

I was right about the noise, that shearing: it was the railings of the lighthouse. They have been entirely ripped away, and the boat has vanished. Torn from its moorings, and swept into the blackness, in a few seconds.

Even if we wanted to take the terrible risk of using the boat – in this darkness, and in this weather – we can't. Not now.

We have no boat. We have no phone. We have no means of communicating with anyone on the mainland, we have no way of reaching Ornsay until the tides are down. We are trapped, and silenced. Me and Lydia.

And whoever else is in here.

I can hear singing.

'Last night as I laid on my pillow, last night as I laid on my bed.'

The singing is coming from the living room. I am barefoot in cold water: but I am shivering from fear, not from cold.

The ghost of my daughter is singing in the darkness.

'Last night as I laid on my pillow, I dreamt that my Bonnie was dead.'

She is in the living room. I lean against the window sill to stop myself from collapsing; then I turn and carry

349

my torch into the living room and I shine it on the sofa – and there she is: alone in the dark, barefoot in her soft pyjamas. It is Lydia. I think.

My daughter regards me, blinking in the torchlight. How did she get here? She is white-faced, and she looks exhausted. The rain flails the windows. It will not stop. I walk closer to the sofa.

'Kirstie is here again,' she says. 'She's in my room. I don't want to see her any more. Mummy, make her go away.'

I want nothing more than for Kirstie to go away. And maybe Lydia too. I am frightened of both of my daughters, the two ghosts in this house, the two ghosts in my head; the Ice Twins, melting, one into the other.

'Let's go into my room and get under the blankets. We can wait for the storm to stop, it will be over soon, it will be light quite soon.'

'OK, Mummy.'

Obediently, she reaches out a hand – but I pick her up bodily and carry her into the bedroom; where I tuck her into the Admiral's Bed and then I close the door. Then I slide the bolt. Whatever is out there, I don't want it to come in here.

Then I get into the bed with my little girl and she snuggles up to me and says, 'I don't believe what Lydia says, Mummy. She says horrible things.'

I am hardly listening to my daughter. I can hear a voice outside the door. Who is it?

It must be her. Kirstie. Or Lydia.

It is indistinct, it sounds like *Mummy Mummy Mummy*.

Now something knocks on the door. It isn't the wind. This is the bedroom door. Then the voice speaks again.

It is her. I am sure. She is outside the door.

I am trembling.

I hug my daughter close and I shut my eyes, trying to block out everything, now: the wind, the rain, the noises, the voices. Everything must end. But this storm will never end, this night will never end, it will just go on and on, I have no choice.

My daughter hugs me under the sheets and then she lifts her face very close to me. I can smell her breath in the darkness, it is sweet, childish, untainted, as if she has been sucking something sugary.

She says, 'Kirstie says it was all your fault. You were with that man. That's why she came back, to hurt you.'

The shards of ice are in me: cold and cutting, in my heart.

'What? What man, darling?'

'The man you were with that night. In the kitchen. I saw you kissing him. So it was your fault, too. I think Nannan knew too, but then she told me I must never say it to anyone.'

I say, 'Yes.'

Because I can remember. All of it.

This is what I have buried in my mind. This was the reason for my denial. This is the memory I lost because the guilt was too intense to bear. This was the self-loathing blurred by drugs.

The dream was telling me: weeks ago. I was shaved because of my shame. I was naked in the kitchen. There were people staring at me. There was a man, staring at my nudity.

I woke up masturbating. Because it was all about sex. But not the sex with my ex, when the twins were tiny.

Something much, much worse.

Angus was going to be very late. Mum and Dad were

351

out. So I asked a guy over. I'd met him in the boatyard bar in Instow a few months before. And I asked him over that night: because I wanted to sleep with him. I was bored with sex with Angus. I always wanted more sex than he did.

And I wanted the thrill of the new.

'Mummy?'

'It's OK, darling, everything is OK. It's OK.'

I kissed him passionately in the kitchen. That's why I was distracted. I was drinking wine with a man I liked and wanted to have sex with – so I kissed him long and deep across the table – and that's when the twins saw me. I was embarrassed and a little drunk; I shouted at them to go away. Then I fucked the man in the spare bedroom on the first floor.

And the guy's name was Simon. I remember it all now. A young, handsome guy, a member of a yacht crew. Younger than Angus: a man like Angus when we first met.

The memories pour into me; the truth rains down. The storm has ripped a hole.

After I'd had sex with Simon, he left, and then I fell asleep on the bed from all the wine and the sex and the house was empty, apart from me and the kids. But then the twins knocked gently on the door of the spare bedroom and again I barked at them, boozily told them to go away *again*; and I fell asleep once more.

And then I woke to hear the scream. The scream that told me what I had done.

I ran upstairs and there was my daughter, shrieking. About her sister. And that scream told me a truth I could not bear, I had been unfaithful, a second time, and this time it had killed my little girl. And that's why I lied, immediately, to everyone – the police, the hospital,

352

Angus, everyone – about the man, about the infidelity, about my neglect. I even told them that my twin fell from the first-floor balcony, trying to distract attention, with a foolish lie, so as to hide my guilt. Because the truth was too much and so my lies became the truth. Even for me. Especially for me.

But they still knew what I had done: my awful crime of neglect, and shame. Angus knew, my mother knew, my doctor knew. But they kept it quiet from everyone else, even the police, to protect me?

But how did Mum know? How did Angus find out?

Perhaps my mother saw something, perhaps my daughter confessed, or maybe this guy just said something in a bar: *I was with her mother, that night the child died*. It doesn't matter. They found out. It was all my fault. I did it. I was with another man – again – and because of that my daughter died. And they've been shielding me from the shattering reality ever since.

'I'm sorry, darling, so sorry, darling.'

'She's coming back now, Mummy. She's outside the door.'

'Kirstie?'

'No, Lydie. She's coming back. Listen.'

The wind is shrieking and the rain is hailing but, yes, I am sure I can hear my dead daughter, outside the bedroom.

Let me in. Let me in. You did it. You must let me in.

I am crying now. My daughter holds me in bed as I cry and my other daughter is outside saying,

Mummy, I'm back now. Let me in. I'm back now.

I kiss my daughter on her forehead and I say, 'She jumped, didn't she?'

My daughter stares at me, with those blue eyes like

353

her grandmother. Sombrely, tremulously, she says, 'No, Mummy. We wanted to climb down, Mummy, from the top balcony. To the other balcony of the other room – the room you were in, Mummy, 'cause we wanted to see why Daddy wasn't there. We were scared to open the bedroom door, 'cause you shouted at us, but Lydie still wanted to see, see through the window, if you were with the man who wasn't Daddy. And – and – and she tried to climb down and then I was climbing down and then she grabbed me, Mummy, she grabbed me because she was falling and she pulled so hard she was pulling me too; so' – my daughter's eyes are now full of tears, big fearful tears – 'that's when I pushed her away, Mummy! And then she fell all the way, it was my fault. You always liked her more and I pushed her off me 'cause I was falling too.'

The tears roll down her face as she speaks.

'So she fell, Mummy, she fell. And I did it, I pushed her 'cause she was pulling me too.'

I am silenced. My guilt is perfected. There is nothing left to know.

My dead daughter is outside. Guiltless and accusing. I need to say a final sorry, the only way I can. So this is it. The timing is immaculate. I am getting out of the bed, jumping into clothes.

Lydia stares at me in the half-light. Tears drying on her cheek. I crouch by the bed, and stroke the sweet blonde hair from my daughter's troubled face. 'Darling,' I say. 'Don't feel guilty. It was all my fault.'

'But it's not all right, Mummy? Is it?'

'No. It is. I am so sorry. It truly wasn't your fault, darling. You were just playing. It was all me, all my fault, everything. Everything has been my fault, all the time. Because of what I did, that night, you've been confused – so confused, for so long. Because of me.' I breathe deep and kiss her forehead. 'And that's why we're going to get away, from here, right now.'

'In the dark? It's too dark, Mummy.'

'That's OK, sweetie, I have a torch.'

'But the wind? And the dark an' everything?'

'It's all right. You can come with me. It's low tide at six. We can cross now in the dark. It won't take so long.'

Lydia looks at me from the bed. She frowns again, deeply puzzled. She rubs the last tears from her eyes with her fist. And I know that if she starts crying again I won't be able to do this terrible thing. So I need to be quick.

'Remember I always loved you. Always. Both of you.'

She is silent for a moment and then she says, 'I'm sorry I fell, Mummy. I'm sorry I tried to climb down to see you. I'm sorry I pulled at Kirstie . . .'

'What?'

'I'm sorry I fell, Mummy. I'm sorry I died.'

I kiss her one more time. 'It doesn't matter, Lydie, it was all my doing. Not anyone else's. But I still love you.' I reach over. 'And now it's time for us to go, to go and find your sister, so we can all be together.'

She nods slowly, and quietly. Then we stand, hand in hand, and we turn and walk to the door, and we unbolt it, and twist the handle. Her overclothes are in the living room: I slip her feet inside her boots, and sleeve her arms in her pink anorak, and I zip her up, tight. Then I put my own coat on, and my wellingtons.

We walk through the gloom and wet of the dining room, and the murk of the kitchen. The rain is dripping from the ceiling. The whole place is crumbling in the storm. It is time for us to leave.

Tightly clutching hands, Lydia and I pull open the kitchen door, and step into the hurling rain; straight into the black and howling wind.

Everything out here is as cold as ice.

27

Angus zipped his raincoat, and buttoned it, too. Then he realized that he was going to need many more levels of clothing than this, to fight the wind and rain, to cross the mudflats at six a.m. in the dark.

He was so drunk, his judgement was failing him. He undid his coat, and sat back down on the bed, listening to the wailing of the wind outside the Selkie. It resembled the hooting of a bunch of kids, trying to sound like ghosts.

The sound was quite convincing.

One more drink.

He reached for the bottle, nearly knocked it over, and poured himself a final glass of Ardbeg. The peaty, spicy whisky burned down his throat and he grimaced as he stood up, once more.

Another zip-up top, another jumper. Then his raincoat, again.

Now he grabbed for his boots, slightly swaying, and laced them tight. They were good, waterproof hiking boots, but they would not keep out the cold, seeping waters of the Torran mudflats. He was going to get horribly wet. But that was tolerable, as long as he made it out there, under cover of dark. Where he would do what he had to do. To save his daughter.

Angus was the only person around as he pushed open the front door of the hotel – against the resisting storm, out into the blackness; the Selkie was silenced by the booming of the wind.

Lights on a wire swung, crazily, in the gale. Torran lighthouse blinked through the murk.

Angus began the walk, down the pier, along the shingle and mud towards Salmadair. The cold dripped down his neck; the mist and rain grew denser as he waded out onto the gaping, endless mudflats.

Was he going the right way? The torch was heavy in his numb hands. He should have worn the head torch, as well. This was a stupid, foolish error. He was very drunk, and making elementary mistakes. And basic errors on these mudflats would be bad.

He looked left, and saw black shapes. In the dark. Black on grey. These were surely boats. But then the wind howled, in the firs of Camuscross, and it sounded like Beany, still alive, still lost on the mud.

'Beany?' He couldn't help himself. He loved that dog. 'Beany? Beano!'

He was shouting into the void. He was now ankle-deep in mud. And he was lost, and drunk, and in trouble.

Angus lifted his boot from the sucking glop and hiked on, desperate now, flinching against the bitterness of the wind, and the rain. No. He was lost. The lighthouse was invisible. Had he gone the wrong way round the bay? Was he heading into the same place where he nearly drowned, trying to save Beany?

There.

A figure? He was sure he could see a figure. Maybe

two figures, an adult and a child. Both of them were hunched against the ferocious wind. But why would an adult and a child be out here, walking across these dreadful muds, in the storm, in the pre-dawn darkness?

It could only be Sarah and Kirstie. And now he could hear his daughter, calling him. He knew that voice so well. *Dada Dada Dada.* Carried on the wind.

Dada.

She was calling him, pleading for him. But could he see her?

He could make out the cold rocks of Salmadair, a lighter grey in the general black. Kirstie and Sarah must be on Salmadair, he just had to reach them and get them all back to the mainland.

'Darling, I'm coming. Hold on!'

Dada.

Angus pulled up short. Gazing into the chains of rain. The figures had completely disappeared. The mist was whorling in places, like flaws in ice. Perhaps he had imagined it? Perhaps there was no one crossing here. It certainly didn't make sense that they would be out here. Why would Sarah and Kirstie leave the cottage to step into this horrific storm? A pointless risk.

And the noise? The voice?

Perhaps it was just the wind. All he could hear was howling. Yes, it might be dogs or children, but it might just be the wind. He was deceived by his fear and desperation.

Leaning low to the gale, Angus trudged on. Slipping left, he pushed a hand into thick mud. Like wet cement. Leaving his mark. And now his right foot plunged into a depth of water: sudden, and sharp, and icy.

Angus cringed, and lifted his heavy, soaking boot

from the seawater. Was the tide coming in already? No. That didn't add up. But how long had he been out here? His sense of time was slipping; he was tired and still drunk, and deafened by the disorienting gales. The rain and mist were so intense, the lighthouse beam was quite obscured.

Or maybe that was it over there: a dull pale throbbing in the grey; like something ominous underwater, like something bad on an X-ray.

For a second the fog split open.

There. That was definitely the lighthouse. And it was not so far away. He was almost around Salmadair. Once he made it to the causeway, it would be easier.

But again he could see a smear of movement, just one figure, rather small, moving in the greyness. Yet the smear of darkness was moving strangely. Left, and then right. Darting. And fast. Not like a child. More like a dog? Was it Beany? Then the movement stopped. And it was gone.

He clambered, painfully, to the top of the rock, where the mist was even thicker.

Whatever it was, it had gone. But now a real gleam of light showed him the way. The lighthouse was truly close: he was running up the causeway, the mud had yielded to rocks and pebbles; the wind was still driving and the rain was still intense, but the beam of the lighthouse displayed the route, every nine seconds.

Up, up, up.

There. He was on the island. There were lights glimmering, in the cottage. In the bedroom? His and Sarah's bedroom?

Angus crouched against the wet and sprinted up the path. The kitchen door was open, flapping hysterically in the brutal wind.

Why had Sarah left the door open? In this storm?

He stepped over the threshold, into the kitchen. The floor was wet, there was water everywhere. His torch showed why: a huge gash in the dining-room ceiling, a great beam of timber protruding.

'Kirstie?'

He was shouting against the wind that boomed outside.

'Kirstie! Sarah! Lydia! It's me!'

Nothing. No one answered. The house was empty. They had gone? Did that explain the two figures he'd maybe seen on the mudflats? Had he just seen his wife and daughter?

'Lydia!' He tried one last time. 'Sarah!'

Again, nothing. What about the bedroom? That's where he'd seen the light. Running through the dining room, he kicked open the bedroom door, and stared, from bed to chair, and from wall to wall, where the Scottish chieftain raised his hand at the crucifix.

The room was empty. The light was on, and the bedding was disturbed. But whoever had been here had recently left.

The house was empty. He'd lost them. They might both die on the flats.

Then he heard the voice. Coming from the far end of Torran cottage.

'I'm still here. I'm still in here!'

Six Months Later

28

It's the first fine day of the summer. The spring has been so wet; endless days of drizzle, and grey. But now the air sparkles, and the hills of Knoydart shine bright across the Sound.

Sgurr an Fhuarain, Sgurr Mor, Fraoch Bheinn.

As we get nearer to Torran, I look to the lighthouse. Just as Molly told me, the railings have been recently repaired. And there is evidence of more building work: big piles of bricks and planks, wheelbarrows parked on the beach. As it's the weekend, our builders are absent.

The new dinghy beaches gently on the shingle. I offer a hand, but Kirstie says,

'No, I can do it by myself now.'

She climbs out of the boat. Together we walk up the heathery path, and push the kitchen door.

A breeze greets me. Like the building is exhaling. Like it has been waiting for me, holding its breath.

But this is my delusion. The breeze comes from that hole in the roof: it forms a wind tunnel. The thin place is thinner than ever; the wildness is reclaiming it.

'It's cold in here,' says Kirstie.

She's right. The day is warm but Torran cottage is still unwarmable.

Together we edge into the dining room. Most of this building work, so far, has been done to the exterior; the interior is much as it was that night. The dining room is entirely wrecked: the rafter that plunged through the dining-room ceiling still protrudes, like a bone in a gruesome fracture. Kirstie gazes around.

'Look at the mess!'

This is my third or fourth reluctant visit, since the storm. I'm putting the traumas of the past behind us; but coming to the island roils these thoughts, again. Torran cottage unnerves me, now. I cannot tolerate being here more than an hour.

Because the memories of that night, and the final hike through those evil gales, will never fade.

'What are we waiting for?'

Kirstie is tugging my sleeve, impatiently. I smile, to disguise my anxiety.

'Nothing, sweetheart, nothing at all. You go and find any toys left behind, this is probably your last visit.'

And she runs off down the hall.

Now I push the door into the living room. Trying to fend off the grief and the fear, trying to be a responsible parent. A single parent. As that is now my job.

We are selling the island, after the renovation is done.

Josh and Molly have sold their plot on Tokavaig, and invested that cash in Torran. This has allowed us to develop the lighthouse-keeper's cottage. Half of the building will be torn down: the damage has, ironically, allowed us to avoid the conservation order. The work should be completed next year. We hope to sell it for two million, at least, and divide the profits equally.

Kirstie and I will be financially secure. Any real monetary anxiety will be gone. All *monetary* anxiety.

The building whispers, as the wind flutes through the hole in the roof. Quickly I pass into the main bedroom – with the Admiral's Bed. I glance at the mirror. It's still here for a very good reason: I don't want it. The mirror represents too many unsettling memories of those tragic weeks.

How many false reflections did we all see, that month we lived on Torran? The abuse, the murder, it was all lies, reflected back and forth; or maybe it was the transparency that confused us: we saw one child through the other: but flawed, and distorted, like seeing things through ice.

Poor Lydia fell. My daughter fell because she climbed down from the top-floor balcony; because she wanted to see her mother. Kirstie pushed her off, to save herself, but it wasn't murder.

I suppress the shudders of guilt, and regret.

The bedroom here in Torran is even colder than the dining room. The Scottish chieftain raises his hand to me – go away, go away. I am keen to obey. When I reach the hall, Kirstie comes running along. She's in yellow leggings and a blue denim skirt. Her favourite clothes.

'Have you got the toys you want?'

Kirstie says,

'There was only one toy left. Under the bed.'

'What was it?'

'Desmond the Dragon.'

The little dragon.

'Not sure I want it anyway.'

She takes the dragon from her One Direction rucksack; I put it in my pocket; I have an urge to throw it away, like something poisonous.

Besides, she is maybe grown out of little toys: Kirstie is eight years old. She has just a few years of childhood left, and I want us to make the most of these years. We are settled in a good, solid house in Ornsay; and Kirstie is now at an excellent school in Broadford. It's a twenty-minute drive, every morning, but I don't mind. The idea of her going back to Kylerdale was disturbingly ridiculous.

Though, strangely enough, she now has friends in the village: kids who knew her at Kylerdale. She is popular. The girl with the story. Kirstie was always that bit more buoyant than Lydia.

'I found something for Beany too.'

'You did?'

She looks in the rucksack again, and takes out a plastic bone. One of Beany's toys.

'Thank you,' I say, taking the toy. 'Beano will love that.'

Beany is waiting for us at the pub, being indulged by Gordon and the locals. His survival is a miracle. The day after the storm, he re-emerged at the Selkie, loping up the pier, muddy, freezing, shivering; like a sodden ghost of a hound. But he is not unmarked. He never comes to the island, he whimpers whenever I try to take him on the boat, or offer to walk him across the mudflats.

Beany's toy is in my jacket pocket. Together Kirstie and I walk out of the cottage, closing the damp kitchen door. It strikes me that one day soon I will close this same door for good – when we sell the island.

I am satisfied with this.

I will always revere Torran, I will always gaze in admiration at its daunting beauty from the seats outside the Selkie. But I am content to keep it at a distance.

Torran has defeated us, with its winds and vermin, with its thunders booming down the Sound from Ardvasar.

I hold Kirstie's hand, very tight, as we walk down to the lighthouse beach. As if the island may try to stop her going.

'OK then, Kirstie-koo. Let's get home.'

'Don't call me that, call me Kirstie!'

The ropes untied, we climb into the boat. With a couple of tugs I get the outboard whirring.

Kirstie is sitting in the back of the boat, she's humming her favourite tune. A pop song, I think. I sigh with barely concealed relief as we steer away from the island. Silence absorbs us. Then a grey seal rises a few yards upstream.

My daughter looks at the seal, and she smiles, and it is very definitely Kirstie's smile: pert, mischievous, alive. She is definitely getting better. Therapy has helped her recover. She no longer feels that Lydie's fall was her fault, we've convinced her of that. But that still leaves my appalling error. I blurred her identity; I made that mistake. One day I will have to forgive *myself*.

The seal has disappeared. Kirstie turns away. And now her face clouds with some further, darker emotion.

'What is it sweetheart?'

Kirstie stares beyond me, at Torran.

Slowly, she says:

'Lydia came back, didn't she?'

'Yes, she did. Just for a bit.'

'But she's gone now, and I'm Kirstie again. Aren't I?'

'Yes,' I say. 'That is who you are. And you always were.'

Kirstie is quiet. The outboard motor churns the clear water. Then she says:

'I miss Mummy. And Lydie.'

371

'I know,' I say. 'So do I, darling.'

And it's true. I do. I miss them every day. But we have what we have, and we have each other.

And we still have little secrets, that might never be revealed. Kirstie's secret is the night of the storm, she has never told me exactly what happened, and what was said in the house, that last night; I have long stopped asking, for fear of upsetting her. Why go back? Why dig it all up?

Equally, I have never told Kirstie the entire truth about her mother.

When I found Kirstie, huddled in the cottage, she apparently had no idea where her mother was. So I searched the house, looking for clues. And finally, as morning paled the mainland skies, Josh and Gordon came over in Gordon's skiff, and rescued us from Torran: ferrying us back to warmth and safety at Josh's house.

And then we heard about Sarah, before the search parties had properly started.

Her body was spotted by a fisherman, floating by the beach at Camuscross. Immediately after that, the police took over Torran. I left them to it, shielding myself and Kirstie from the journalists and the detectives. We hid ourselves in Josh's house, staring at the shivering rowans beyond the big windows.

Within a week the police reached their conclusion: Sarah had quit the cottage, for whatever reason – perhaps in some strange attempt to get help; but she had fallen in the mud and the darkness, and drowned. It was so easily done. Too easily done. It was an accident.

But was it, truly? I am haunted by that phrase I heard at the Freedlands': *All love is a form of suicide*. Maybe Sarah wanted to join her dead daughter. Or maybe she was deranged with guilt, by what she read in the bottom drawer of the kist. I found the letter from her doctor, scattered on the floor of the bedroom, that same night I found Kirstie. I destroyed it.

The questions will plague me, always: would she really leave her daughter behind in the cottage? Did I really see one or two figures, through the mist, as I made my own way to Torran?

There will never be an answer. Though there were clues, and these are the clues I will not reveal to Kirstie. Not as long as I live.

When they found Sarah's solitary body, floating in the tide, they found her holding Lydia's pink coat, by the sleeve.

And when the forensic scientists conducted the post mortem, they discovered sad, wet strands of fine blonde hair, clutched in Sarah's fingers, as if she had been grasping desperately at someone in those final minutes: trying to save her child from drowning.

Kirstie is looking south, to Mallaig; I have my back to Torran island.

It is a fine, calm day in early June; the skies are mirrored in the silent sea lochs. And yet a cold wind still whips off those beautiful hills.

Sgurr an Fhuarain, Sgurr Mor, Fraoch Bheinn.